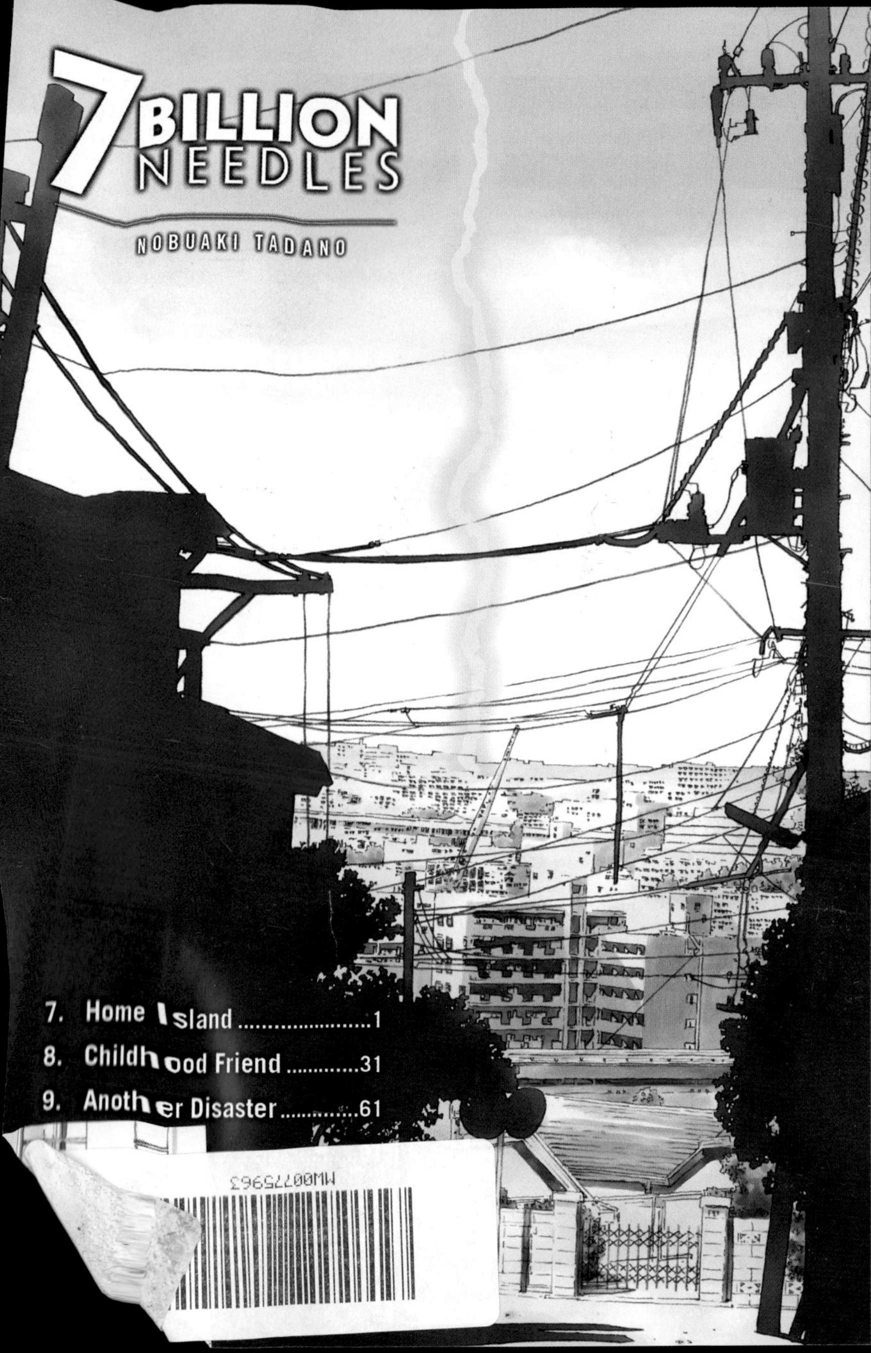

7 BILLION NEEDLES

NOBUAKI TADANO

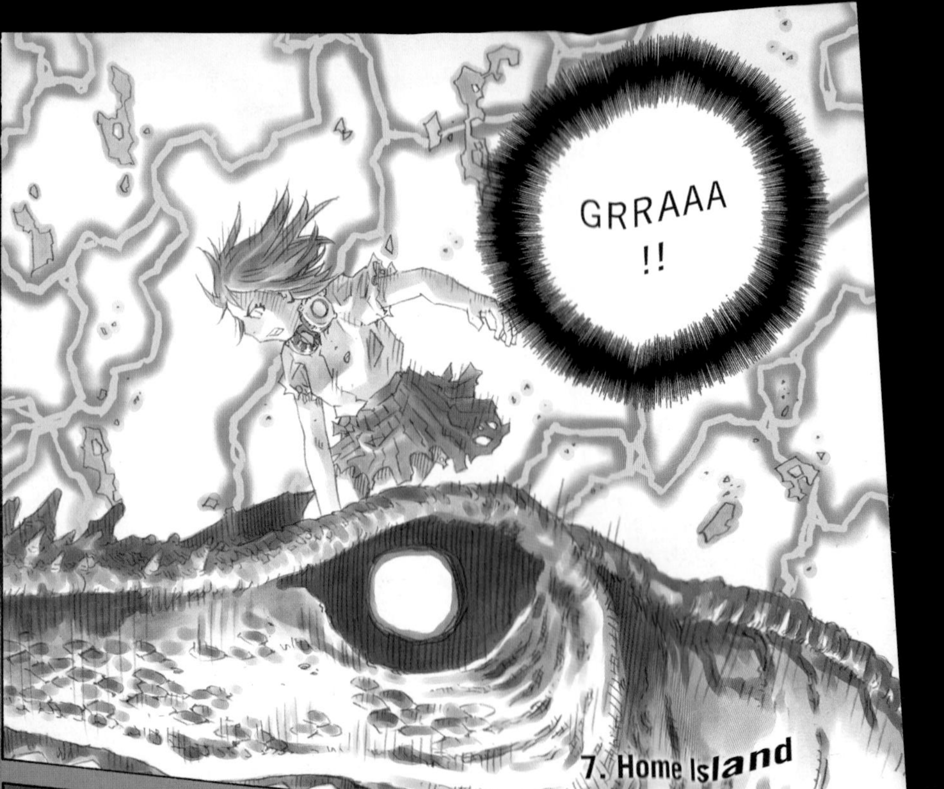
GRRAAA
!!
7. Home Island

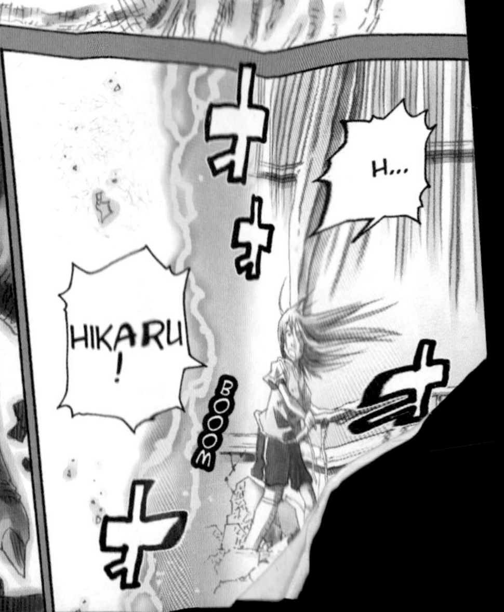
H...
HIKARU
!
BOOOM

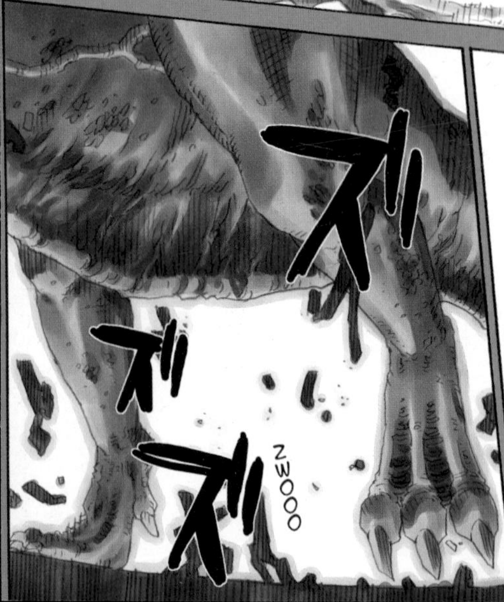
ZWOOO

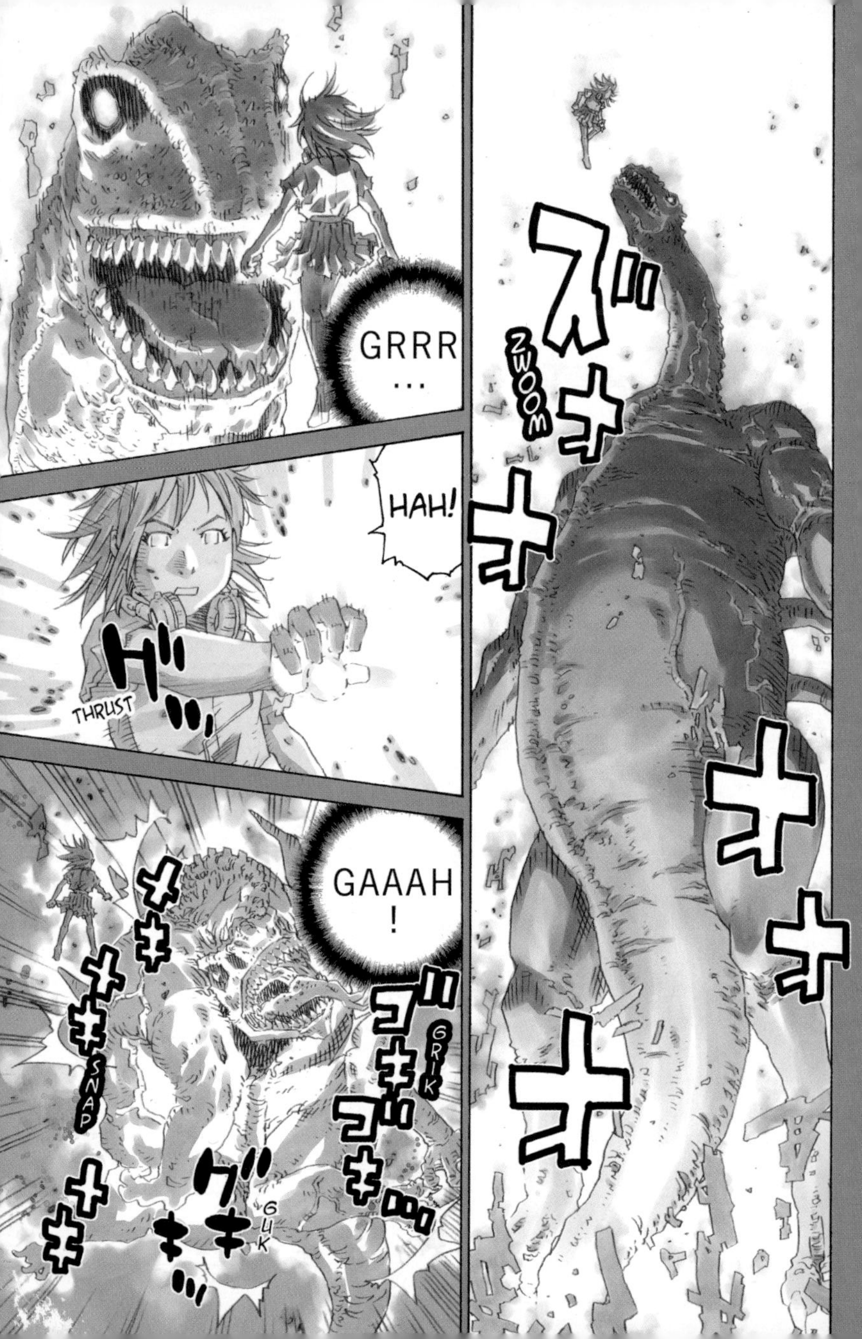
ZWOOM
GRRR...
HAH!
THRUST
GAAAH!
GRIK
SNAP
GUK

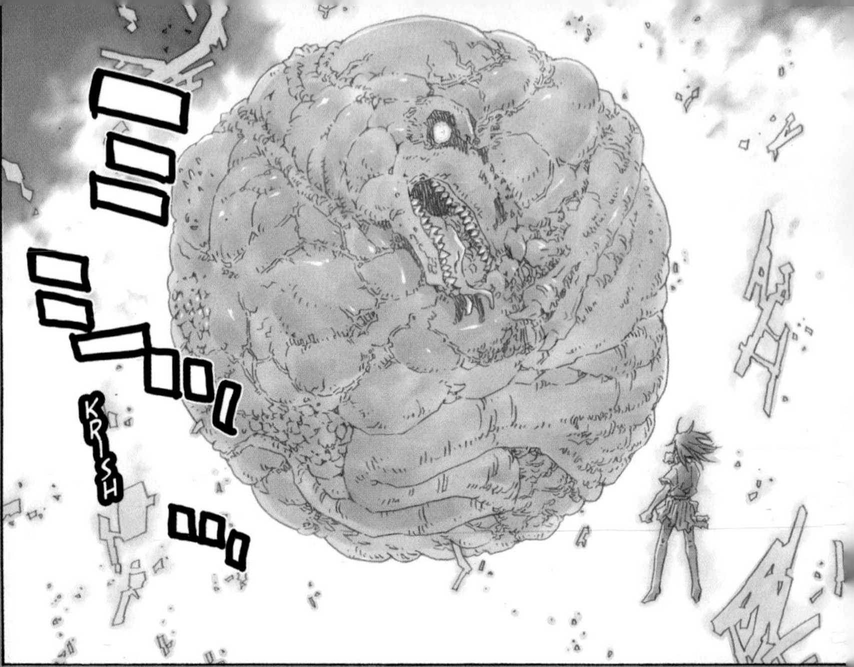
KRISH
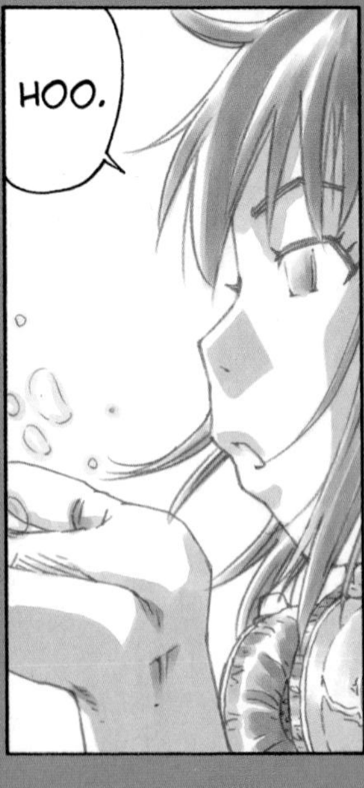
HOO.
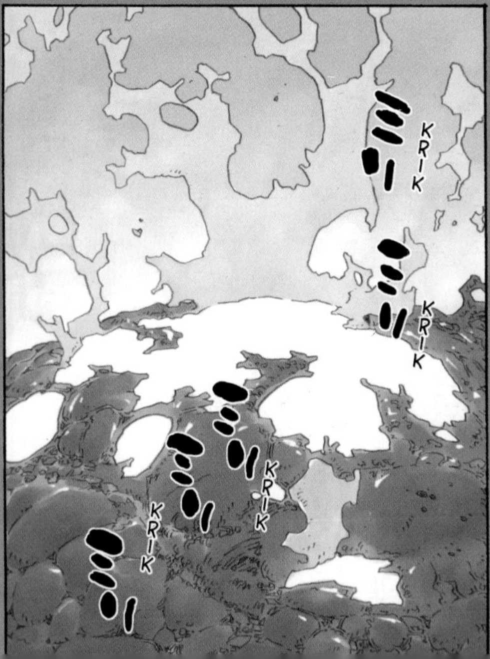
KRIK
KRIK
KRIK
KRIK

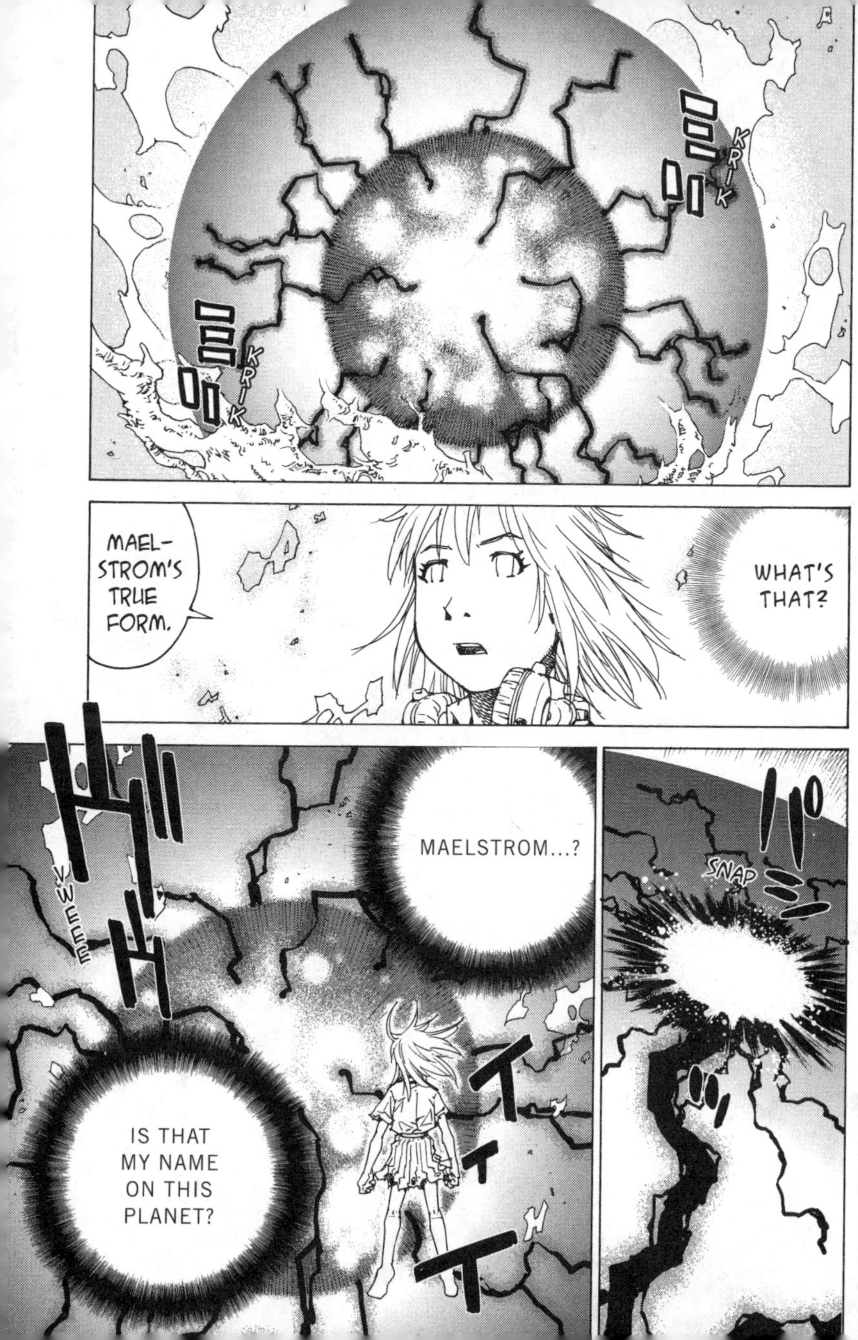
KRIK
KRIK
WHAT'S THAT?
MAEL-STROM'S TRUE FORM.
SNAP
MAELSTROM...?
VWEEE
IS THAT MY NAME ON THIS PLANET?

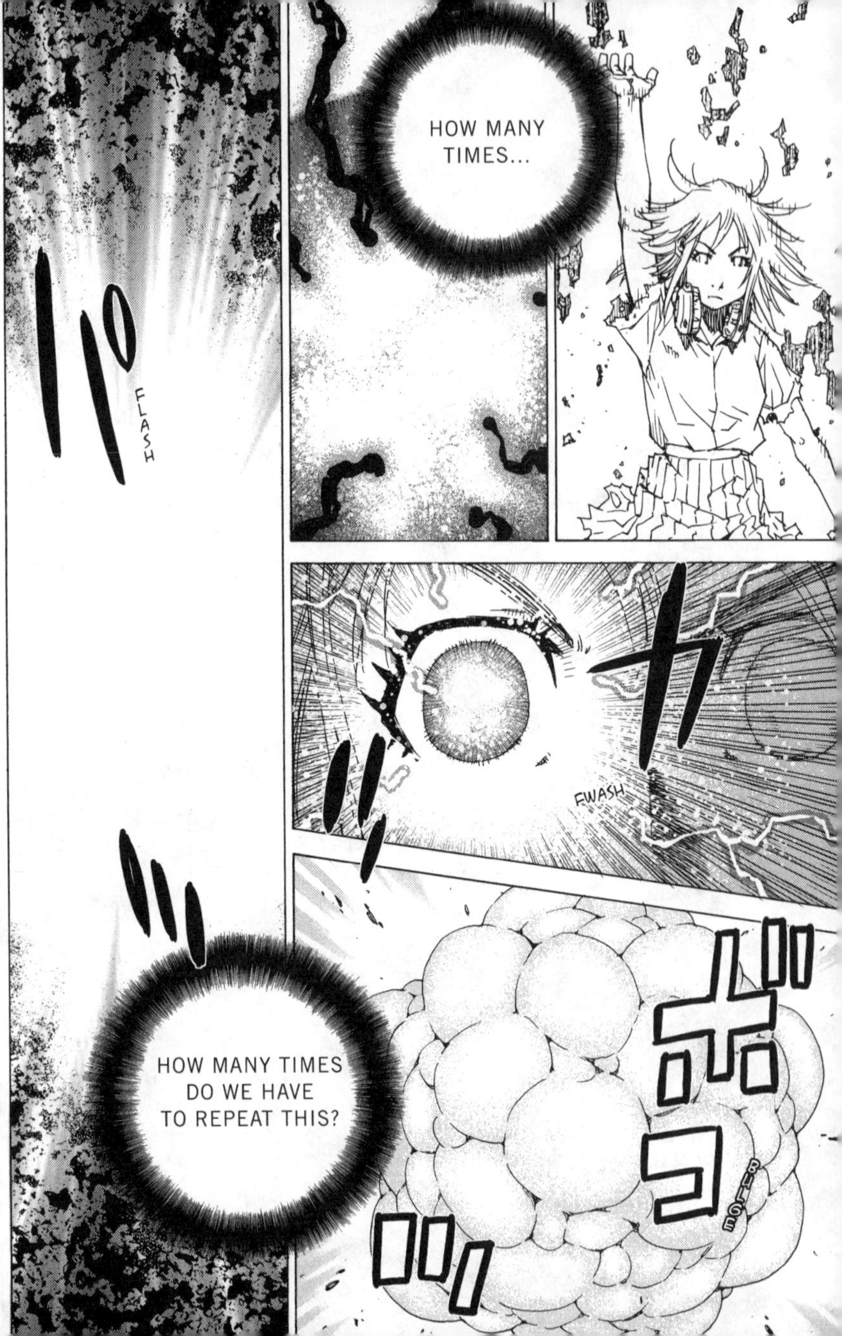
HOW MANY TIMES...
FWASH
BULGE
FLASH
HOW MANY TIMES DO WE HAVE TO REPEAT THIS?

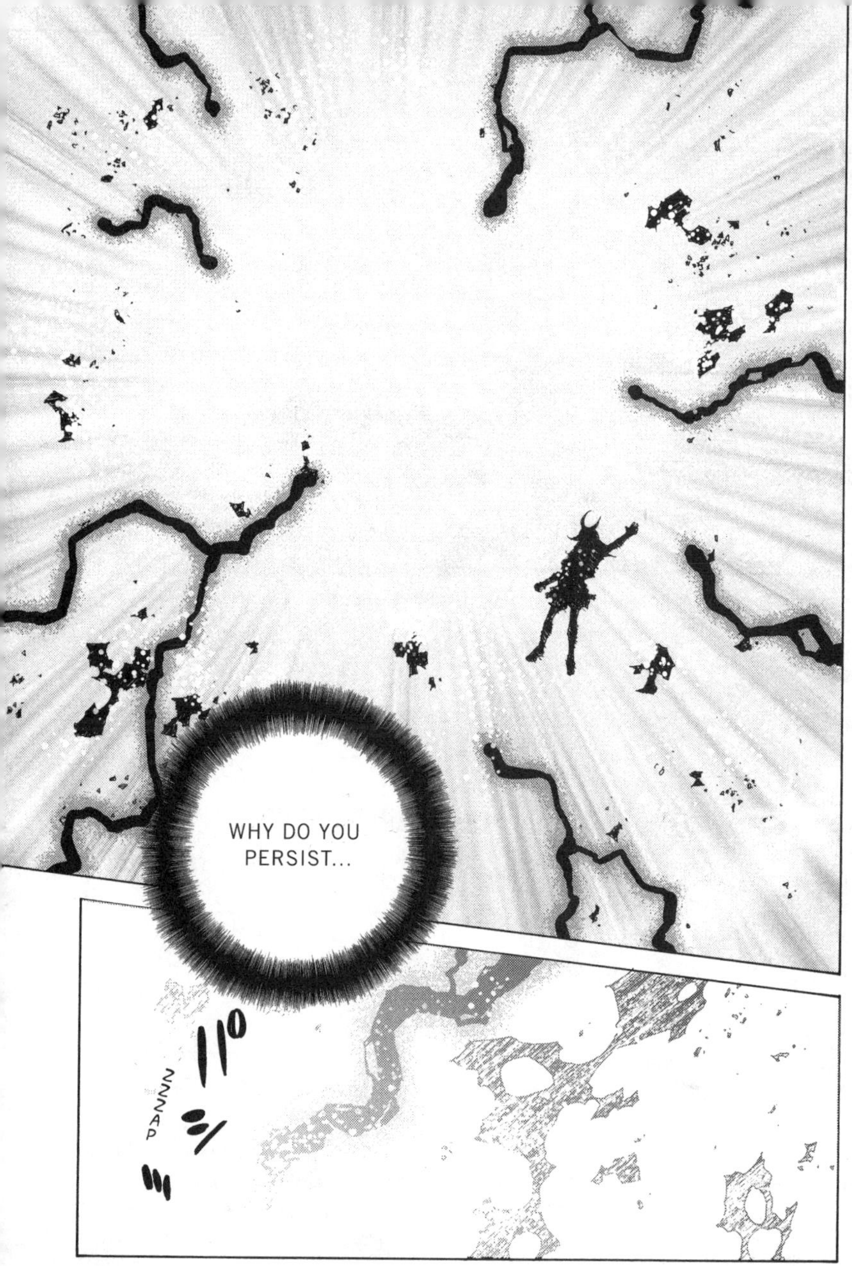
WHY DO YOU PERSIST...
ZZZAP

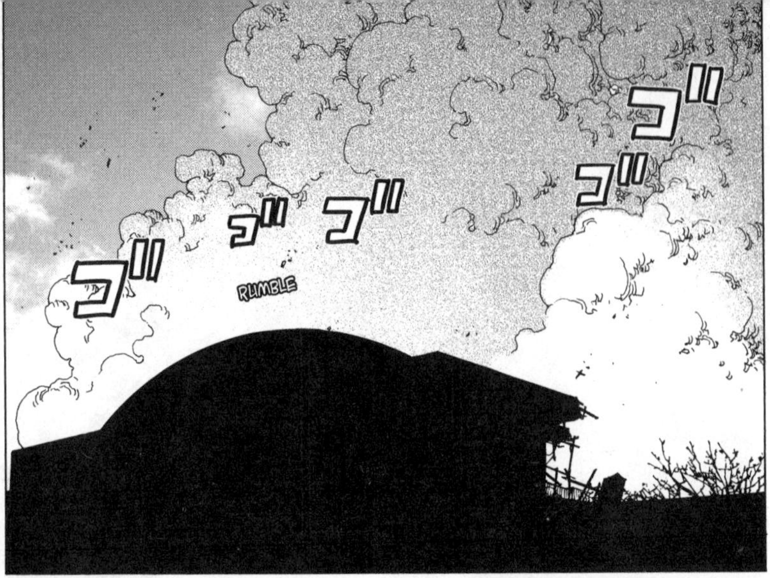
ゴ
ゴ
ゴ
ゴ
ゴ
RUMBLE

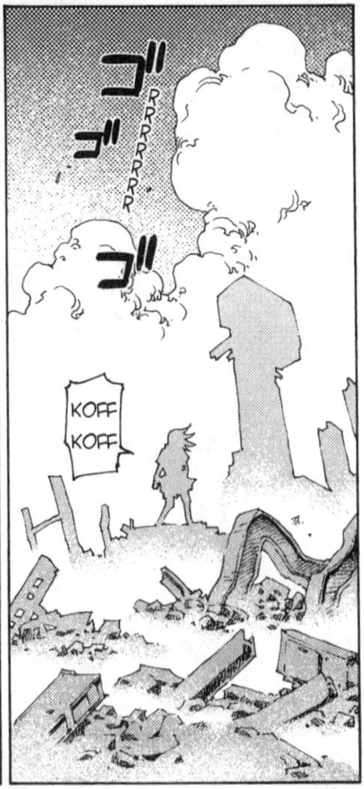
ゴ
ゴ
RRRRRRR
ゴ
KOFF
KOFF

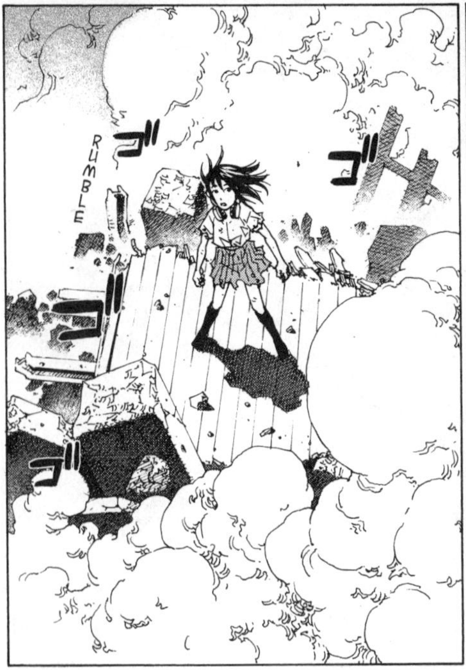
ゴ
RUMBLE
ゴ
ゴ
ゴ

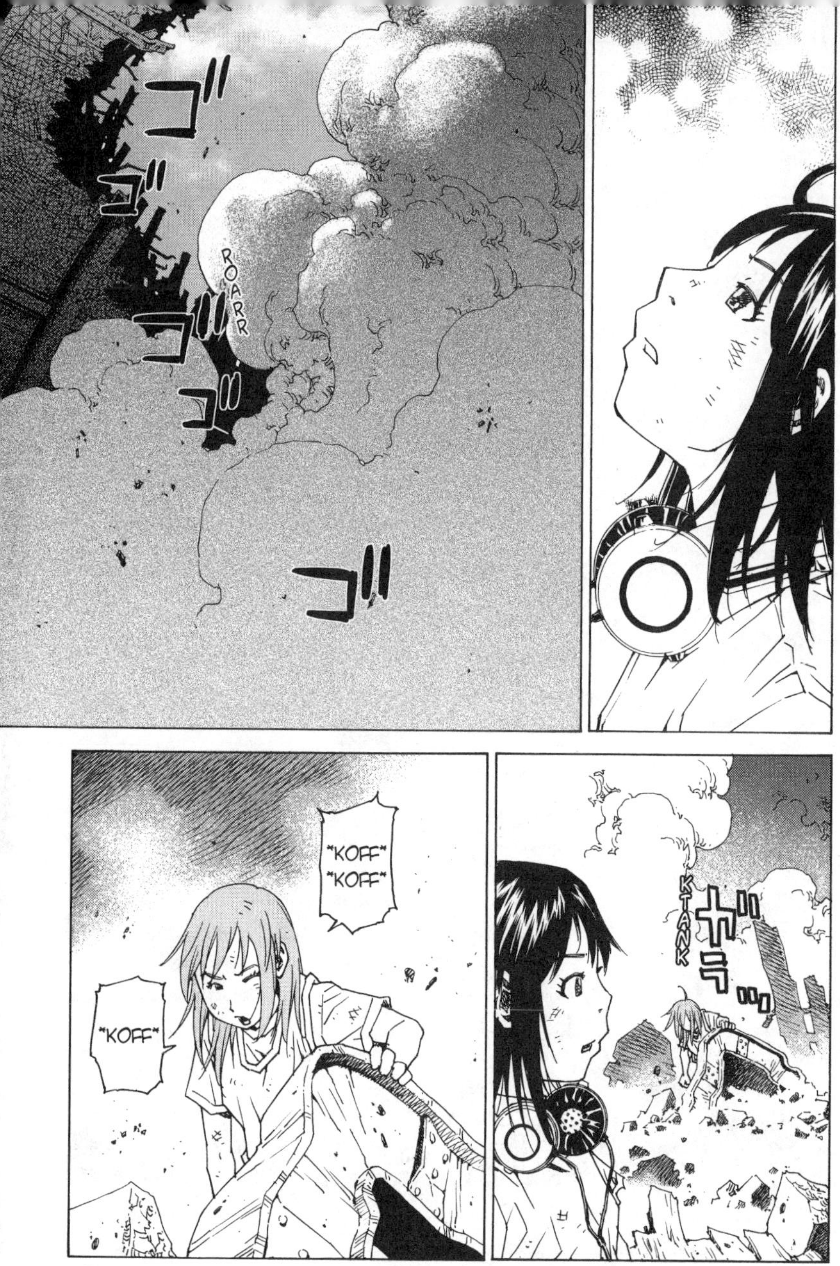
ゴゴゴゴゴ
ROARR
ガラッ
KTANK
KOFF
KOFF *KOFF*

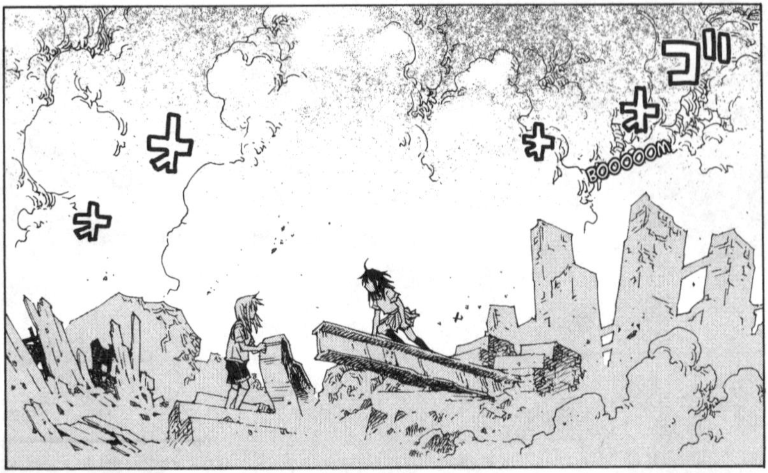
ゴ
オ
オ
オ
オ
BOOOOOM
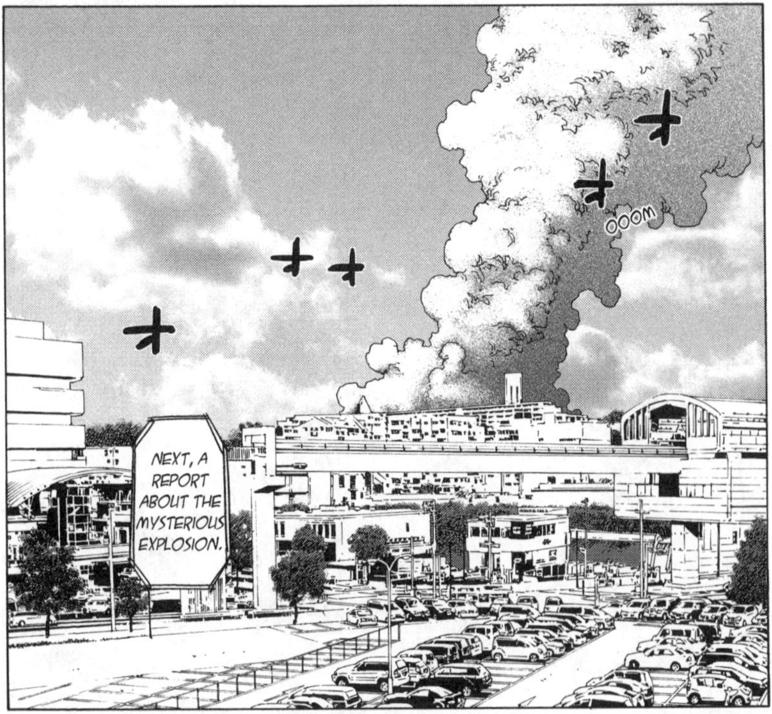
オ
オ
OOOM
オ
オ
オ
NEXT, A REPORT ABOUT THE MYSTERIOUS EXPLOSION.

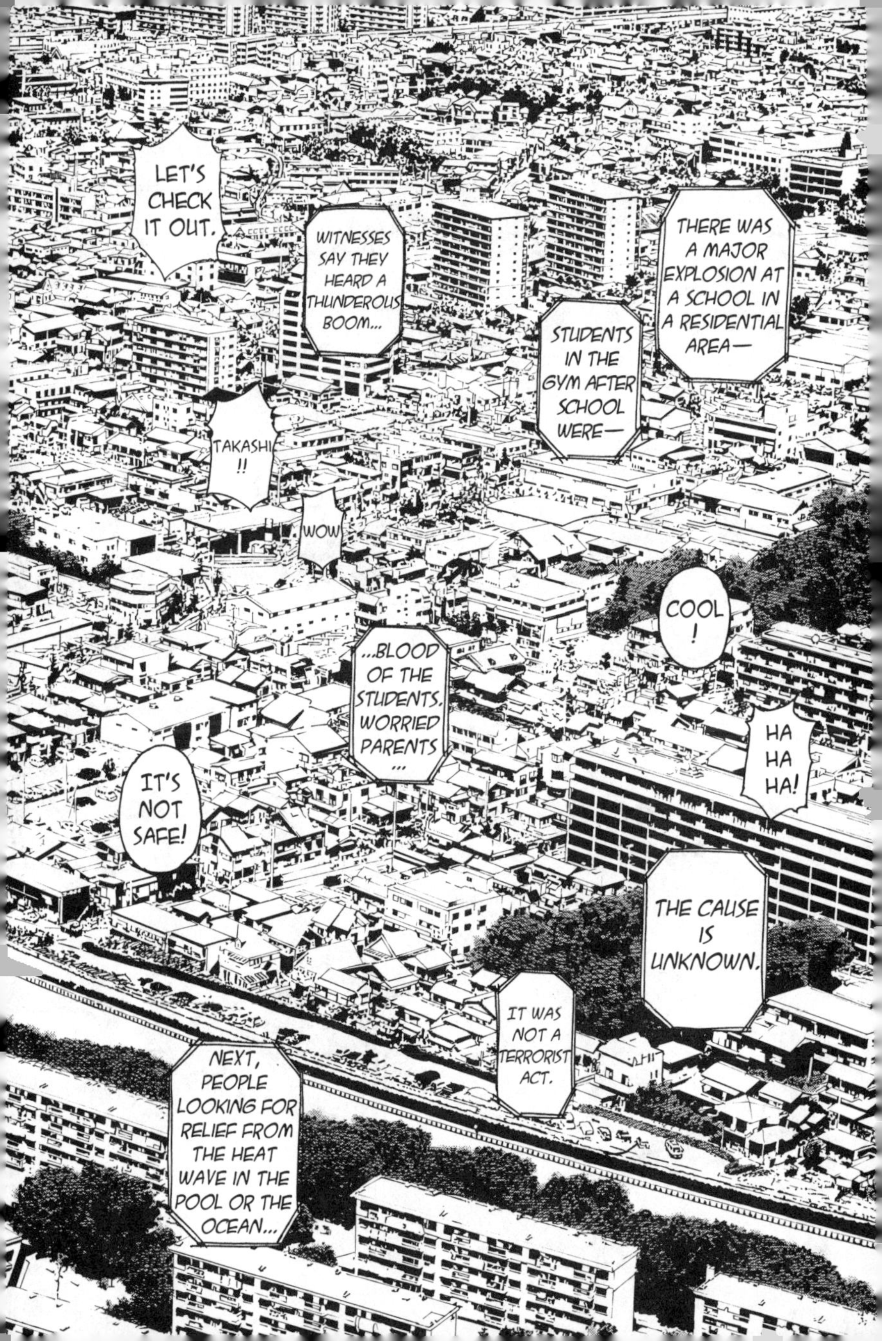
THERE WAS A MAJOR EXPLOSION AT A SCHOOL IN A RESIDENTIAL AREA—
STUDENTS IN THE GYM AFTER SCHOOL WERE—
WITNESSES SAY THEY HEARD A THUNDEROUS BOOM...
LET'S CHECK IT OUT.
TAKASHI !!
WOW
COOL !
...BLOOD OF THE STUDENTS, WORRIED PARENTS ...
HA HA HA!
IT'S NOT SAFE!
THE CAUSE IS UNKNOWN.
IT WAS NOT A TERRORIST ACT.
NEXT, PEOPLE LOOKING FOR RELIEF FROM THE HEAT WAVE IN THE POOL OR THE OCEAN...

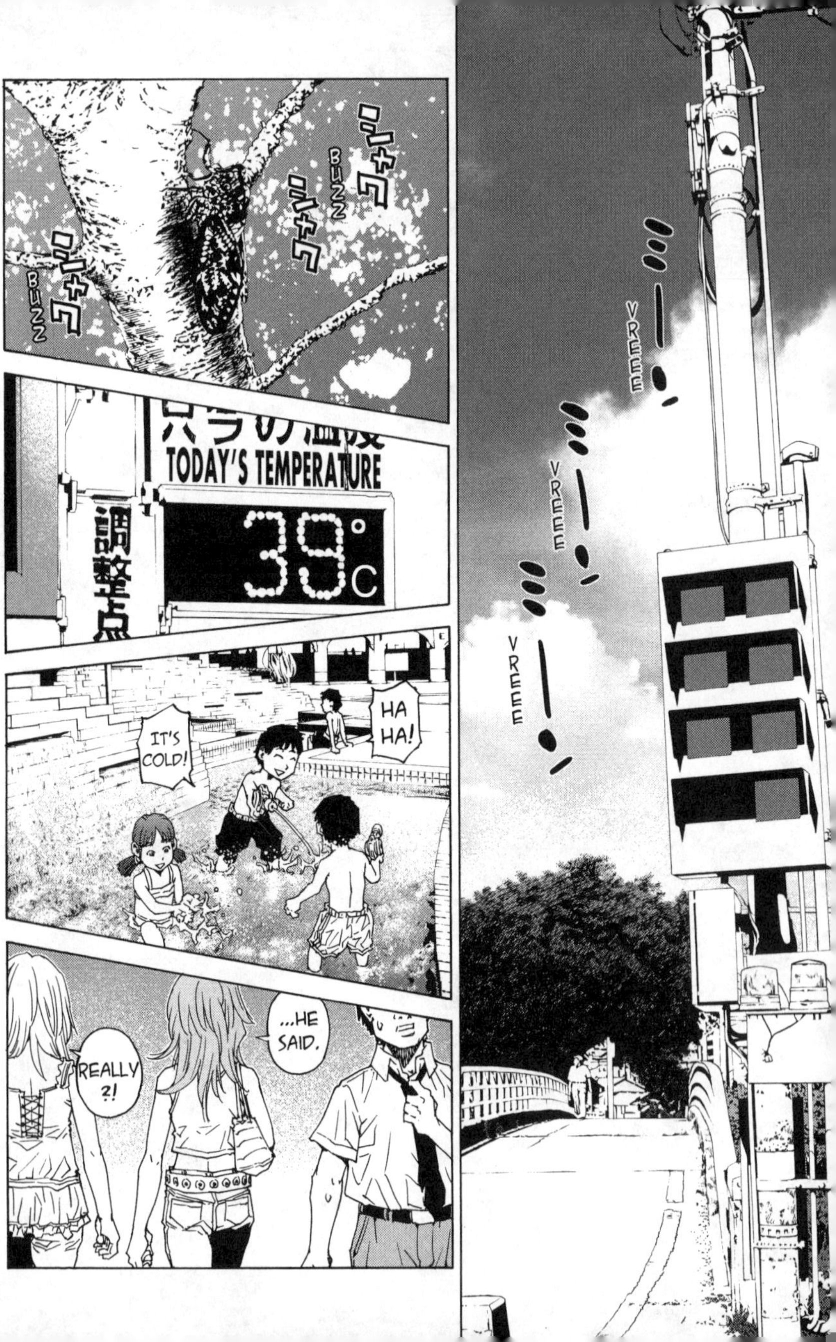
VREEE
VREEE
VREEE
BUZZ
BUZZ
TODAY'S TEMPERATURE
調整点
39°C
HA HA!
IT'S COLD!
...HE SAID.
REALLY ?!

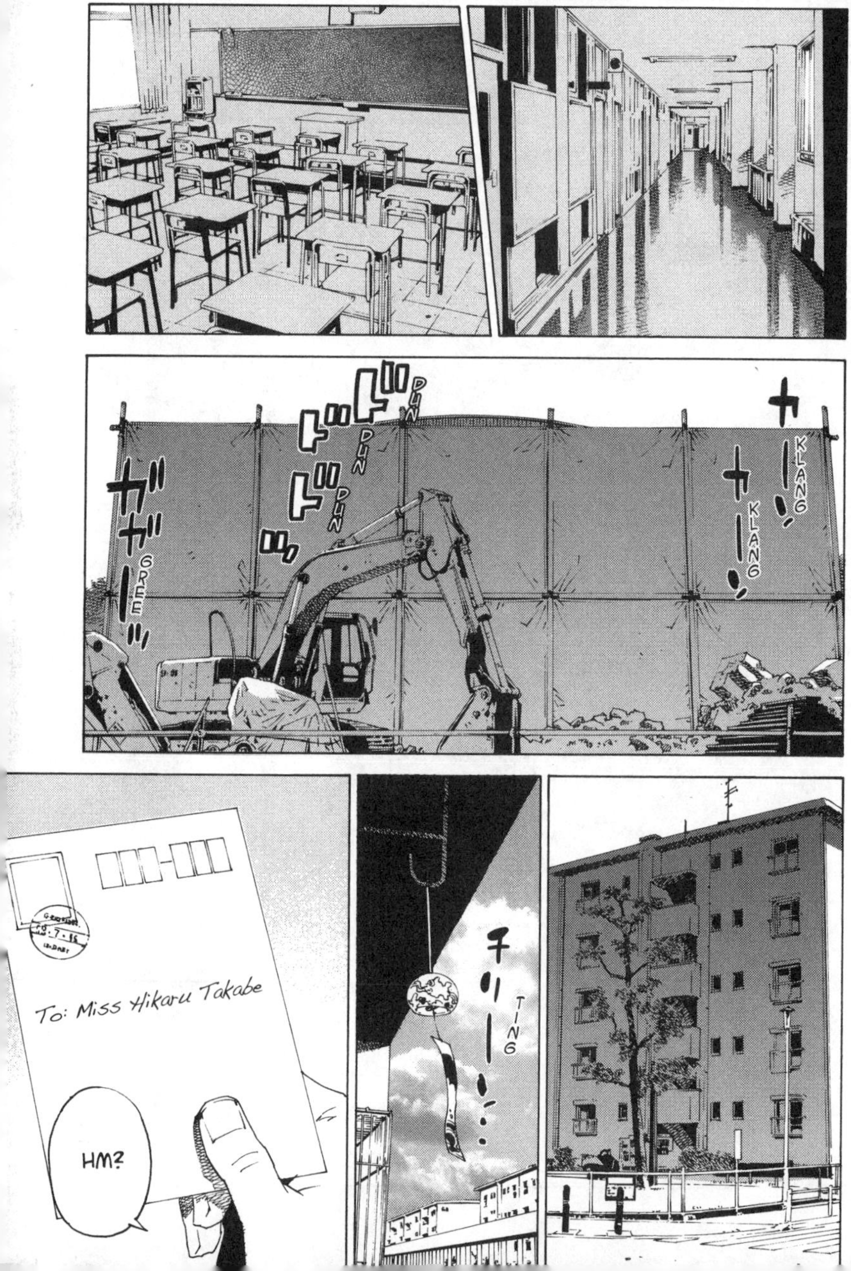
KLANG
KLANG
DUN
DUN
DUN
GREE
チリー…
TING
To: Miss Hikaru Takabe
HM?

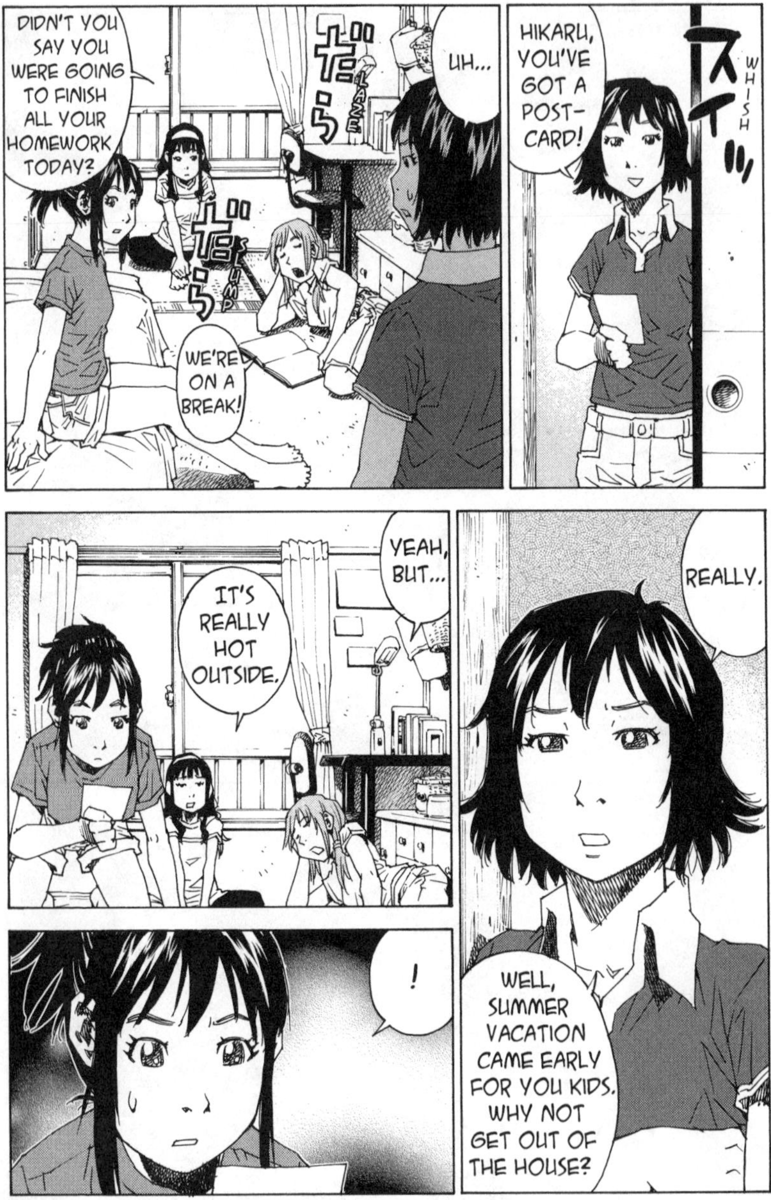

スイッ
WHISH
HIKARU, YOU'VE GOT A POST-CARD!
UH...
LAZE
DIDN'T YOU SAY YOU WERE GOING TO FINISH ALL YOUR HOMEWORK TODAY?
SLUMP
WE'RE ON A BREAK!
REALLY.
WELL, SUMMER VACATION CAME EARLY FOR YOU KIDS. WHY NOT GET OUT OF THE HOUSE?
YEAH, BUT...
IT'S REALLY HOT OUTSIDE.
!

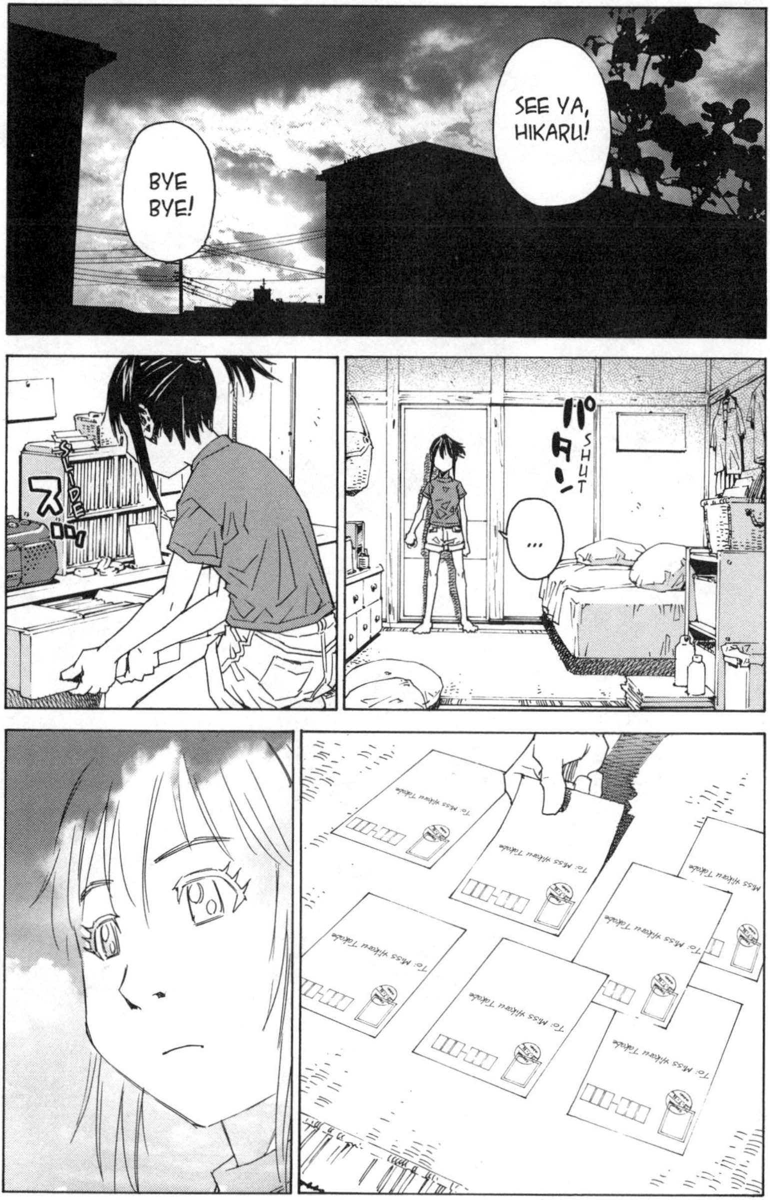
SEE YA, HIKARU!
BYE BYE!
SHUT
...
SLIDE
To: Miss Hikaru Takabe

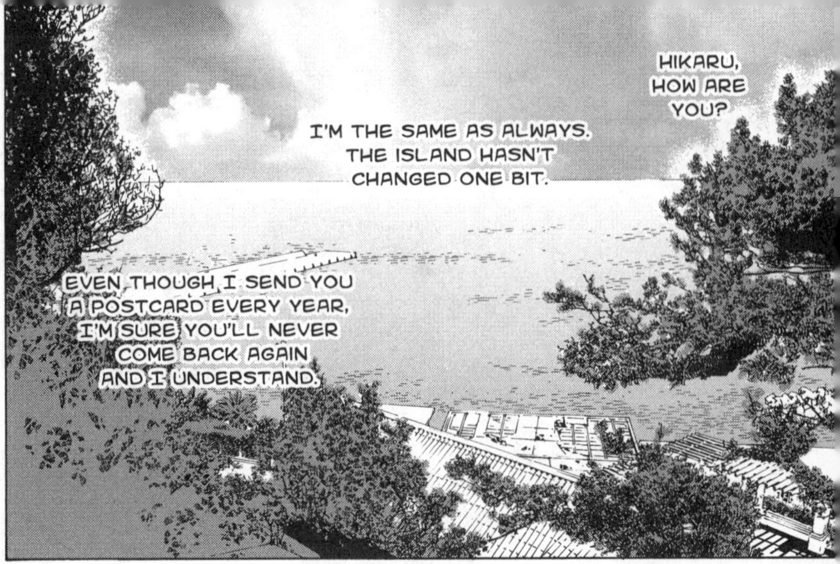
HIKARU, HOW ARE YOU?
I'M THE SAME AS ALWAYS. THE ISLAND HASN'T CHANGED ONE BIT.
EVEN THOUGH I SEND YOU A POSTCARD EVERY YEAR, I'M SURE YOU'LL NEVER COME BACK AGAIN AND I UNDERSTAND.

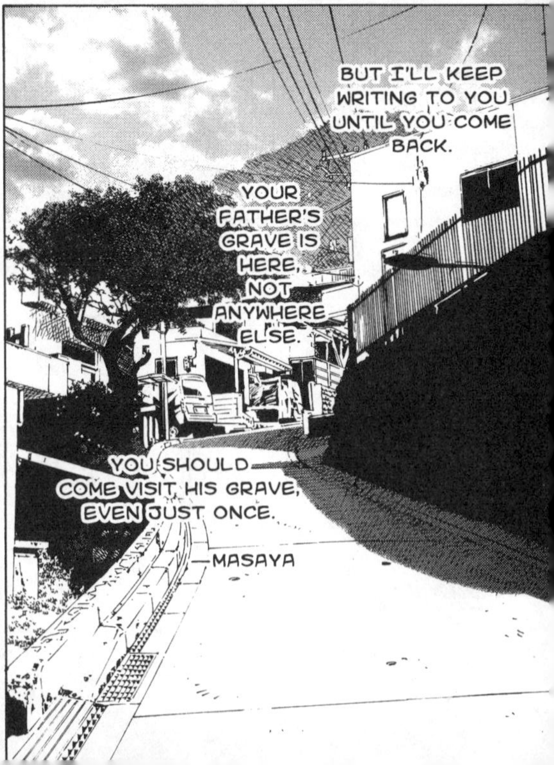
BUT I'LL KEEP WRITING TO YOU UNTIL YOU COME BACK.
YOUR FATHER'S GRAVE IS HERE, NOT ANYWHERE ELSE.
YOU SHOULD COME VISIT HIS GRAVE, EVEN JUST ONCE.
—MASAYA

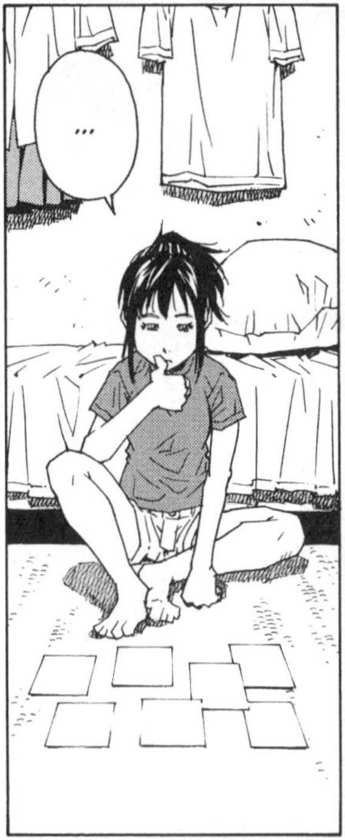
...

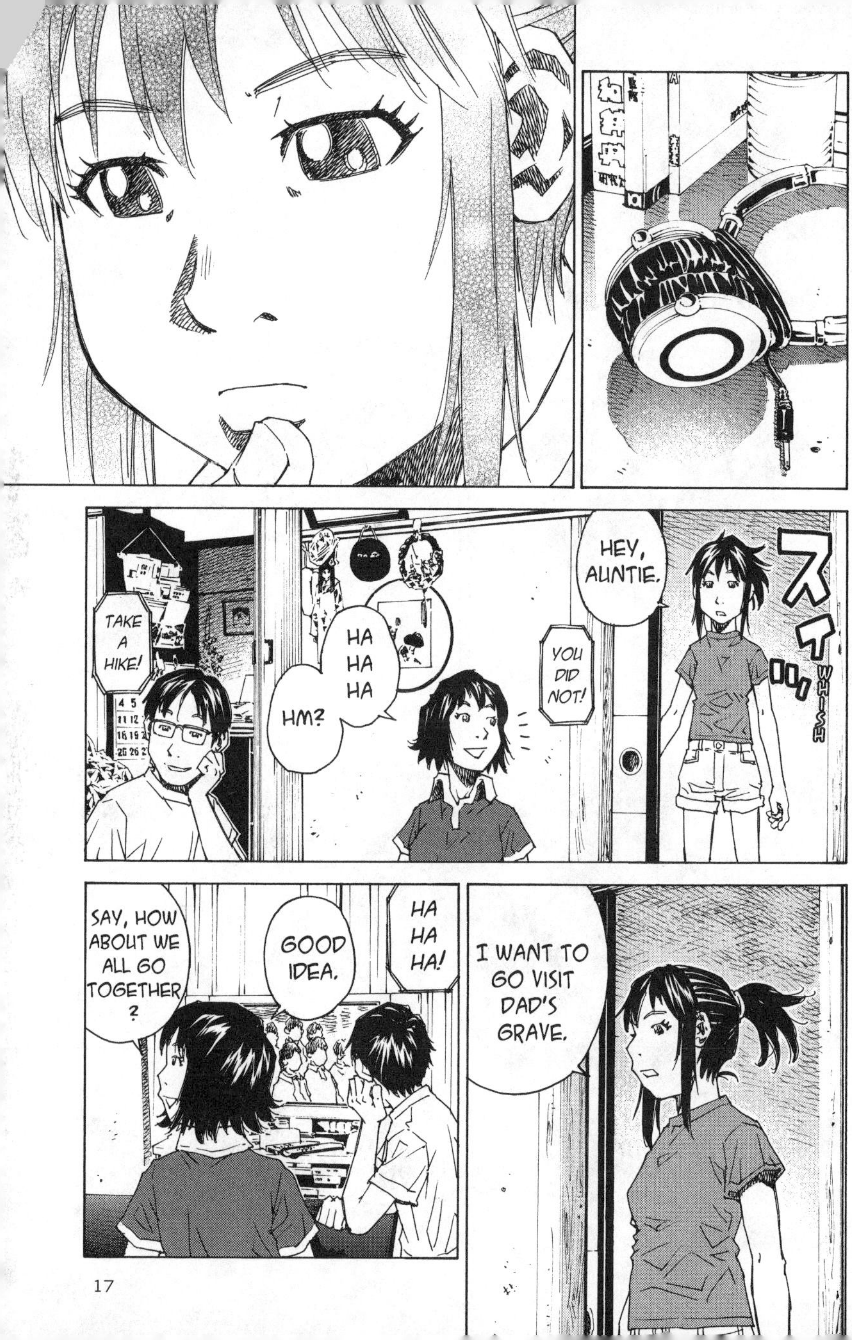
スイ
WHISH
HEY, AUNTIE.
YOU DID NOT!
HA HA HA
HM?
TAKE A HIKE!
I WANT TO GO VISIT DAD'S GRAVE.
HA HA HA!
GOOD IDEA.
SAY, HOW ABOUT WE ALL GO TOGETHER?

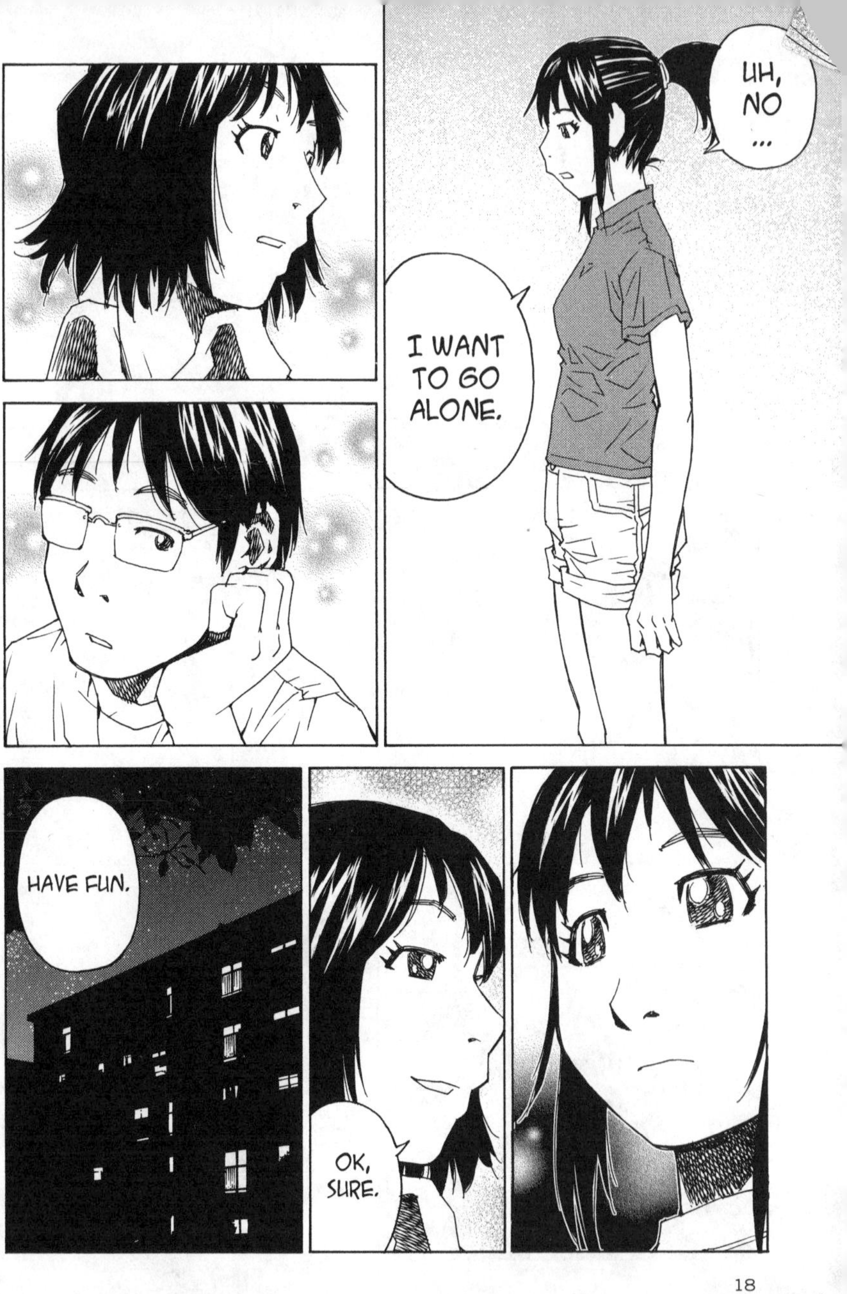
UH, NO ...
I WANT TO GO ALONE.
OK, SURE.
HAVE FUN.

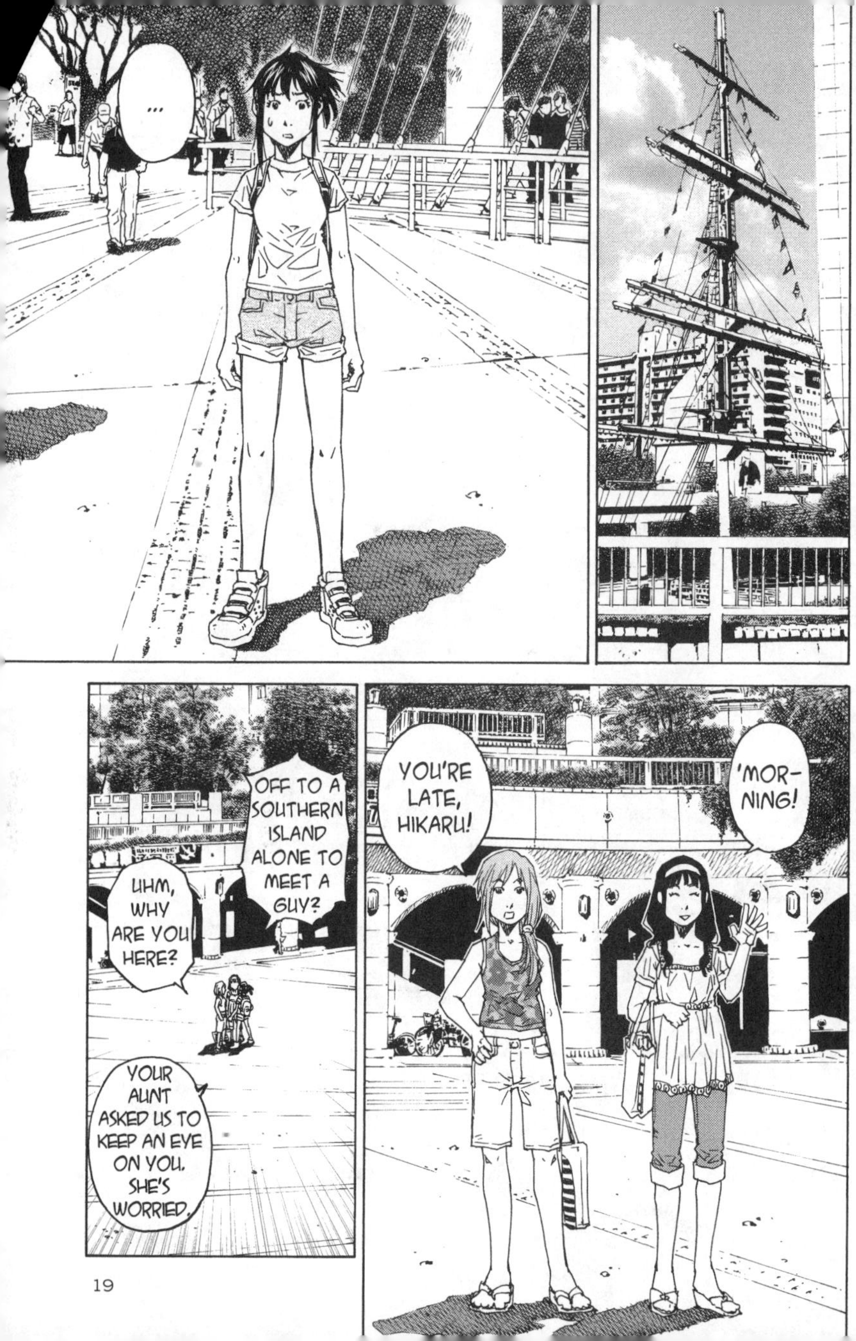
...
'MOR-NING!
YOU'RE LATE, HIKARU!
OFF TO A SOUTHERN ISLAND ALONE TO MEET A GUY?
UHM, WHY ARE YOU HERE?
YOUR AUNT ASKED US TO KEEP AN EYE ON YOU. SHE'S WORRIED.

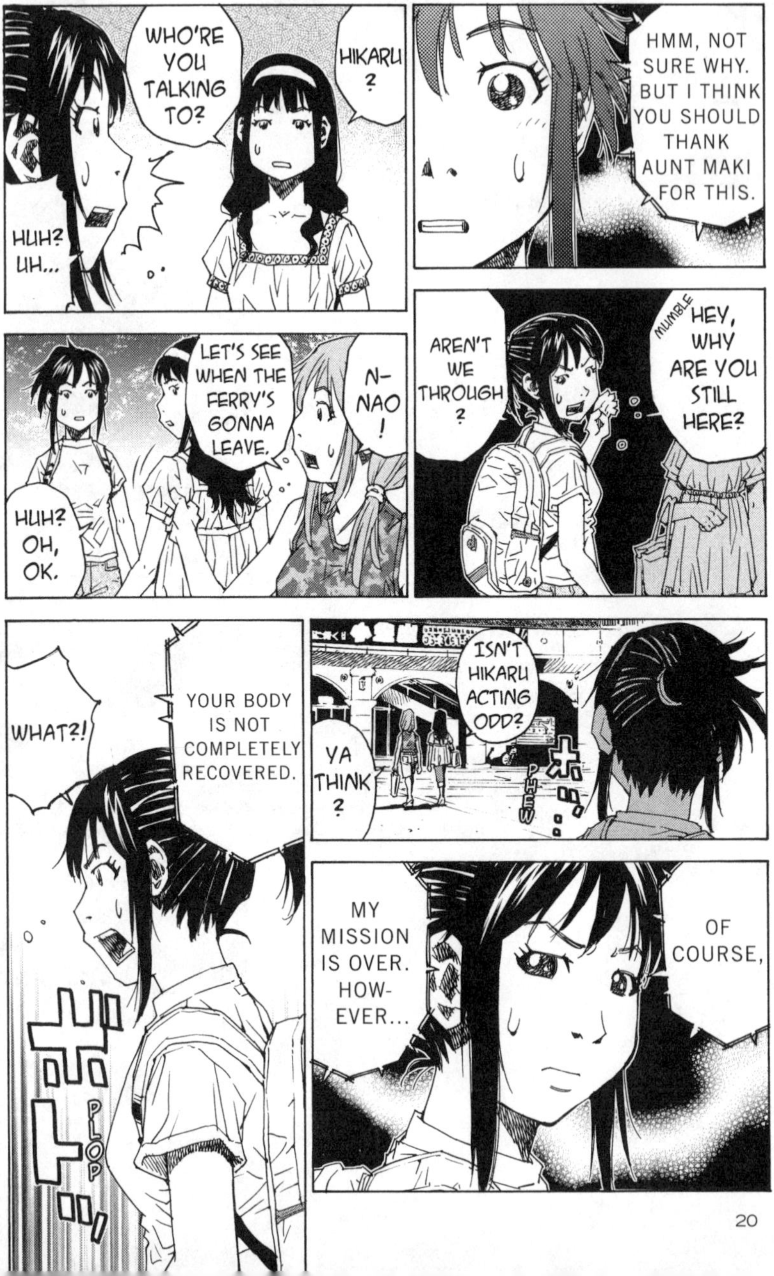
HMM, NOT SURE WHY. BUT I THINK YOU SHOULD THANK AUNT MAKI FOR THIS.
HIKARU?
WHO'RE YOU TALKING TO?
HUH? UH...
MUMBLE
HEY, WHY ARE YOU STILL HERE?
AREN'T WE THROUGH?
N-NAO!
LET'S SEE WHEN THE FERRY'S GONNA LEAVE.
HUH? OH, OK.
ISN'T HIKARU ACTING ODD?
YA THINK?
PHEW
OF COURSE,
MY MISSION IS OVER. HOW-EVER...
YOUR BODY IS NOT COMPLETELY RECOVERED.
WHAT?!
PLOP

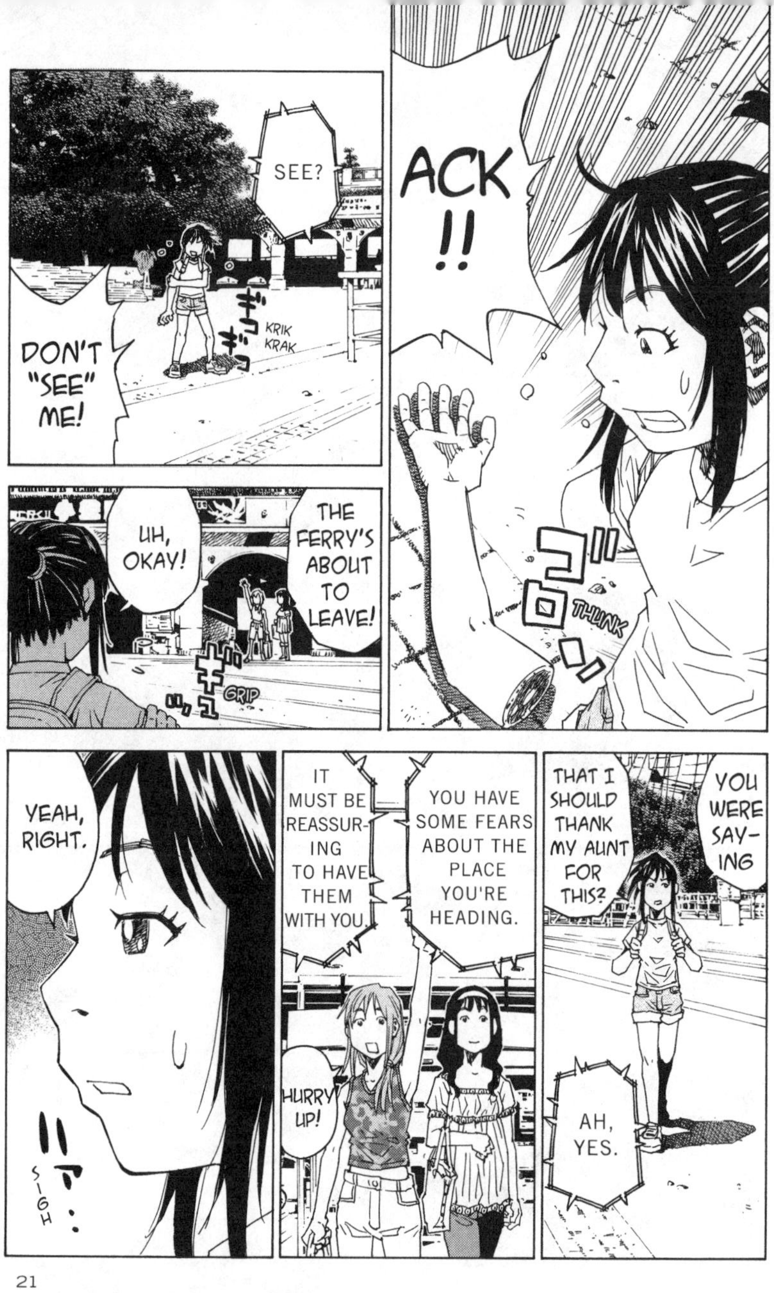
ACK !!
THUNK
SEE?
KRIK KRAK
DON'T "SEE" ME!
THE FERRY'S ABOUT TO LEAVE!
UH, OKAY!
GRIP
YOU WERE SAY-ING
THAT I SHOULD THANK MY AUNT FOR THIS?
AH, YES.
YOU HAVE SOME FEARS ABOUT THE PLACE YOU'RE HEADING.
IT MUST BE REASSUR-ING TO HAVE THEM WITH YOU.
HURRY UP!
YEAH, RIGHT.
SIGH

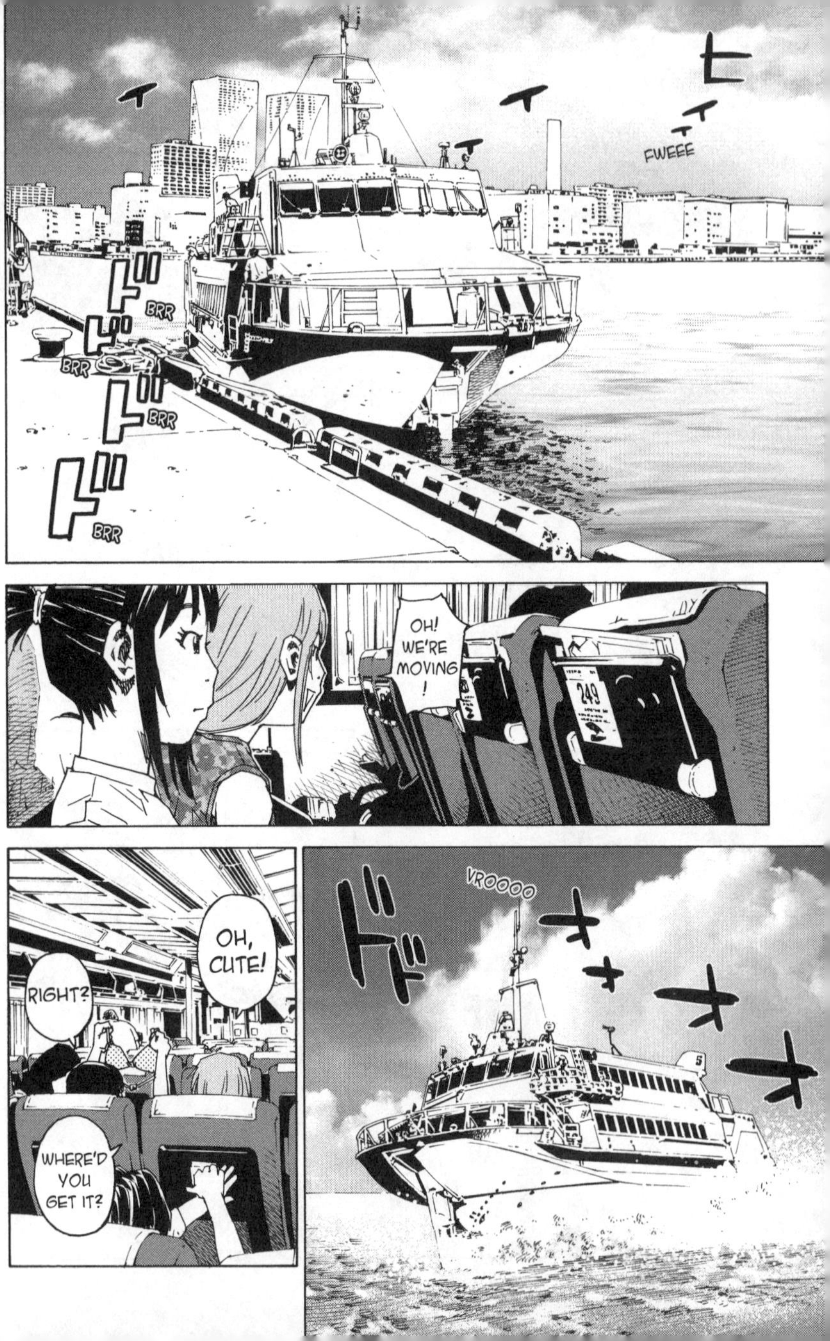
FWEEE
BRR
BRR
BRR
BRR
OH! WE'RE MOVING!
VROOOO
OH, CUTE!
RIGHT?
WHERE'D YOU GET IT?

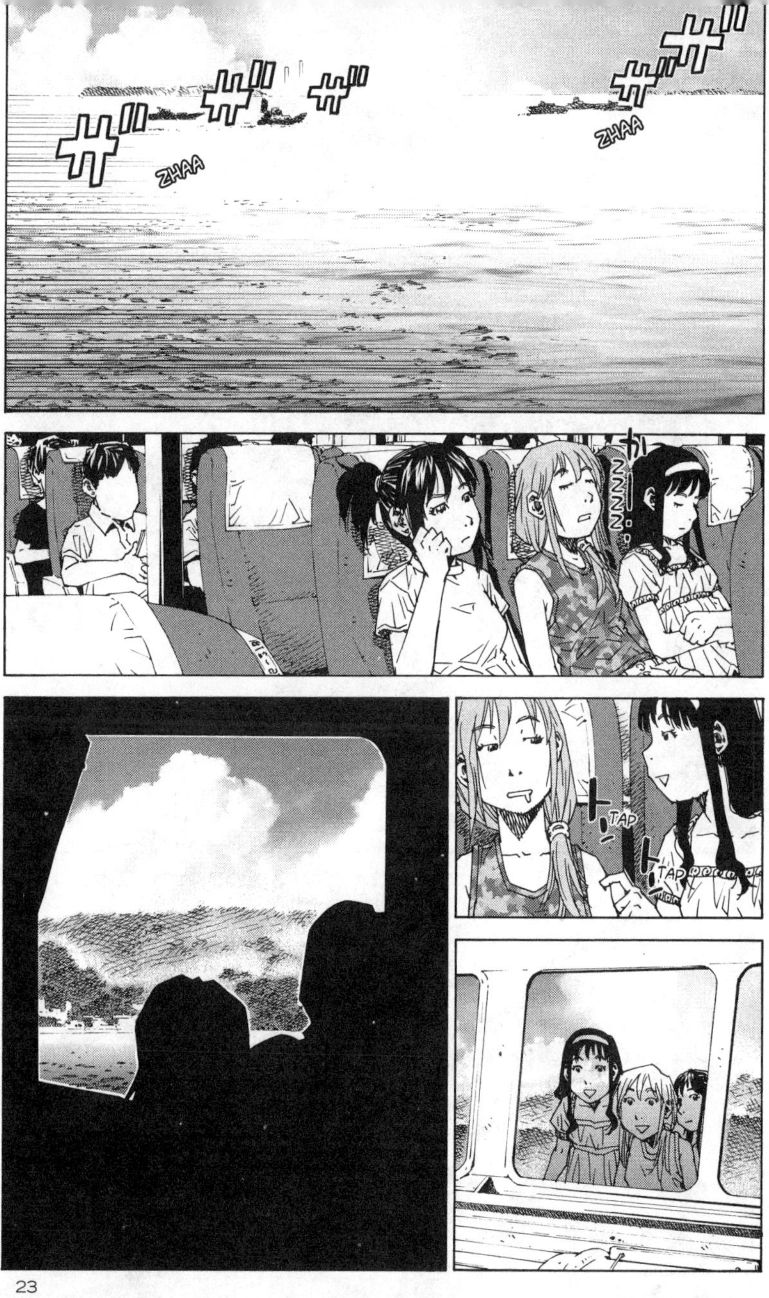
ZHAA
ZHAA
ZZZZ...
TAP
TAP

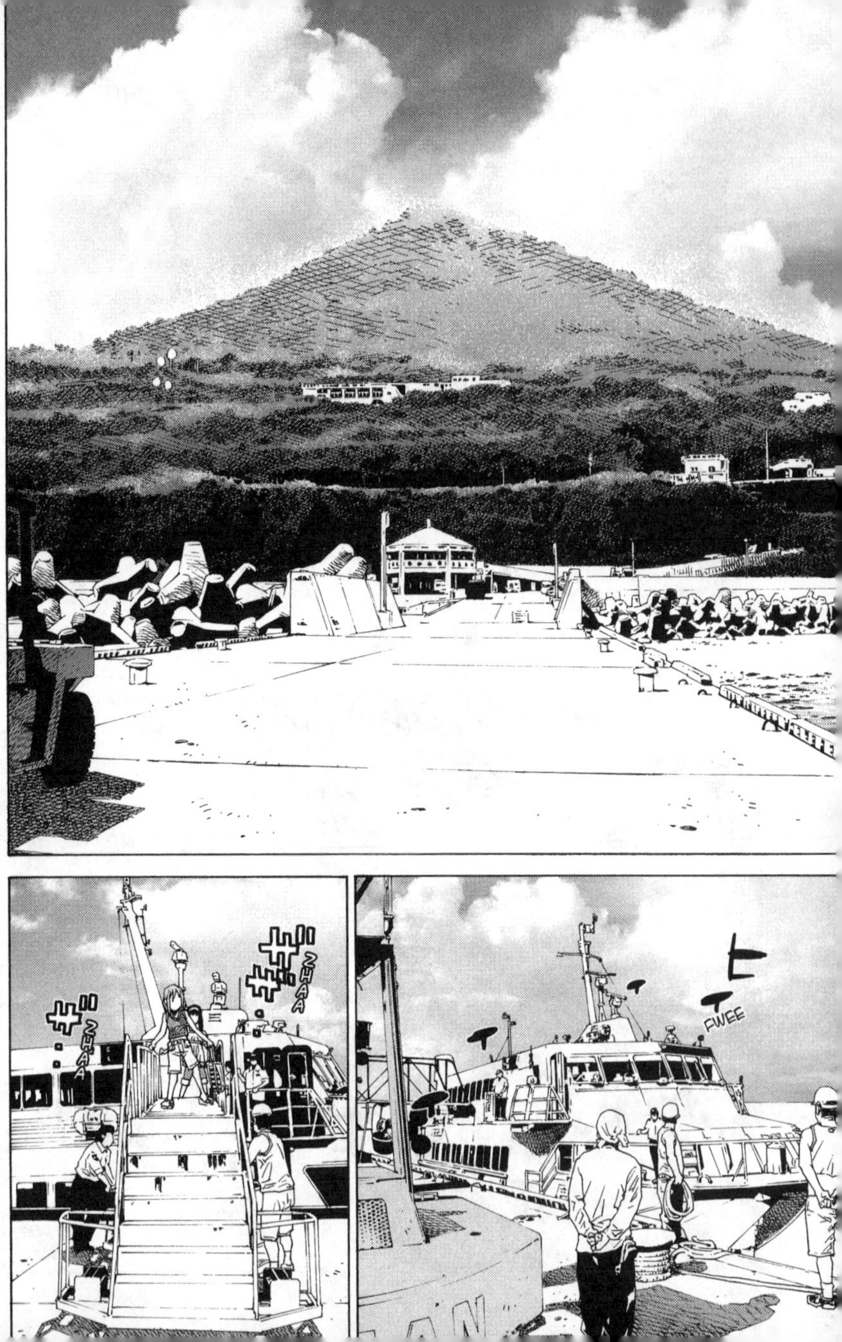
FWEE
ZHAA
ZHAA

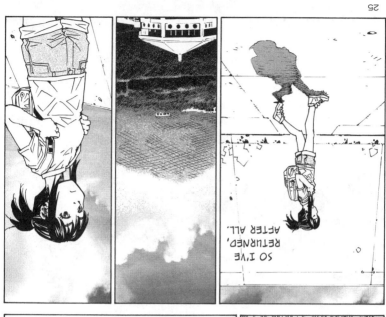

SO I'VE
RETURNED,
AFTER ALL.

AN
ISLAND
!!

YAY!

WHOA!

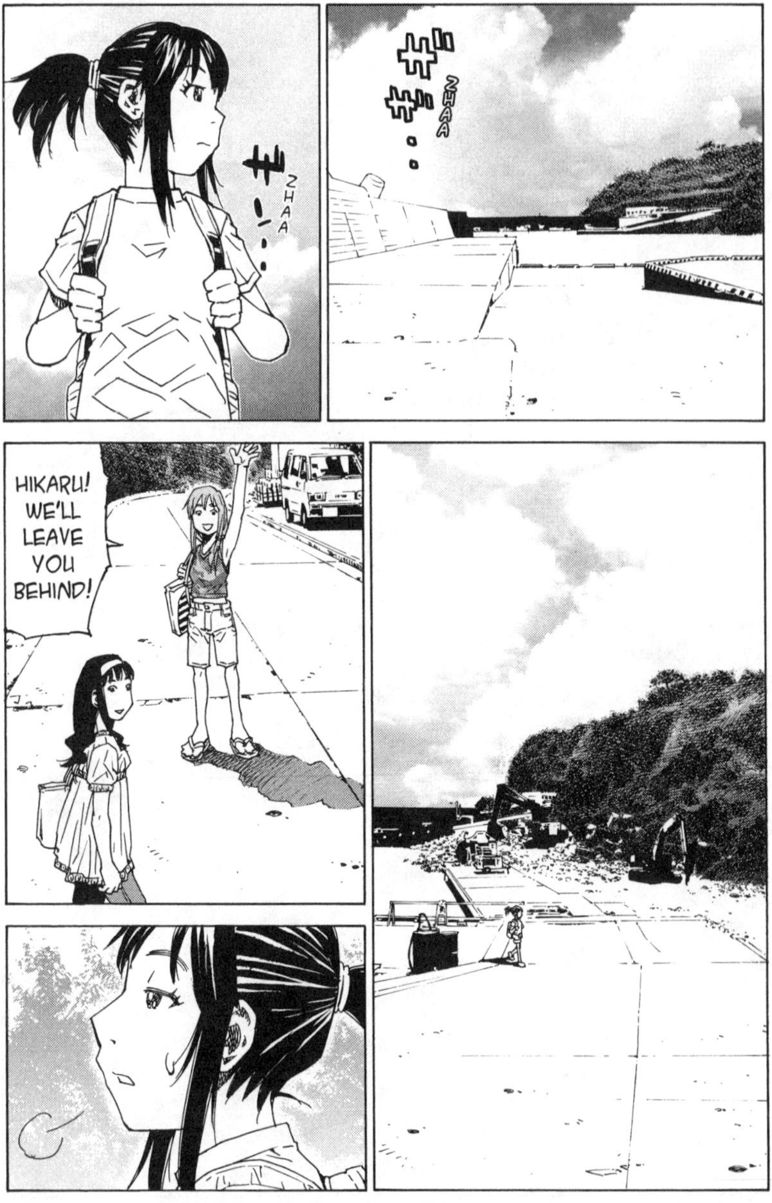
ZHAA
ZHAA
HIKARU! WE'LL LEAVE YOU BEHIND!

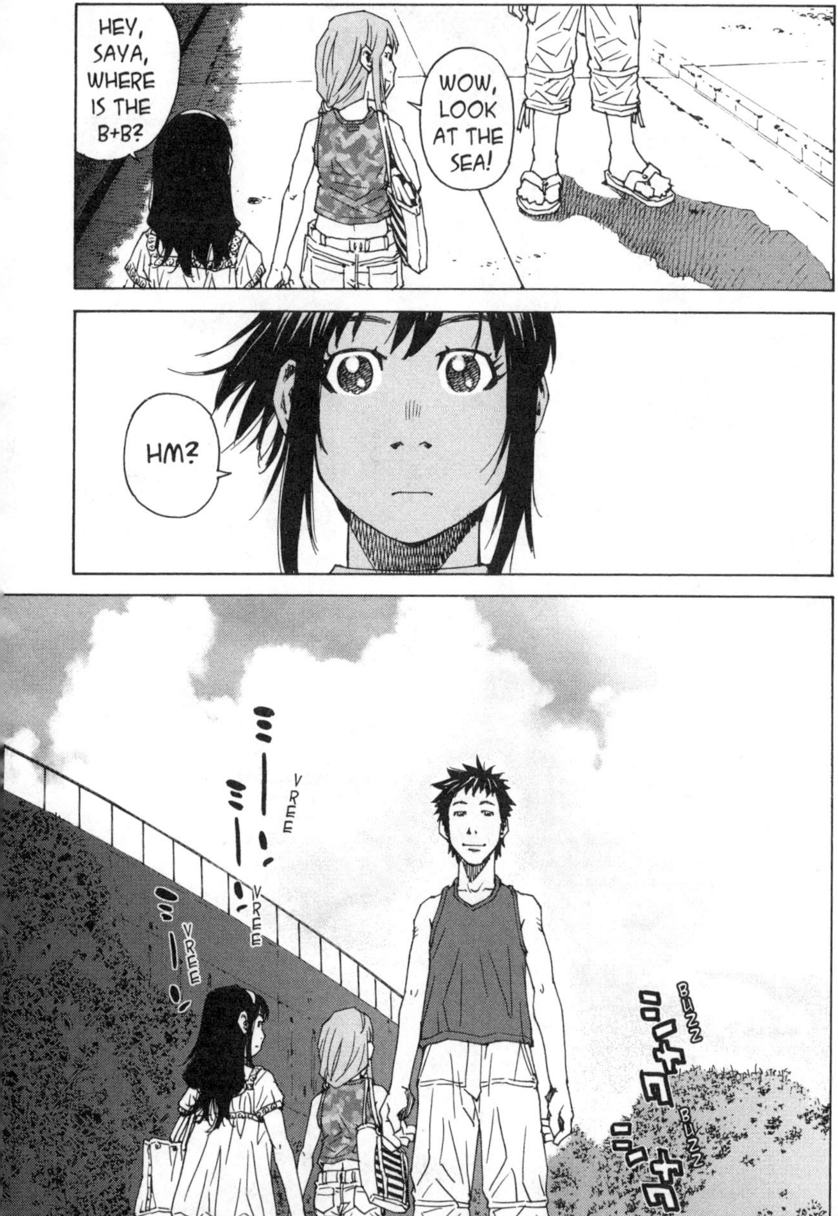
WOW, LOOK AT THE SEA!
HEY, SAYA, WHERE IS THE B+B?
HM?
BUZZ
BUZZ
VREE
VREE
VREE

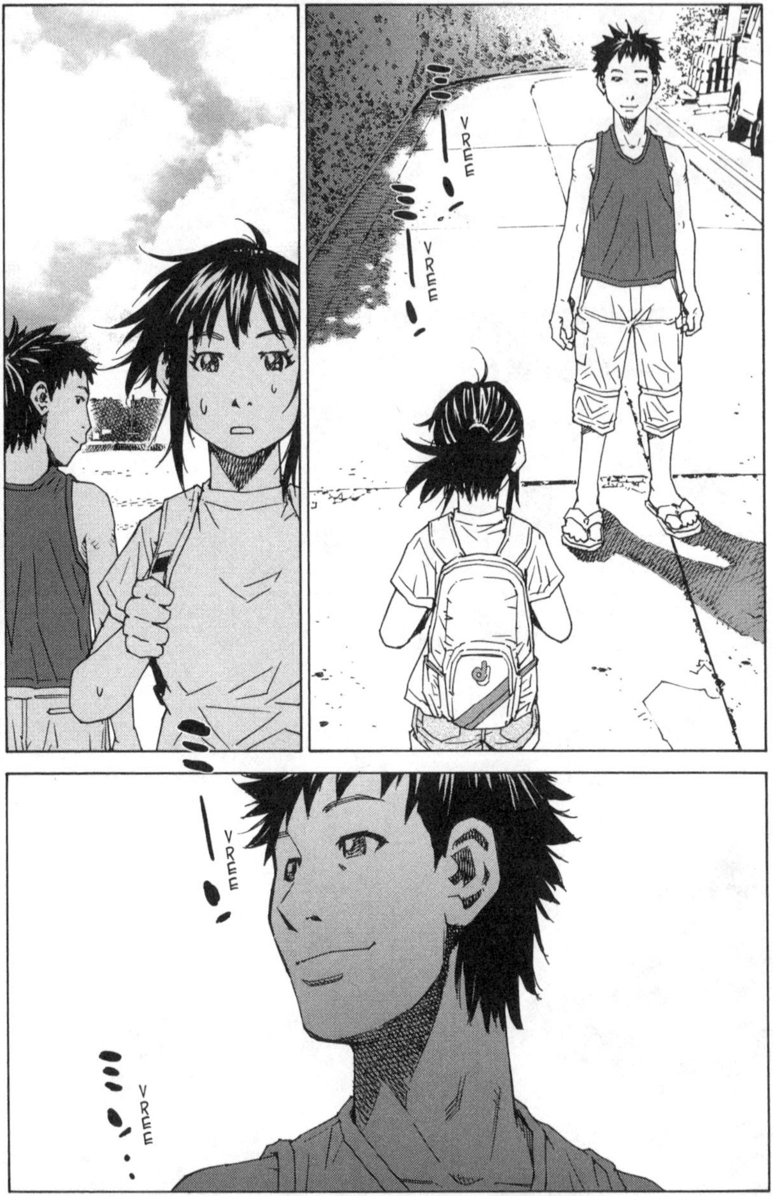
VREE
VREE
VREE
VREE

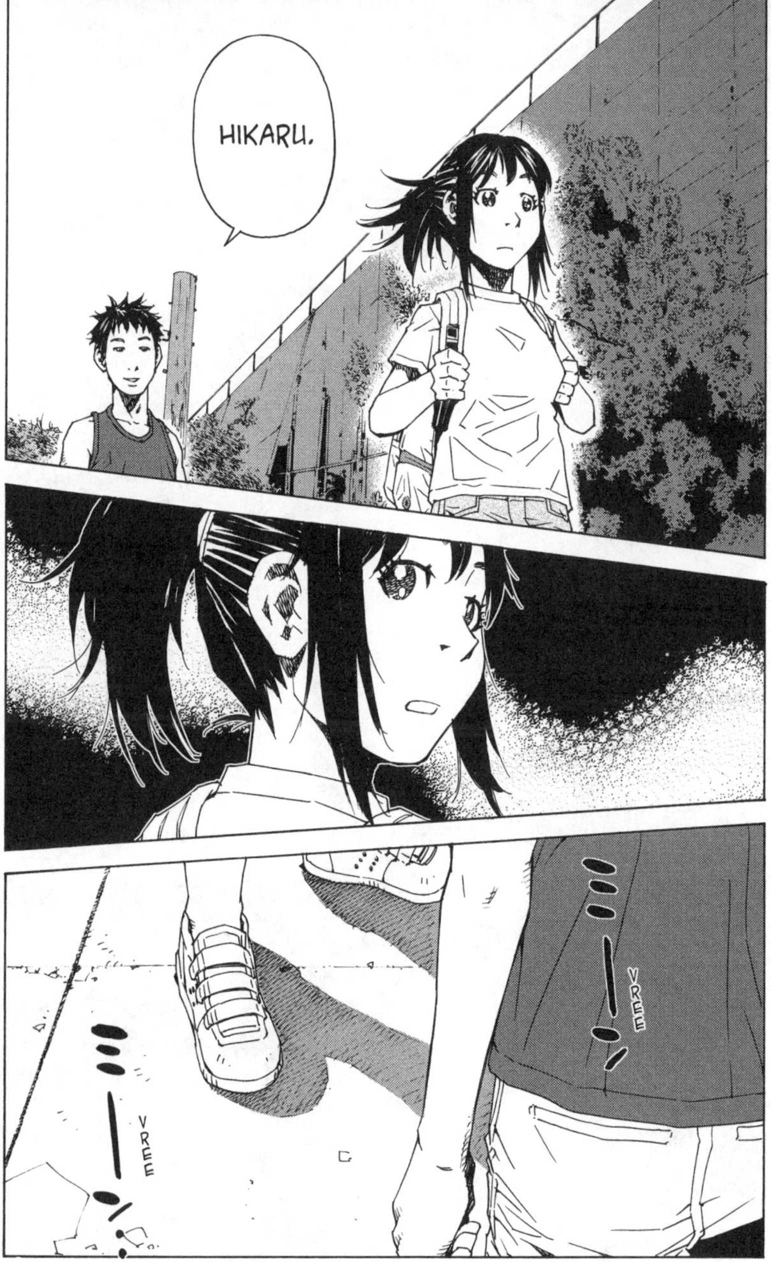
HIKARU.
VREE
VREE

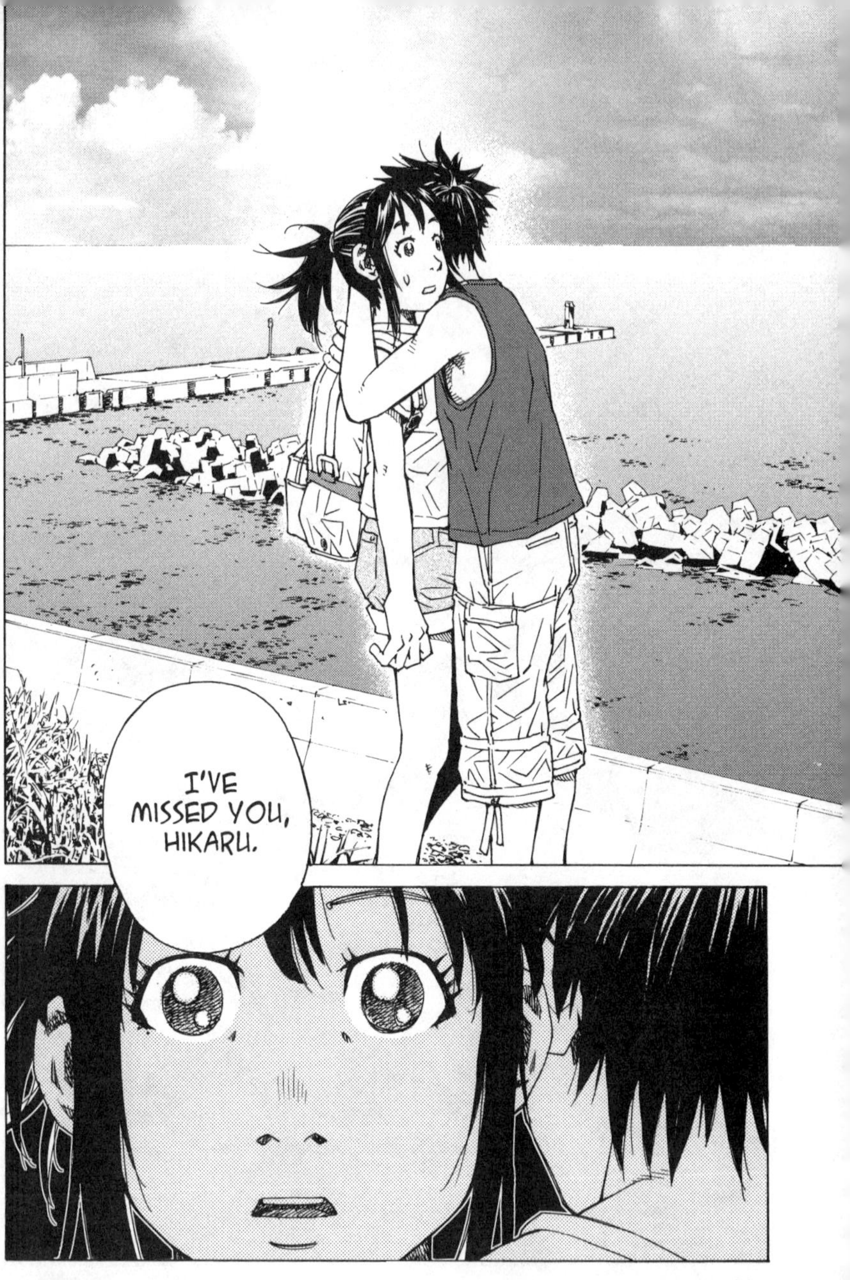
I'VE MISSED YOU, HIKARU.

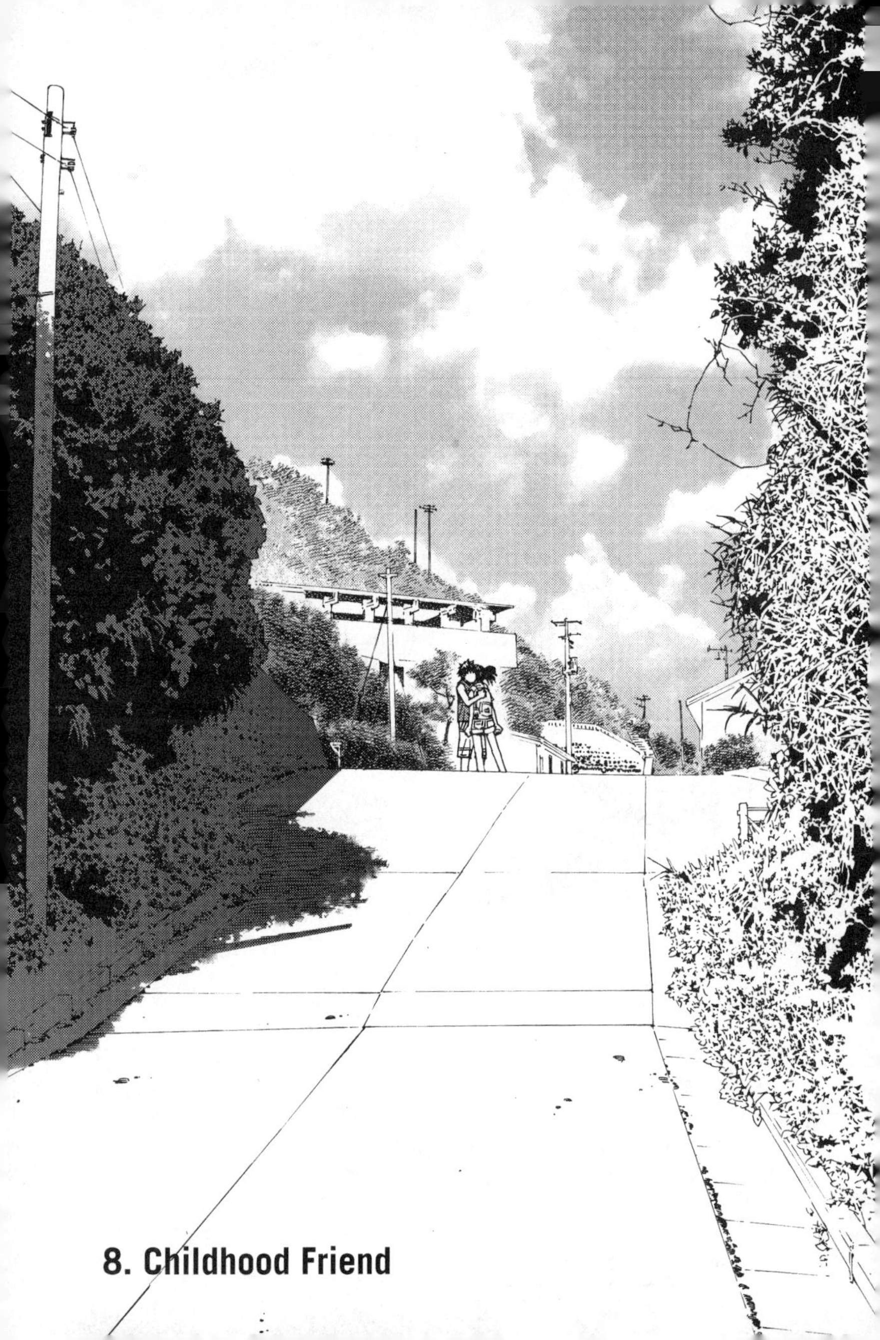
8. Childhood Friend

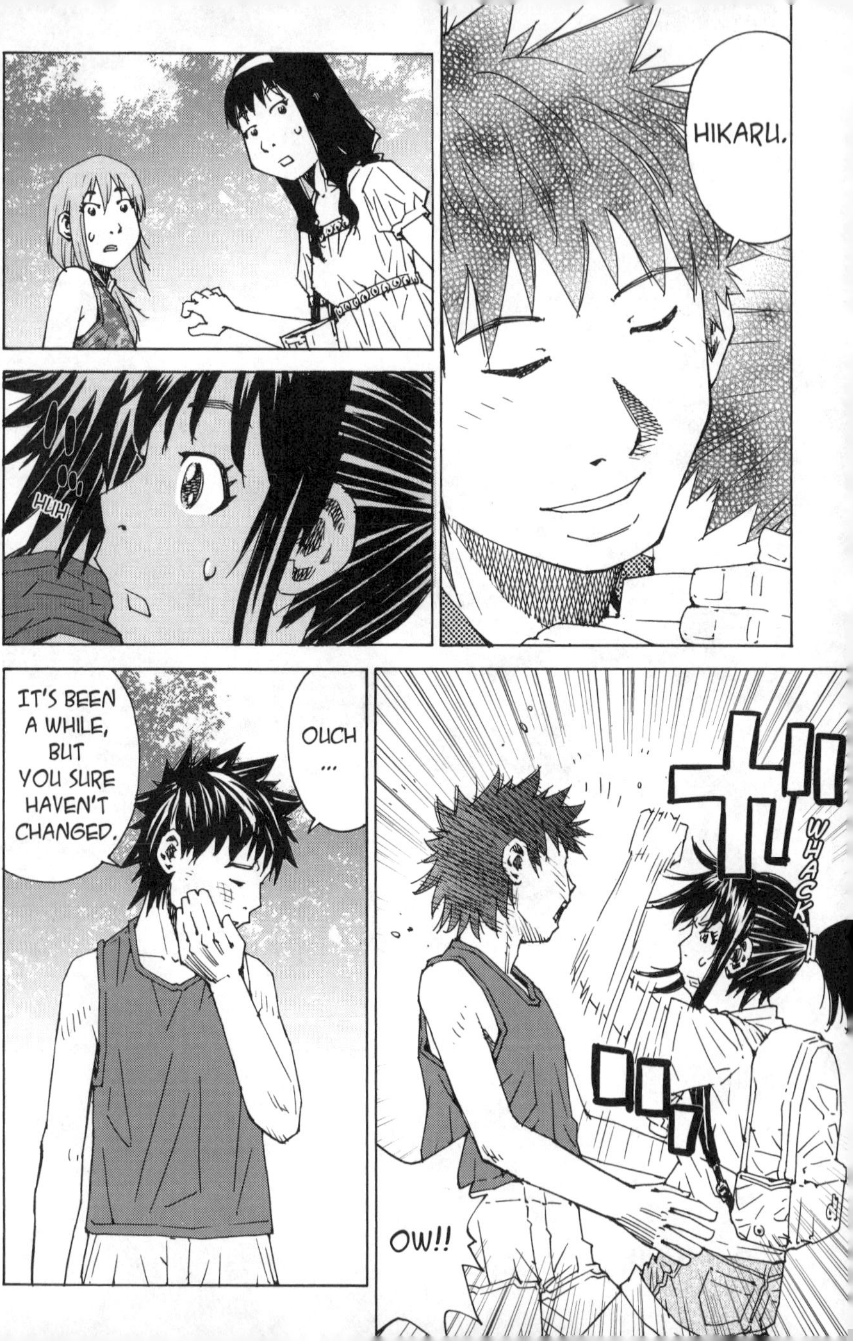
HIKARU.
HUH
WHACK
OW!!
IT'S BEEN A WHILE, BUT YOU SURE HAVEN'T CHANGED.
OUCH ...

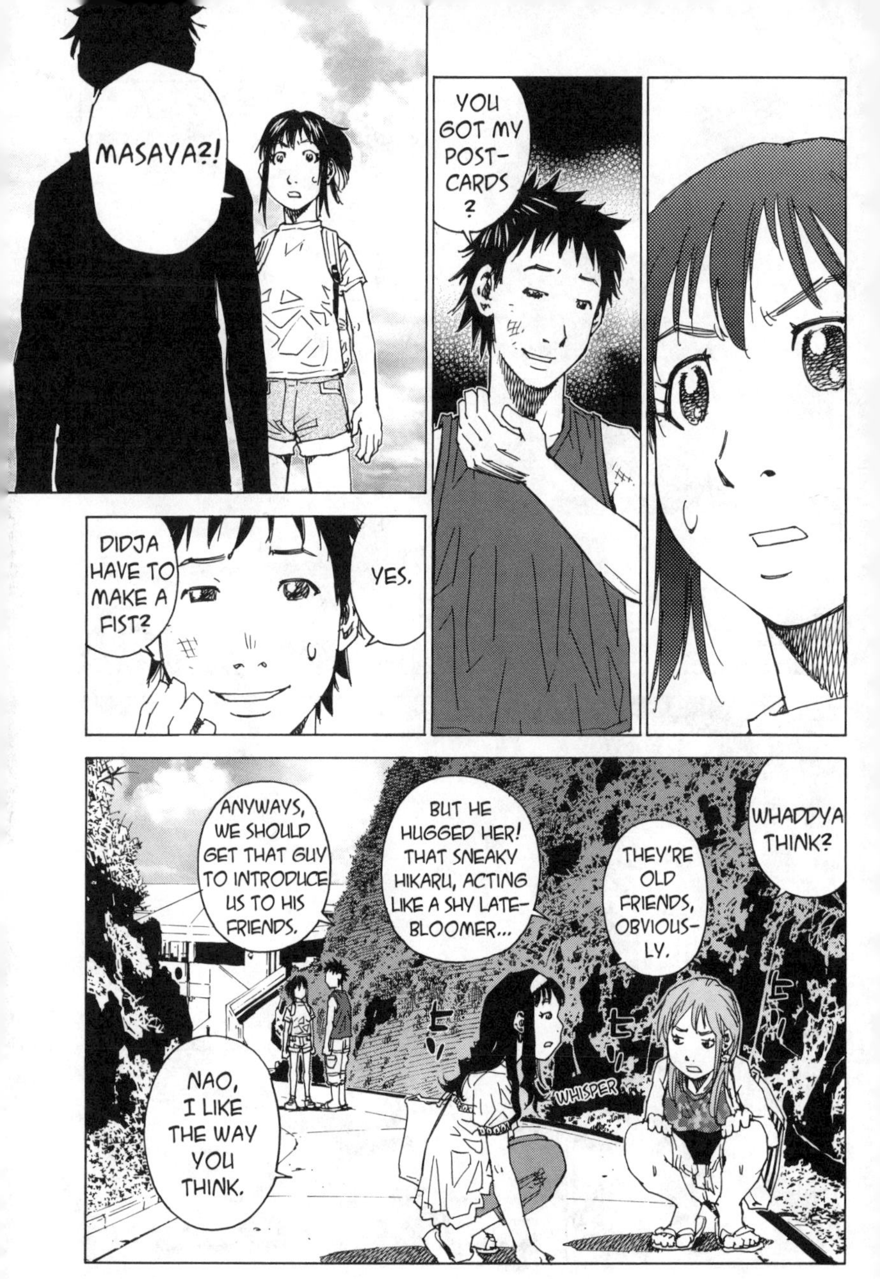
YOU GOT MY POST-CARDS?
MASAYA?!
DIDJA HAVE TO MAKE A FIST?
YES.
WHADDYA THINK?
THEY'RE OLD FRIENDS, OBVIOUS-LY.
BUT HE HUGGED HER! THAT SNEAKY HIKARU, ACTING LIKE A SHY LATE-BLOOMER...
WHISPER
ANYWAYS, WE SHOULD GET THAT GUY TO INTRODUCE US TO HIS FRIENDS.
NAO, I LIKE THE WAY YOU THINK.

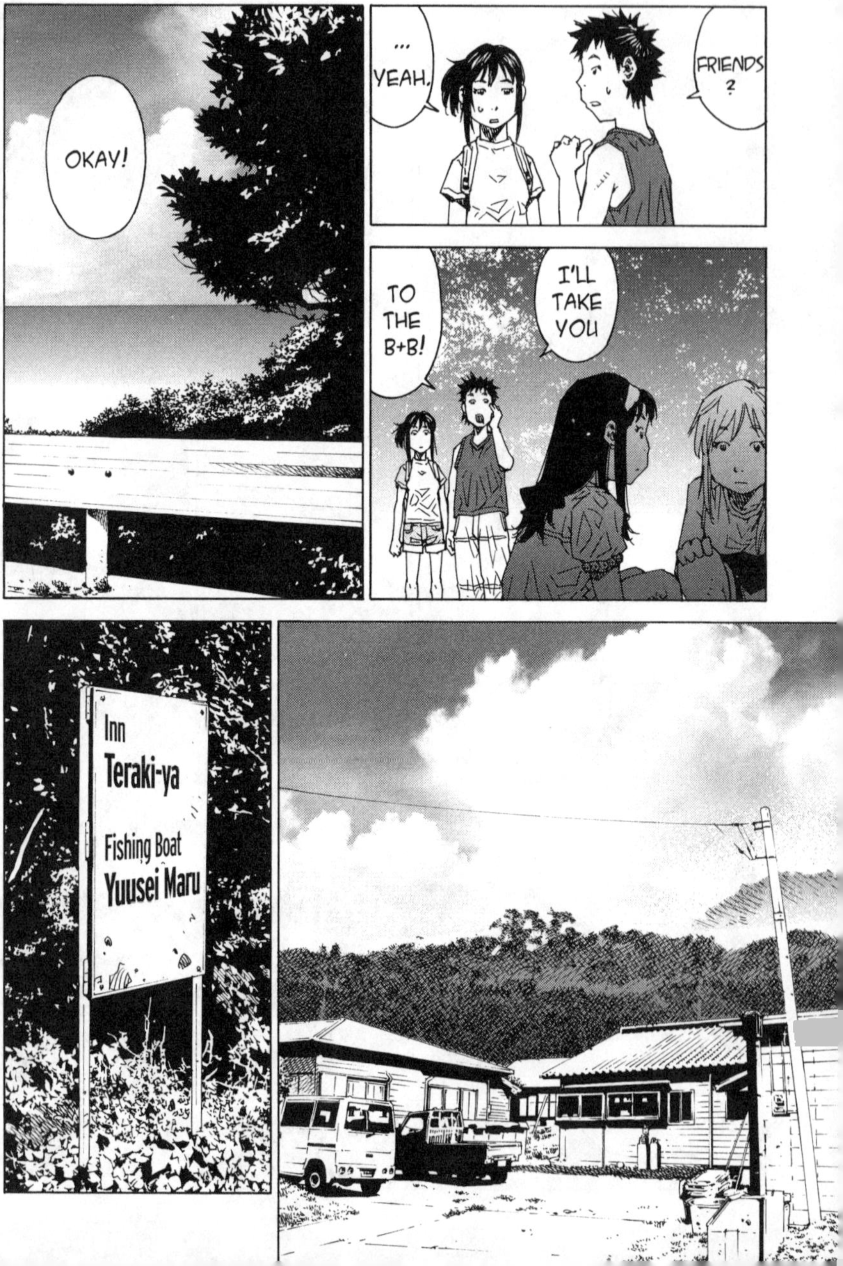
FRIENDS ?
... YEAH,
I'LL TAKE YOU
TO THE B+B!
OKAY!
Inn
Teraki-ya
Fishing Boat
Yuusei Maru

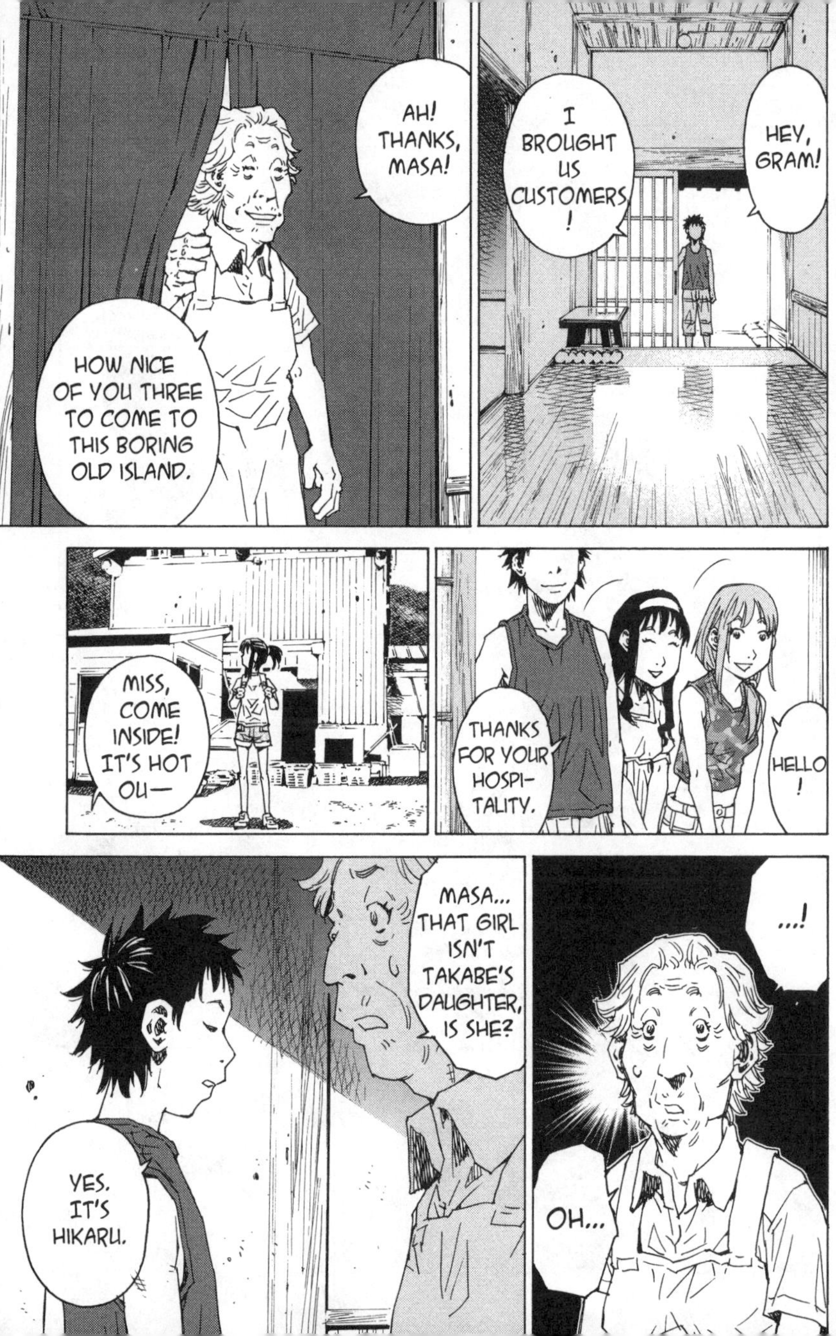
HEY, GRAM!
I BROUGHT US CUSTOMERS!
AH! THANKS, MASA!
HOW NICE OF YOU THREE TO COME TO THIS BORING OLD ISLAND.
HELLO!
THANKS FOR YOUR HOSPI-TALITY.
MISS, COME INSIDE! IT'S HOT OU—
...!
OH...
MASA... THAT GIRL ISN'T TAKABE'S DAUGHTER, IS SHE?
YES. IT'S HIKARU.

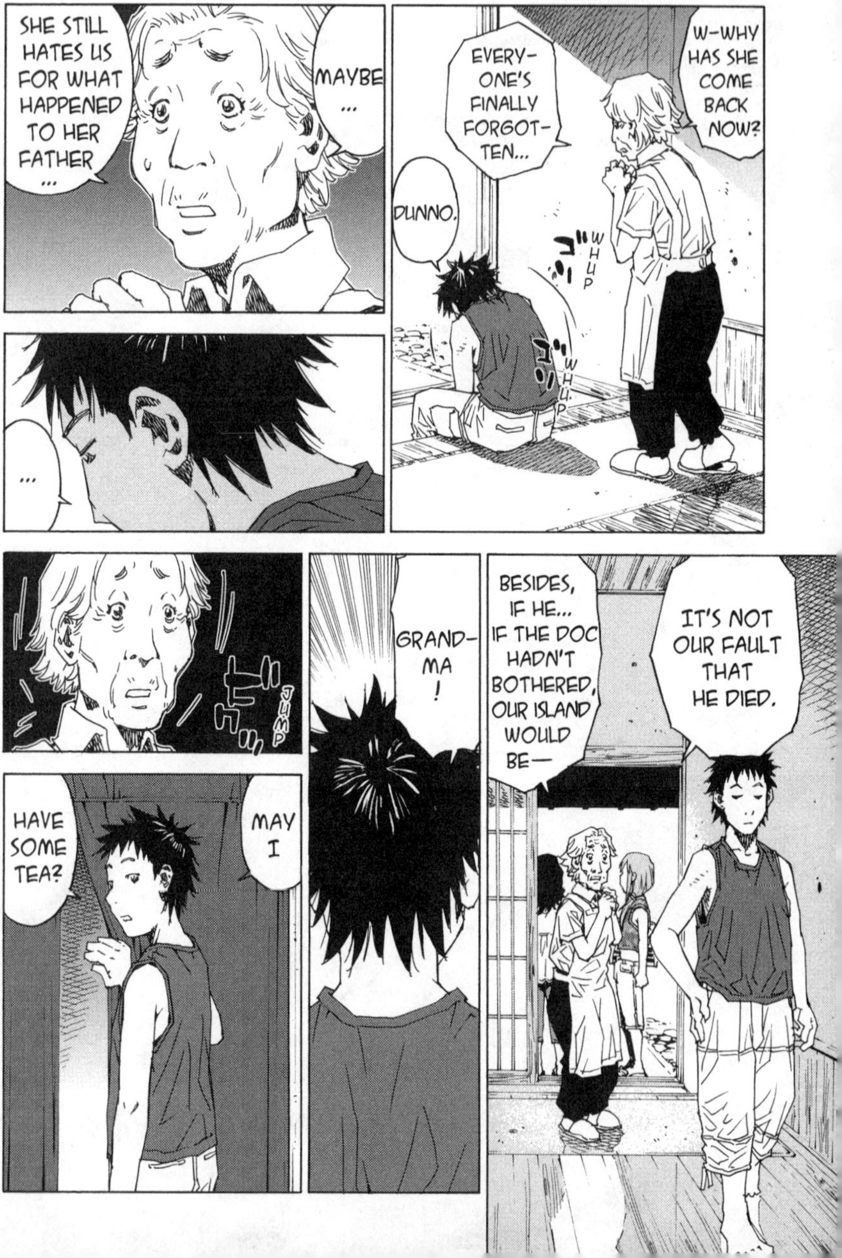
W-WHY HAS SHE COME BACK NOW?
EVERYONE'S FINALLY FORGOTTEN...
DUNNO.
WHUP
WHUP
SHE STILL HATES US FOR WHAT HAPPENED TO HER FATHER ...
MAYBE ...
...
IT'S NOT OUR FAULT THAT HE DIED.
BESIDES, IF HE... IF THE DOC HADN'T BOTHERED, OUR ISLAND WOULD BE—
GRANDMA!
JUMP
MAY I
HAVE SOME TEA?

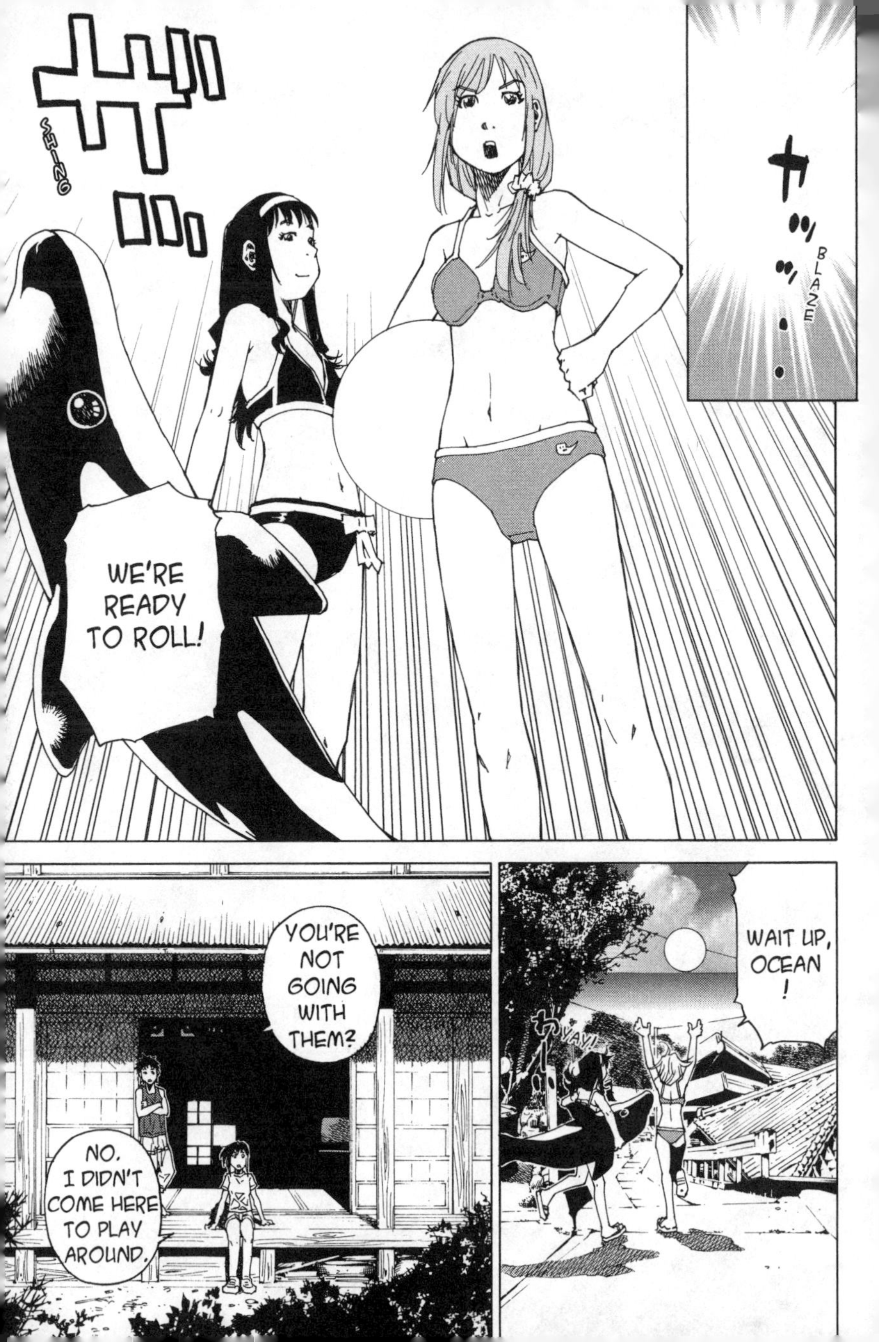
BLAZE
SHING
WE'RE READY TO ROLL!
WAIT UP, OCEAN!
YAY!
YOU'RE NOT GOING WITH THEM?
NO. I DIDN'T COME HERE TO PLAY AROUND.

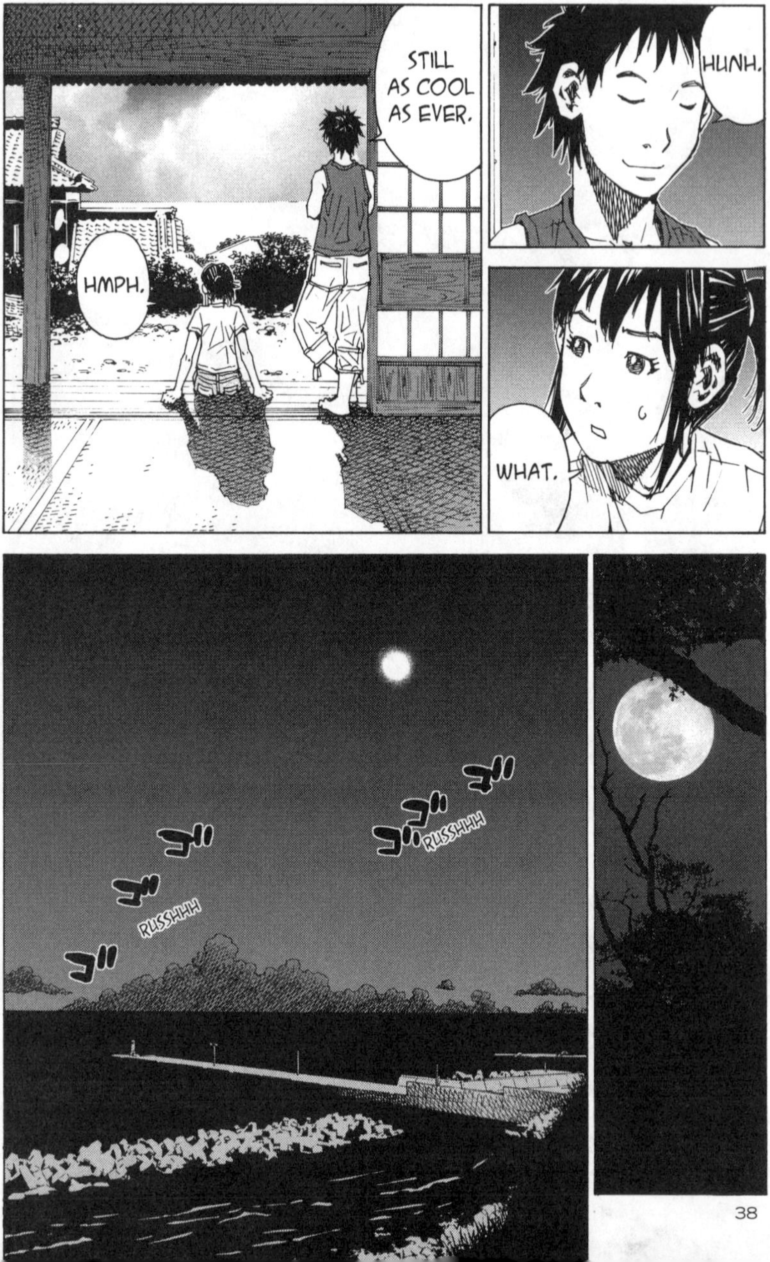
HUNH.
WHAT.
STILL AS COOL AS EVER.
HMPH.
RUSSHHH
RUSSHHH

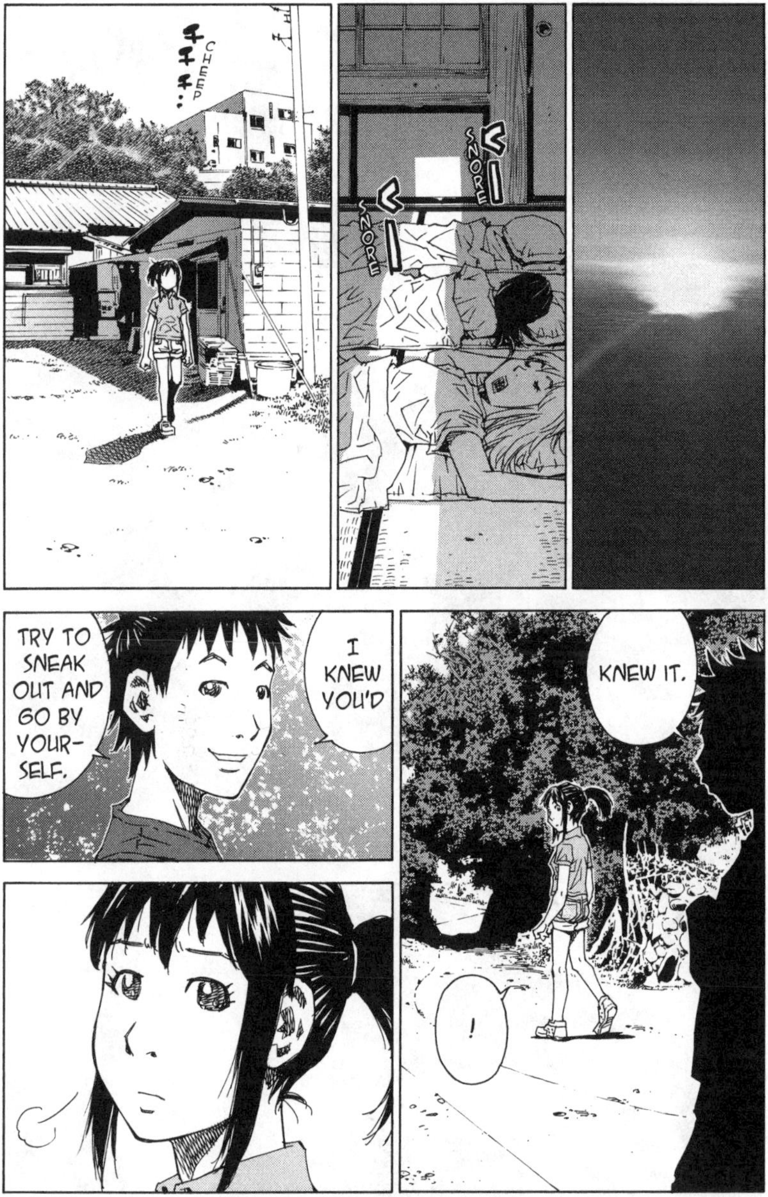
SNORE
SNORE
チチチ
CHEEP
KNEW IT.
I KNEW YOU'D
TRY TO SNEAK OUT AND GO BY YOUR-SELF.
!

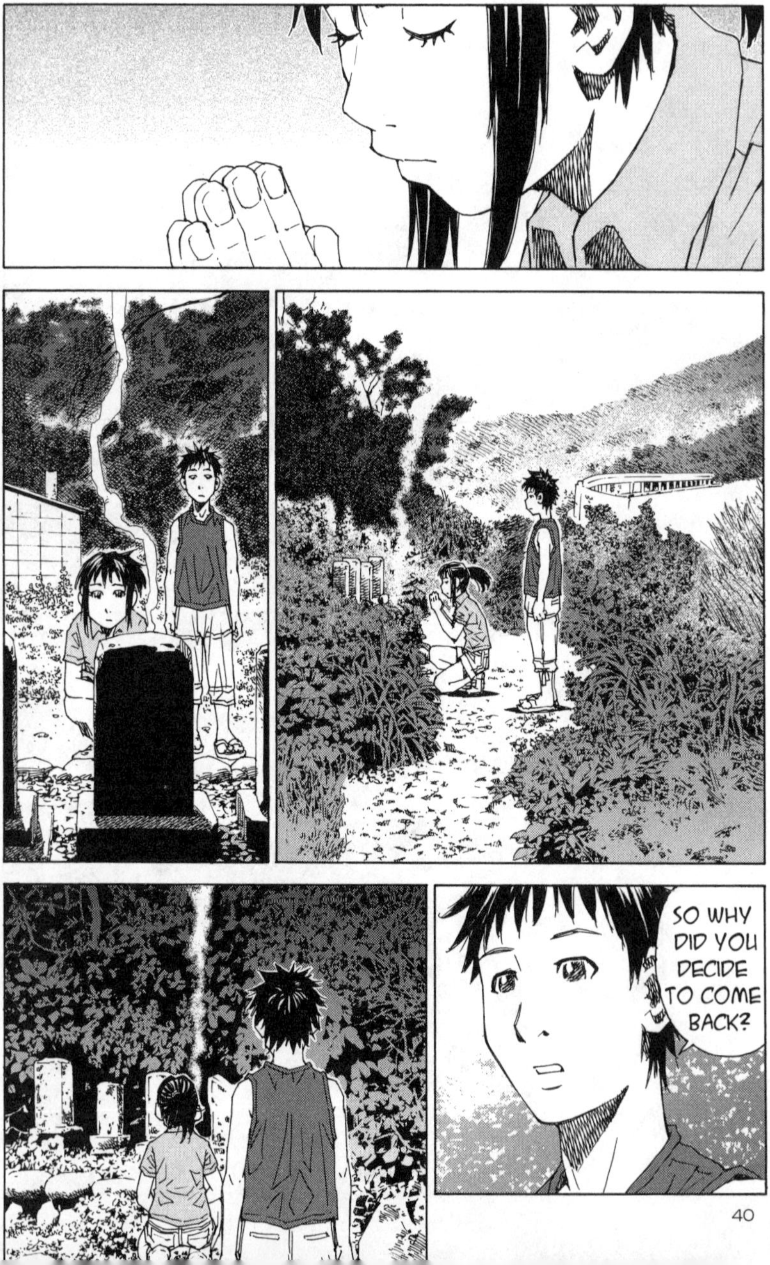
SO WHY DID YOU DECIDE TO COME BACK?

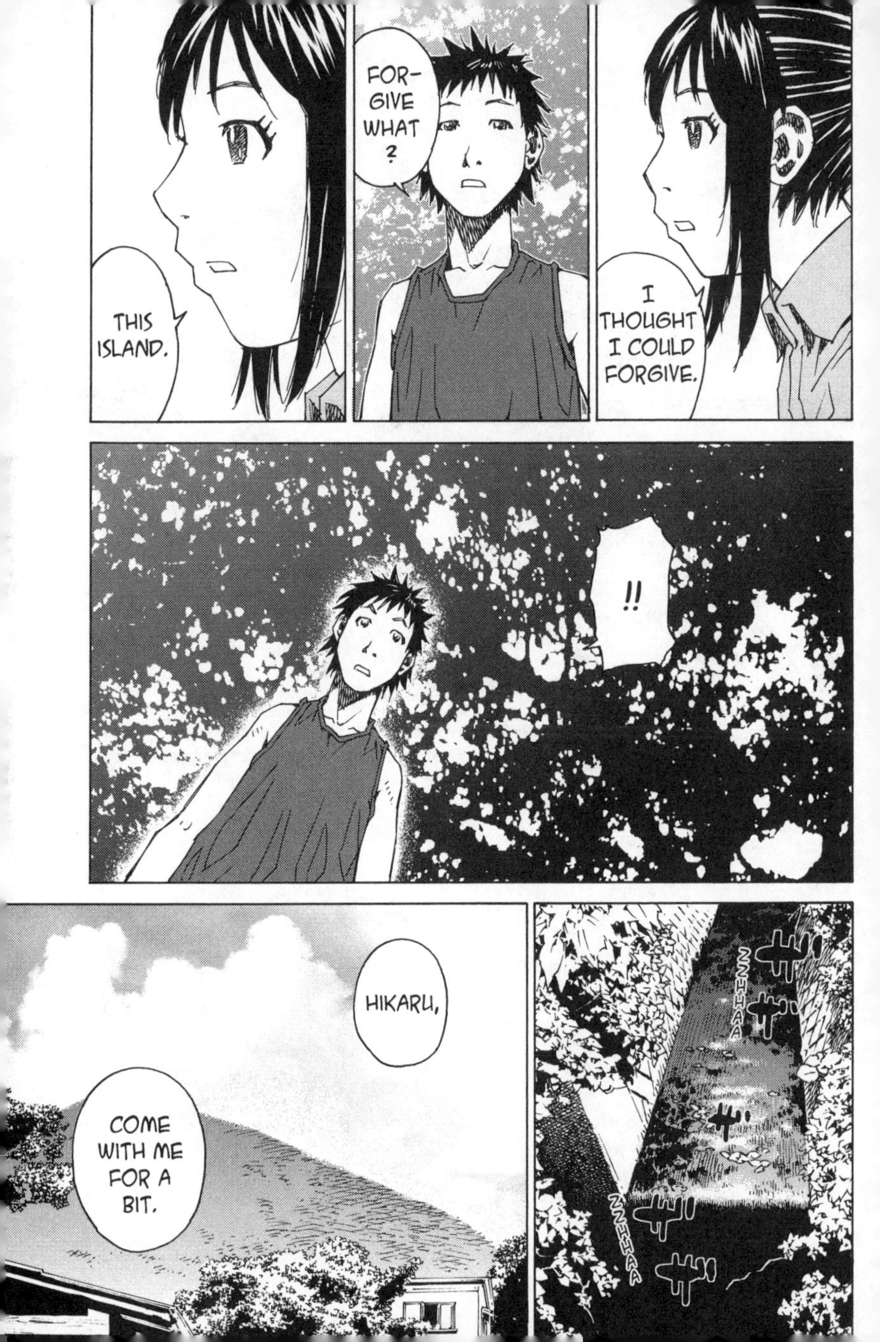
I THOUGHT I COULD FORGIVE.
FOR-GIVE WHAT?
THIS ISLAND.
!!
ZZHHAA
ZZHHAA
HIKARU,
COME WITH ME FOR A BIT.

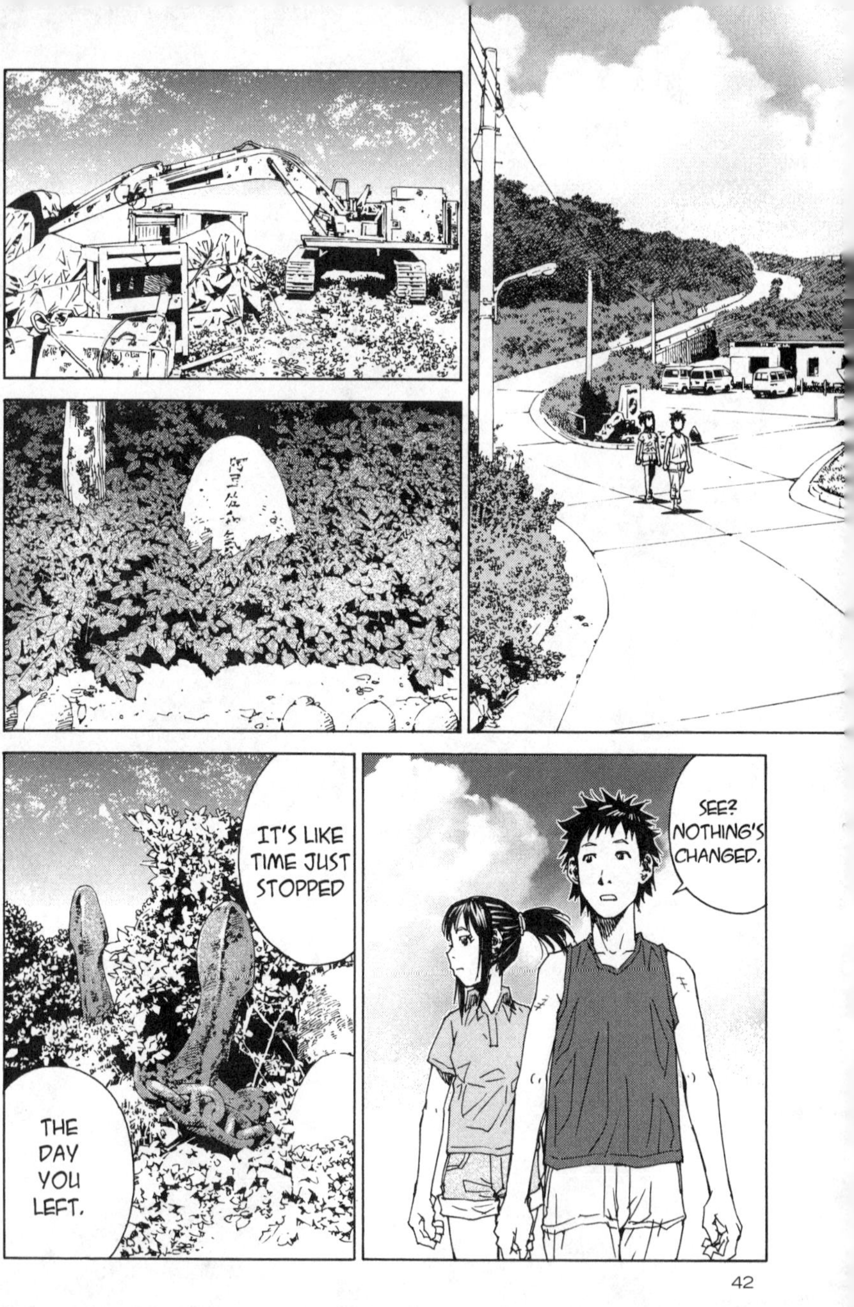
SEE? NOTHING'S CHANGED.
IT'S LIKE TIME JUST STOPPED
THE DAY YOU LEFT.

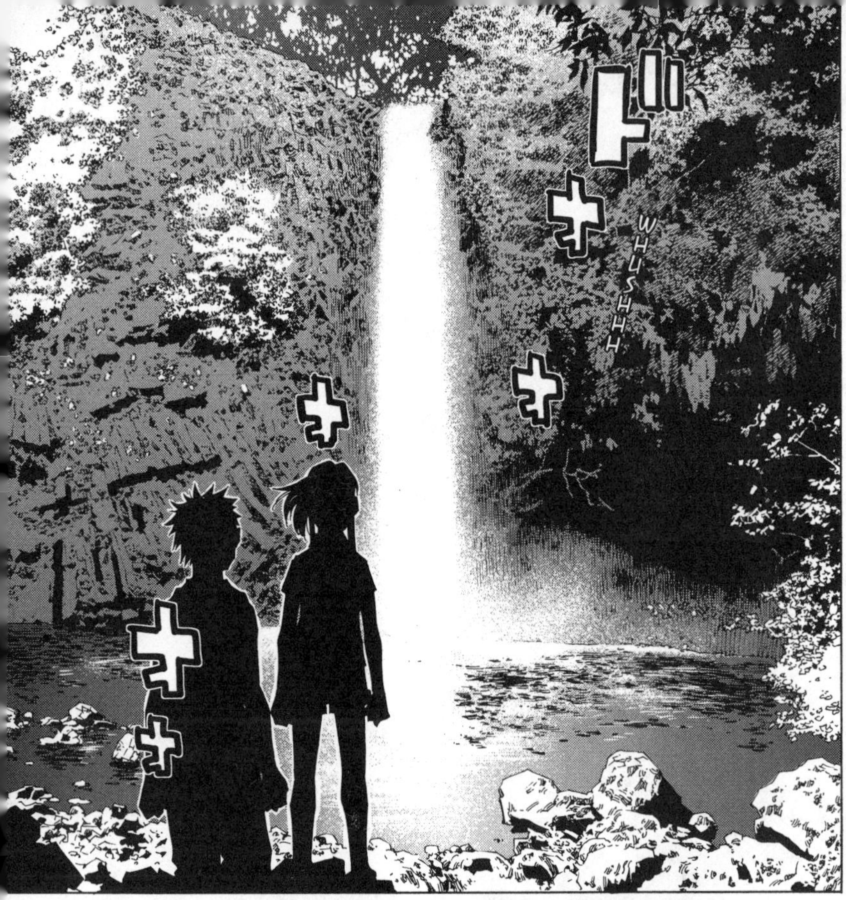
WHUSHHH

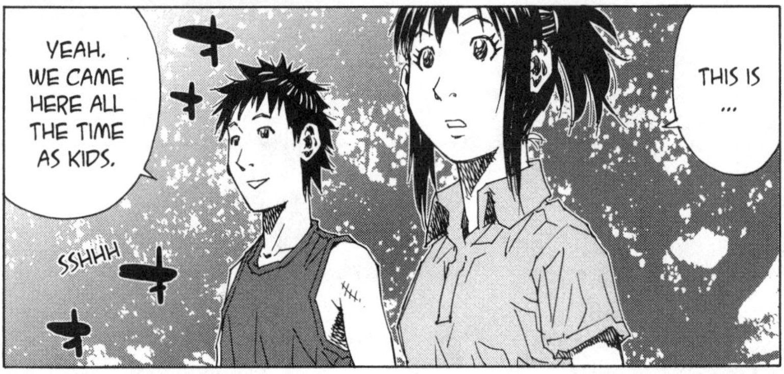
THIS IS
...
YEAH. WE CAME HERE ALL THE TIME AS KIDS.
SSHHH

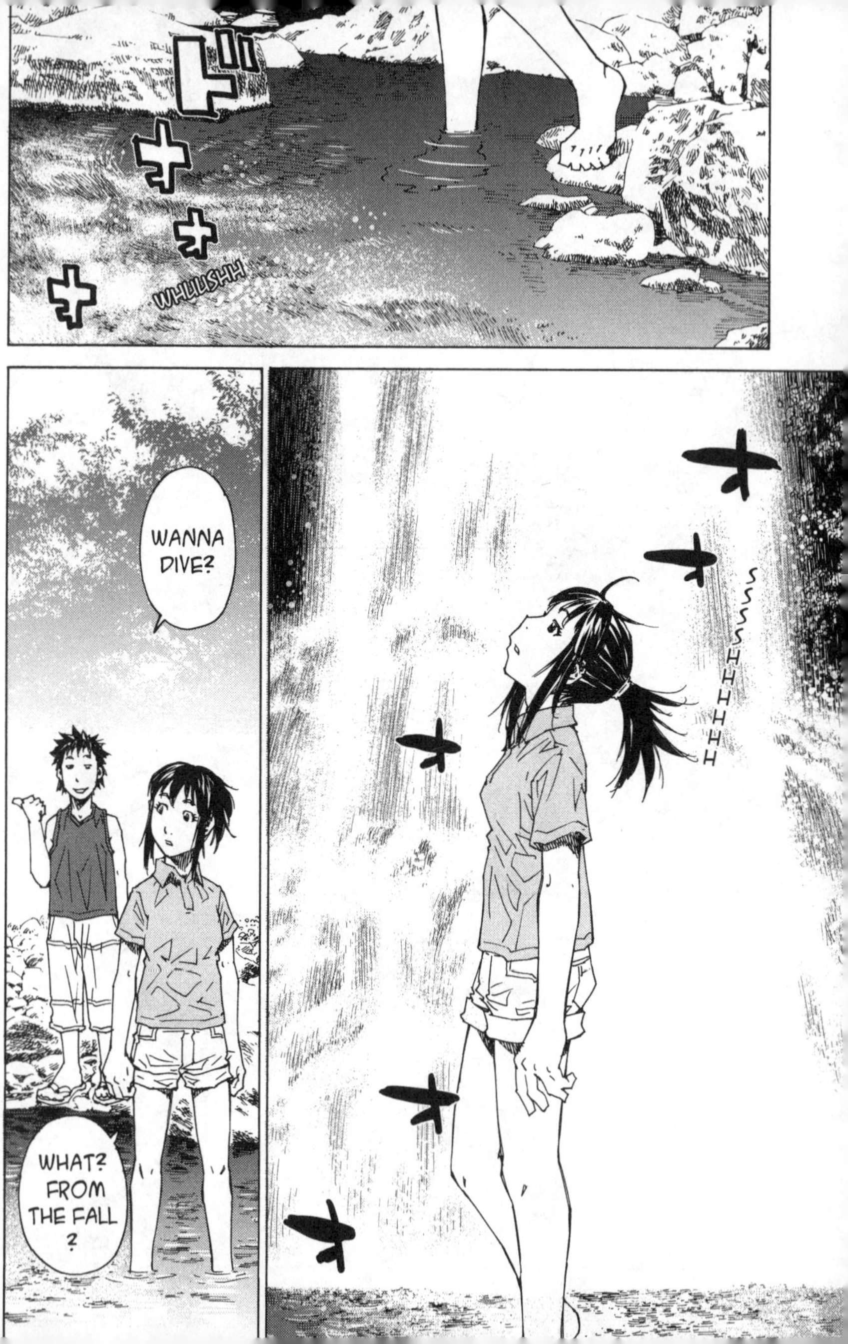
WHLLLSHH
SSSSHHHHHHH
WANNA DIVE?
WHAT? FROM THE FALL ?

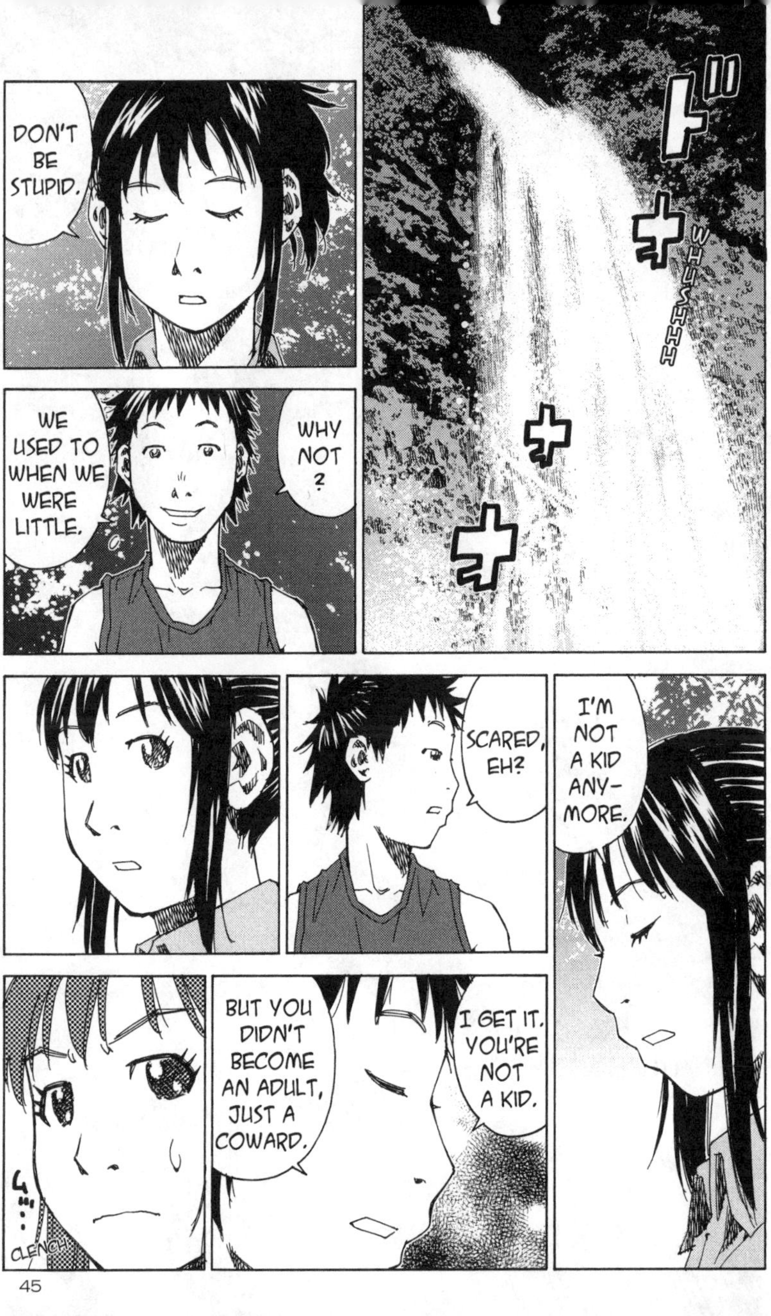
WHUSHHH
DON'T BE STUPID.
WHY NOT?
WE USED TO WHEN WE WERE LITTLE.
I'M NOT A KID ANY-MORE.
SCARED, EH?
I GET IT. YOU'RE NOT A KID.
BUT YOU DIDN'T BECOME AN ADULT, JUST A COWARD.
...
CLENCH

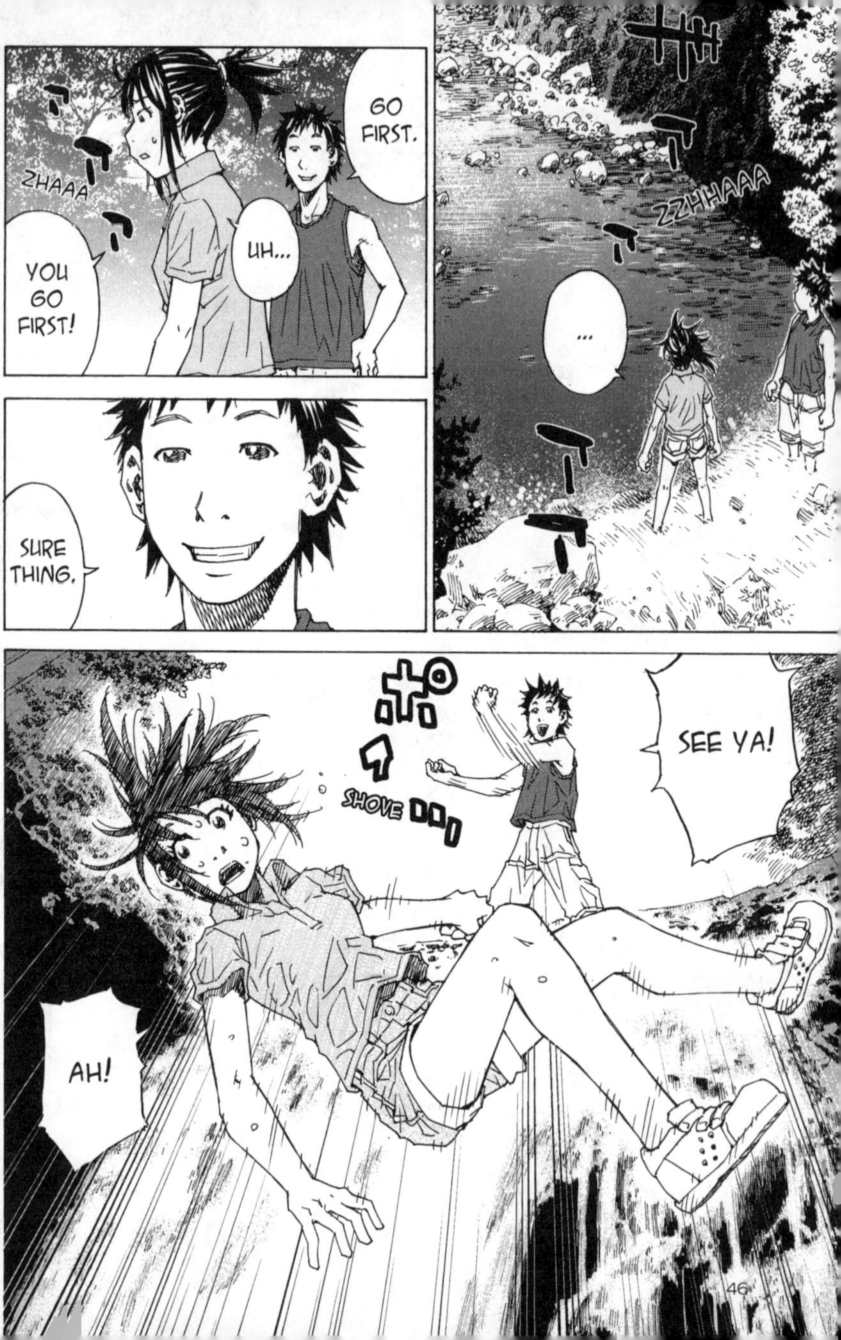
ZZHHAAA
...
GO FIRST.
UH...
YOU GO FIRST!
ZHAAA
SURE THING.
SEE YA!
SHOVE
AH!

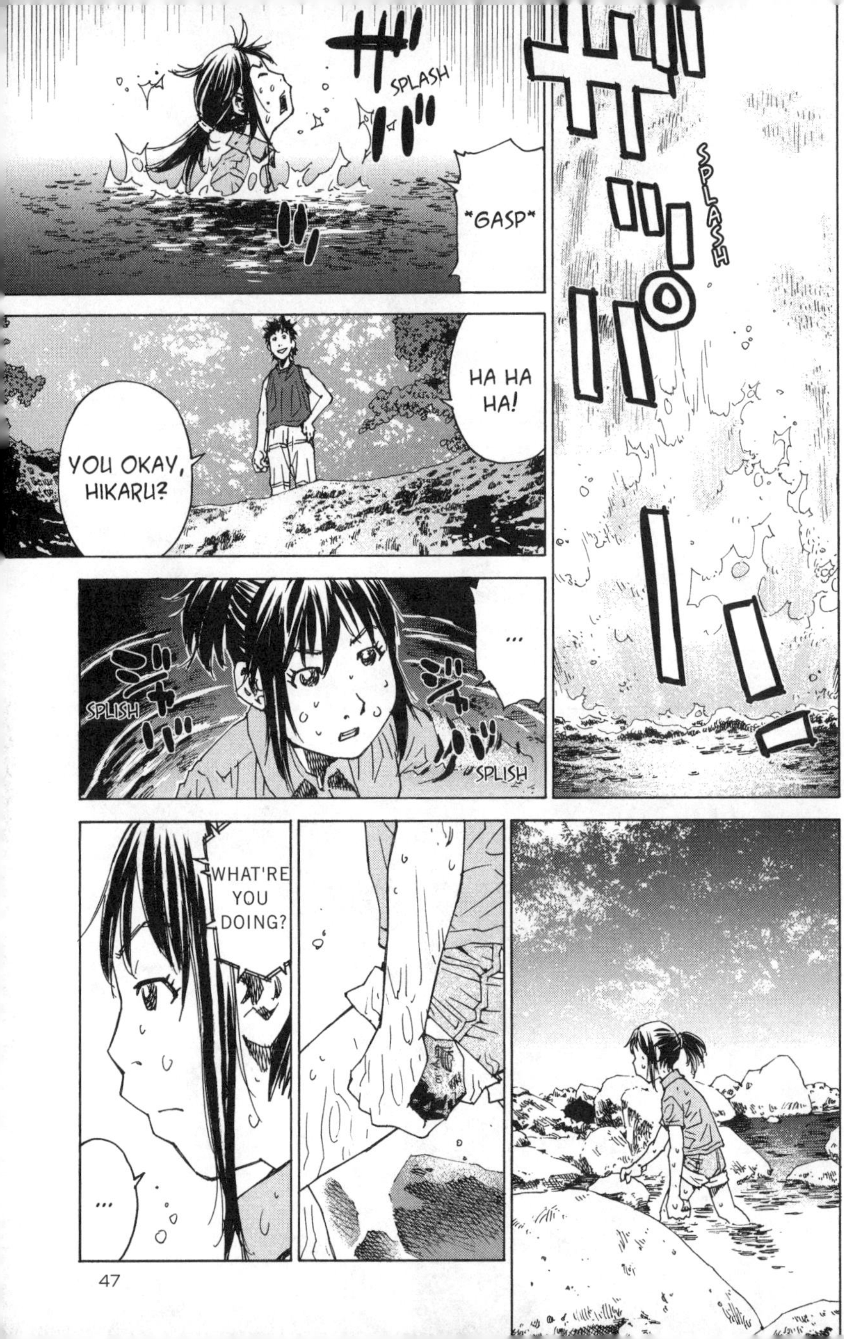
SPLASH
SPLASH
GASP
HA HA HA!
YOU OKAY, HIKARU?
...
SPLISH
SPLISH
WHAT'RE YOU DOING?
...

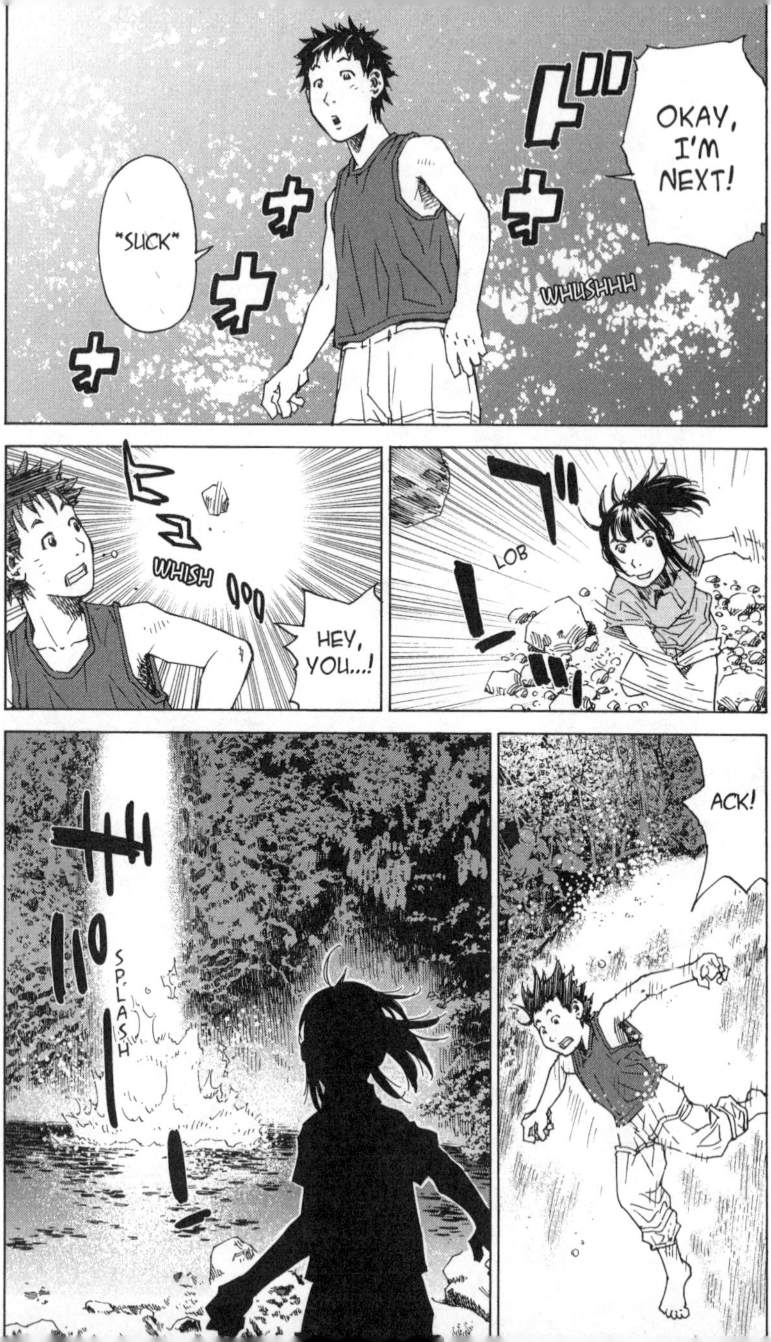
OKAY, I'M NEXT!
SUCK
WHUSHHH
LOB
WHISH
HEY, YOU...!
ACK!
SPLASH

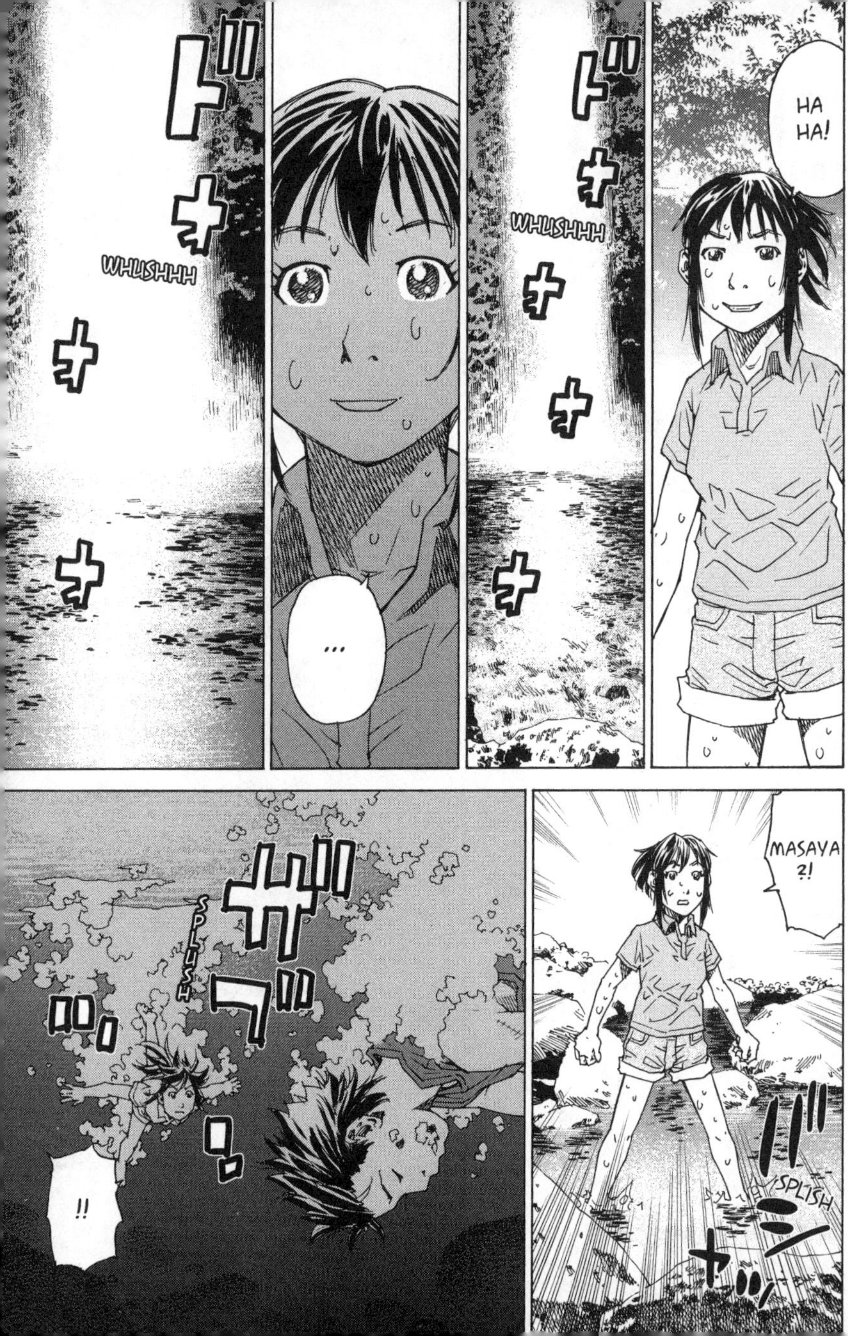
HA HA!
WHUSHHH
...
WHUSHHH
MASAYA ?!
SPLISH
SPLISH
!!

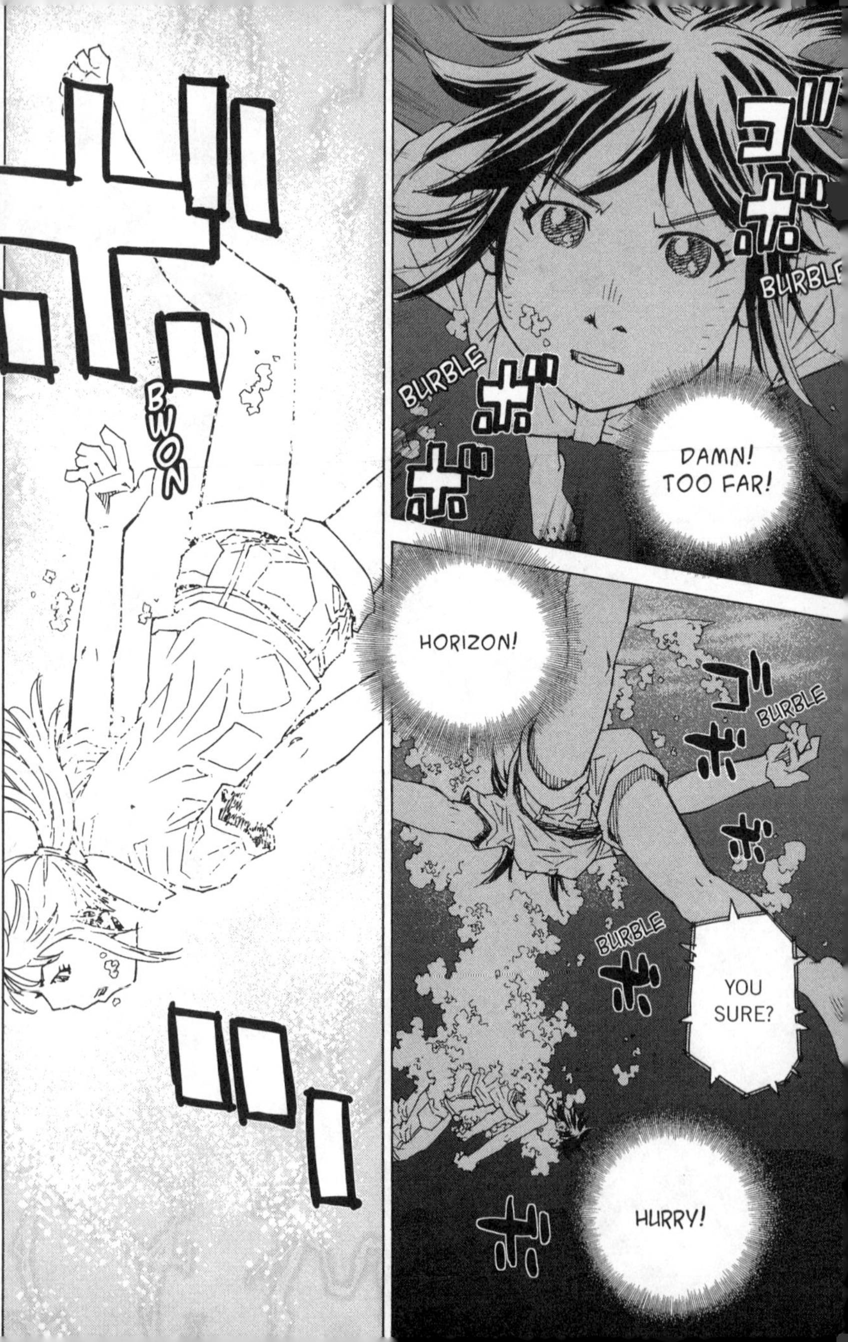
BURBLE
BURBLE
DAMN! TOO FAR!
HORIZON!
BURBLE
BURBLE
YOU SURE?
HURRY!
BWON

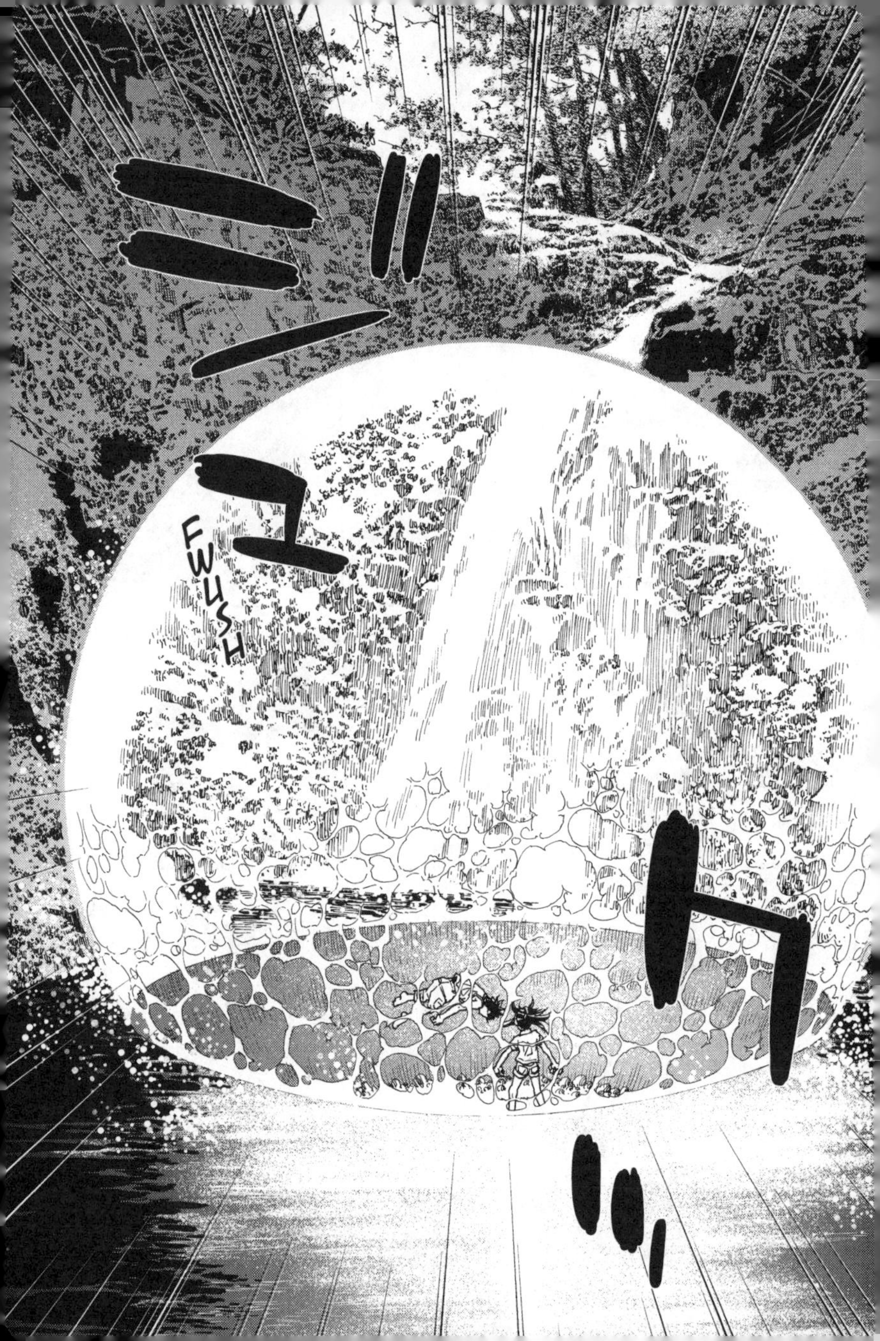
ジュワッ
FWUSH

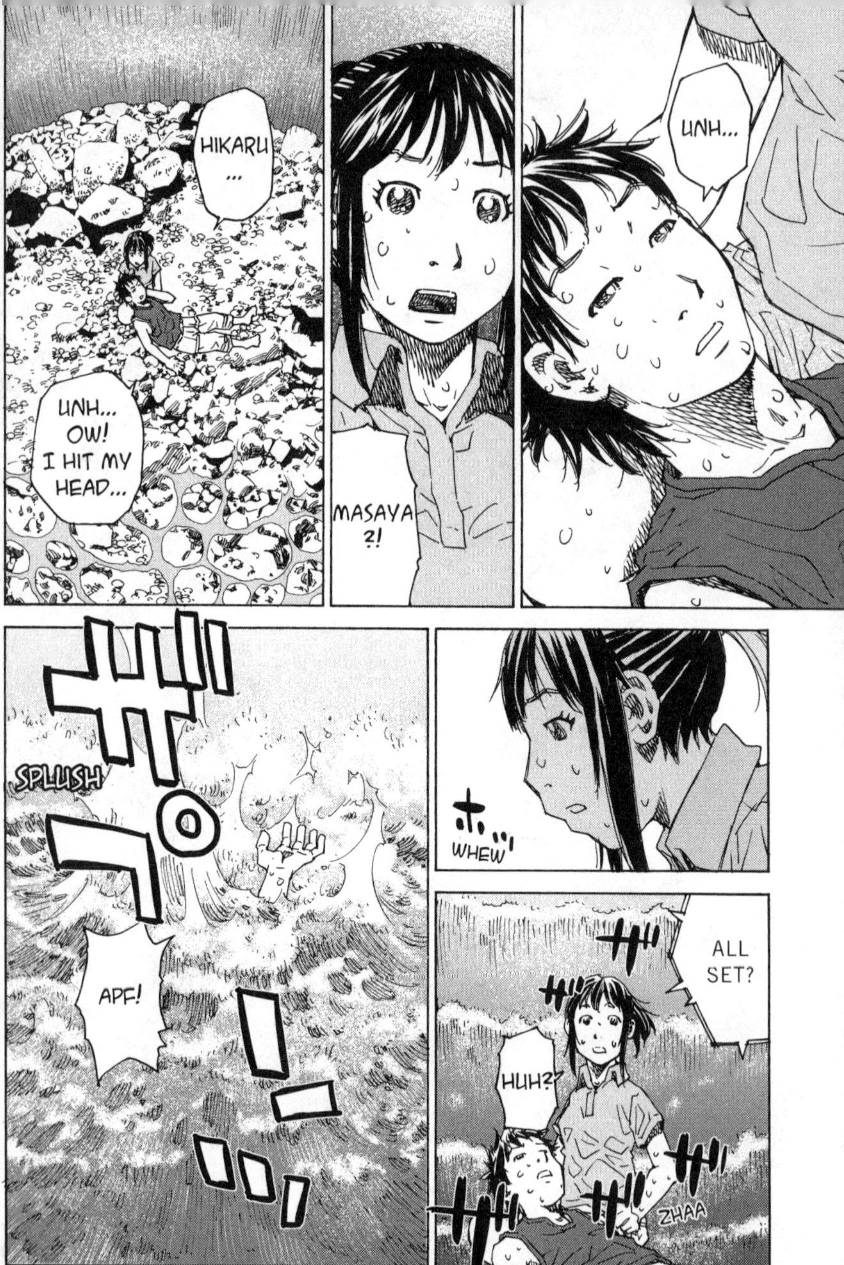
UNH...
MASAYA ?!
HIKARU ...
UNH... OW! I HIT MY HEAD...
WHEW
ALL SET?
HUH?
ZHAA
SPLUSH
APF!

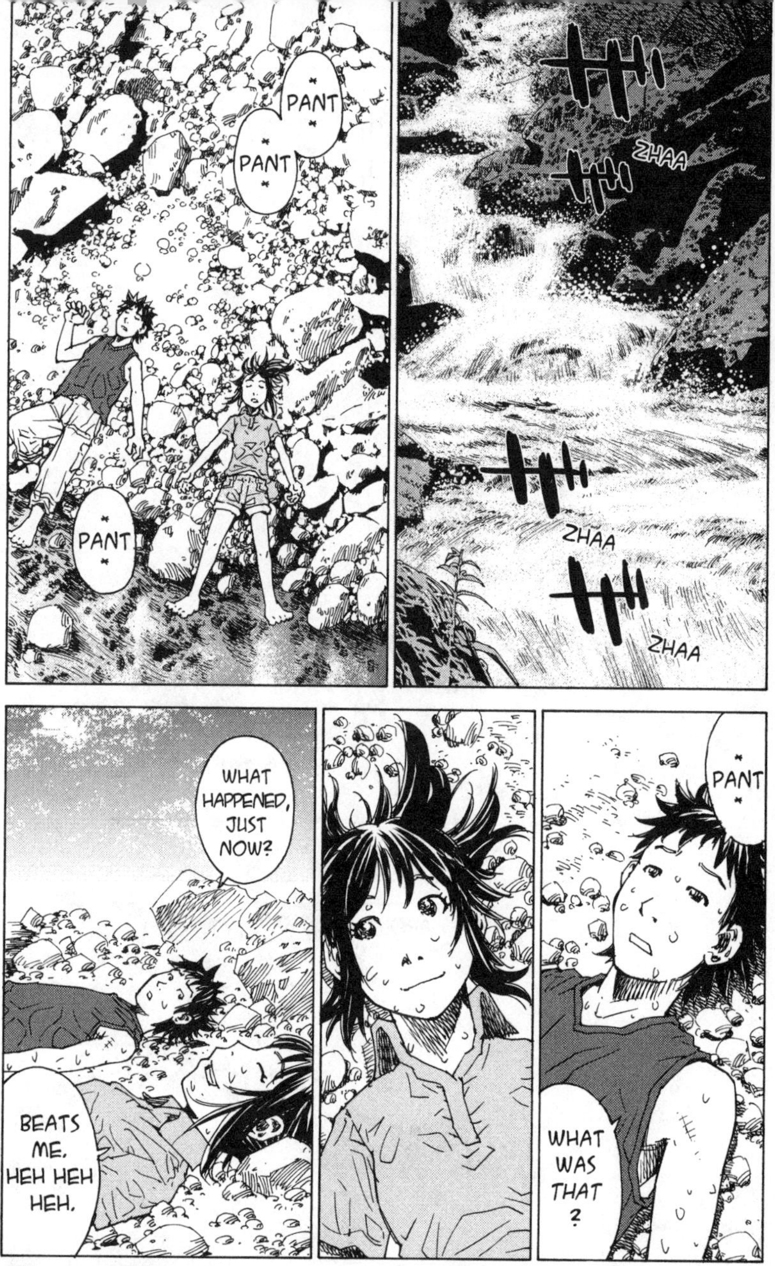
ZHAA
ZHAA
ZHAA
* PANT *
* PANT *
* PANT *
* PANT *
WHAT WAS THAT ?
WHAT HAPPENED, JUST NOW?
BEATS ME. HEH HEH HEH.

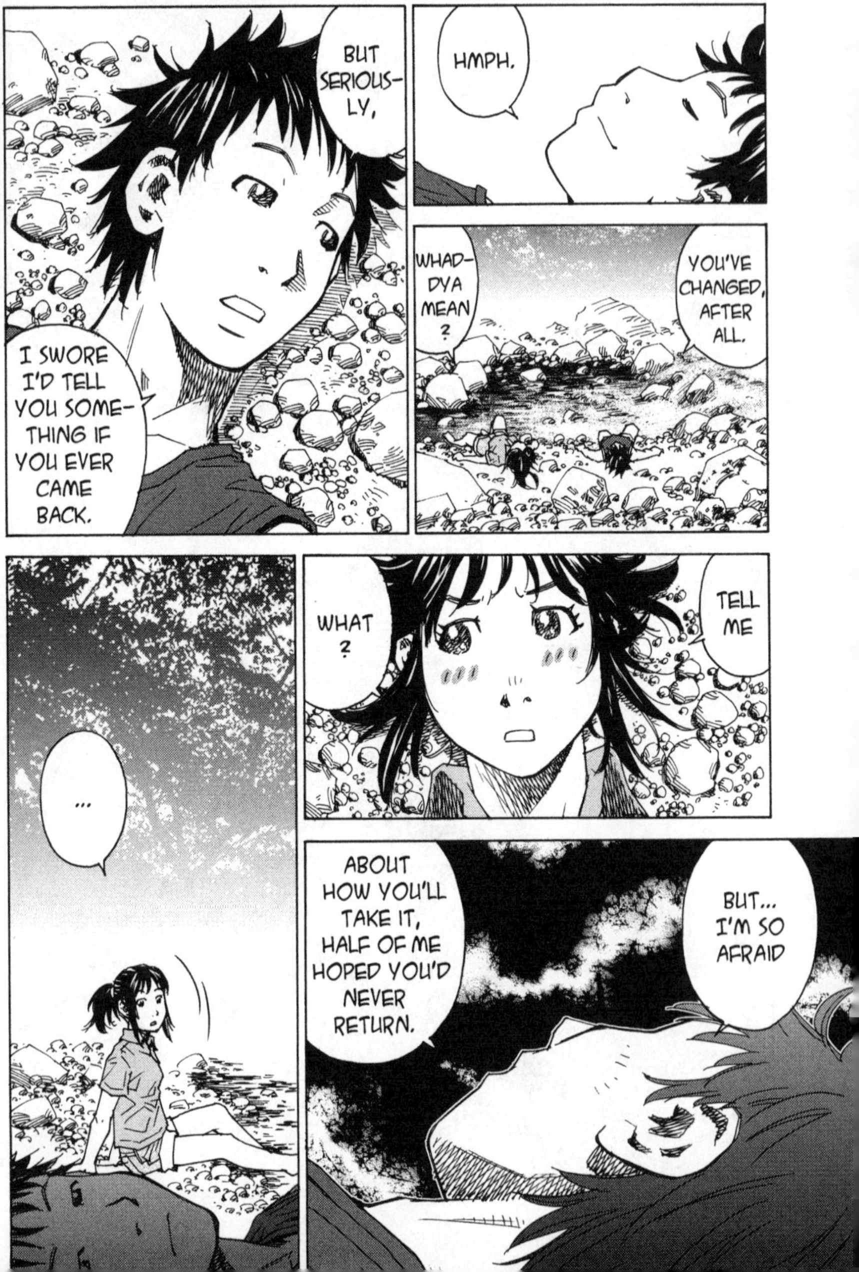
HMPH.
YOU'VE CHANGED, AFTER ALL.
WHAD-DYA MEAN?
BUT SERIOUS-LY,
I SWORE I'D TELL YOU SOME-THING IF YOU EVER CAME BACK.
TELL ME
WHAT?
BUT... I'M SO AFRAID
ABOUT HOW YOU'LL TAKE IT, HALF OF ME HOPED YOU'D NEVER RETURN.
...

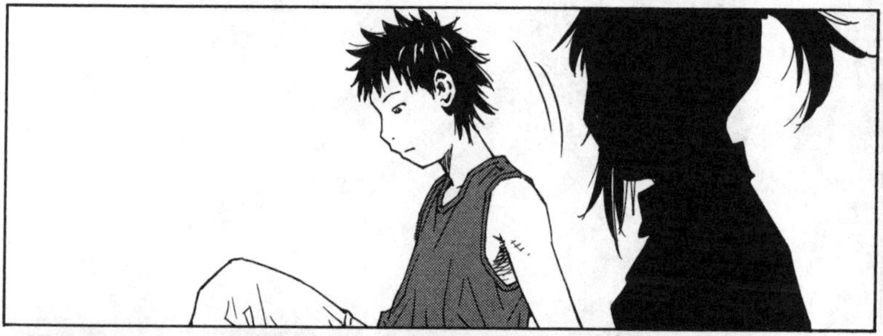
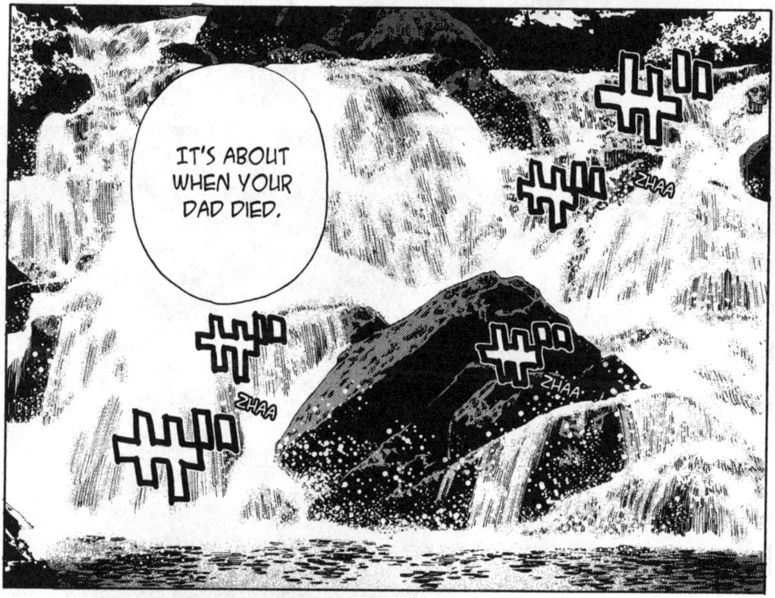
ZHAA
ZHAA
IT'S ABOUT WHEN YOUR DAD DIED.
ZHAA
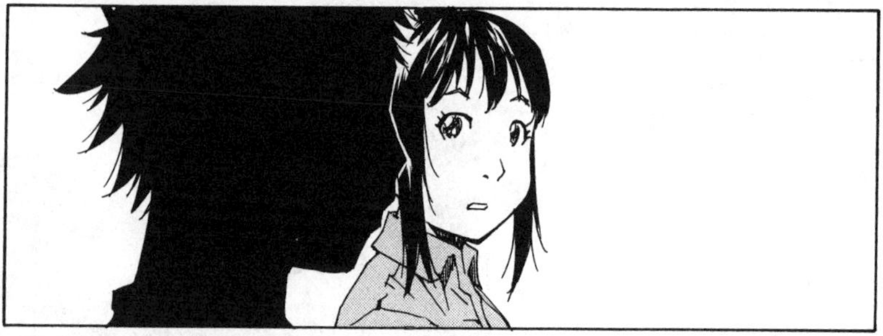

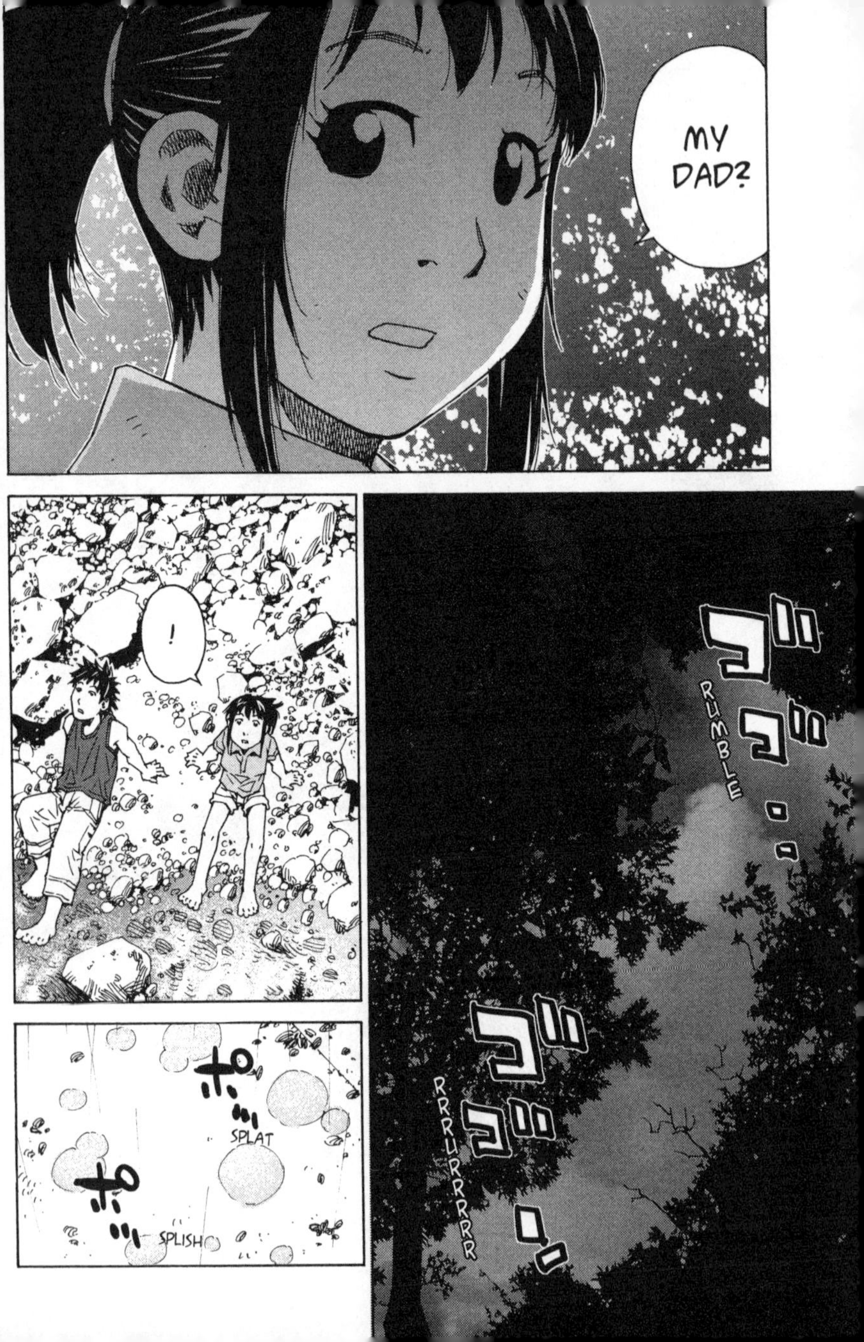
MY DAD?
RUMBLE
RRRURRRRR
!
SPLAT
SPLISH

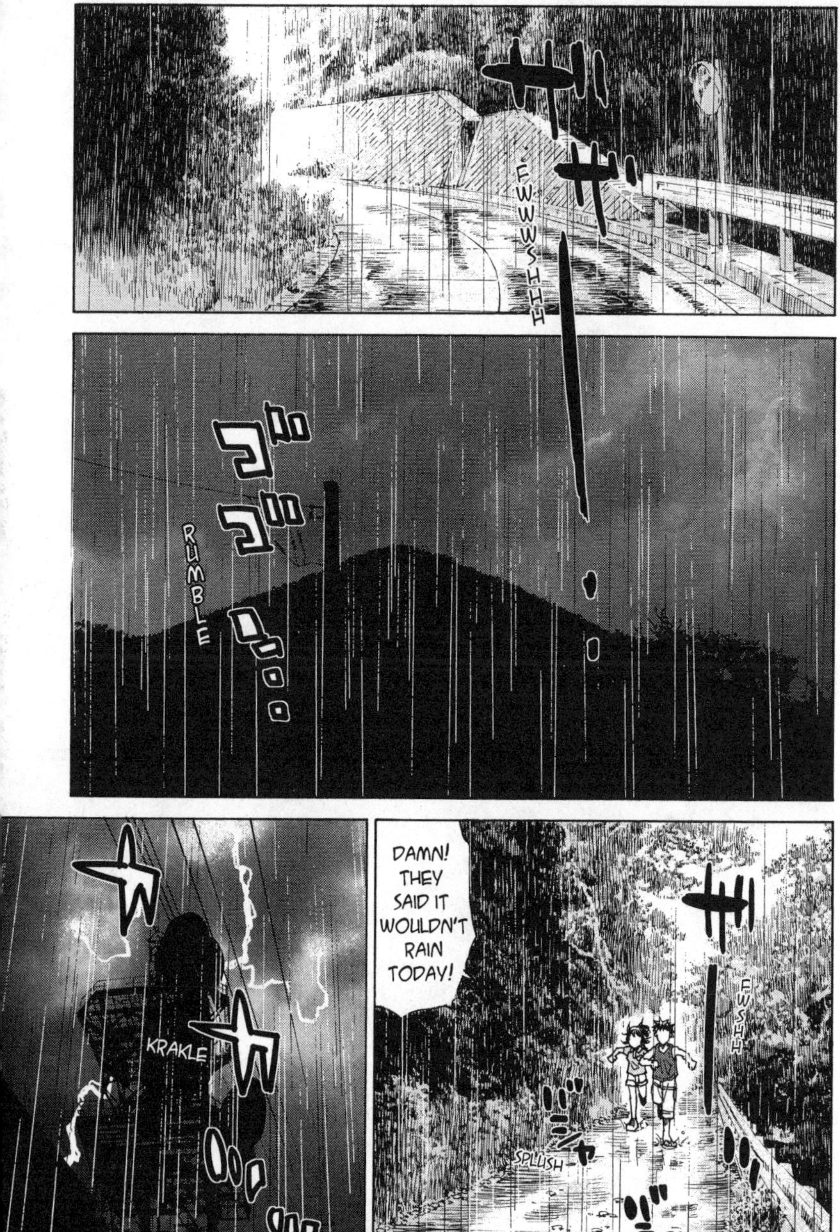
FWWWSHHH
RUMBLE
DAMN! THEY SAID IT WOULDN'T RAIN TODAY!
FWSHH
SPLUSH
SPLUSH
KRAKLE

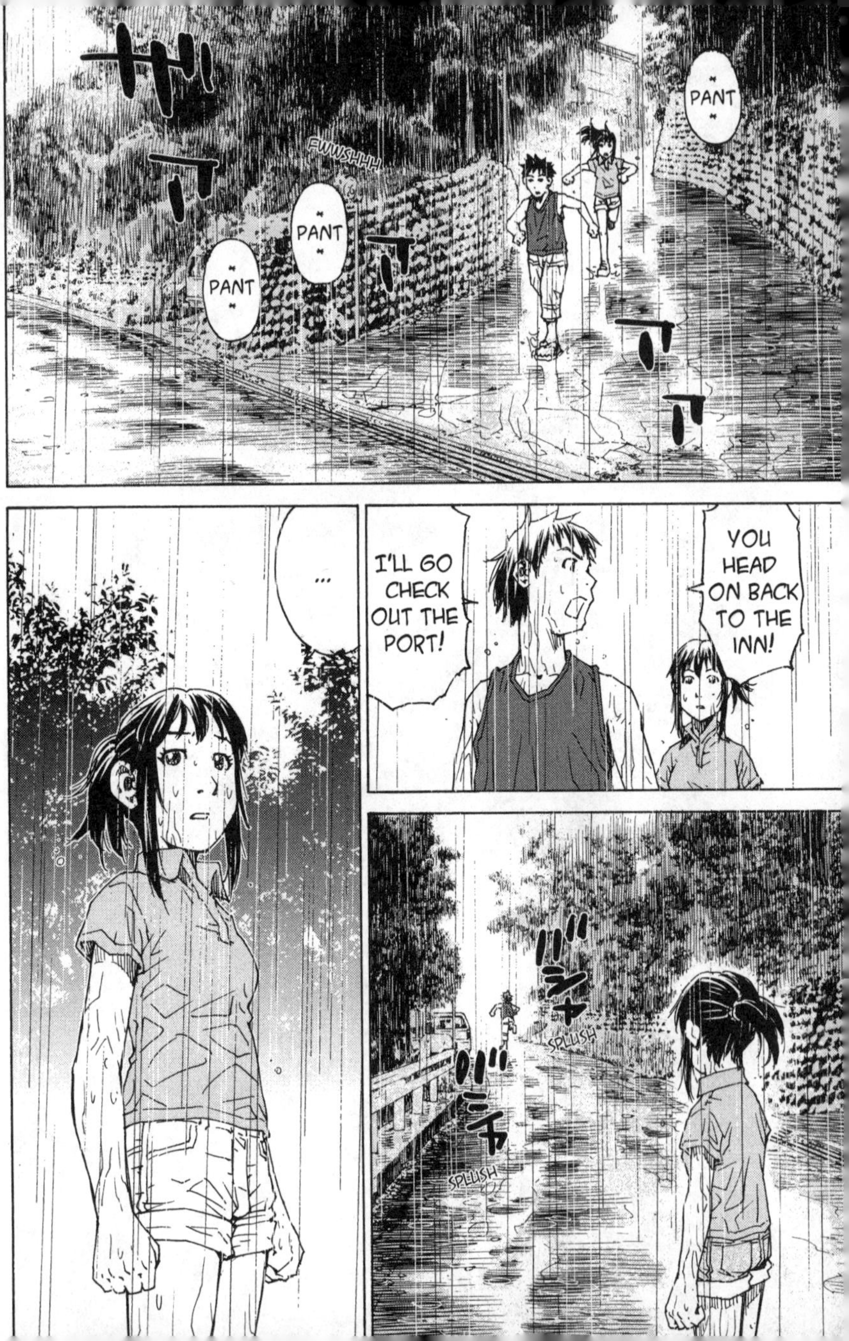
PANT
PANT
PANT
FWWSHHH
YOU HEAD ON BACK TO THE INN!
I'LL GO CHECK OUT THE PORT!
SPLLISH
SPLLISH
...

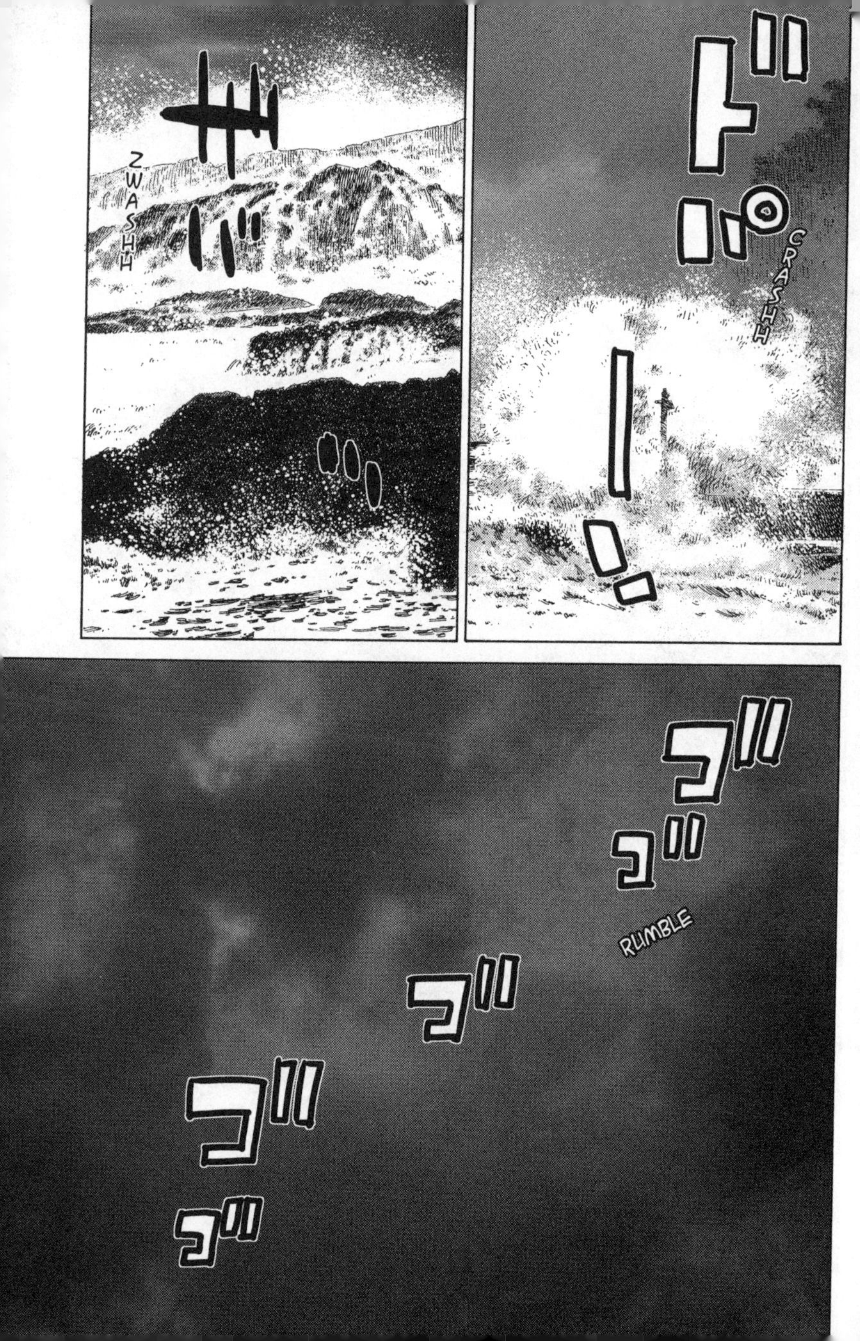
CRASHH
ZWASHH
RUMBLE

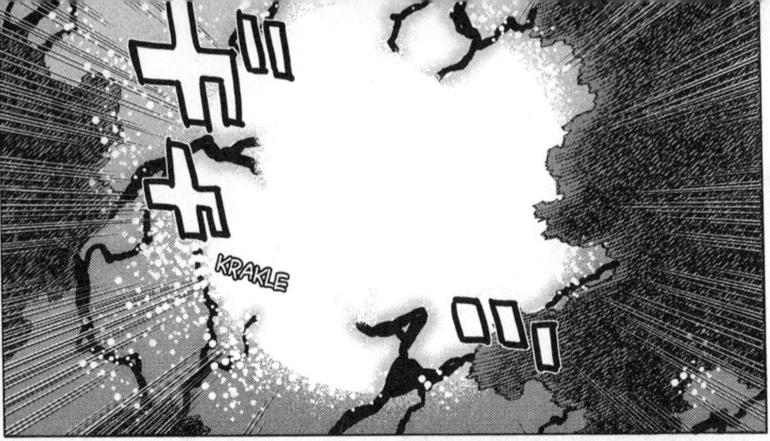
KRAKLE

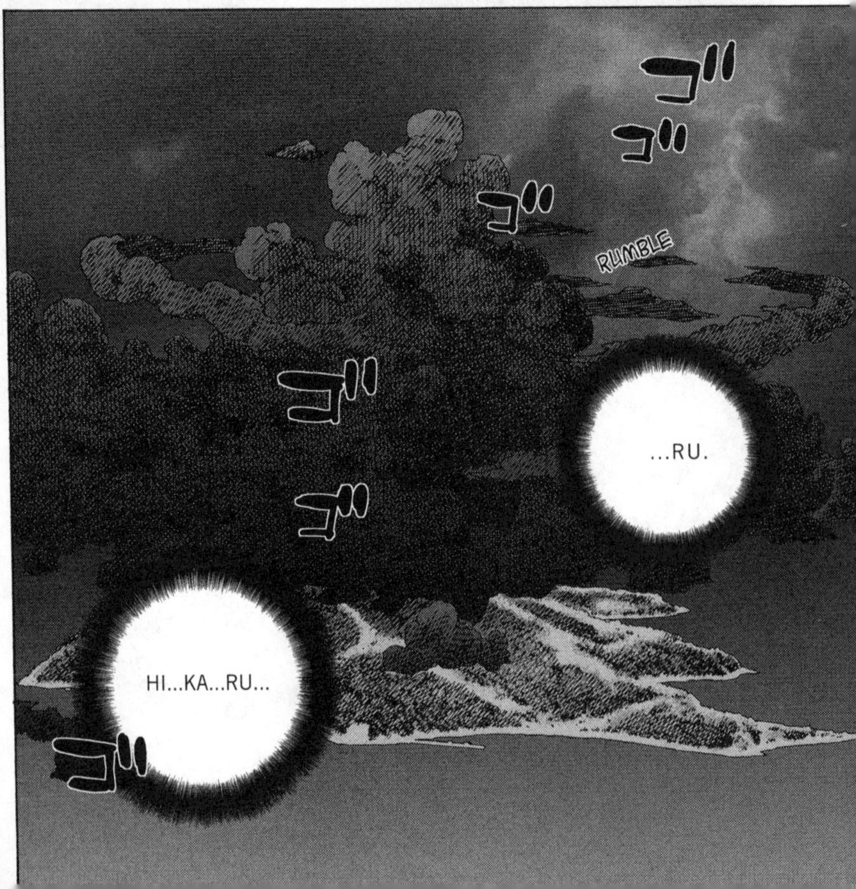
ゴゴ
ゴ
RUMBLE
ゴ
...RU.
ゴ
HI...KA...RU...
ゴ

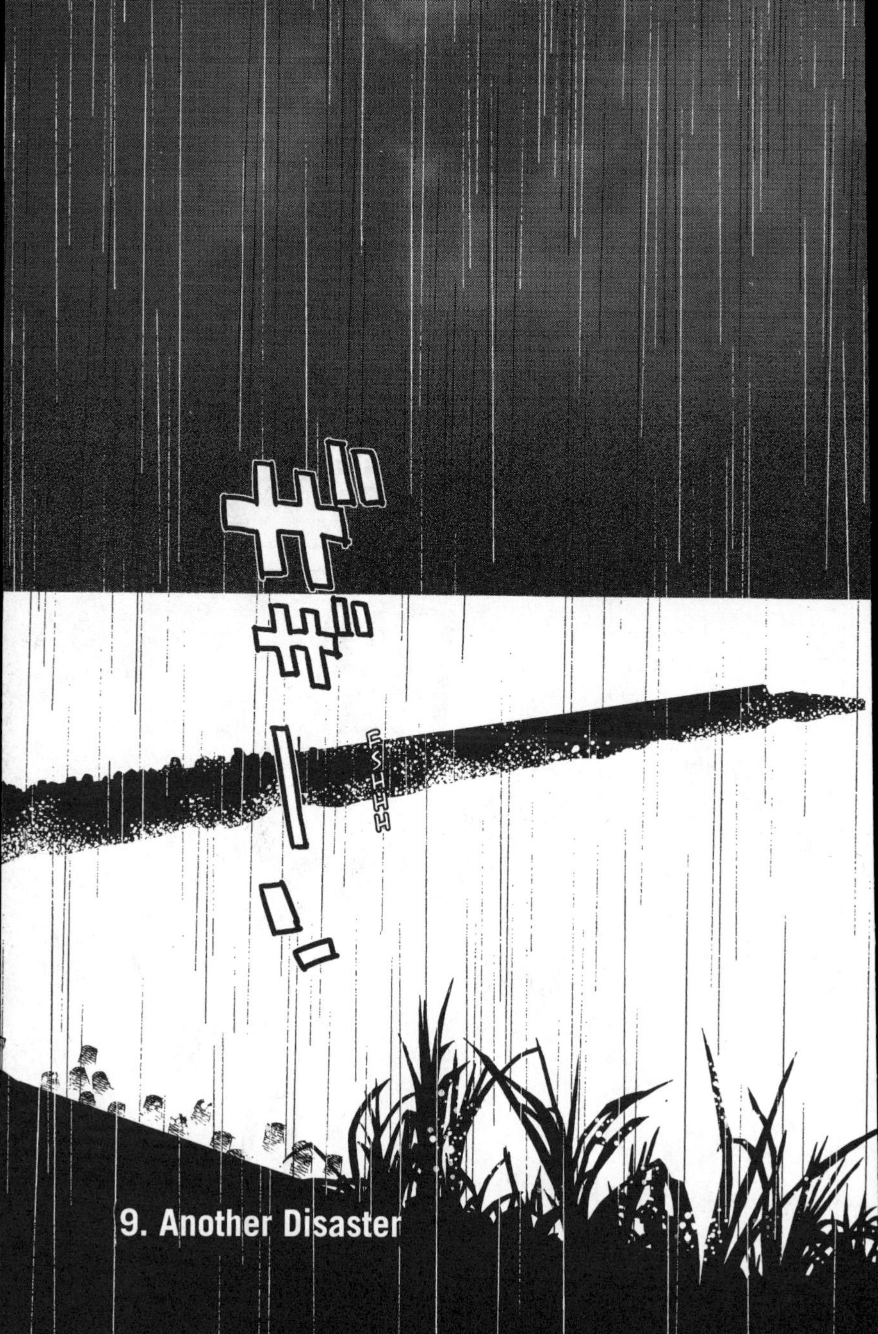
ザザーッ
FSHHH

9. Another Disaster

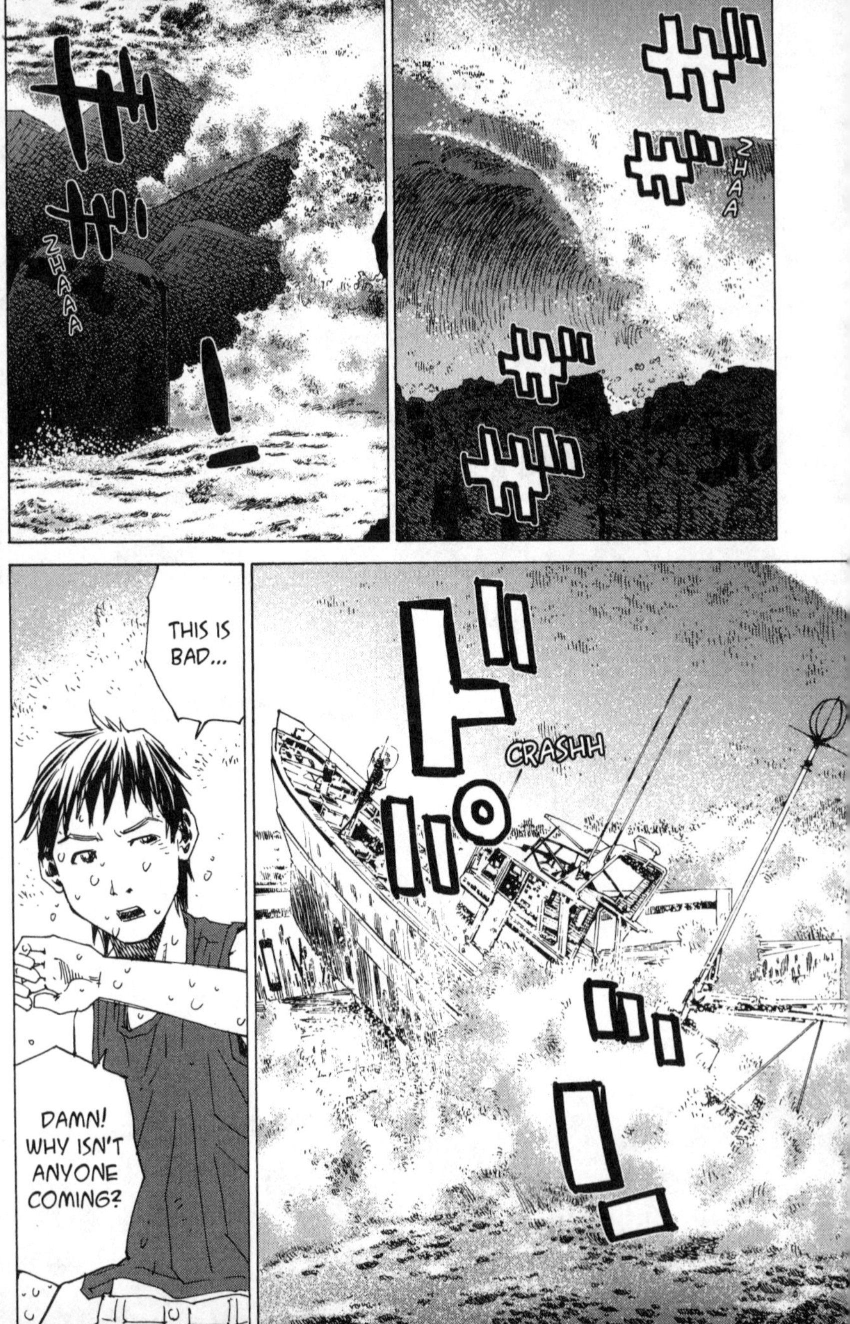
ZHAA
ZHAAAA
CRASHH
THIS IS BAD...
DAMN! WHY ISN'T ANYONE COMING?

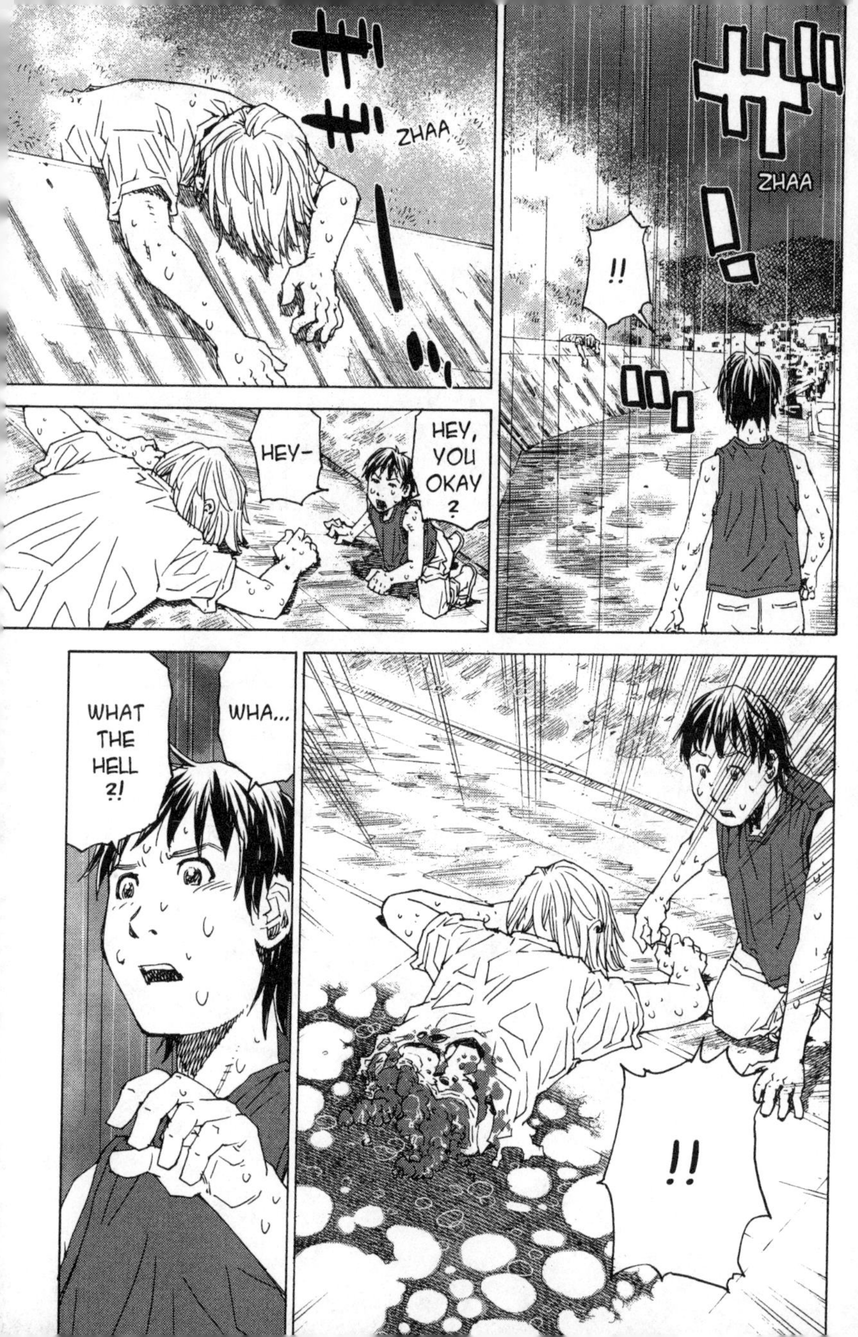
ZHAA
!!
ZHAA
HEY, YOU OKAY?
HEY-
!!
WHA...
WHAT THE HELL?!

GLARE

ARE YOU HIKARU?

JUMP

?!

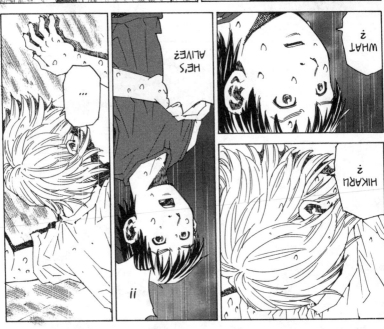

WHAT ?

HE'S ALIVE?

...

HIKARU ?

!!

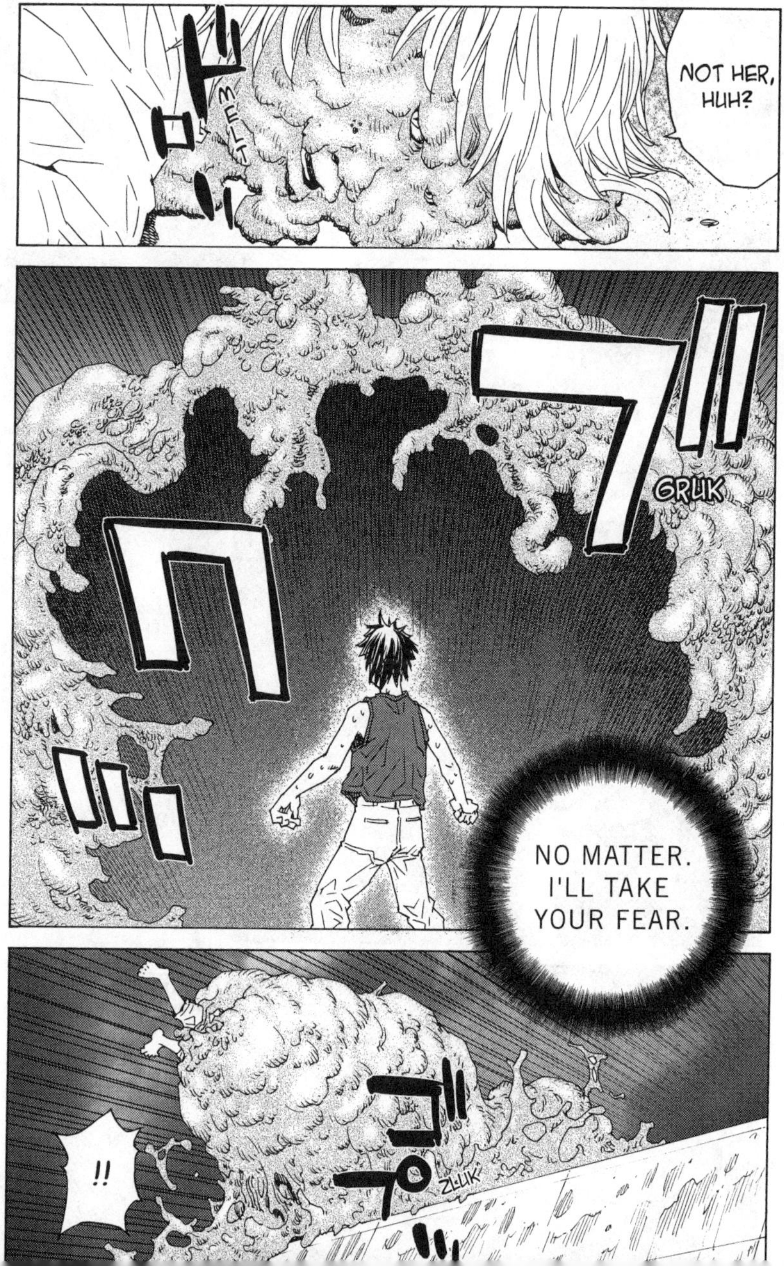
NOT HER, HUH?
MELT
GRUK
NO MATTER. I'LL TAKE YOUR FEAR.
ZLUK
!!

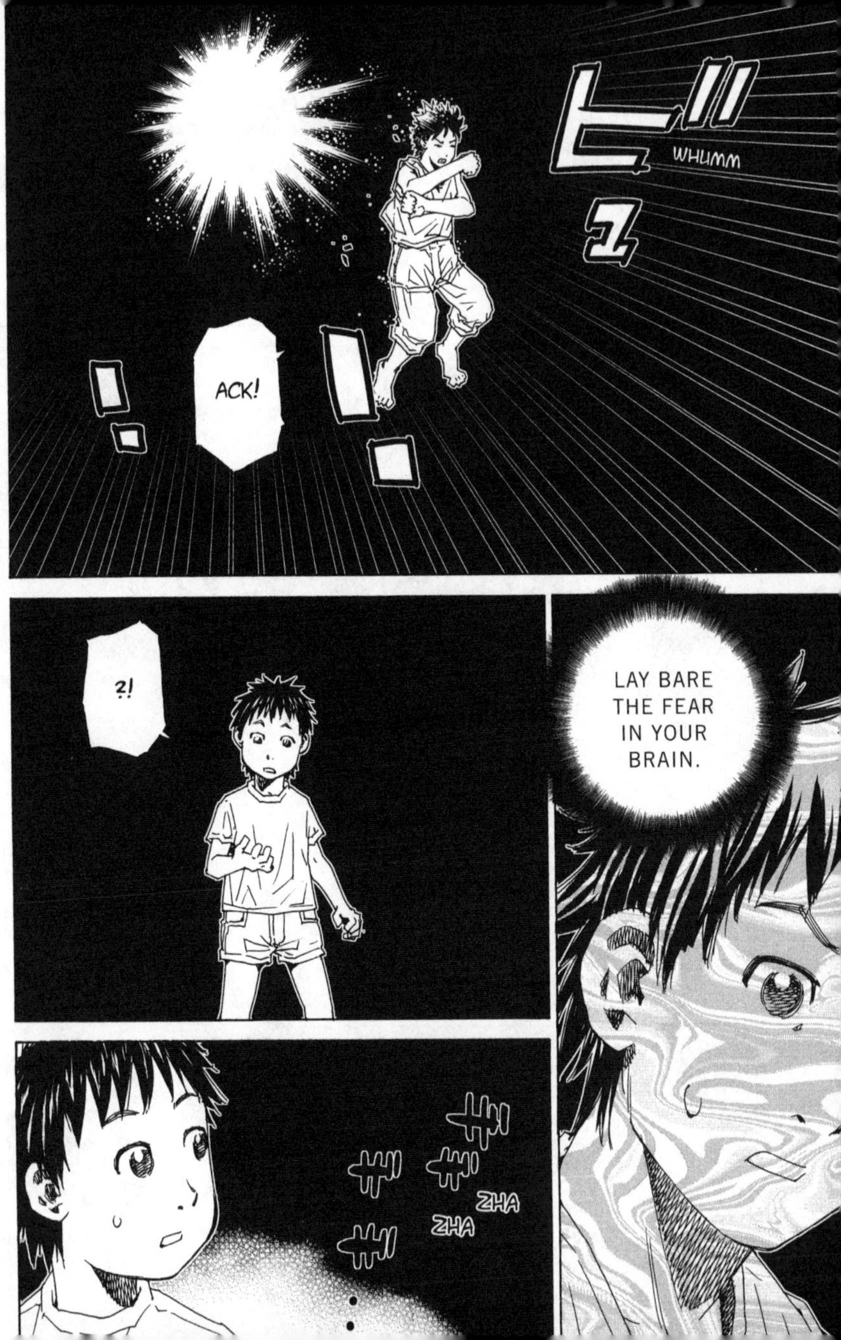
WHUMM
ACK!
LAY BARE THE FEAR IN YOUR BRAIN.
?!
ZHA
ZHA
...

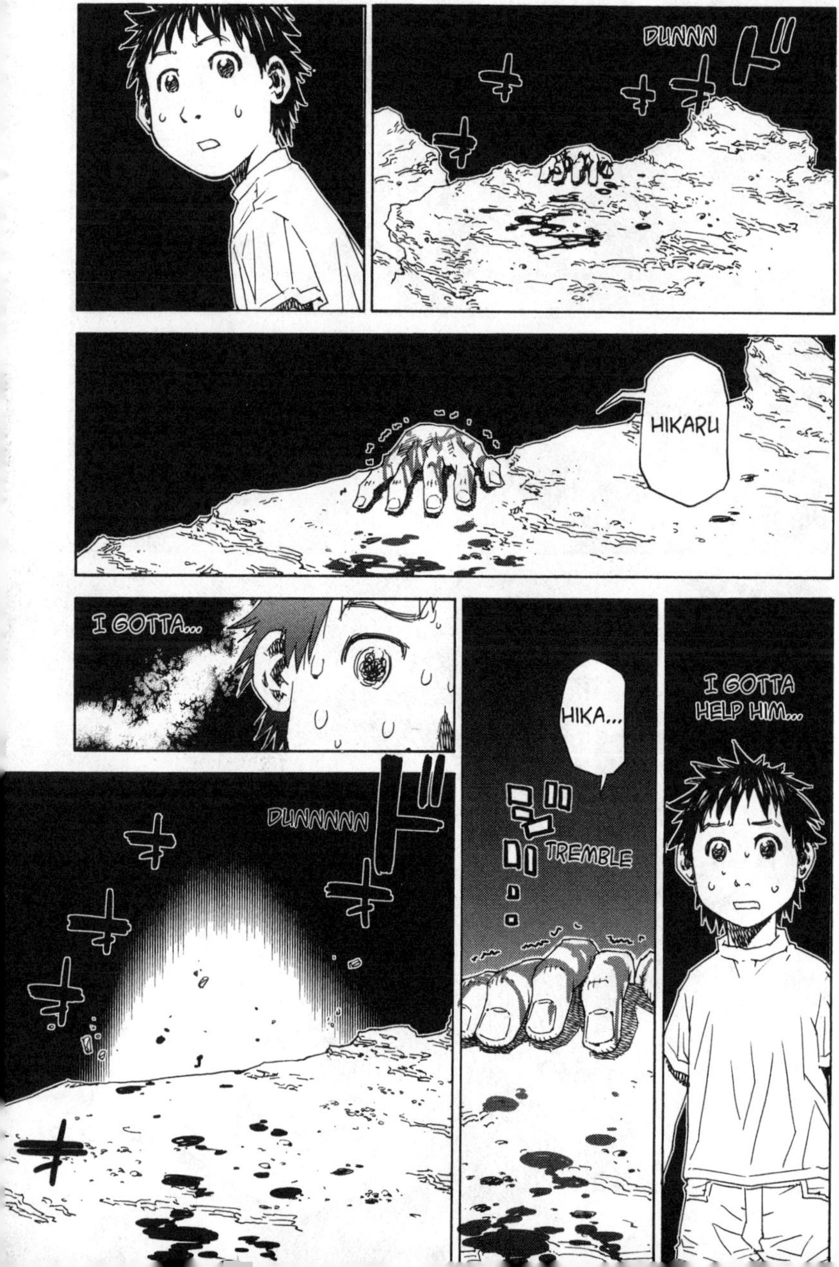
DUNNN
HIKARU
I GOTTA
HELP HIM...
HIKA...
TREMBLE
I GOTTA...
DUNNNNN

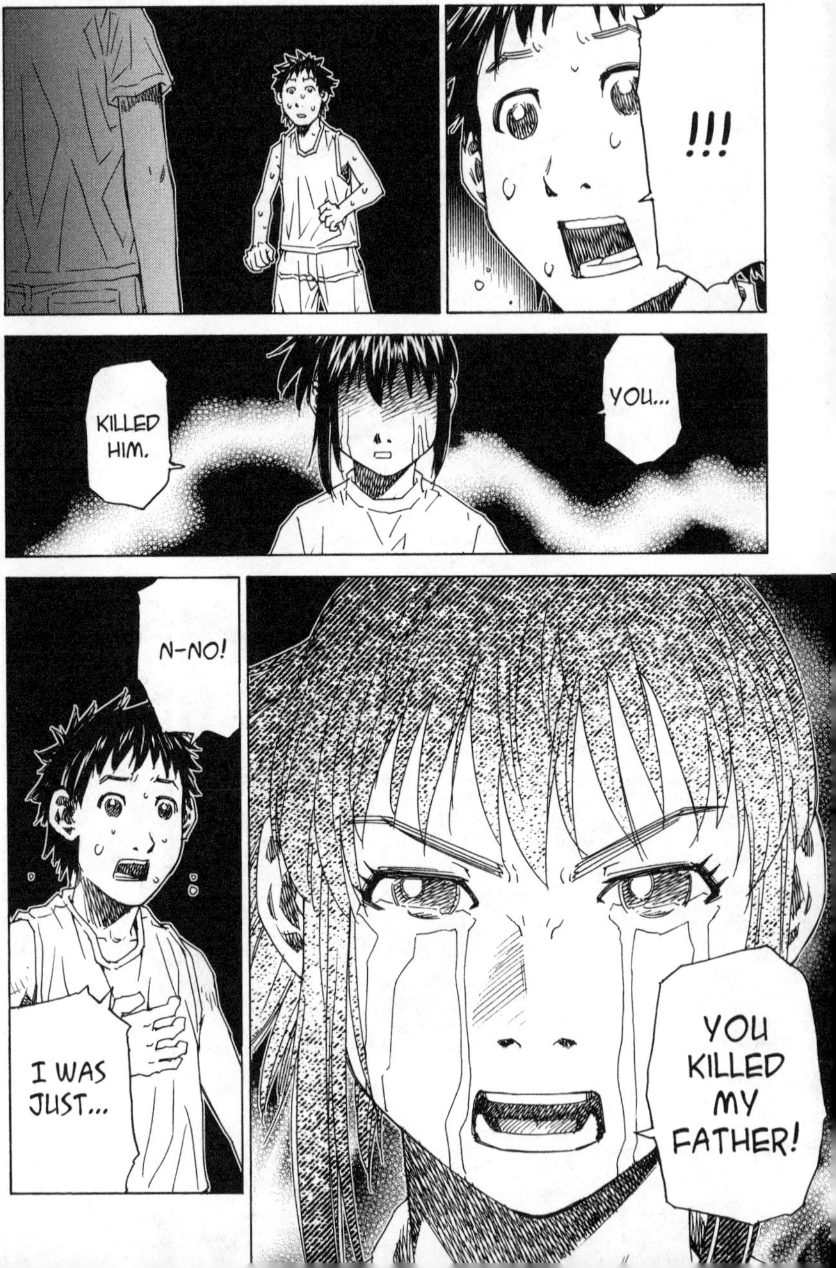
!!!
YOU...
KILLED HIM.
YOU KILLED MY FATHER!
N-NO!
I WAS JUST...

!!
ARRRG!
GRIK
GRIK
GRIK
GRIK
YOU'RE WRONG! STOP IT!
GRIK
GRIK
GRIK
AH!
AAAAH!
POW

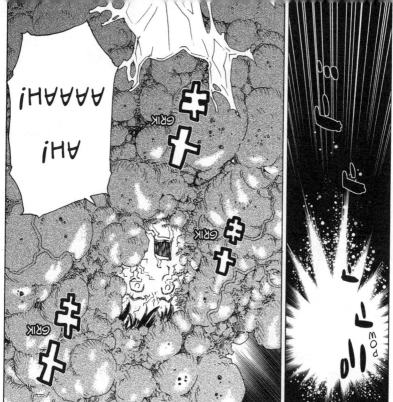

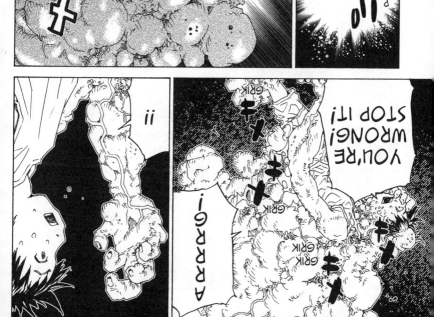

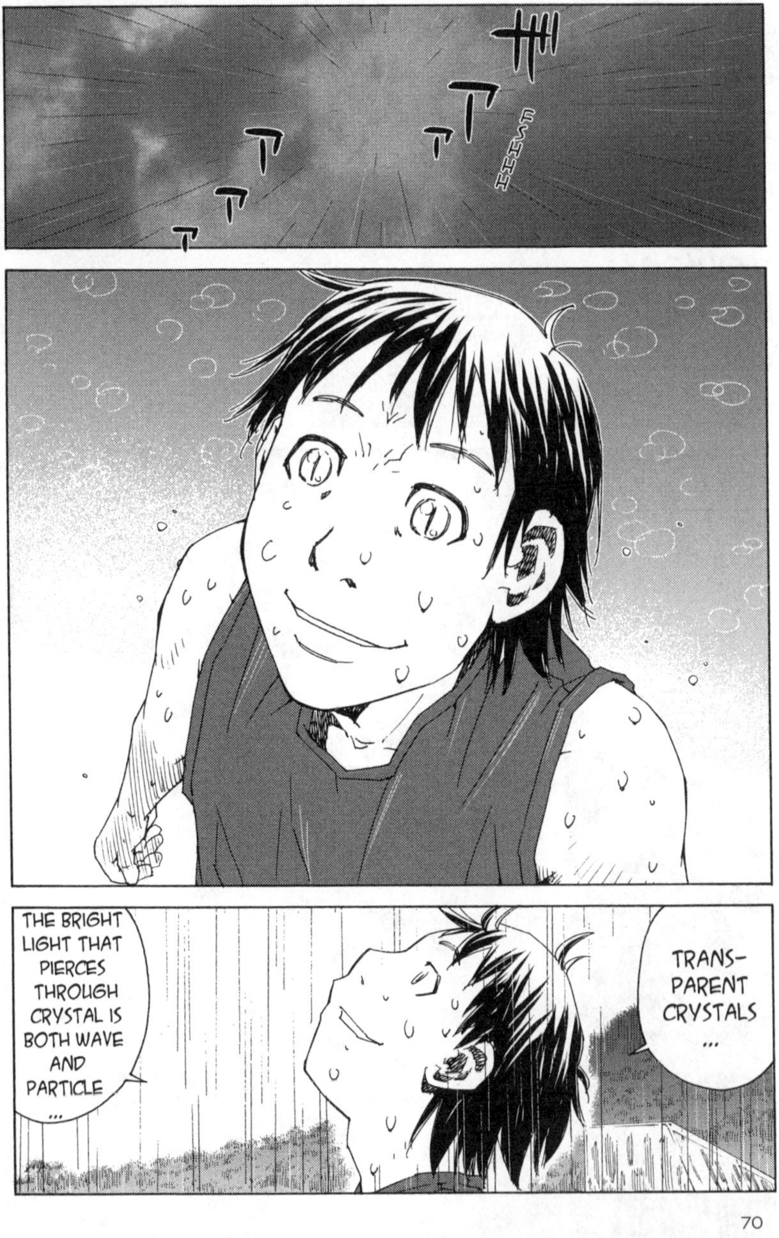
ザアァアアァ
FSHHH
TRANS-PARENT CRYSTALS ...
THE BRIGHT LIGHT THAT PIERCES THROUGH CRYSTAL IS BOTH WAVE AND PARTICLE ...

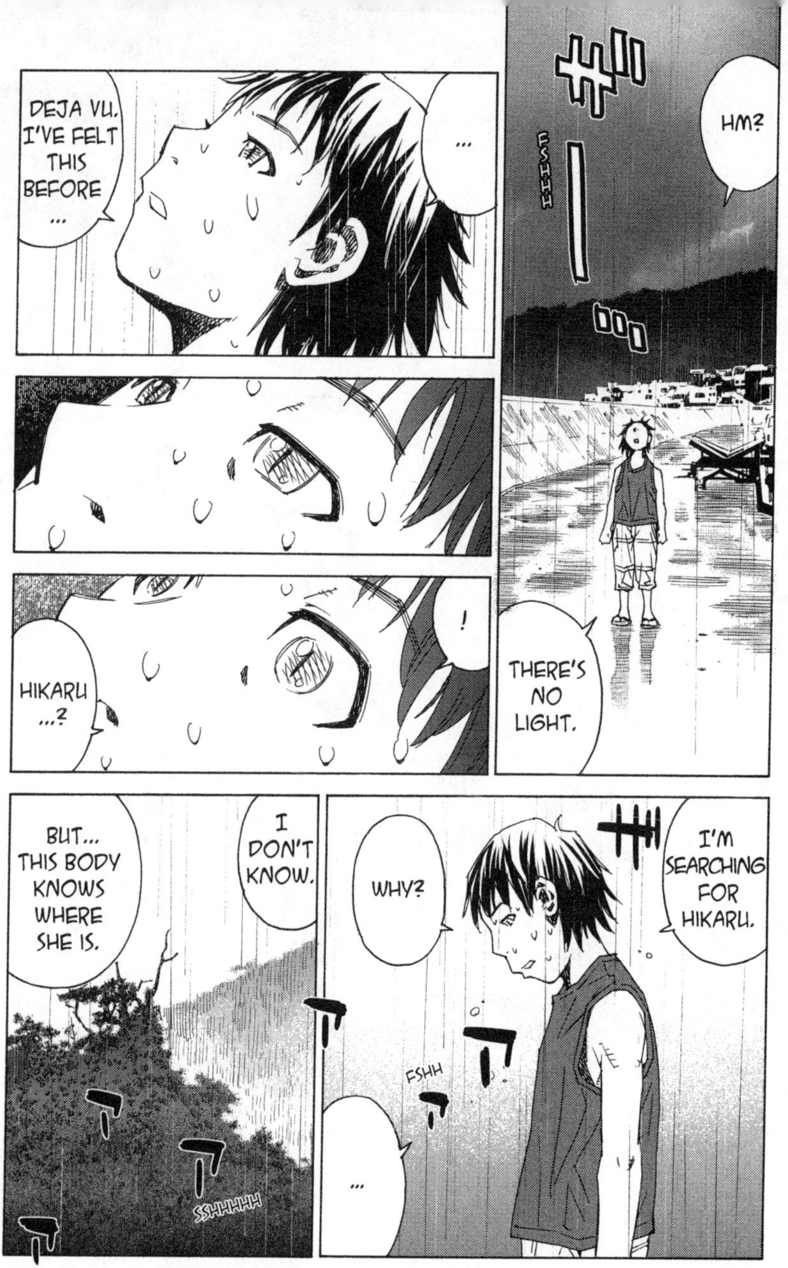
HM?
FSHHH
THERE'S NO LIGHT.
DEJA VU, I'VE FELT THIS BEFORE ...
...
!
HIKARU ...?
I'M SEARCHING FOR HIKARU.
WHY?
FSHH
...
I DON'T KNOW.
BUT... THIS BODY KNOWS WHERE SHE IS.
SSHHHHH

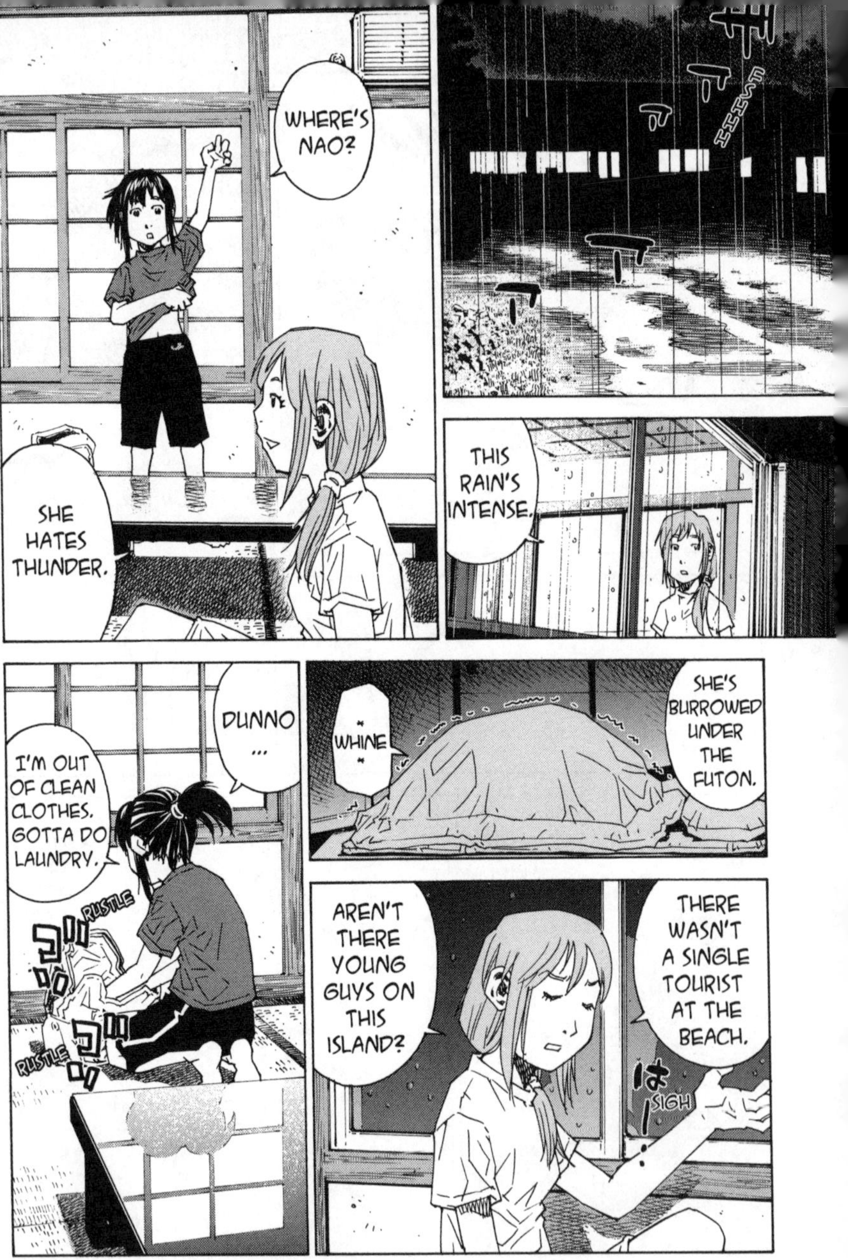
THIS RAIN'S INTENSE.
WHERE'S NAO?
SHE HATES THUNDER.
SHE'S BURROWED UNDER THE FUTON.
* WHINE *
THERE WASN'T A SINGLE TOURIST AT THE BEACH.
SIGH
AREN'T THERE YOUNG GUYS ON THIS ISLAND?
DUNNO ...
I'M OUT OF CLEAN CLOTHES. GOTTA DO LAUNDRY.
RUSTLE
RUSTLE

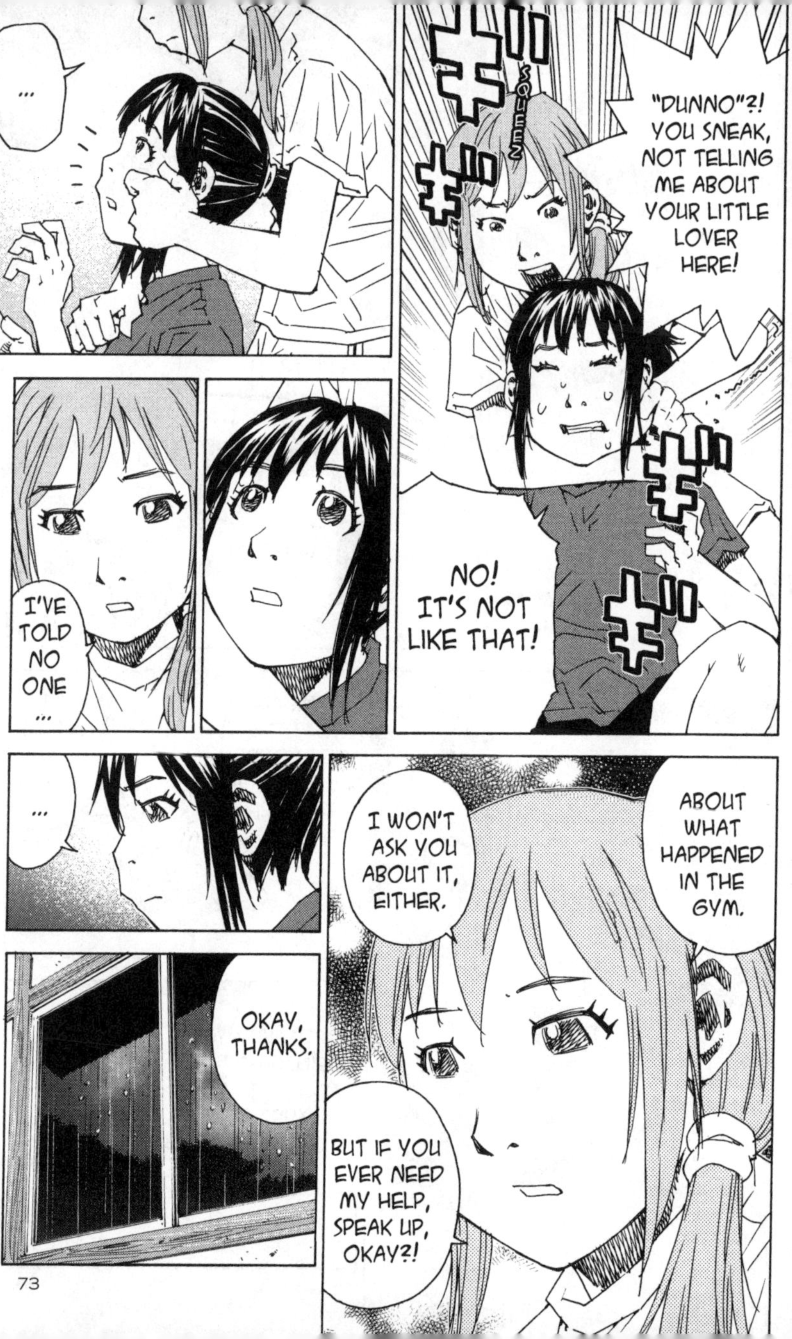
"DUNNO"?! YOU SNEAK, NOT TELLING ME ABOUT YOUR LITTLE LOVER HERE!
SQUEEZ
NO! IT'S NOT LIKE THAT!
...
I'VE TOLD NO ONE ...
ABOUT WHAT HAPPENED IN THE GYM.
I WON'T ASK YOU ABOUT IT, EITHER.
BUT IF YOU EVER NEED MY HELP, SPEAK UP, OKAY?!
...
OKAY, THANKS.

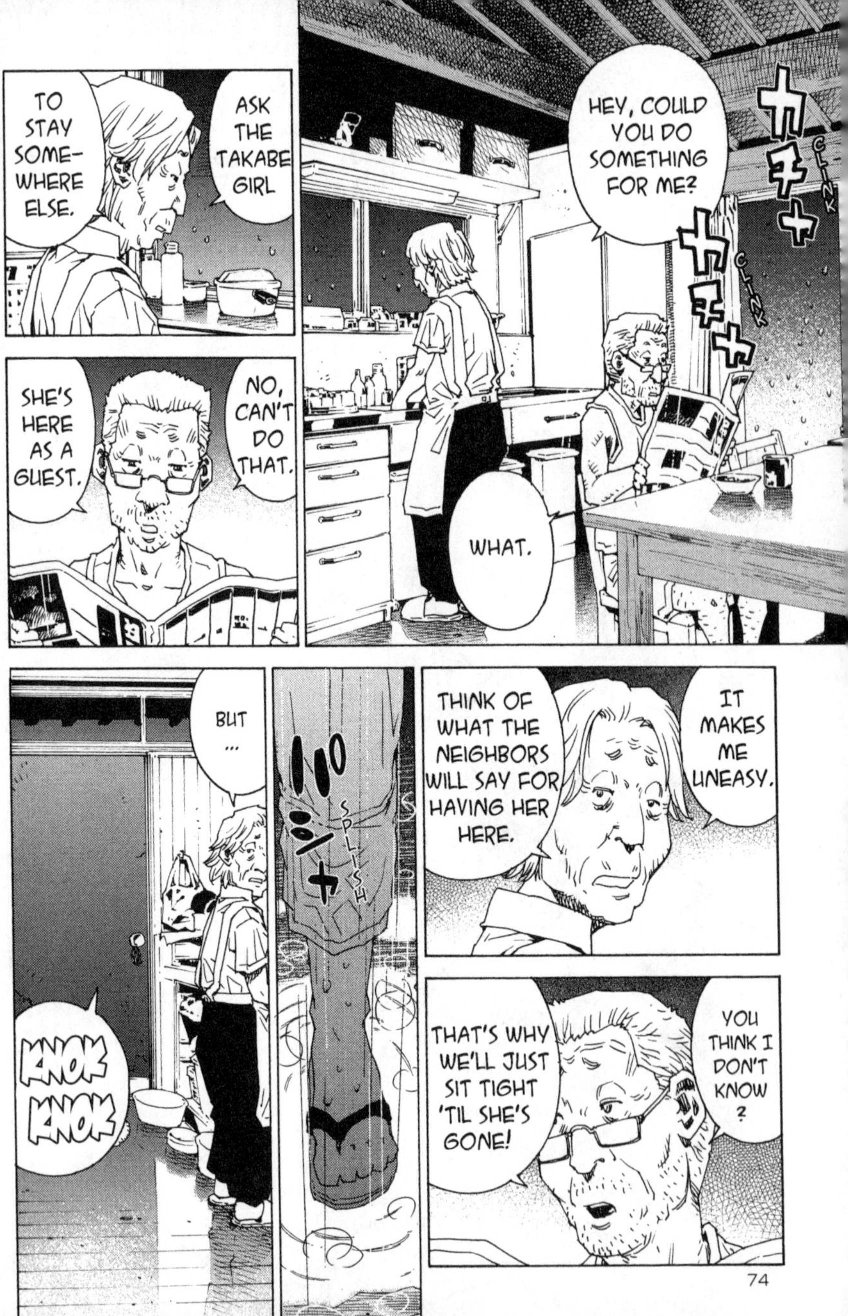
CLINK
CLINK
HEY, COULD YOU DO SOMETHING FOR ME?
WHAT.
ASK THE TAKABE GIRL
TO STAY SOME-WHERE ELSE.
NO, CAN'T DO THAT.
SHE'S HERE AS A GUEST.
IT MAKES ME UNEASY.
THINK OF WHAT THE NEIGHBORS WILL SAY FOR HAVING HER HERE.
YOU THINK I DON'T KNOW ?
THAT'S WHY WE'LL JUST SIT TIGHT 'TIL SHE'S GONE!
SPLISH
BUT ...
KNOK KNOK

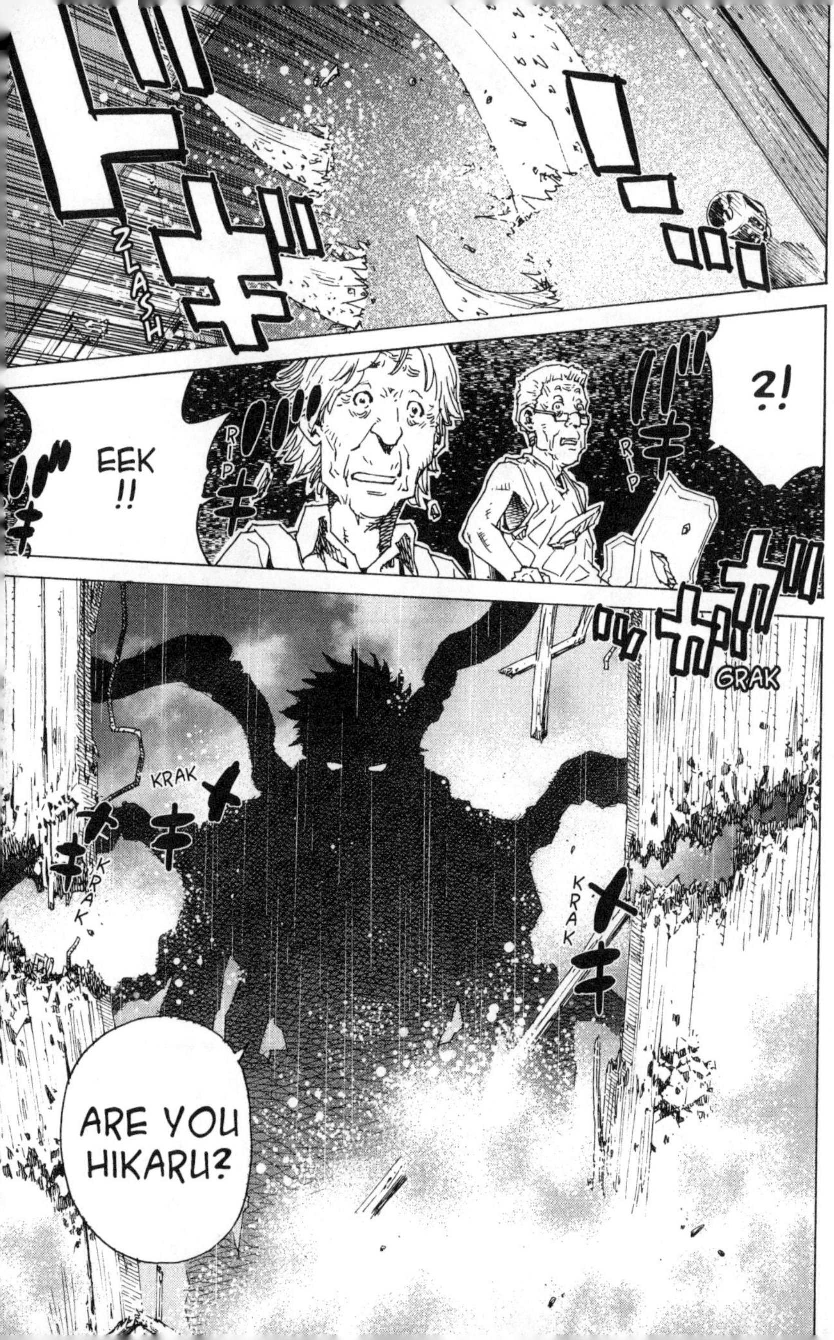
ZLASH
?!
RIP
RIP
EEK !!
GRAK
KRAK
KRAK
KRAK
ARE YOU HIKARU?

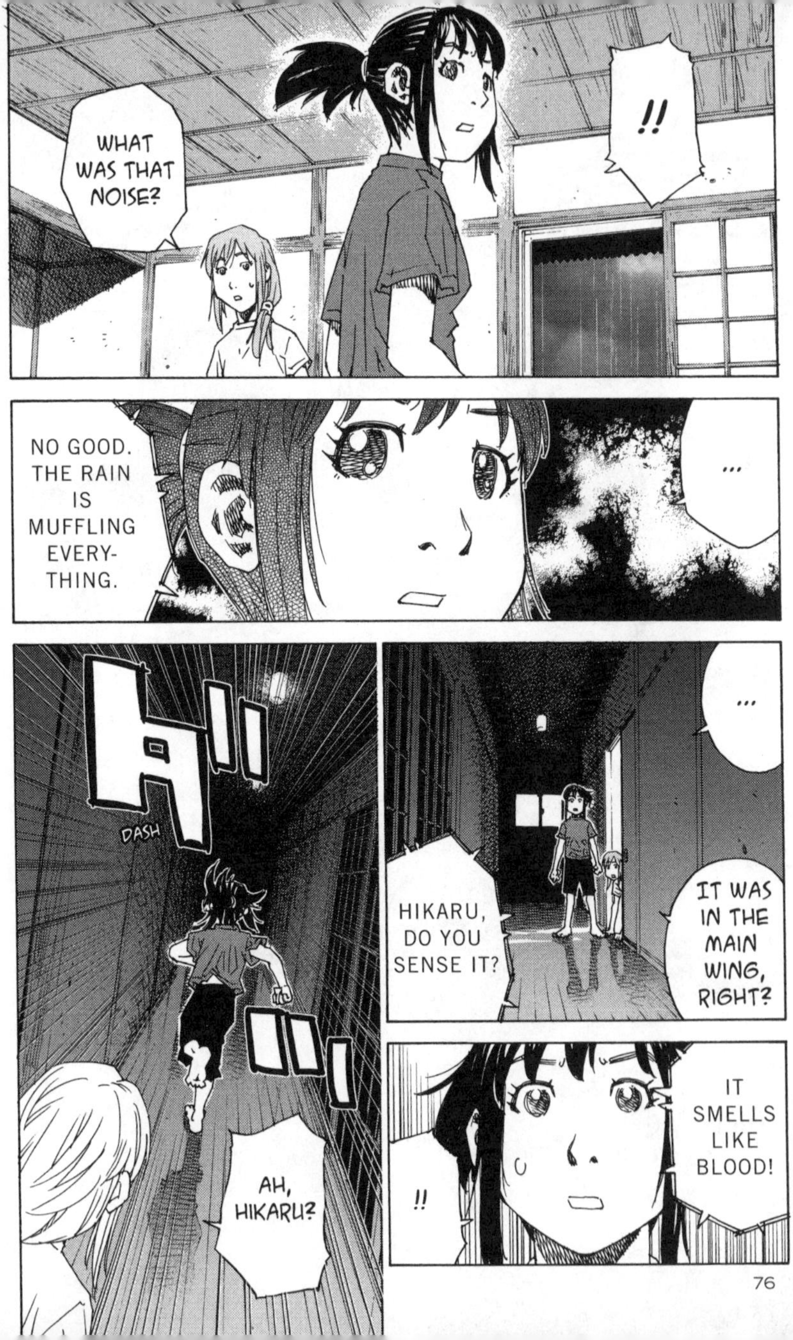
!!
WHAT WAS THAT NOISE?
...
NO GOOD. THE RAIN IS MUFFLING EVERY-THING.
...
IT WAS IN THE MAIN WING, RIGHT?
HIKARU, DO YOU SENSE IT?
IT SMELLS LIKE BLOOD!
!!
DASH
AH, HIKARU?

...

IT'S LIKE AT THE GYM...

THIS CAN'T BE...

...

WHAT THE....

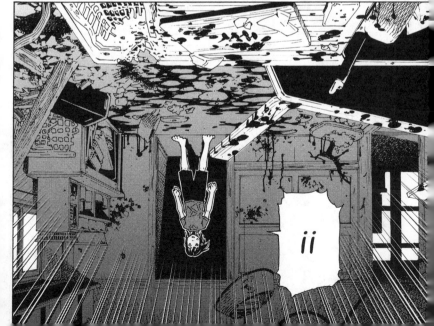

!!

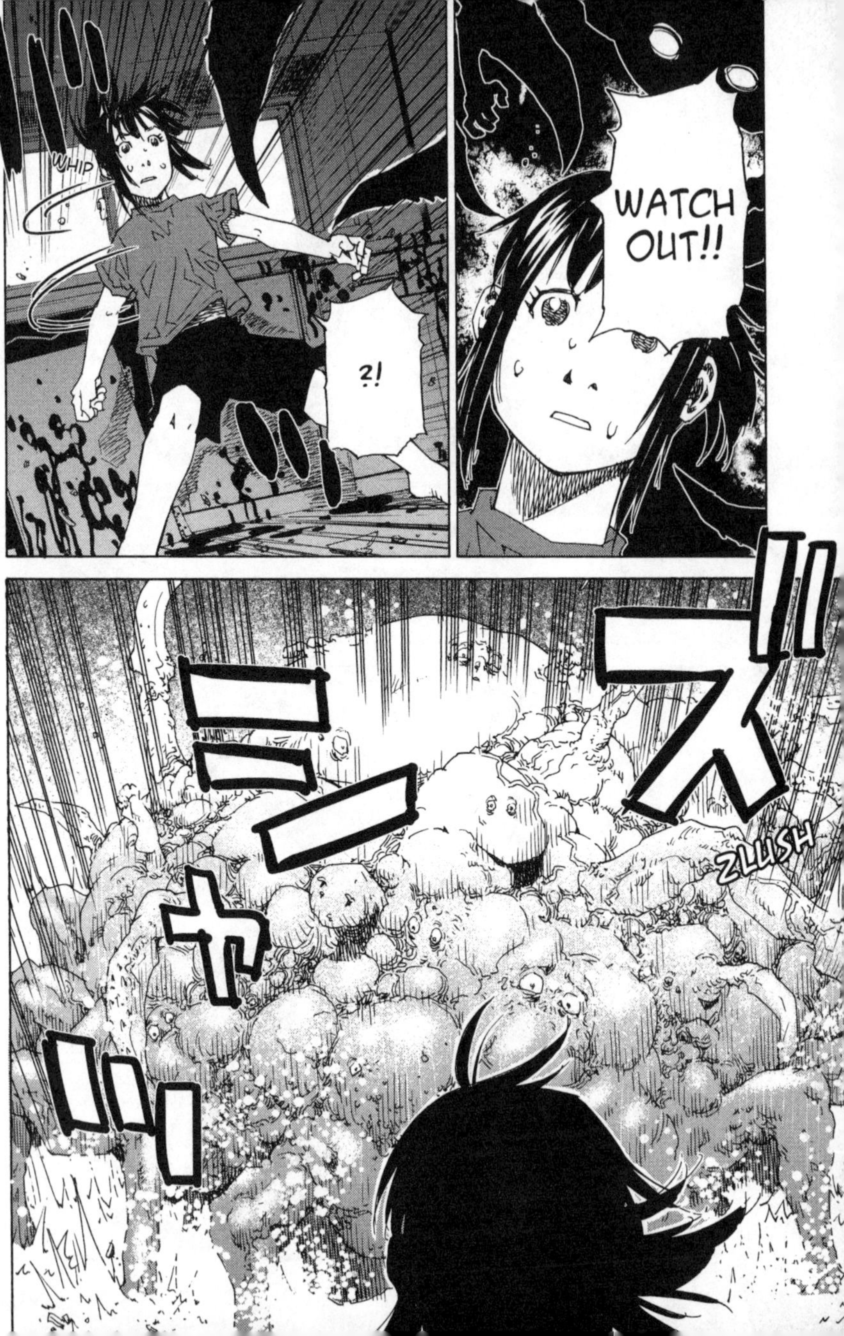
WATCH OUT!!
WHIP
?!
ZLUSH

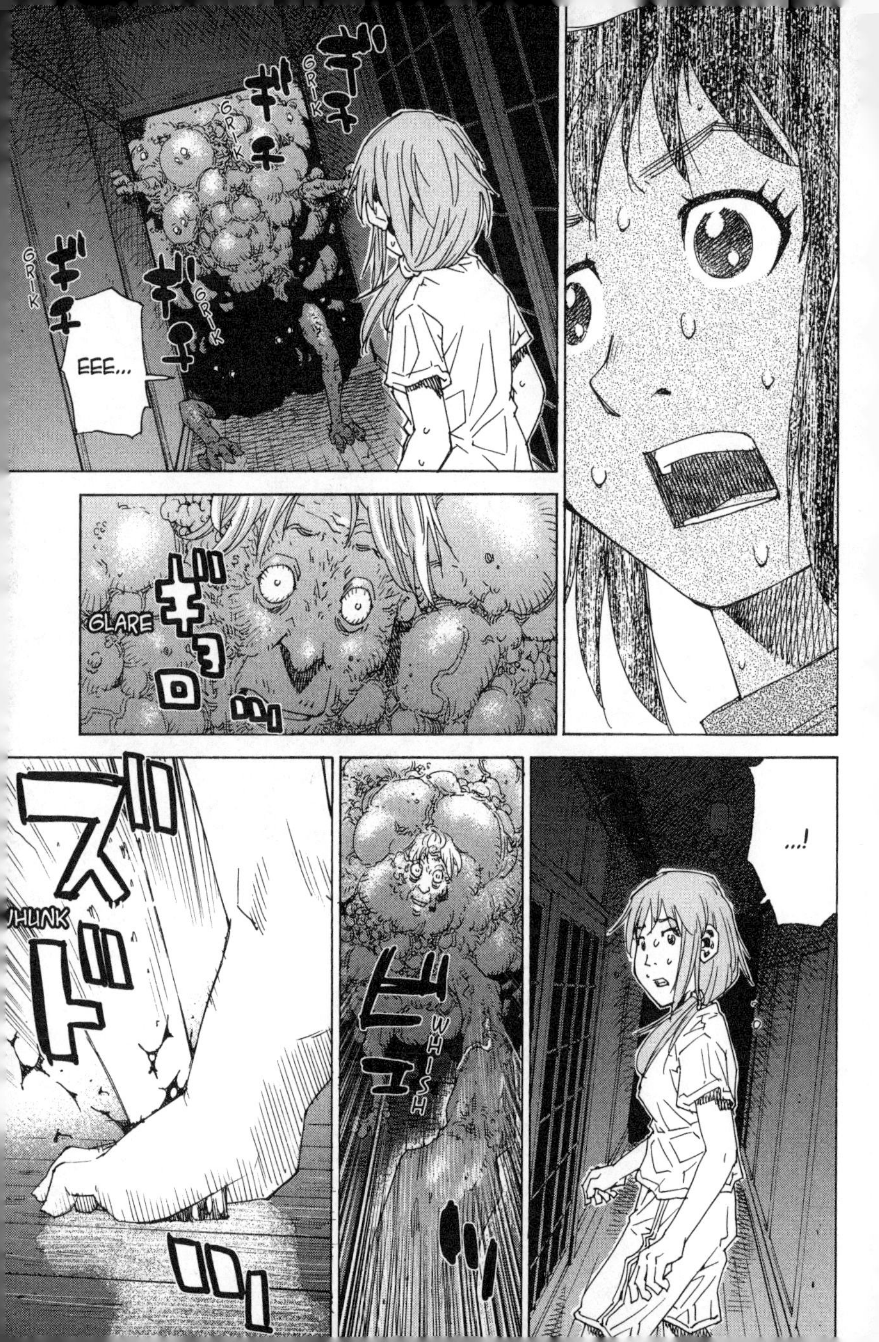
GRIK
GRIK
GRIK
GRIK
EEE...
GLARE
...!
WHISH
WHUNK

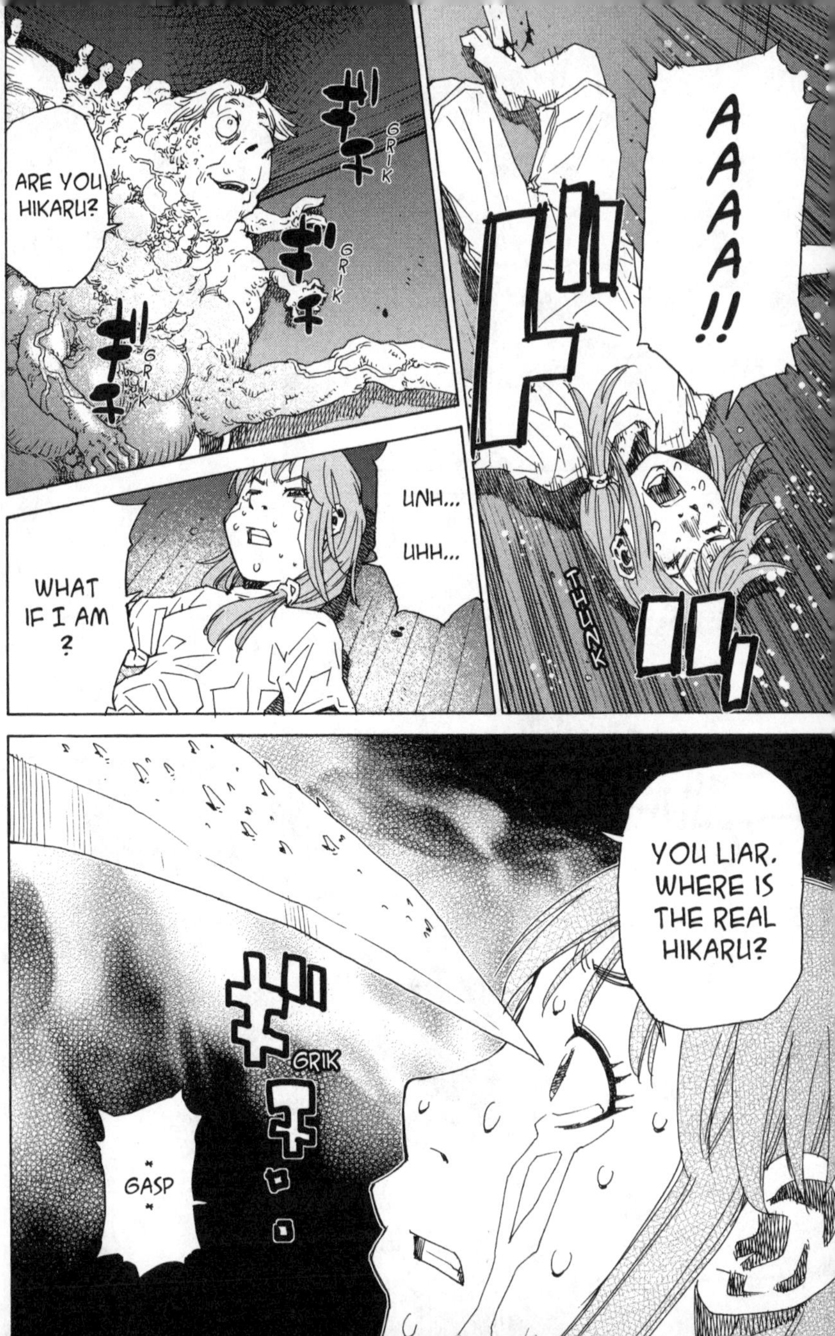
AAAAA!!
THUNK
ARE YOU HIKARU?
GRIK
GRIK
GRIK
UNH...
UHH...
WHAT IF I AM?
YOU LIAR. WHERE IS THE REAL HIKARU?
GRIK
* GASP *

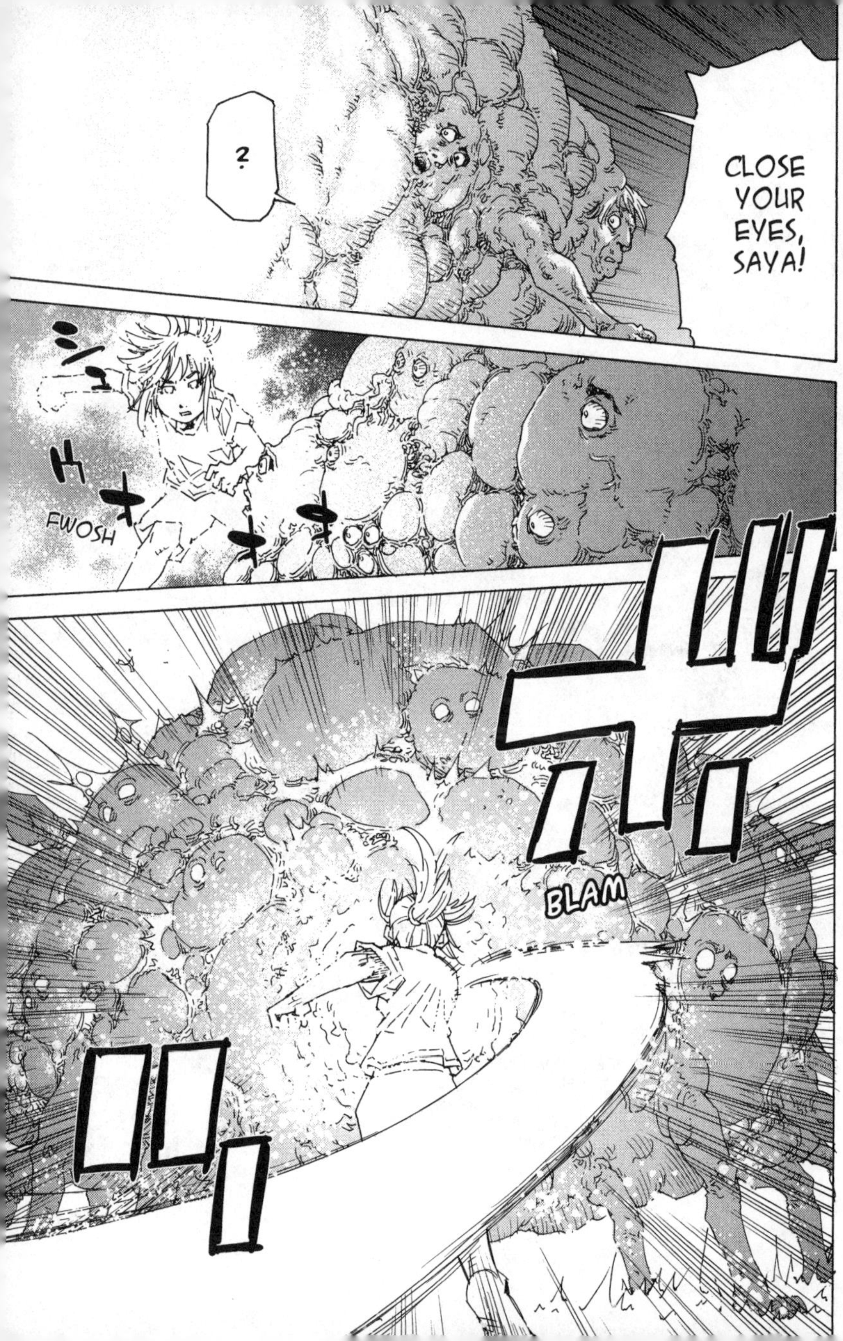
CLOSE YOUR EYES, SAYA!
?
FWOSH
BLAM

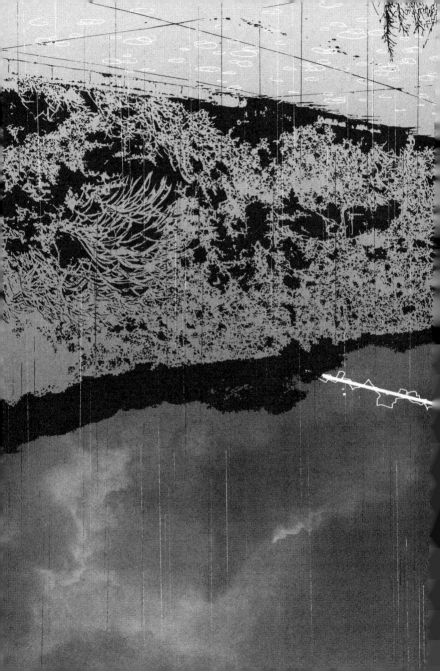

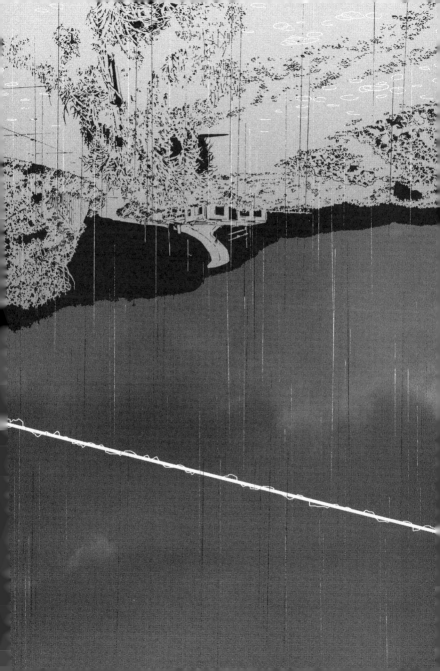

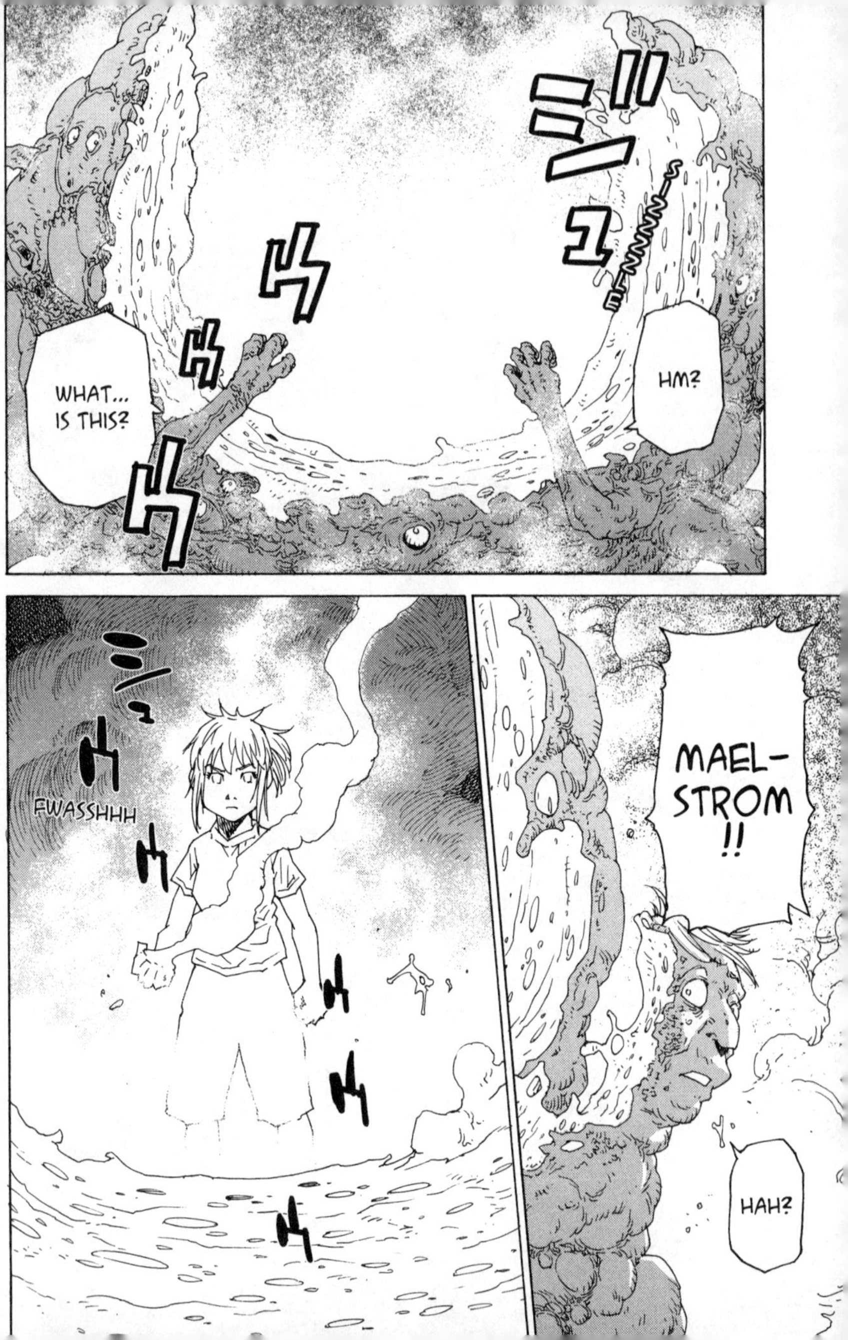
S-NNNNN-M
HM?
WHAT... IS THIS?
MAEL-STROM!!
HAH?
FWASSHHH

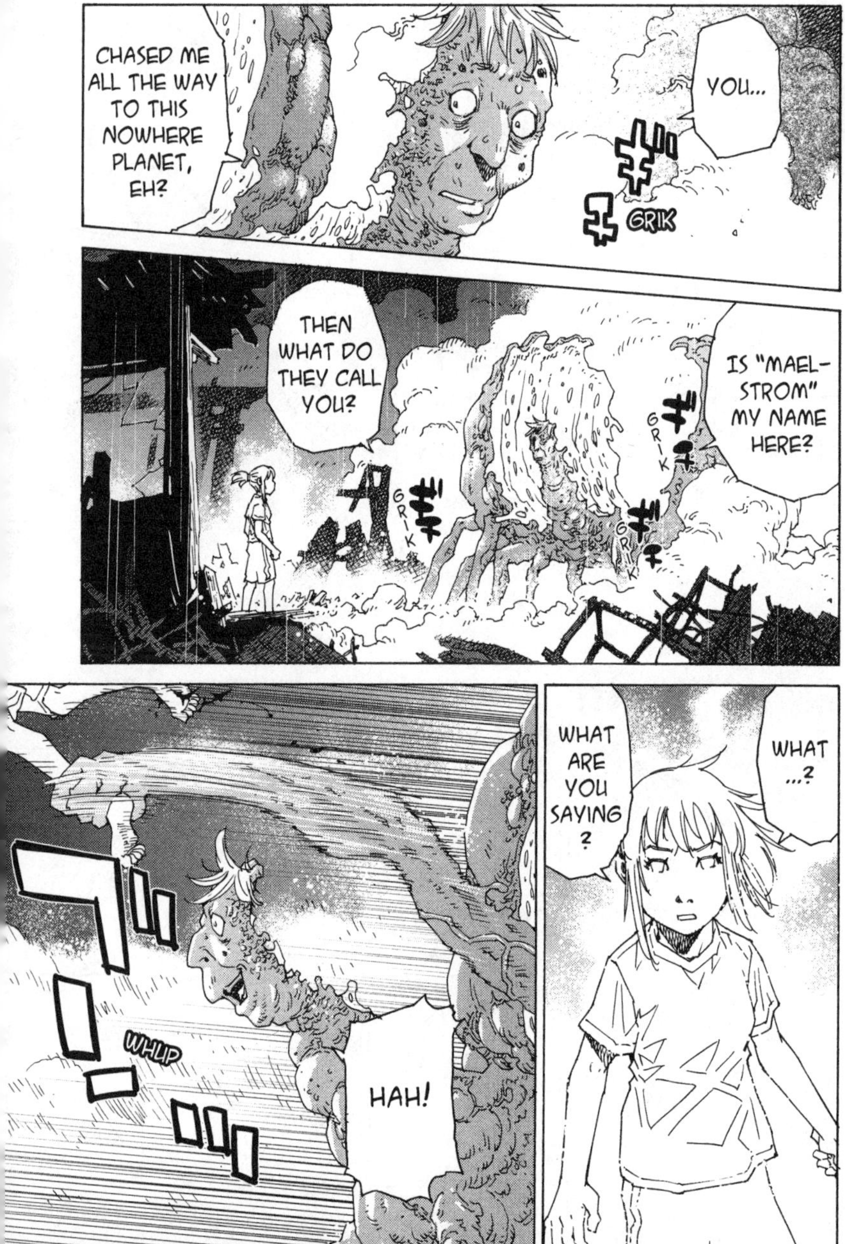
YOU...
GRIK
CHASED ME ALL THE WAY TO THIS NOWHERE PLANET, EH?
IS "MAEL-STROM" MY NAME HERE?
GRIK
GRIK
GRIK
THEN WHAT DO THEY CALL YOU?
WHAT ...?
WHAT ARE YOU SAYING ?
WHUP
HAH!

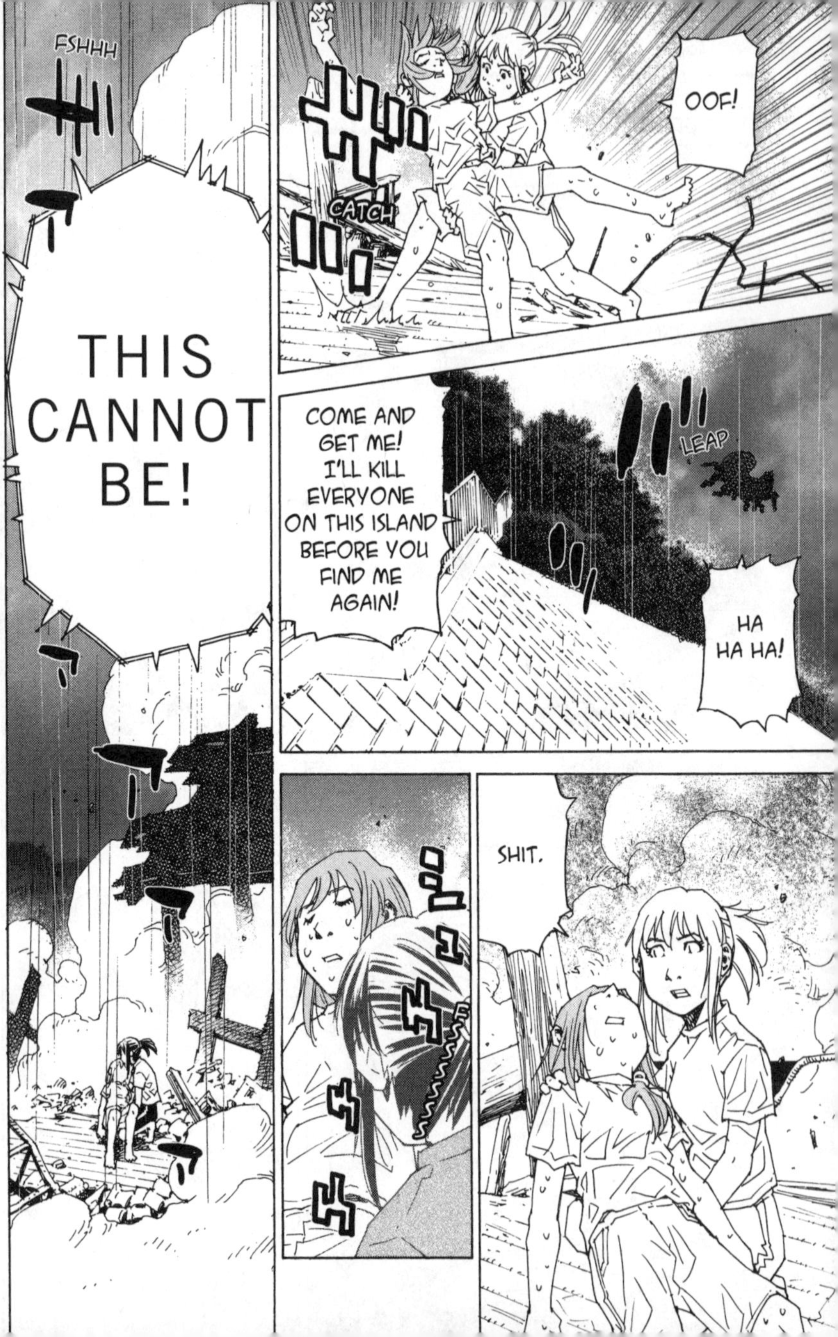
OOF!
CATCH
HA HA HA!
LEAP
COME AND GET ME! I'LL KILL EVERYONE ON THIS ISLAND BEFORE YOU FIND ME AGAIN!
SHIT.
FSHHH
THIS CANNOT BE!

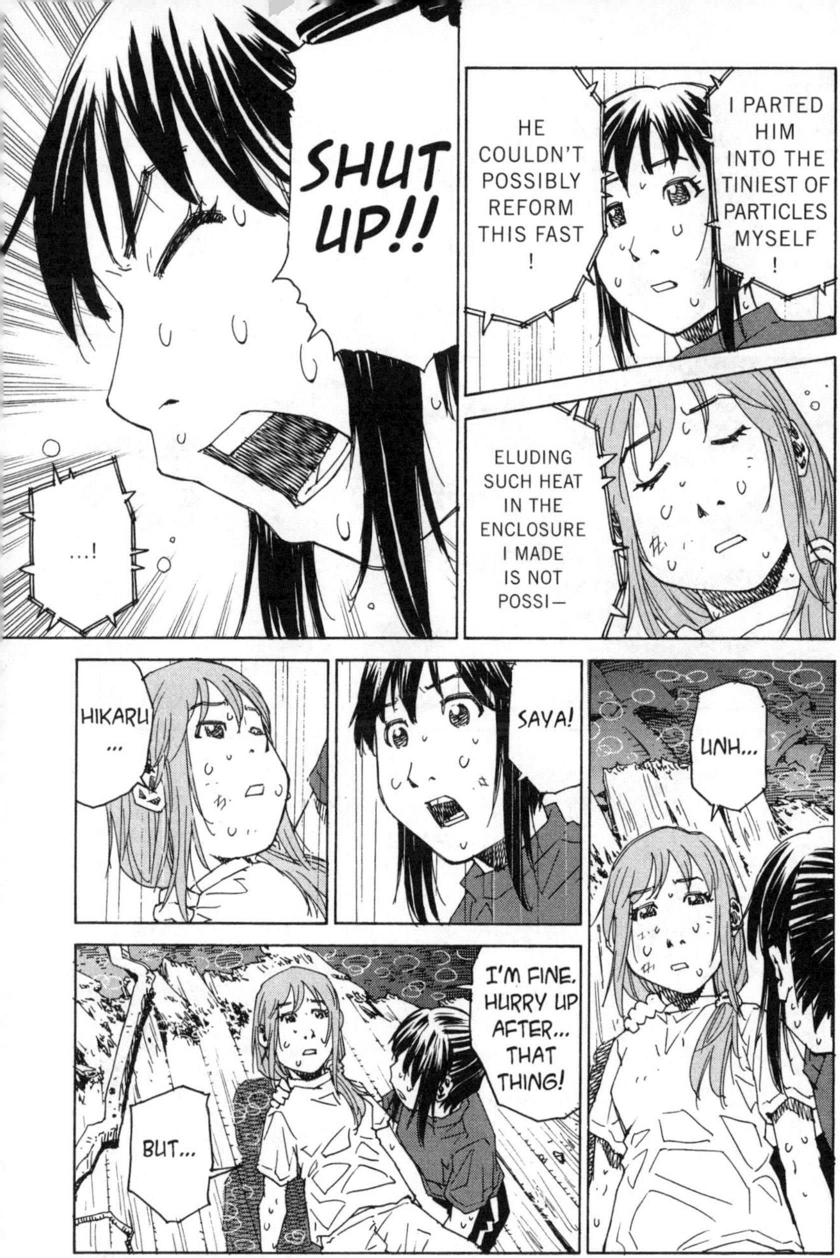
I PARTED HIM INTO THE TINIEST OF PARTICLES MYSELF !
HE COULDN'T POSSIBLY REFORM THIS FAST !
ELUDING SUCH HEAT IN THE ENCLOSURE I MADE IS NOT POSSI—
SHUT UP!!
...!
UNH...
SAYA!
HIKARU ...
I'M FINE. HURRY UP AFTER... THAT THING!
BUT...

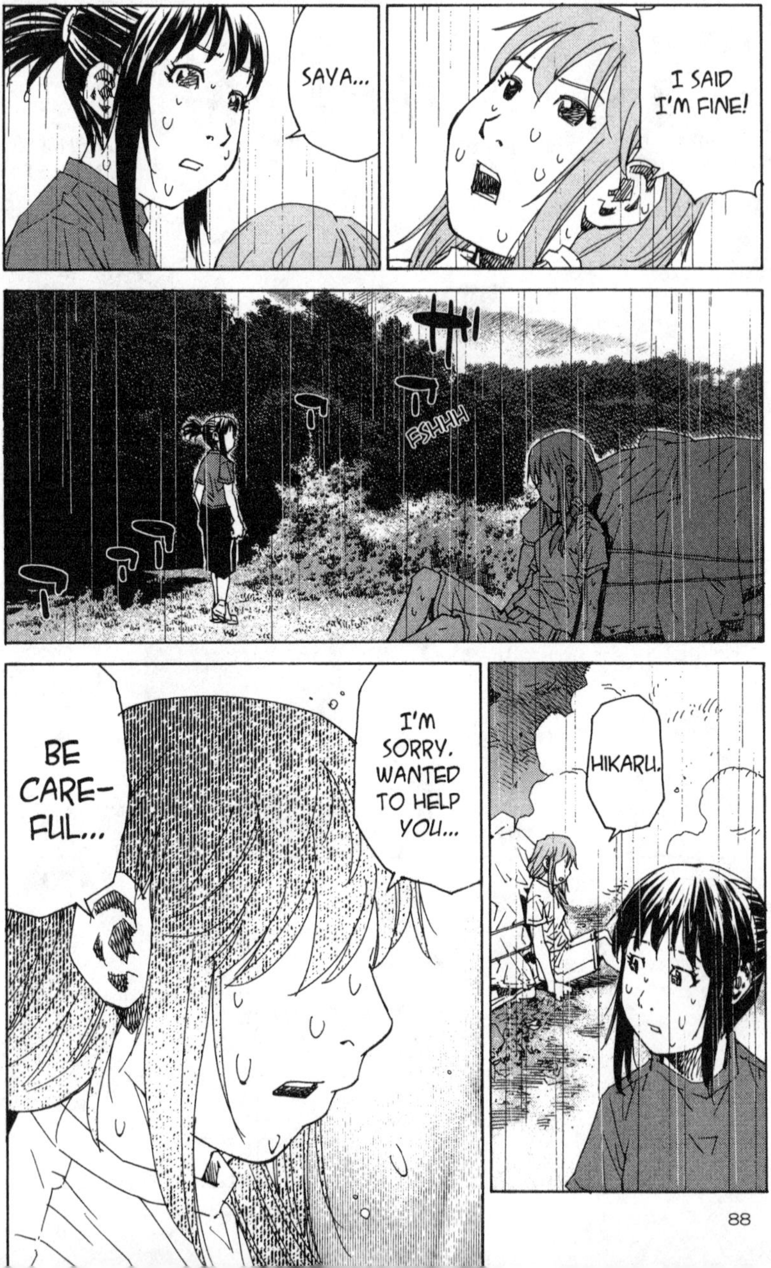
I SAID
I'M FINE!
SAYA...
FSHHH
HIKARU.
I'M SORRY. WANTED TO HELP YOU...
BE CARE-FUL...

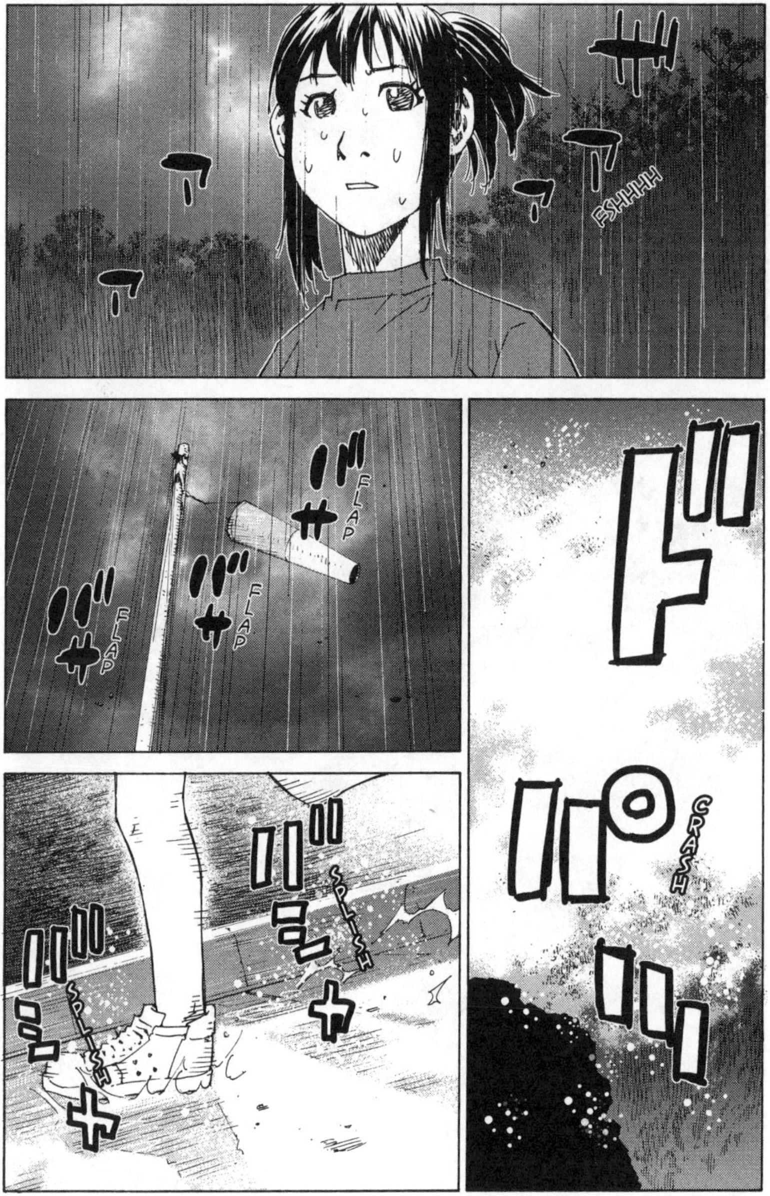
FSHHHH
CRASH
FLAP
FLAP
FLAP
SPLISH
SPLISH

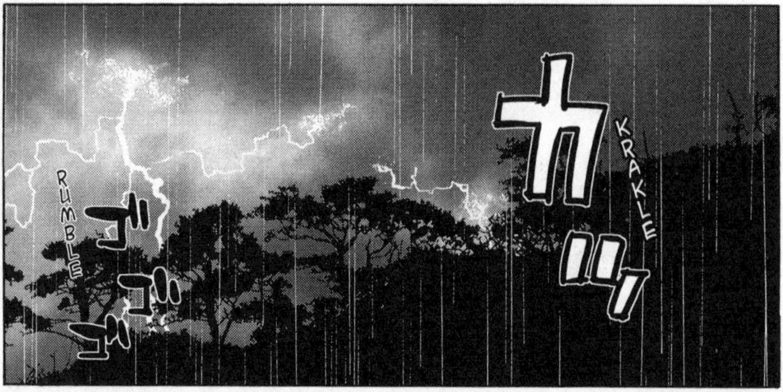
カッ
KRAKLE
ゴゴゴ
RUMBLE
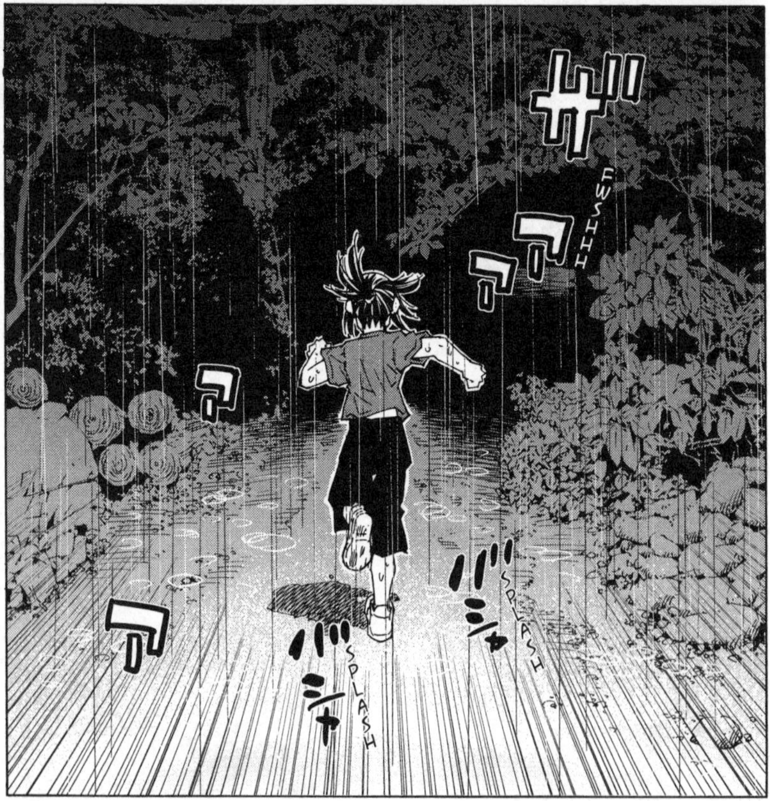
ザァァァ
FWSHHH
バシャ
SPLASH
バシャ
SPLASH

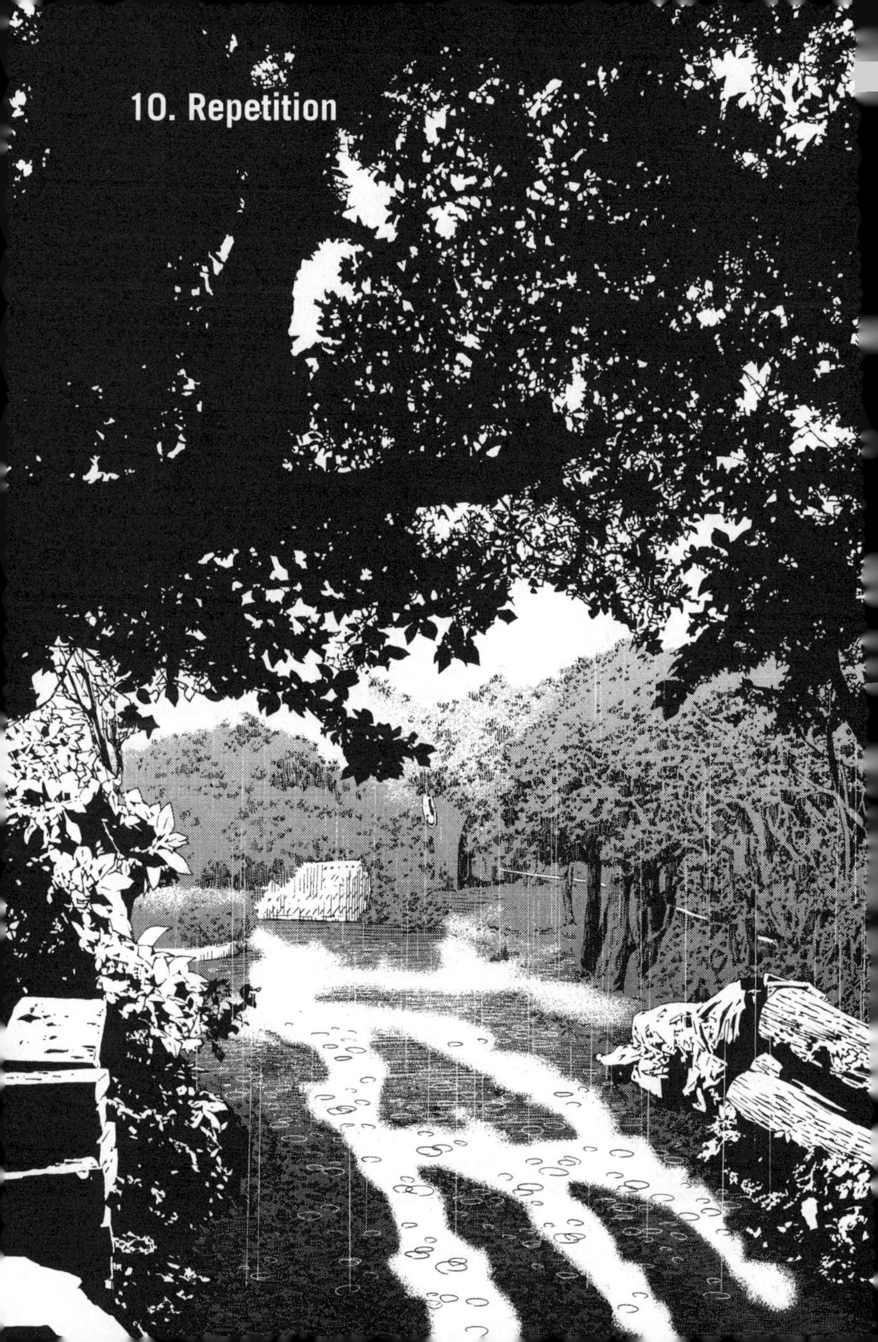
10. Repetition

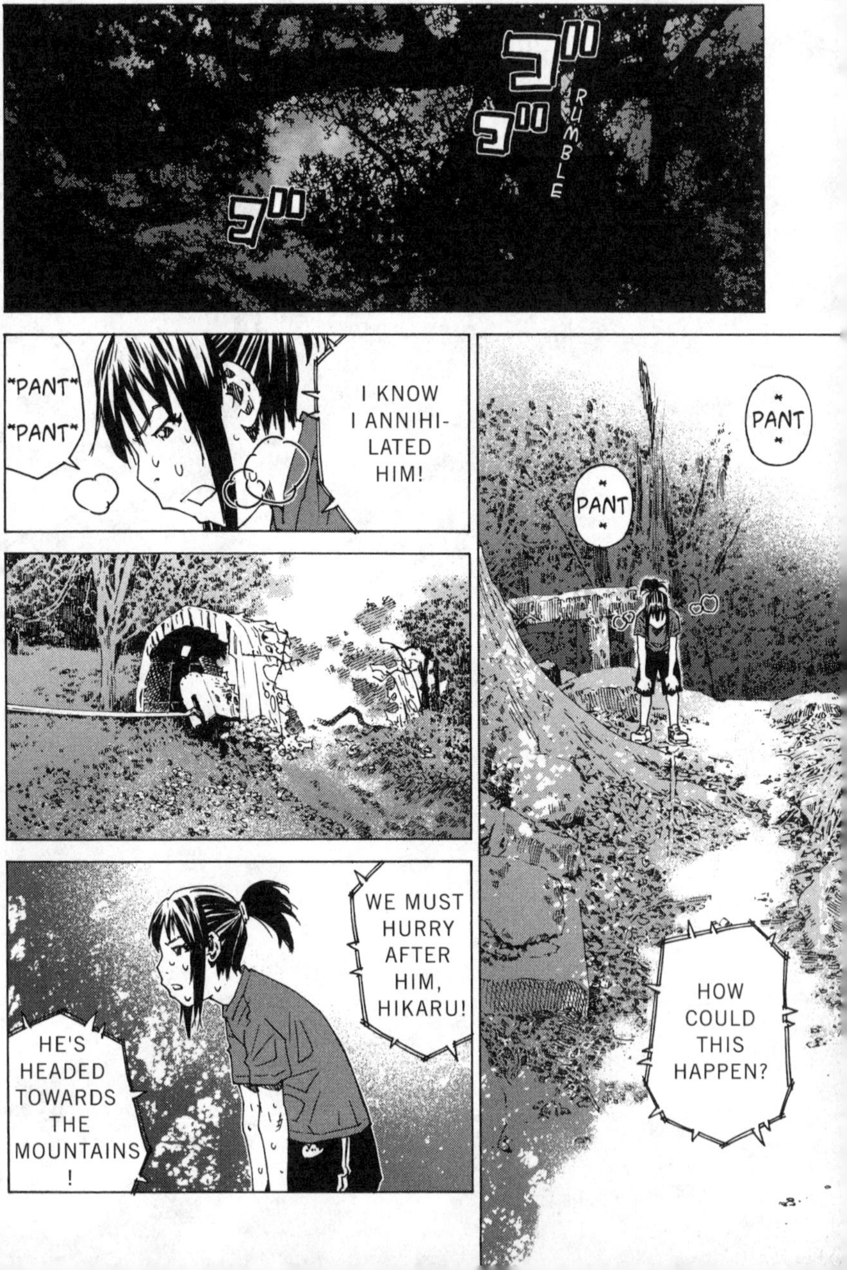
RUMBLE
PANT
PANT
HOW COULD THIS HAPPEN?
PANT *PANT*
I KNOW I ANNIHI-LATED HIM!
WE MUST HURRY AFTER HIM, HIKARU!
HE'S HEADED TOWARDS THE MOUNTAINS!

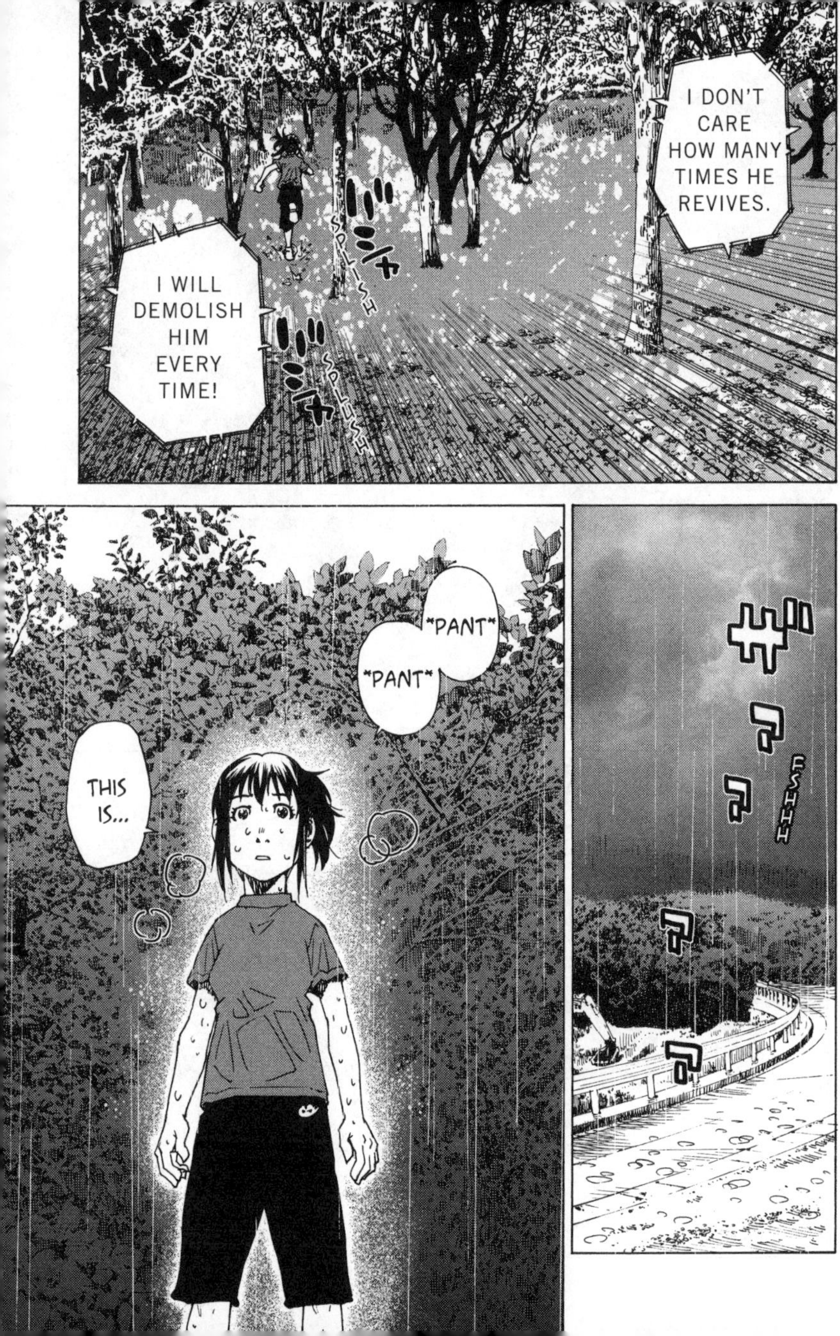
I DON'T CARE HOW MANY TIMES HE REVIVES.
SPLISH
I WILL DEMOLISH HIM EVERY TIME!
SPLISH
FSHHH
PANT
PANT
THIS IS...

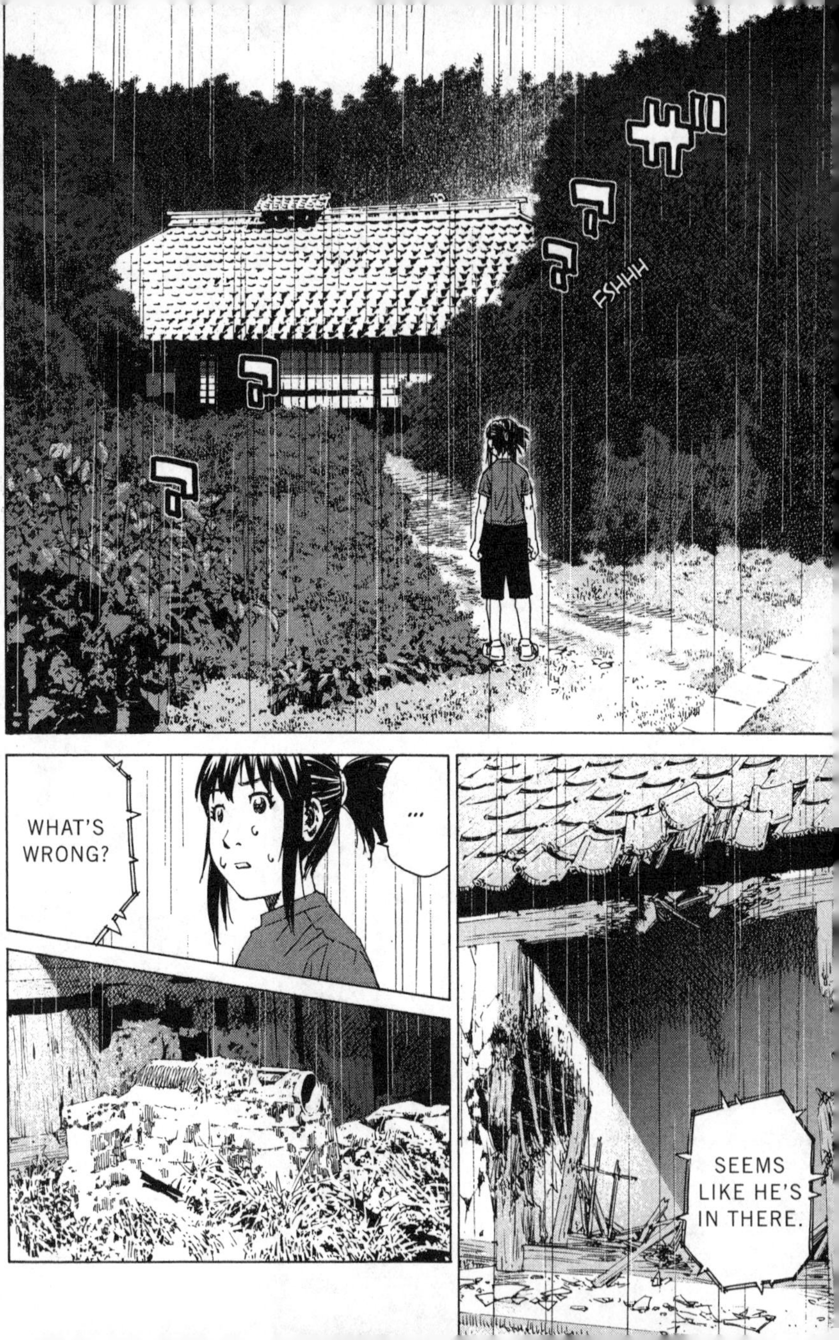
FSHHH
SEEMS LIKE HE'S IN THERE.
...
WHAT'S WRONG?

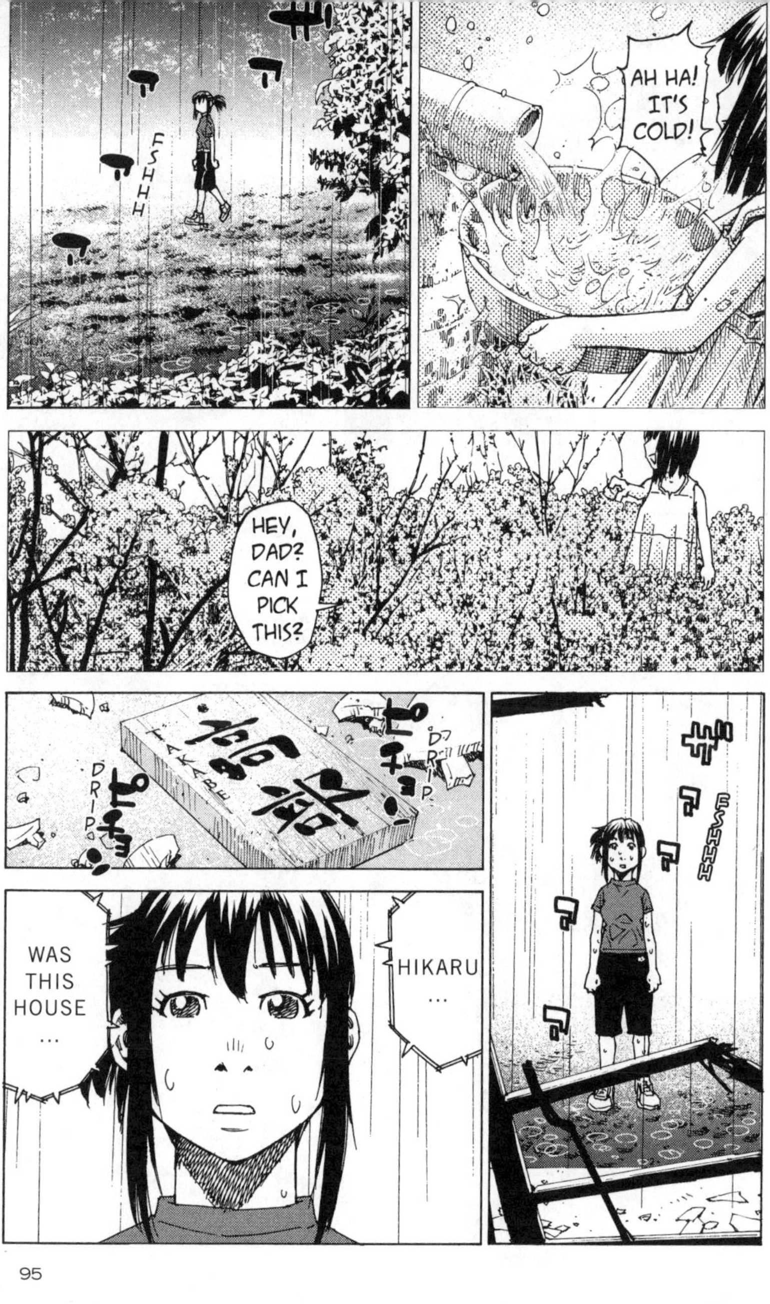
AH HA! IT'S COLD!
FSHHH
HEY, DAD? CAN I PICK THIS?
TAKABE
DRIP
DRIP
HIKARU ...
WAS THIS HOUSE ...

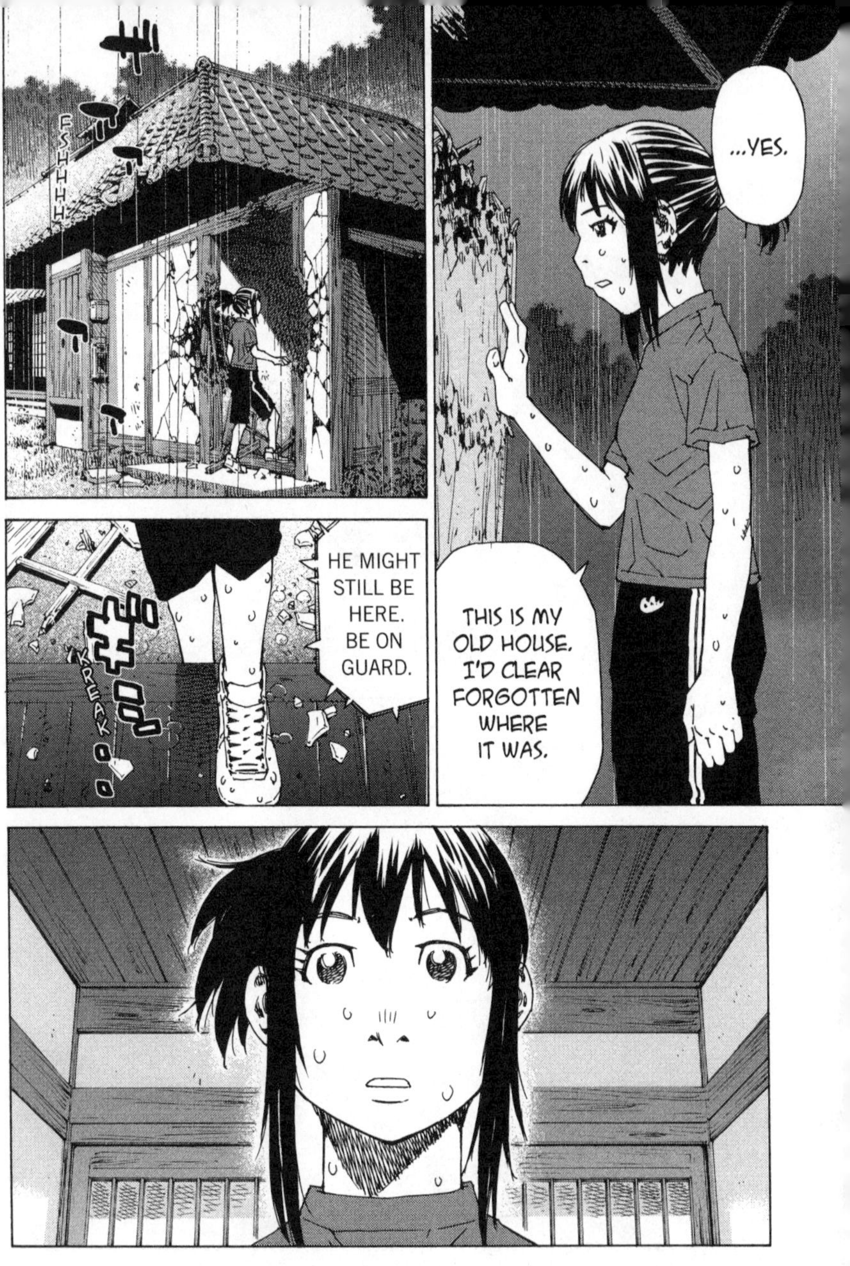
...YES.
THIS IS MY OLD HOUSE. I'D CLEAR FORGOTTEN WHERE IT WAS.
FSHHHH
HE MIGHT STILL BE HERE. BE ON GUARD.
KREAK

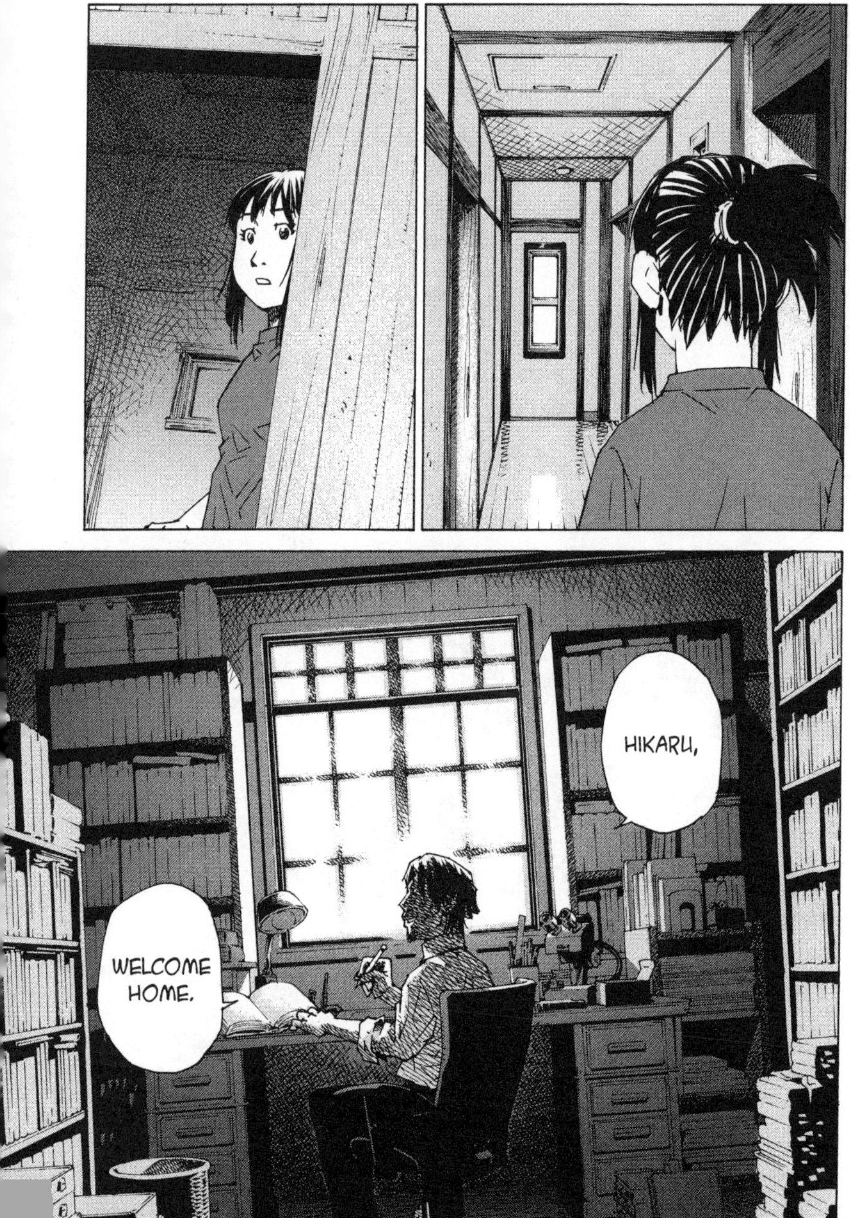
HIKARU,
WELCOME HOME.

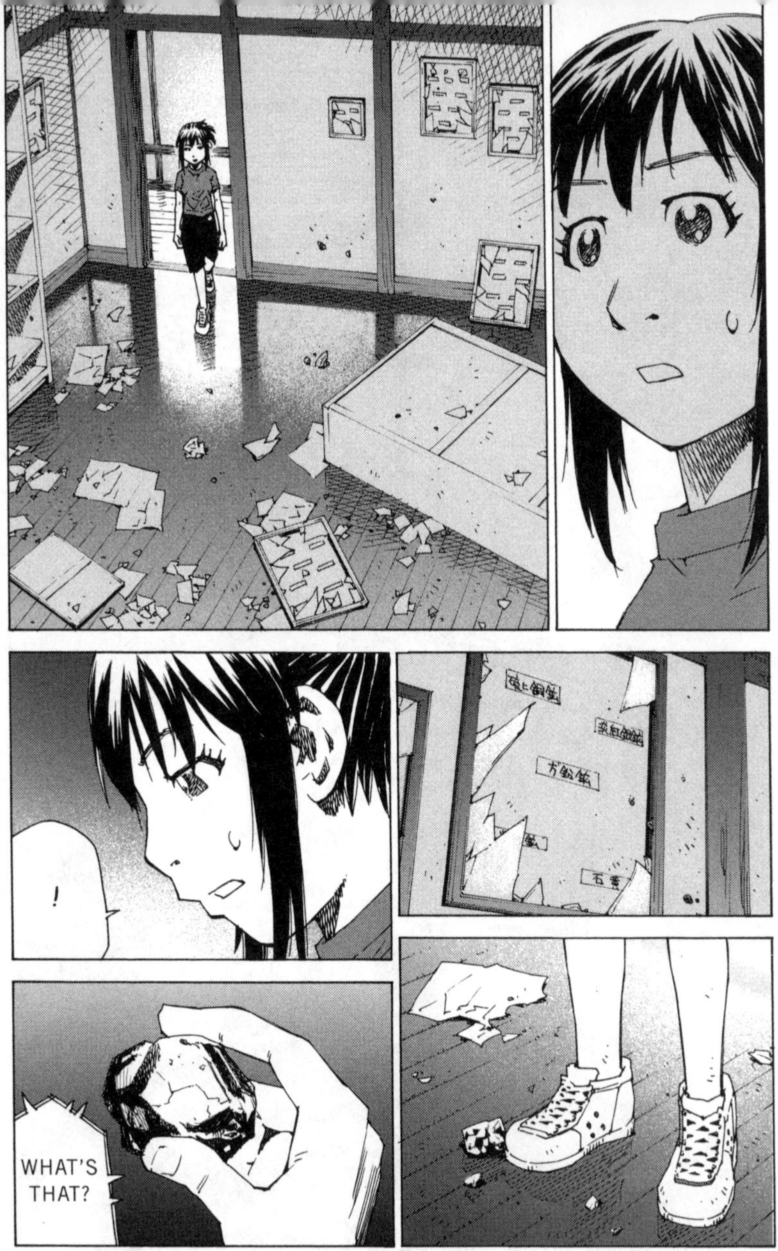
方鉛鉱
石膏
!
WHAT'S THAT?

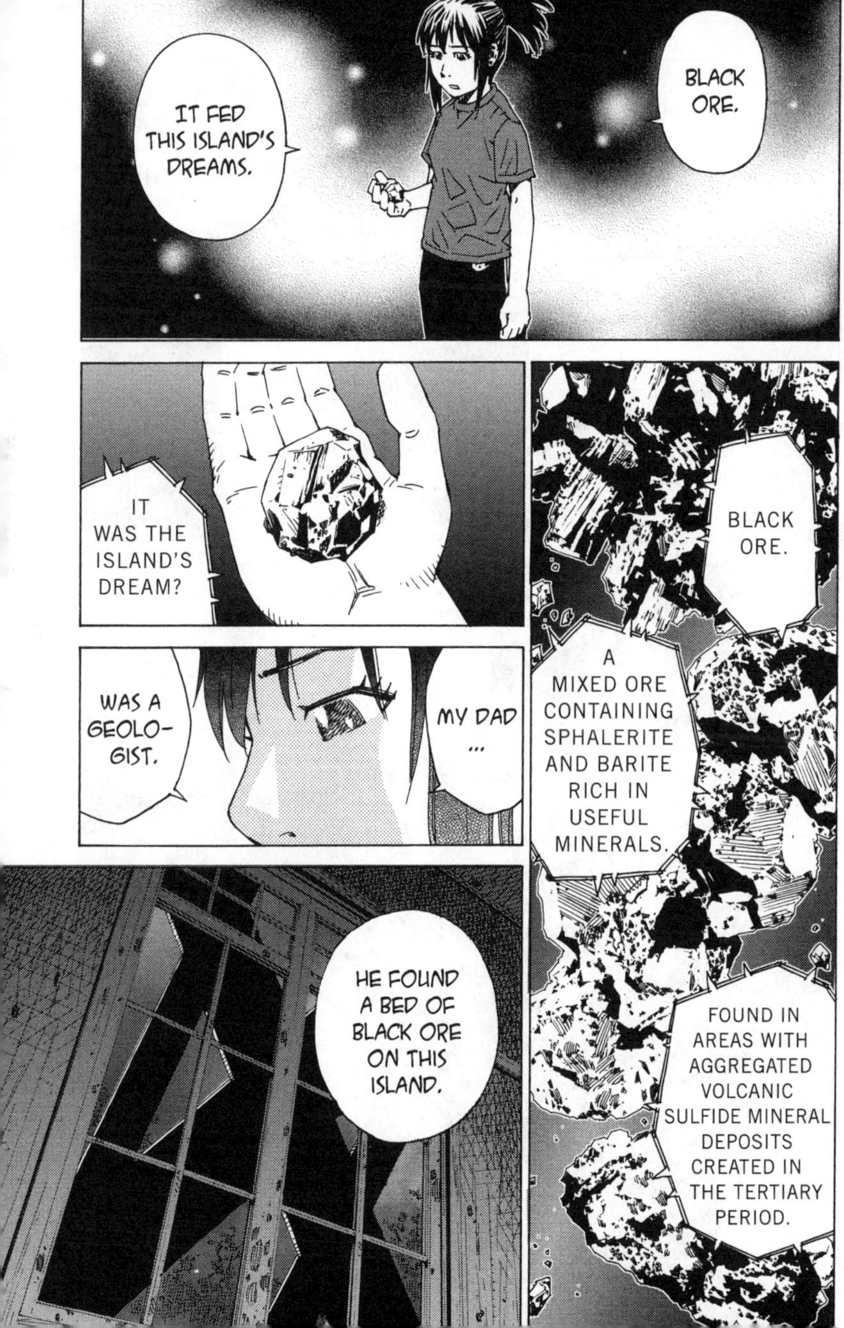
BLACK ORE.
IT FED THIS ISLAND'S DREAMS.
BLACK ORE.
A MIXED ORE CONTAINING SPHALERITE AND BARITE RICH IN USEFUL MINERALS.
FOUND IN AREAS WITH AGGREGATED VOLCANIC SULFIDE MINERAL DEPOSITS CREATED IN THE TERTIARY PERIOD.
IT WAS THE ISLAND'S DREAM?
MY DAD ...
WAS A GEOLO-GIST.
HE FOUND A BED OF BLACK ORE ON THIS ISLAND.

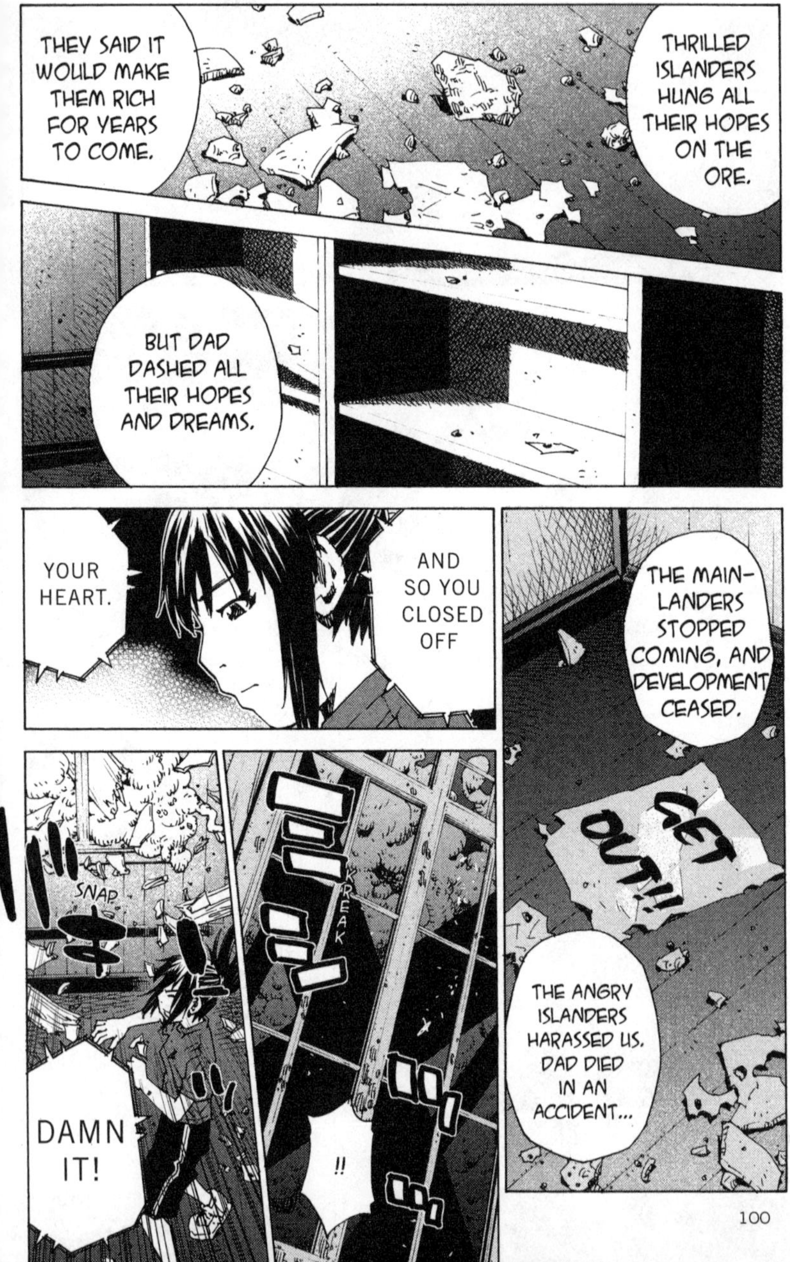
THRILLED ISLANDERS HUNG ALL THEIR HOPES ON THE ORE.
THEY SAID IT WOULD MAKE THEM RICH FOR YEARS TO COME.
BUT DAD DASHED ALL THEIR HOPES AND DREAMS.
THE MAIN-LANDERS STOPPED COMING, AND DEVELOPMENT CEASED.
GET OUT!!
THE ANGRY ISLANDERS HARASSED US. DAD DIED IN AN ACCIDENT...
AND SO YOU CLOSED OFF
YOUR HEART.
KREAK
!!
SNAP
DAMN IT!

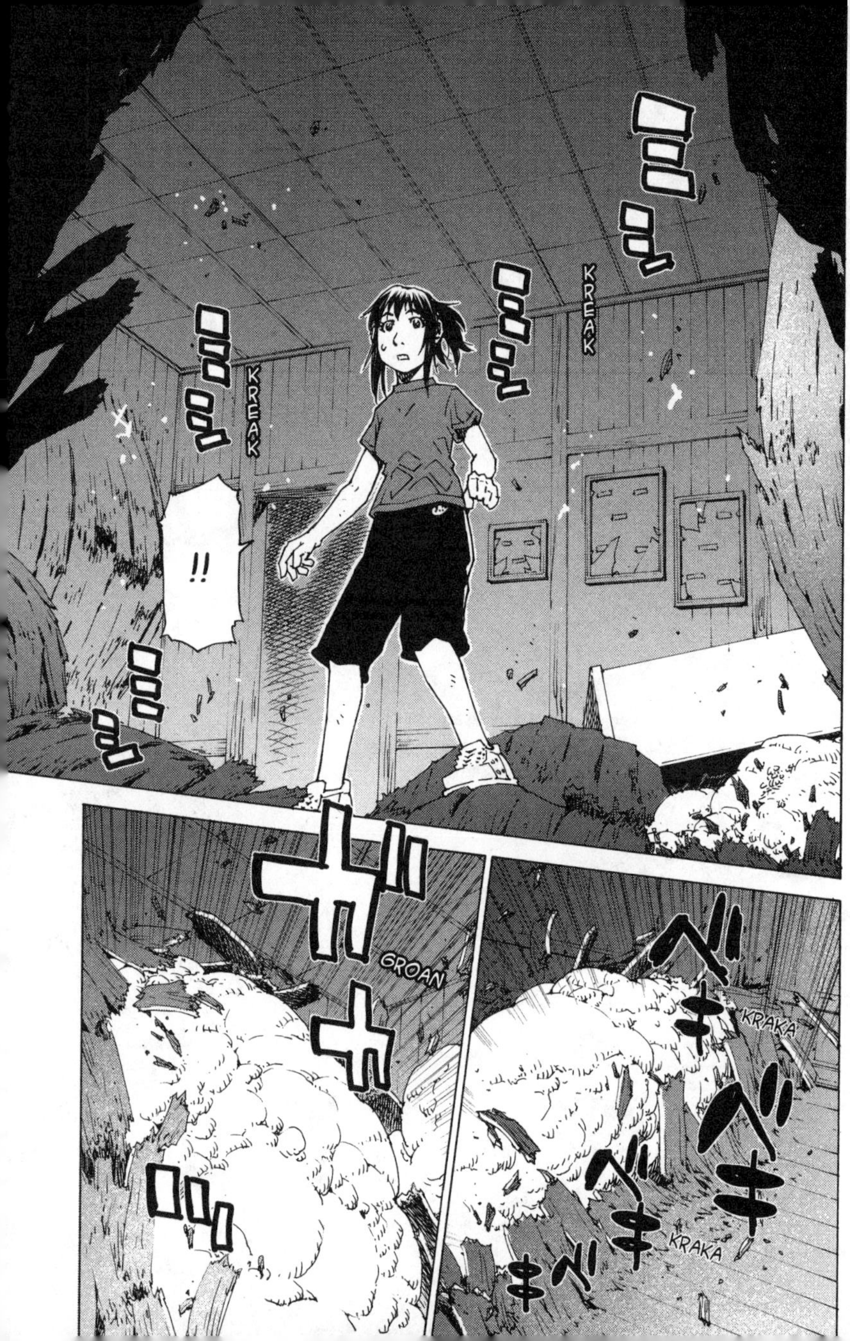
ゴゴゴ
KREAK
ゴゴゴゴ
ゴゴゴ
KREAK
!!
ゴゴゴ
ベキベキベキ
KRAKA
KRAKA
ギギ
GROAN
ゴゴ

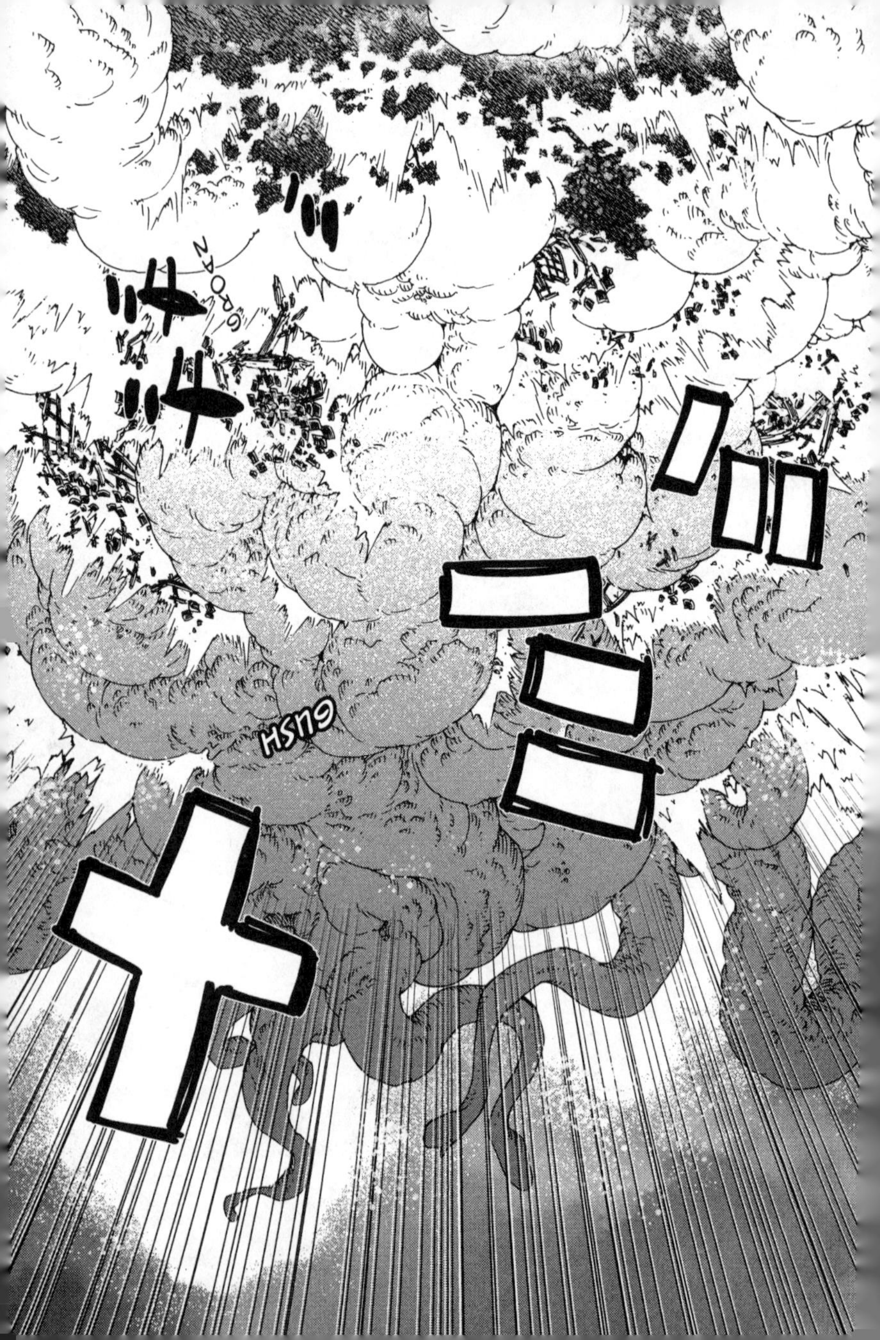
GROAN
GUSH

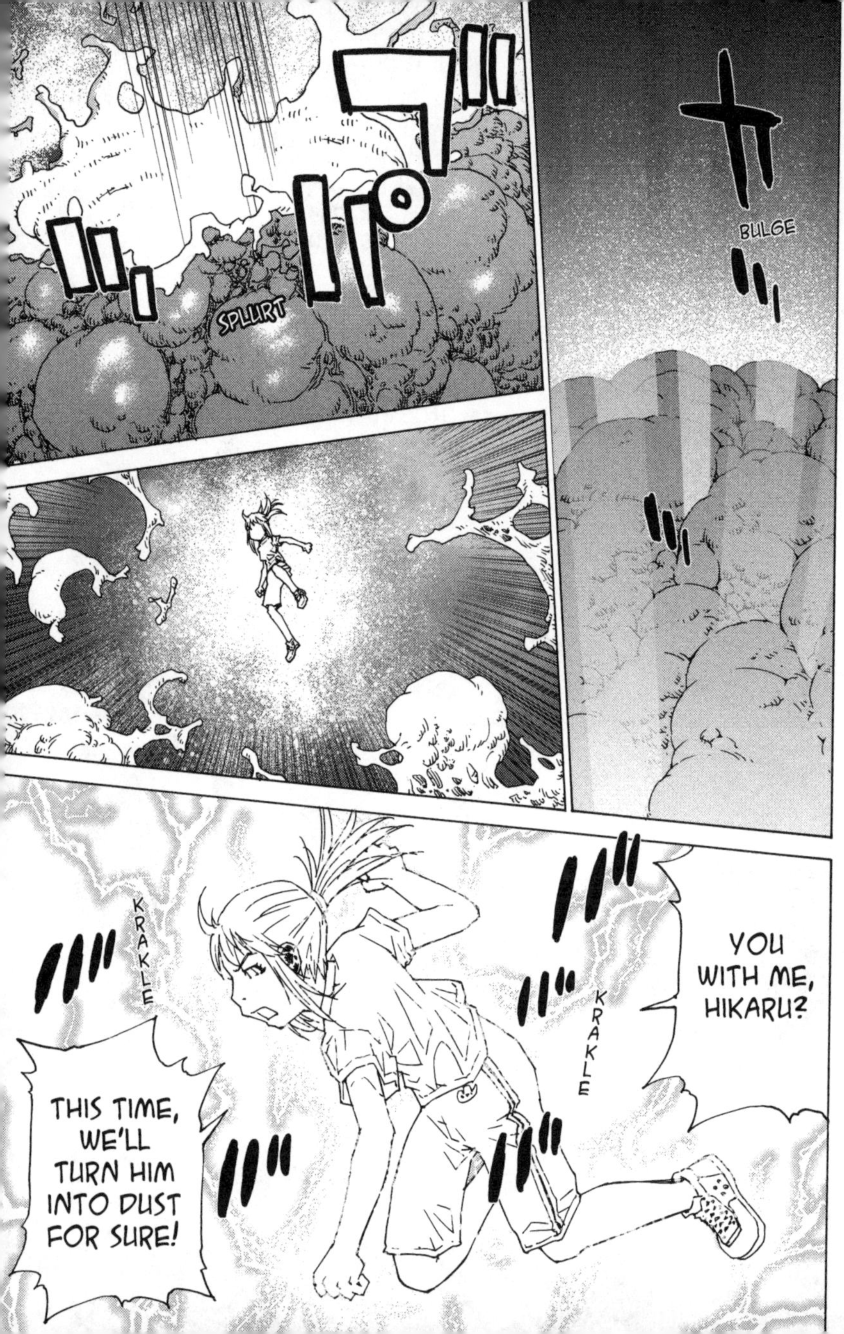
BULGE
SPLURT
YOU WITH ME, HIKARU?
KRAKLE
KRAKLE
THIS TIME, WE'LL TURN HIM INTO DUST FOR SURE!

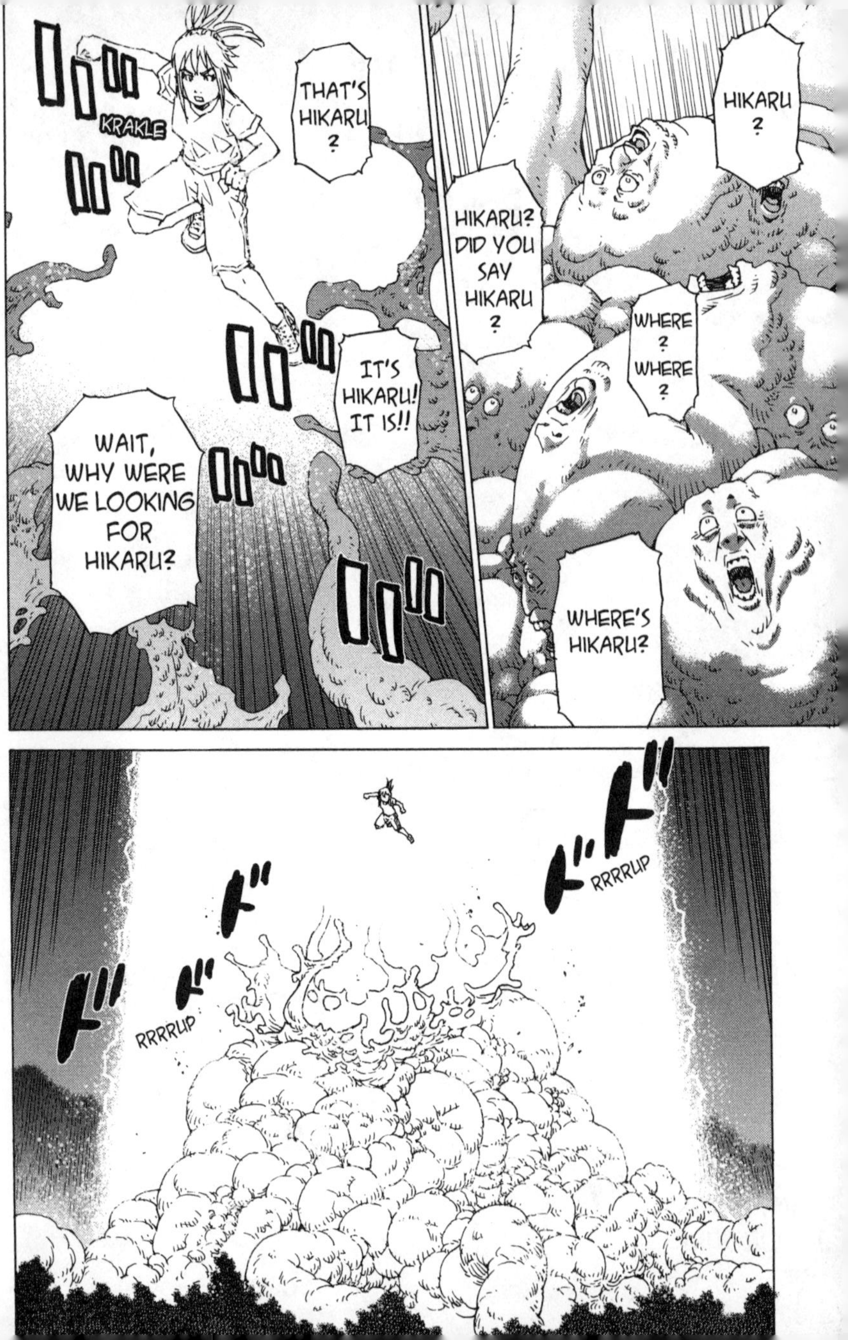
HIKARU ?
HIKARU? DID YOU SAY HIKARU ?
WHERE ? WHERE ?
WHERE'S HIKARU?
THAT'S HIKARU ?
KRAKLE
IT'S HIKARU! IT IS!!
WAIT, WHY WERE WE LOOKING FOR HIKARU?
RRRRUP
RRRRUP

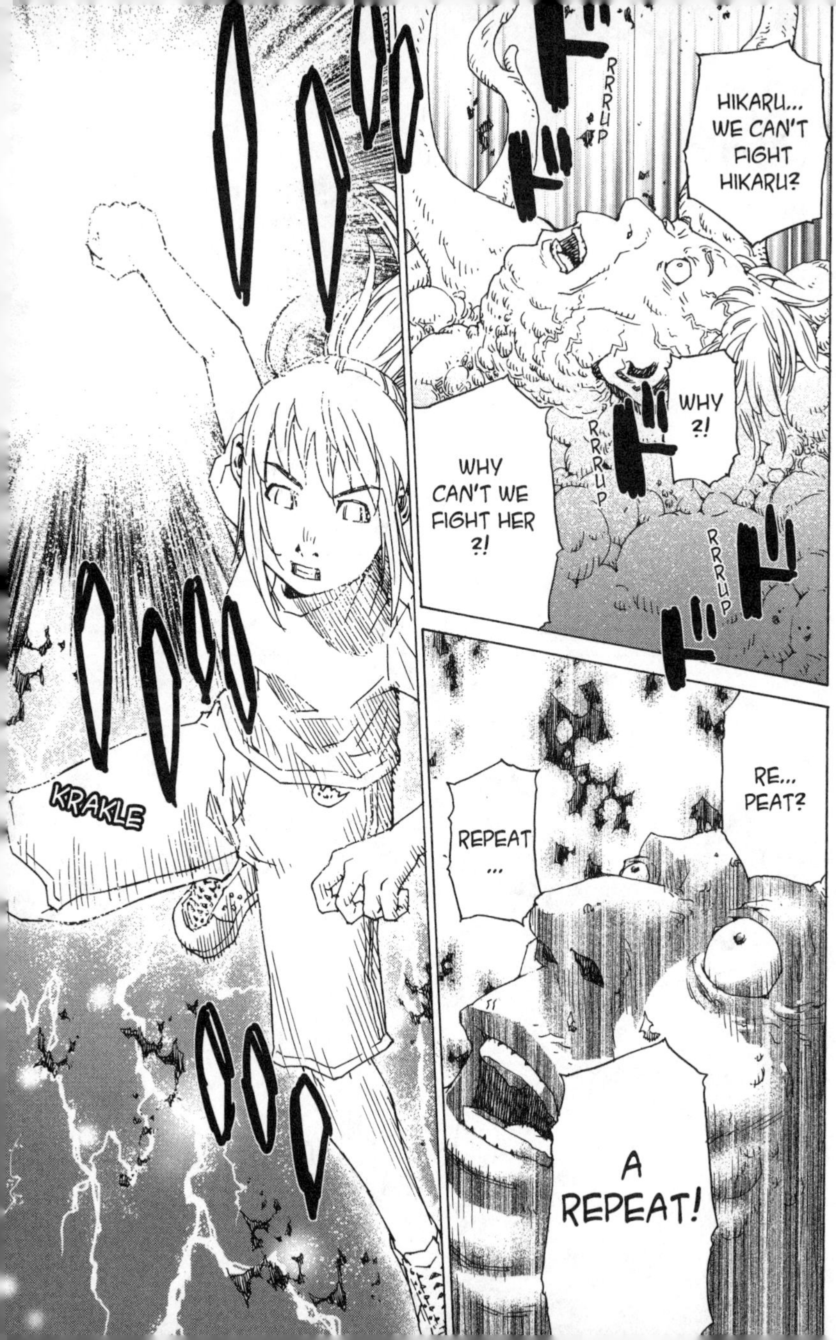
HIKARU... WE CAN'T FIGHT HIKARU?
RRRUP
WHY ?!
RRRUP
RRRUP
WHY CAN'T WE FIGHT HER ?!
RE... PEAT?
REPEAT ...
A REPEAT!
KRAKLE

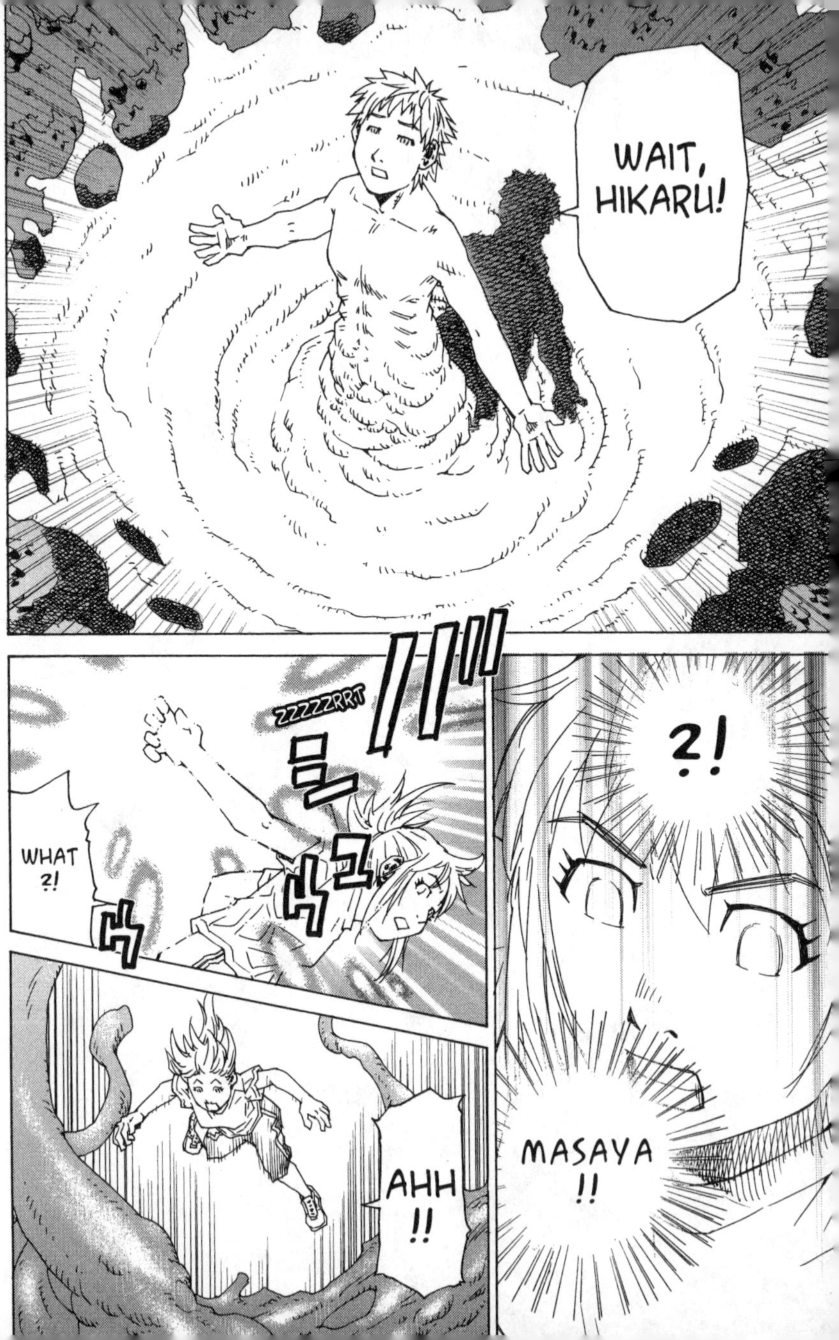
WAIT, HIKARU!
?!
MASAYA !!
ZZZZZRRT
WHAT ?!
AHH !!

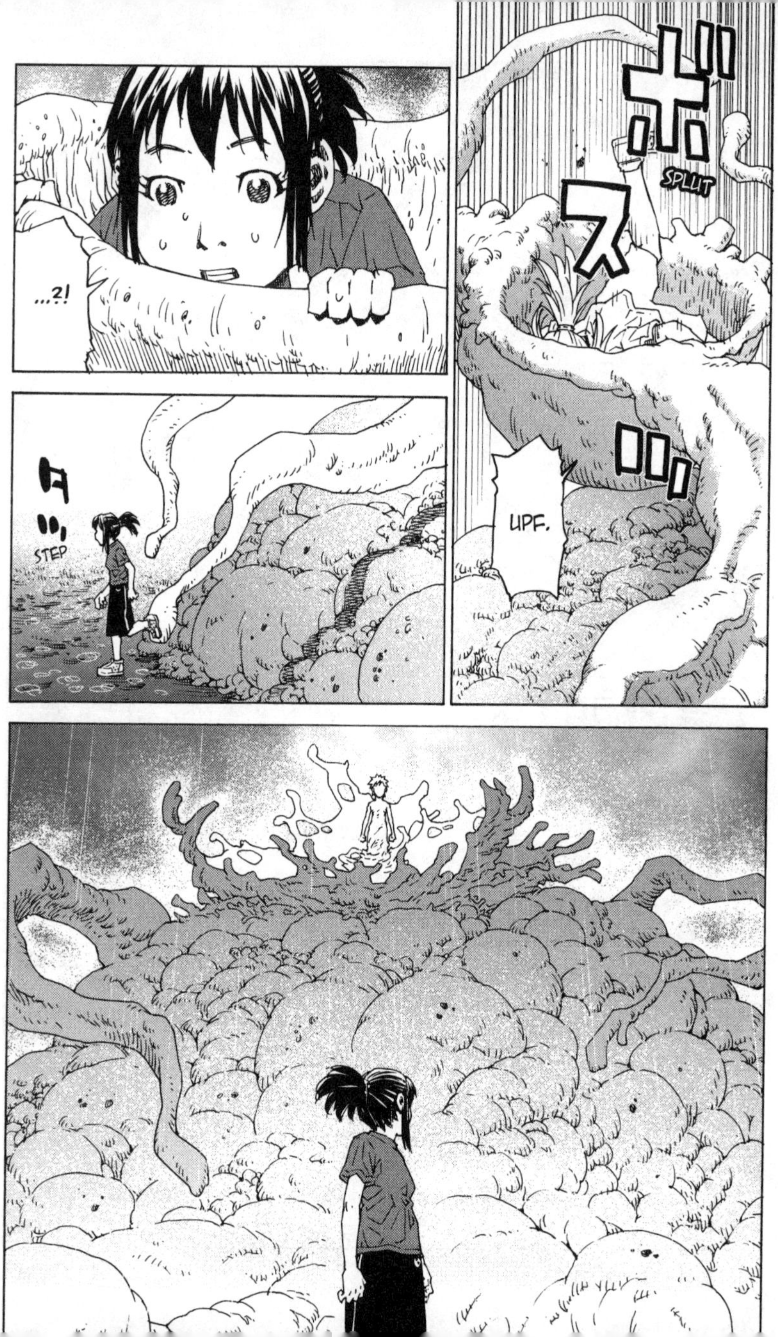
SPLUT
UPF.
...?!
STEP

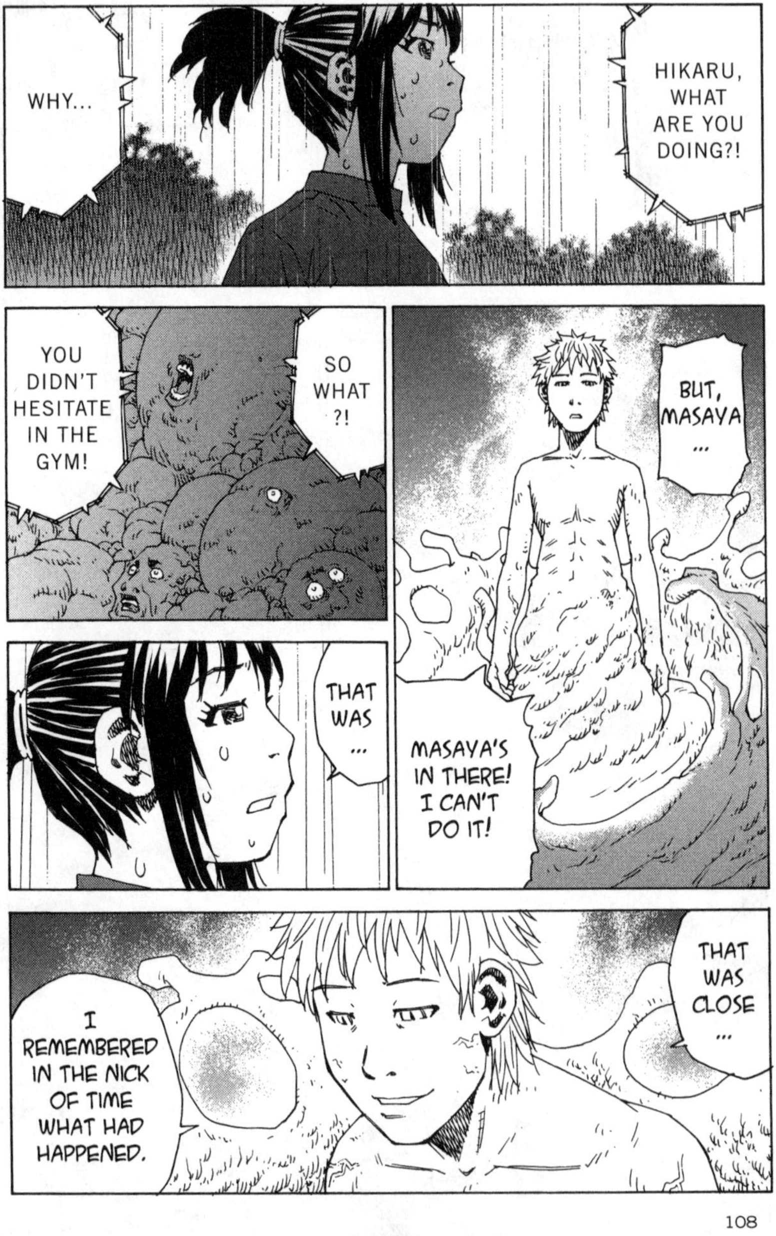
HIKARU, WHAT ARE YOU DOING?!
WHY...
BUT, MASAYA ...
MASAYA'S IN THERE! I CAN'T DO IT!
SO WHAT ?!
YOU DIDN'T HESITATE IN THE GYM!
THAT WAS ...
THAT WAS CLOSE ...
I REMEMBERED IN THE NICK OF TIME WHAT HAD HAPPENED.

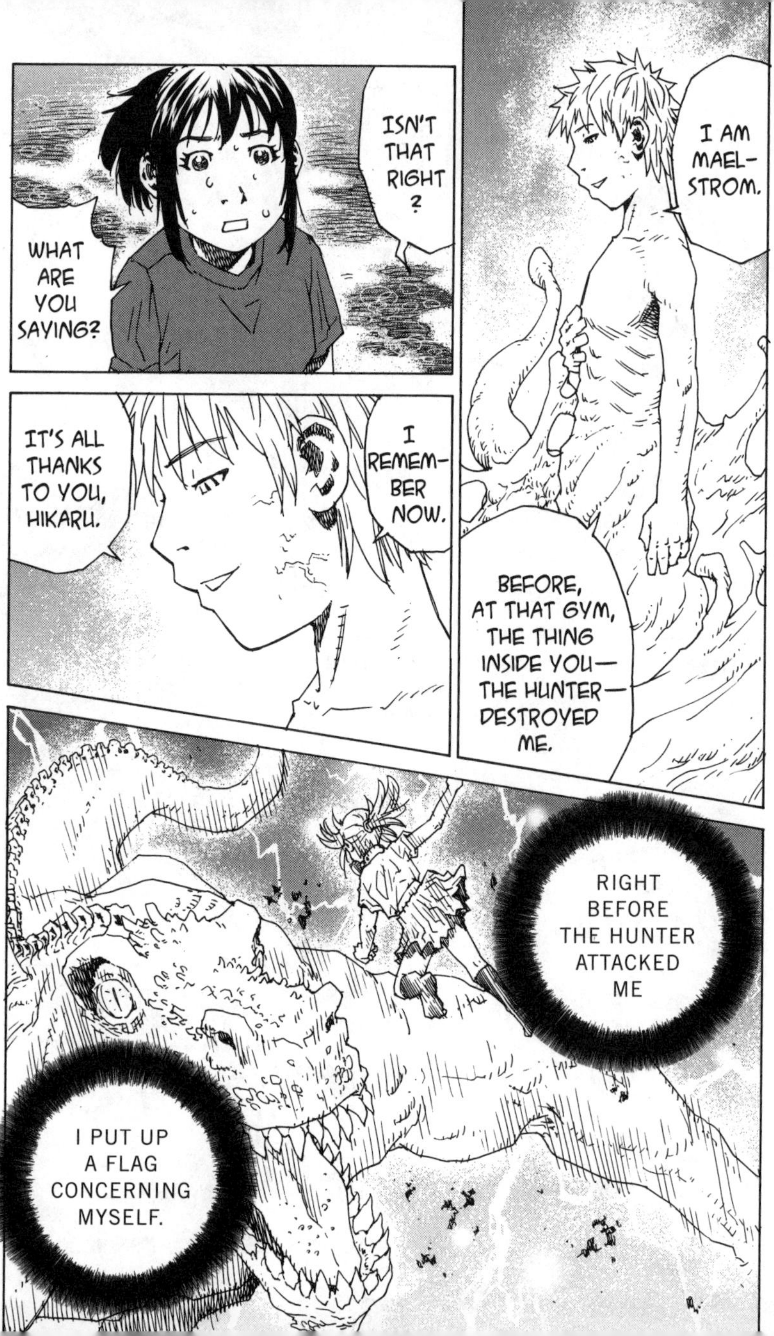
I AM MAEL-STROM.
BEFORE, AT THAT GYM, THE THING INSIDE YOU—THE HUNTER—DESTROYED ME.
ISN'T THAT RIGHT?
WHAT ARE YOU SAYING?
I REMEMBER NOW.
IT'S ALL THANKS TO YOU, HIKARU.
RIGHT BEFORE THE HUNTER ATTACKED ME
I PUT UP A FLAG CONCERNING MYSELF.

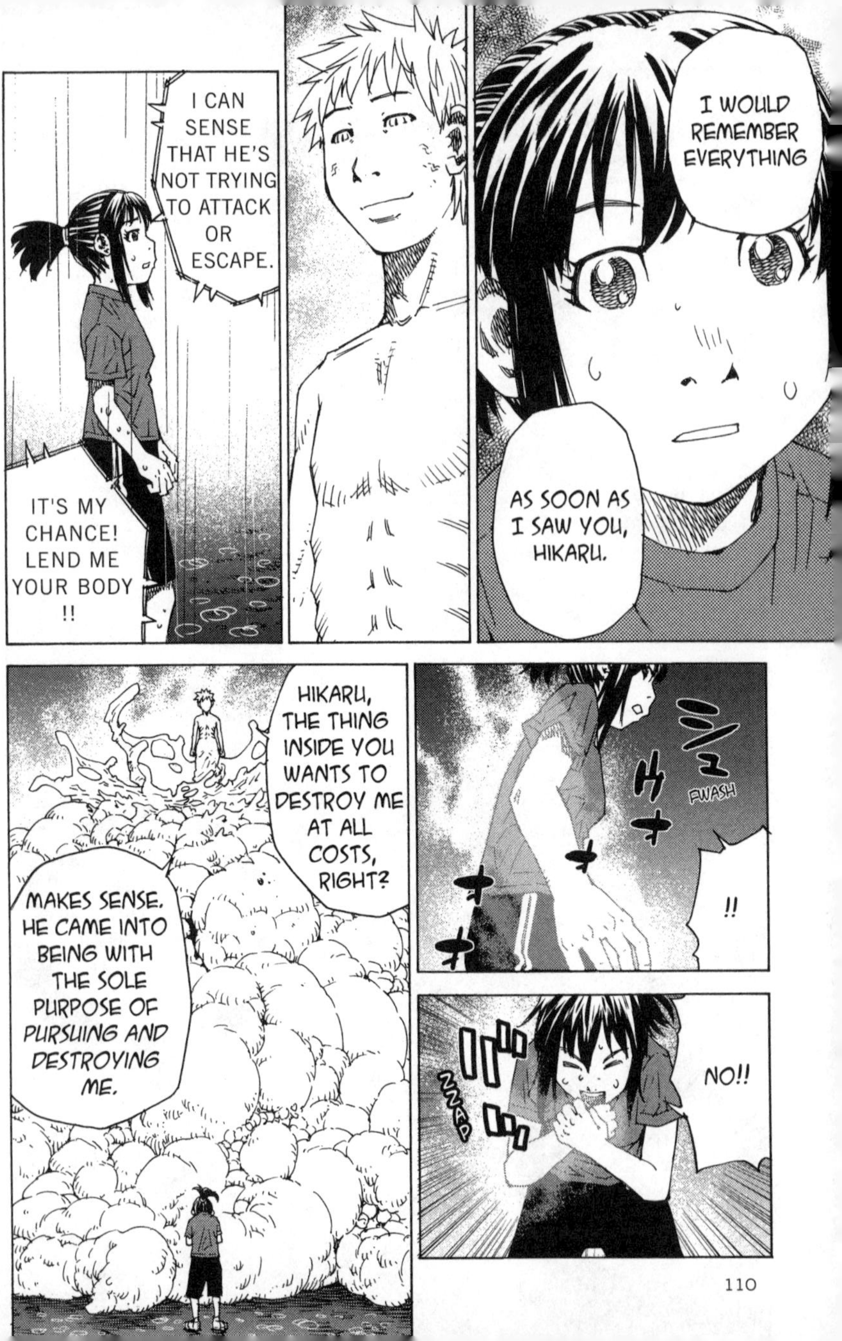
I WOULD REMEMBER EVERYTHING
AS SOON AS I SAW YOU, HIKARU.
I CAN SENSE THAT HE'S NOT TRYING TO ATTACK OR ESCAPE.
IT'S MY CHANCE! LEND ME YOUR BODY !!
FWASH
!!
NO!!
ZZZAP
HIKARU, THE THING INSIDE YOU WANTS TO DESTROY ME AT ALL COSTS, RIGHT?
MAKES SENSE. HE CAME INTO BEING WITH THE SOLE PURPOSE OF PURSUING AND DESTROYING ME.

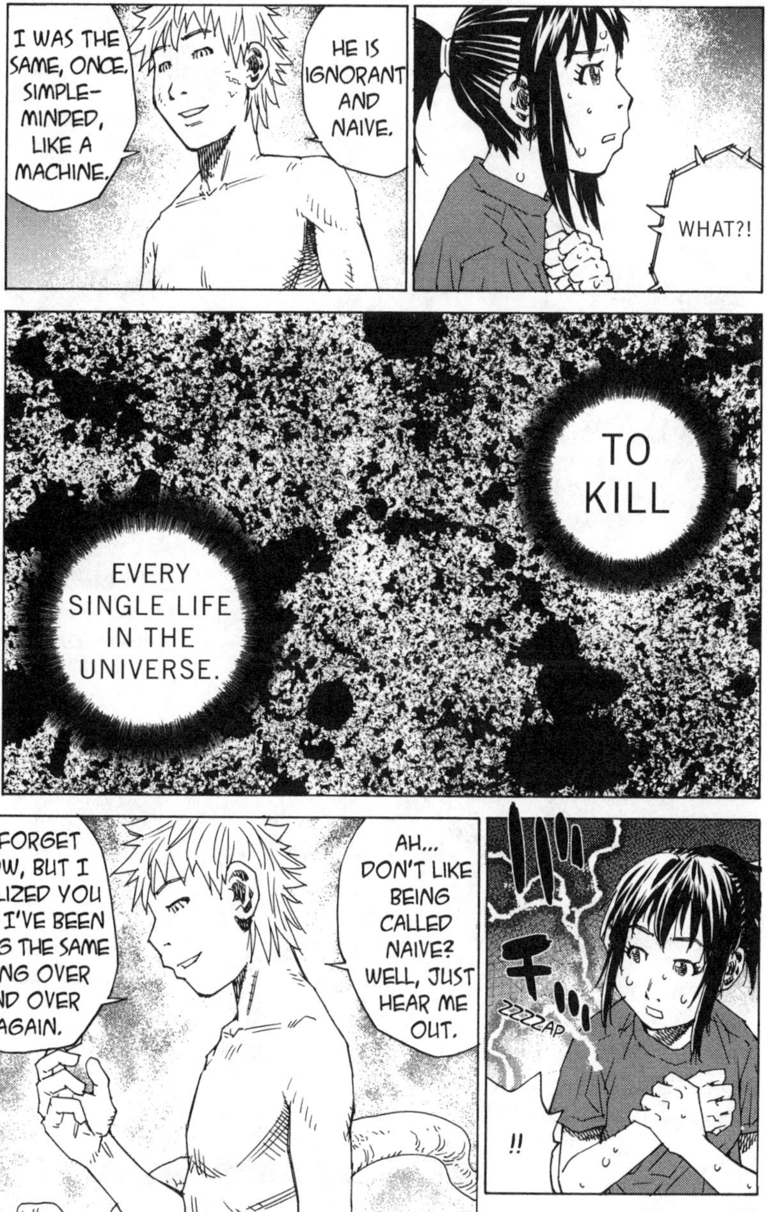
WHAT?!
HE IS IGNORANT AND NAIVE.
I WAS THE SAME, ONCE. SIMPLE-MINDED, LIKE A MACHINE.
TO KILL
EVERY SINGLE LIFE IN THE UNIVERSE.
!!
ZZZZAP
AH... DON'T LIKE BEING CALLED NAIVE? WELL, JUST HEAR ME OUT.
I FORGET HOW, BUT I REALIZED YOU AND I'VE BEEN DOING THE SAME THING OVER AND OVER AGAIN.

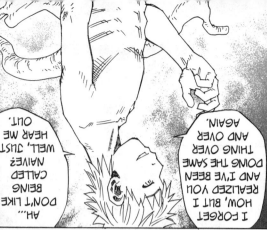

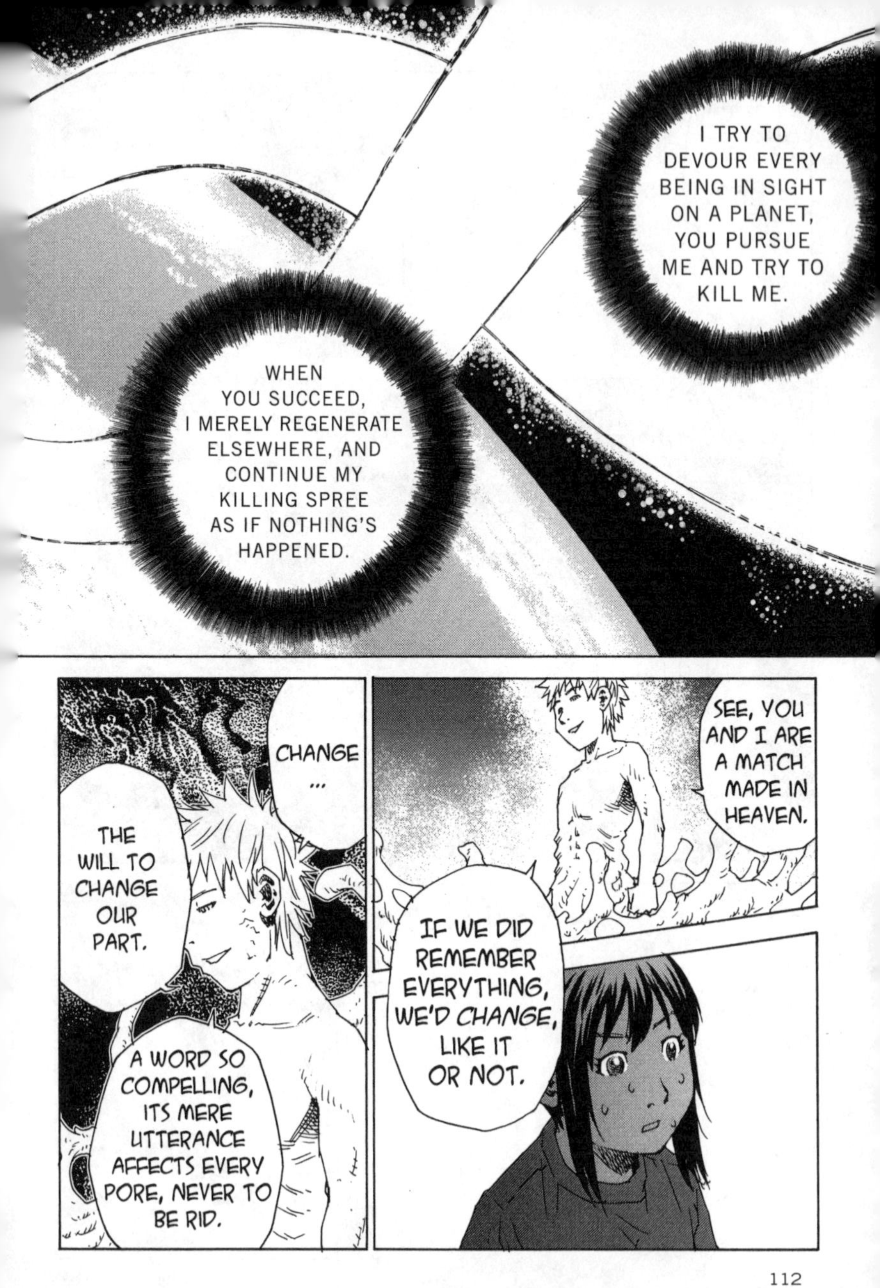
I TRY TO DEVOUR EVERY BEING IN SIGHT ON A PLANET, YOU PURSUE ME AND TRY TO KILL ME.
WHEN YOU SUCCEED, I MERELY REGENERATE ELSEWHERE, AND CONTINUE MY KILLING SPREE AS IF NOTHING'S HAPPENED.
SEE, YOU AND I ARE A MATCH MADE IN HEAVEN.
IF WE DID REMEMBER EVERYTHING, WE'D CHANGE, LIKE IT OR NOT.
CHANGE ...
THE WILL TO CHANGE OUR PART.
A WORD SO COMPELLING, ITS MERE UTTERANCE AFFECTS EVERY PORE, NEVER TO BE RID.

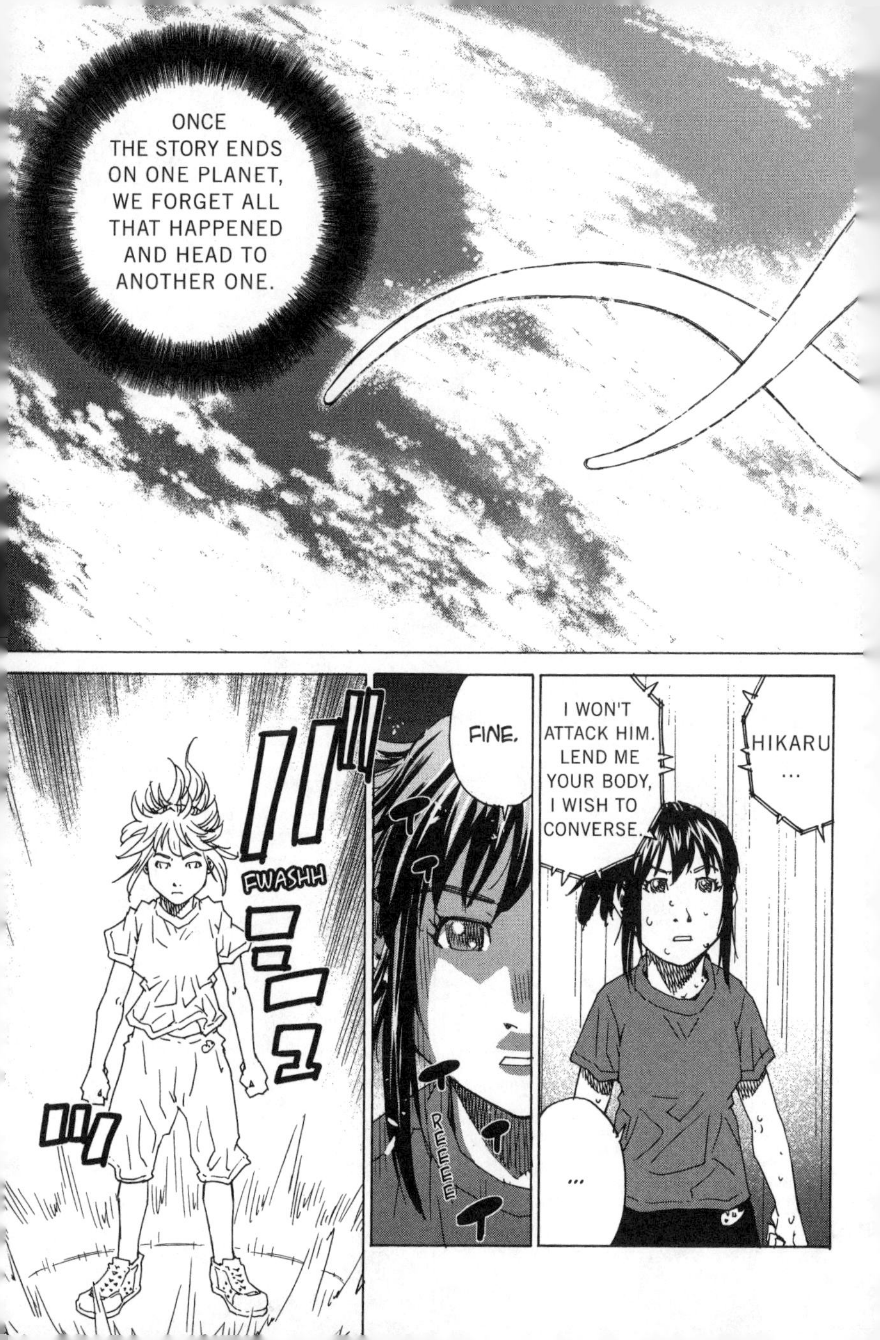
ONCE THE STORY ENDS ON ONE PLANET, WE FORGET ALL THAT HAPPENED AND HEAD TO ANOTHER ONE.
HIKARU ...
I WON'T ATTACK HIM. LEND ME YOUR BODY, I WISH TO CONVERSE.
...
FINE.
REEEEE
FWASHH

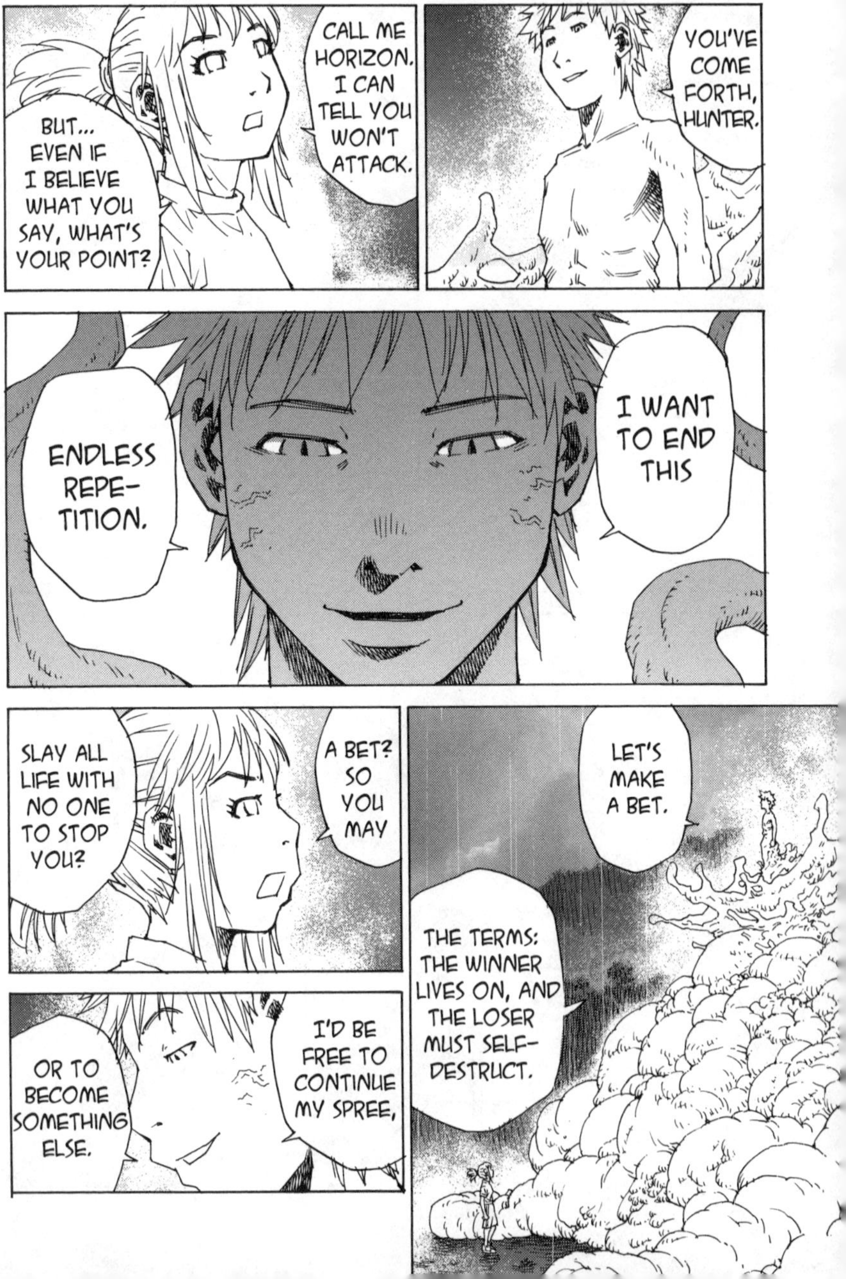
YOU'VE COME FORTH, HUNTER.
CALL ME HORIZON. I CAN TELL YOU WON'T ATTACK.
BUT... EVEN IF I BELIEVE WHAT YOU SAY, WHAT'S YOUR POINT?
I WANT TO END THIS
ENDLESS REPE-TITION.
LET'S MAKE A BET.
THE TERMS: THE WINNER LIVES ON, AND THE LOSER MUST SELF-DESTRUCT.
A BET? SO YOU MAY
SLAY ALL LIFE WITH NO ONE TO STOP YOU?
I'D BE FREE TO CONTINUE MY SPREE,
OR TO BECOME SOMETHING ELSE.

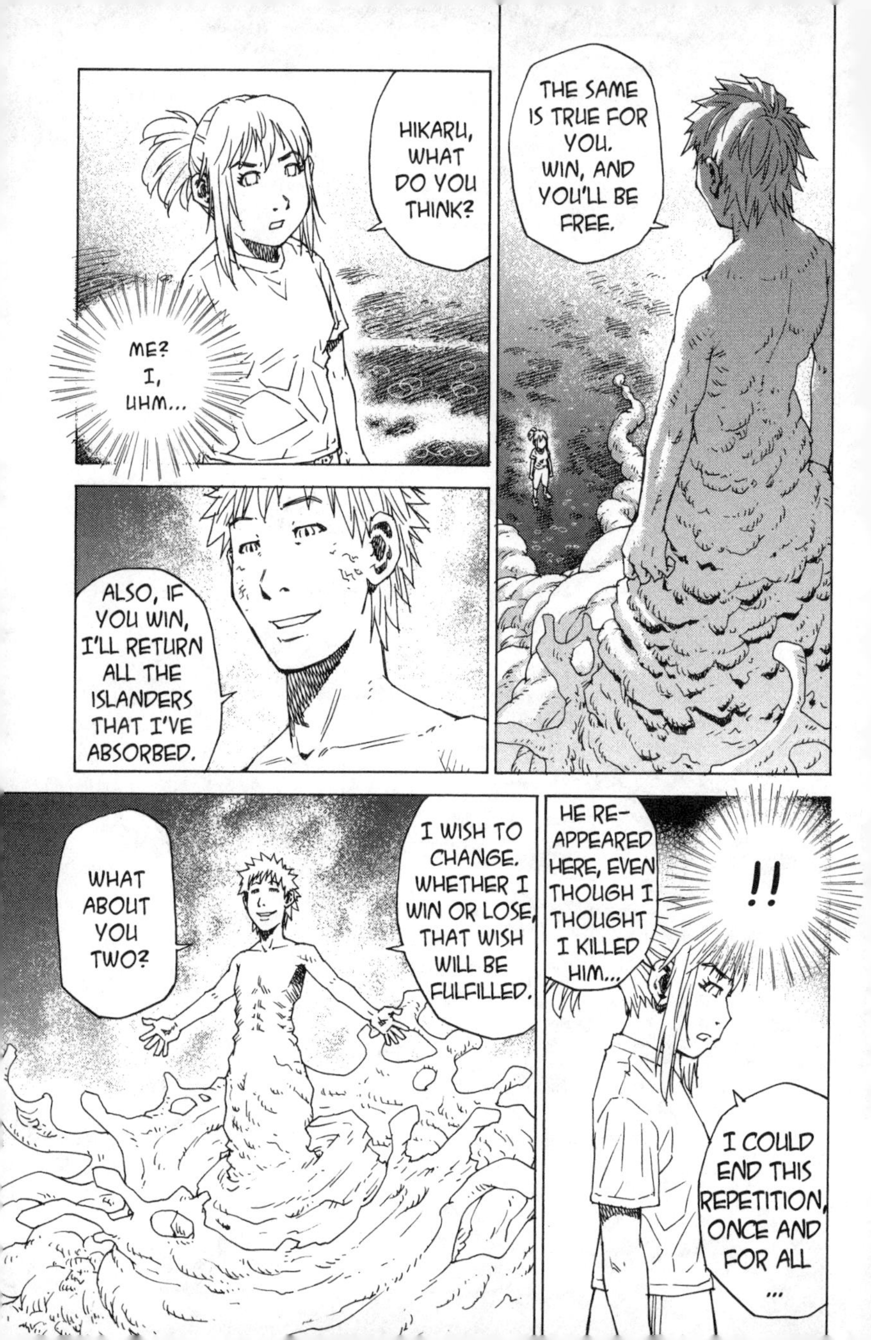
THE SAME IS TRUE FOR YOU. WIN, AND YOU'LL BE FREE.
HIKARU, WHAT DO YOU THINK?
ME? I, UHM...
ALSO, IF YOU WIN, I'LL RETURN ALL THE ISLANDERS THAT I'VE ABSORBED.
!!
HE RE-APPEARED HERE, EVEN THOUGH I THOUGHT I KILLED HIM...
I COULD END THIS REPETITION, ONCE AND FOR ALL ...
I WISH TO CHANGE. WHETHER I WIN OR LOSE, THAT WISH WILL BE FULFILLED.
WHAT ABOUT YOU TWO?

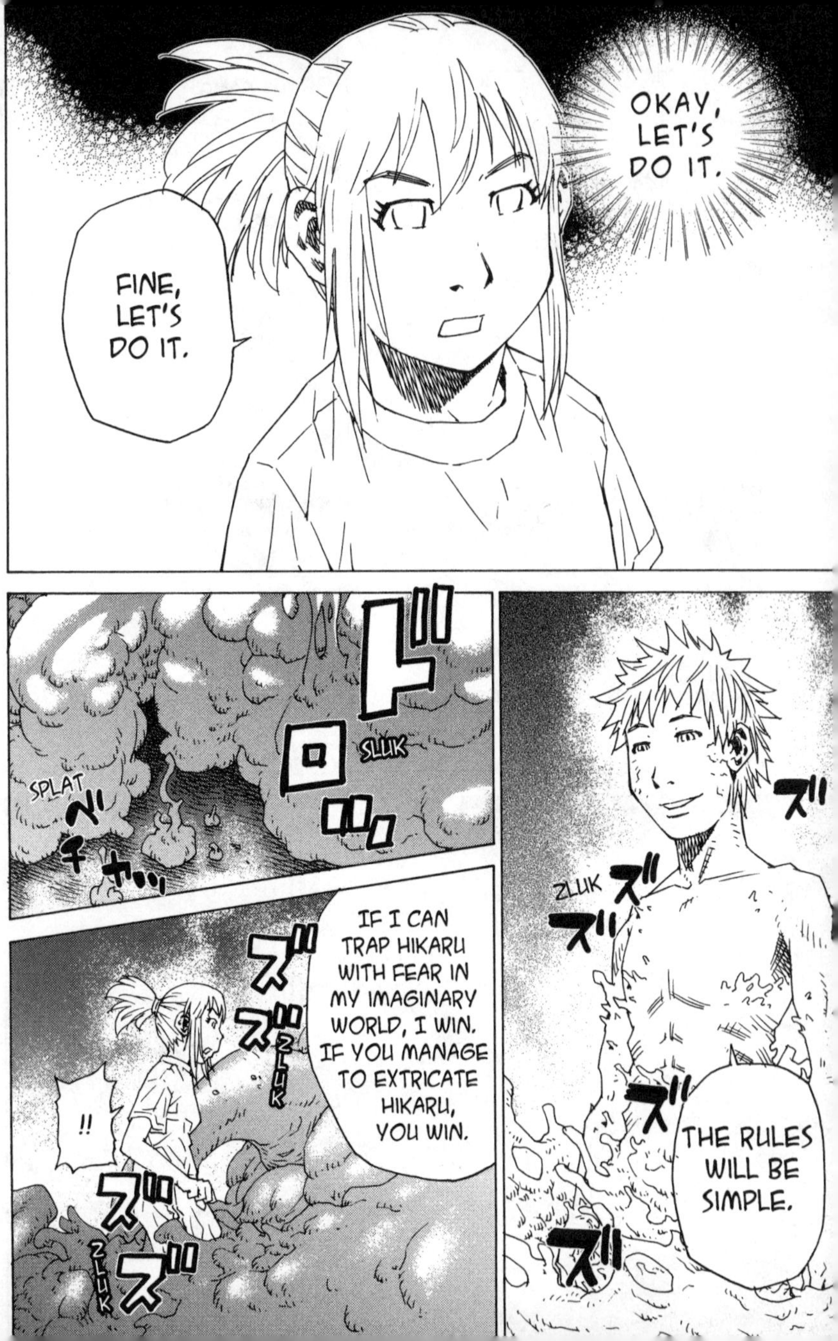
OKAY, LET'S DO IT.
FINE, LET'S DO IT.
ZLUK
THE RULES WILL BE SIMPLE.
SLUK
SPLAT
IF I CAN TRAP HIKARU WITH FEAR IN MY IMAGINARY WORLD, I WIN. IF YOU MANAGE TO EXTRICATE HIKARU, YOU WIN.
ZLUK
!!
ZLUK

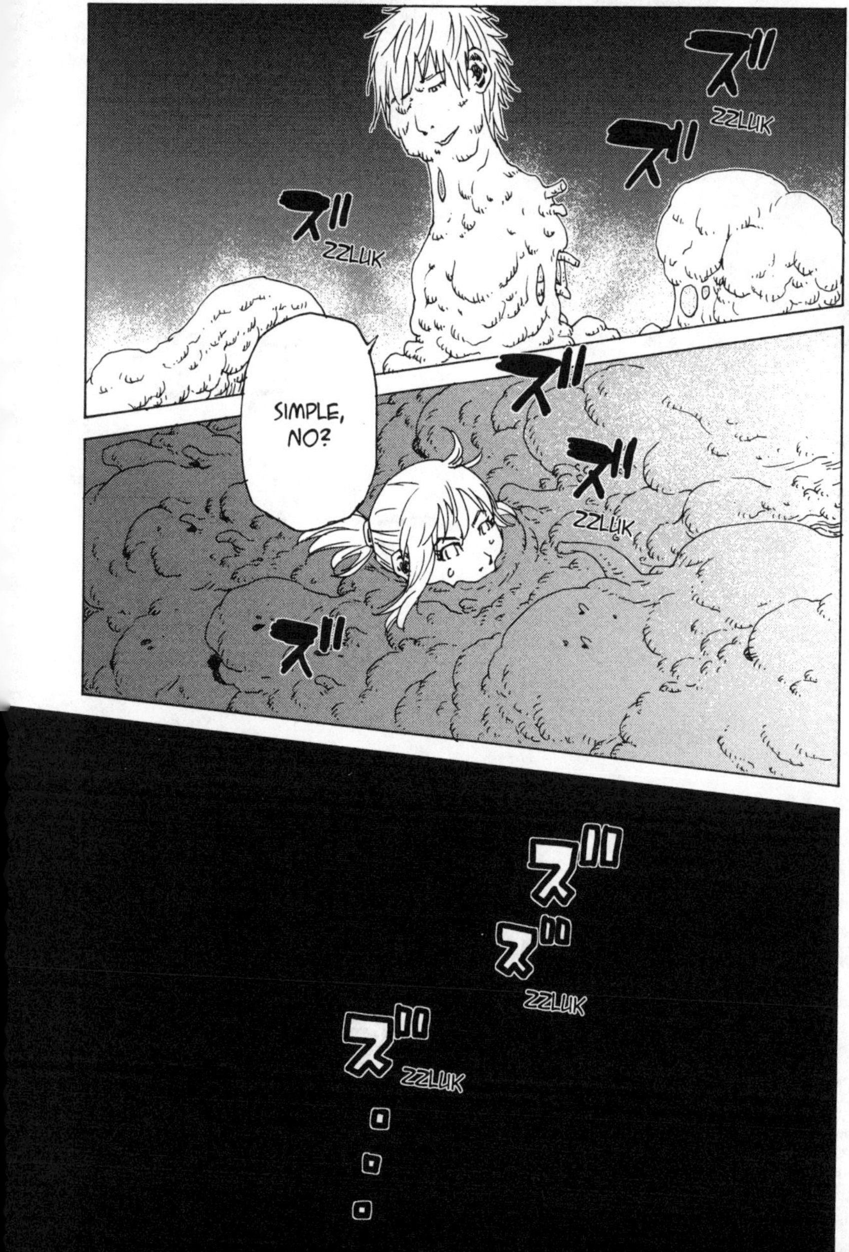
ZZLUK
ZZLUK
SIMPLE, NO?
ZZLUK
ZZLUK
ZZLUK

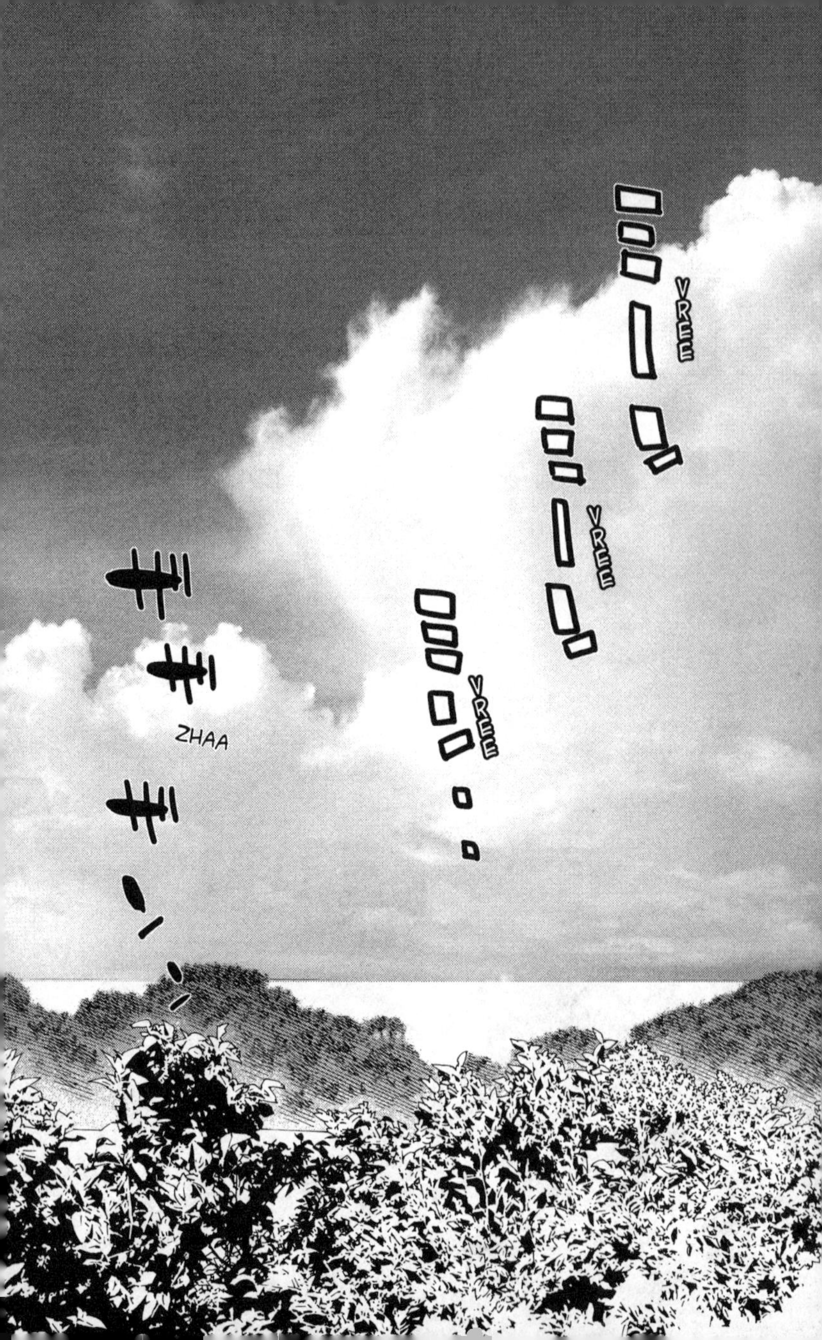
VREE
VREE
VREE
ZHAA

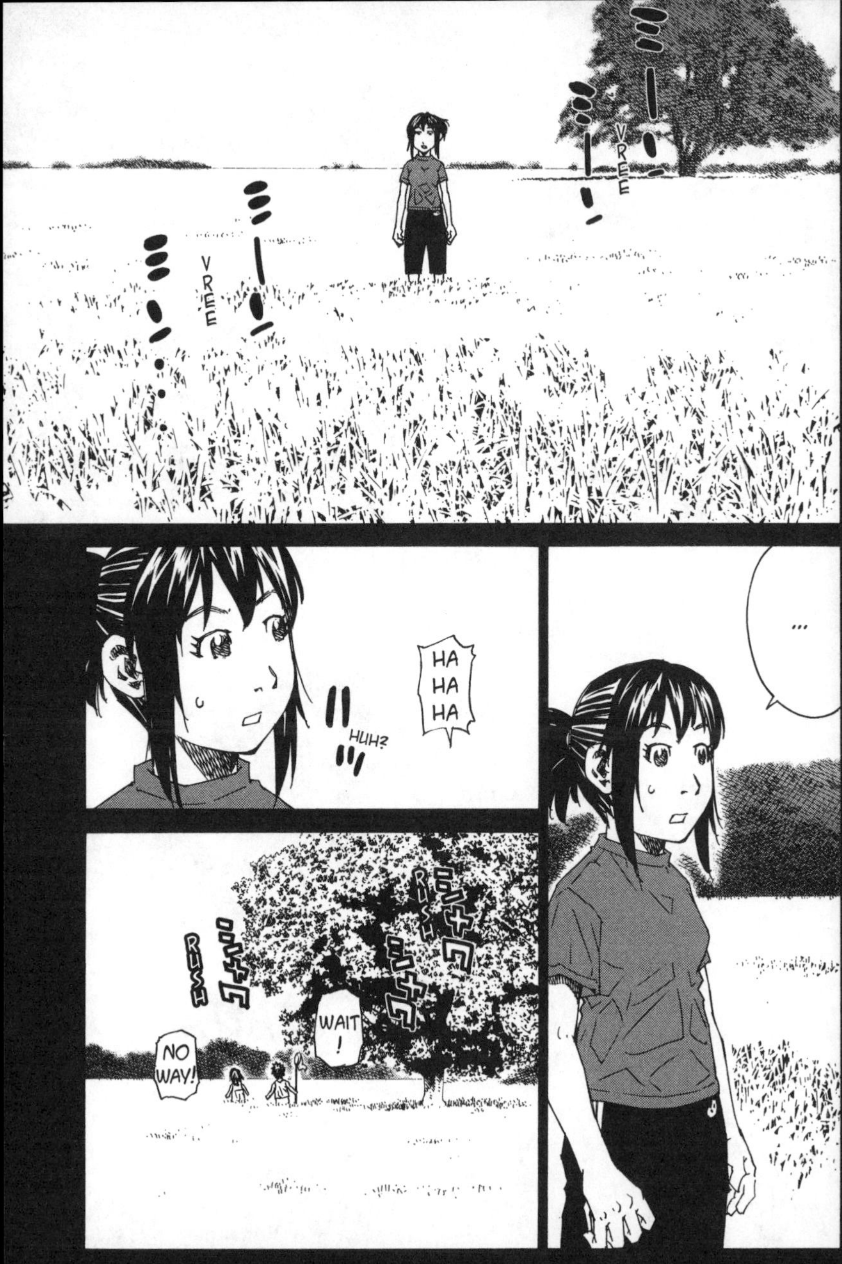
VREE
VREE
...
HA HA HA
HUH?
RUSH
RUSH
WAIT!
NO WAY!

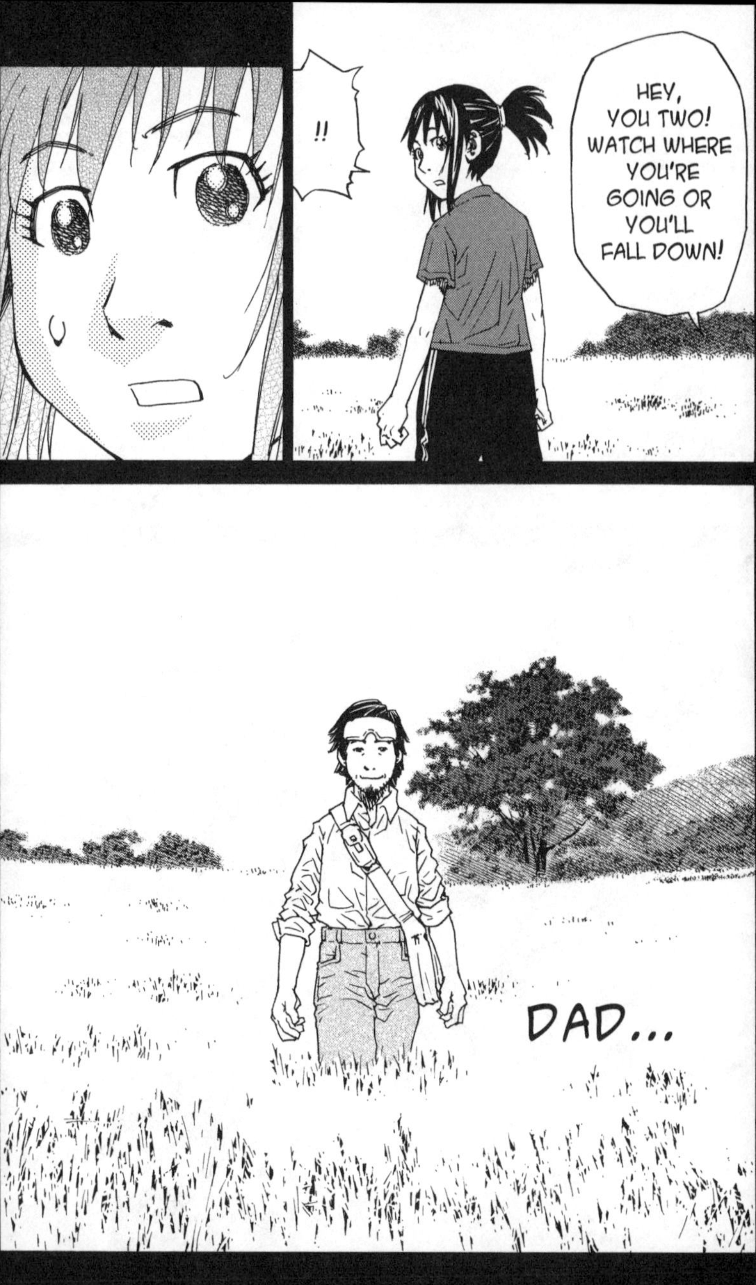
HEY, YOU TWO! WATCH WHERE YOU'RE GOING OR YOU'LL FALL DOWN!
!!
DAD...

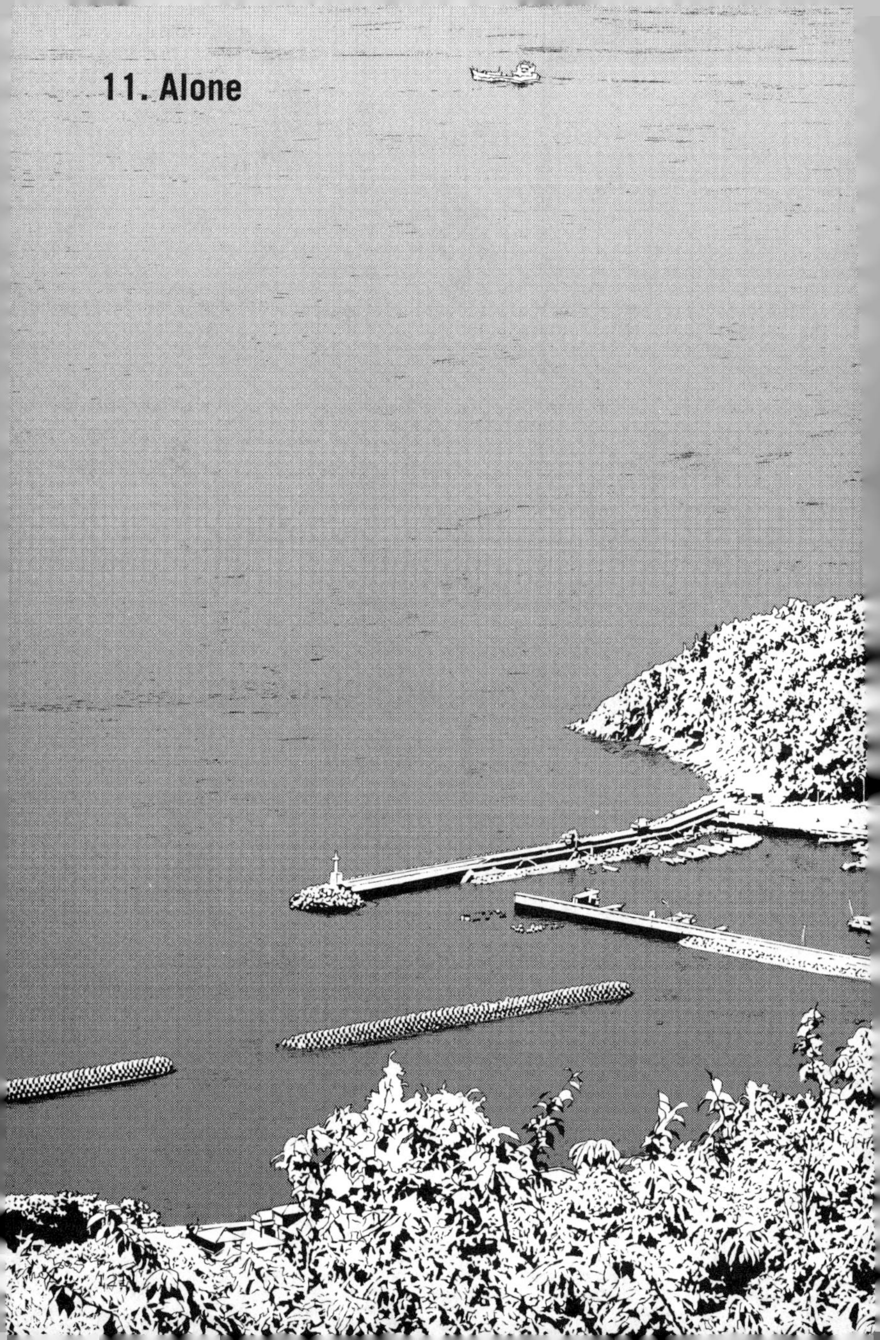
11. Alone

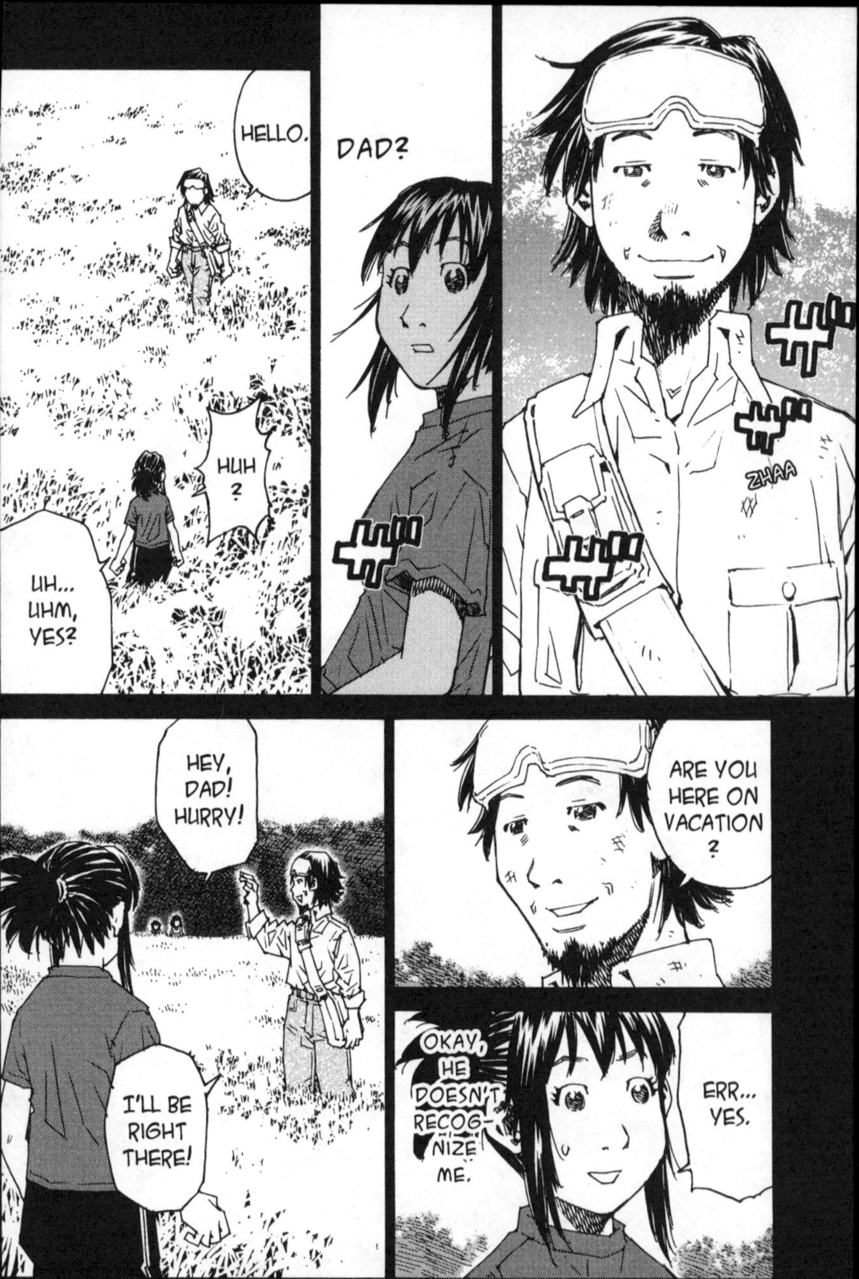
ZHAA
DAD?
HELLO.
HUH?
UH... UHM, YES?
ARE YOU HERE ON VACATION?
ERR... YES.
OKAY, HE DOESN'T RECOG-NIZE ME.
HEY, DAD! HURRY!
I'LL BE RIGHT THERE!

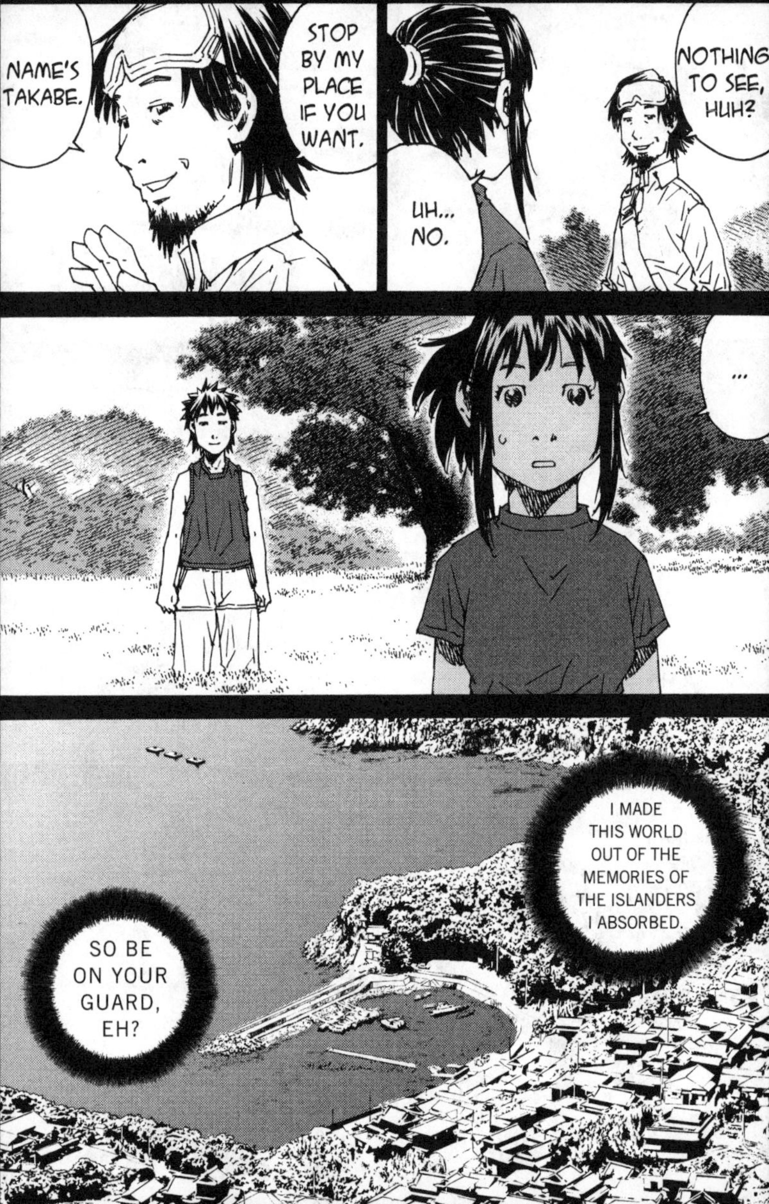
NOTHING TO SEE, HUH?
UH... NO.
NAME'S TAKABE.
STOP BY MY PLACE IF YOU WANT.
...
I MADE THIS WORLD OUT OF THE MEMORIES OF THE ISLANDERS I ABSORBED.
SO BE ON YOUR GUARD, EH?

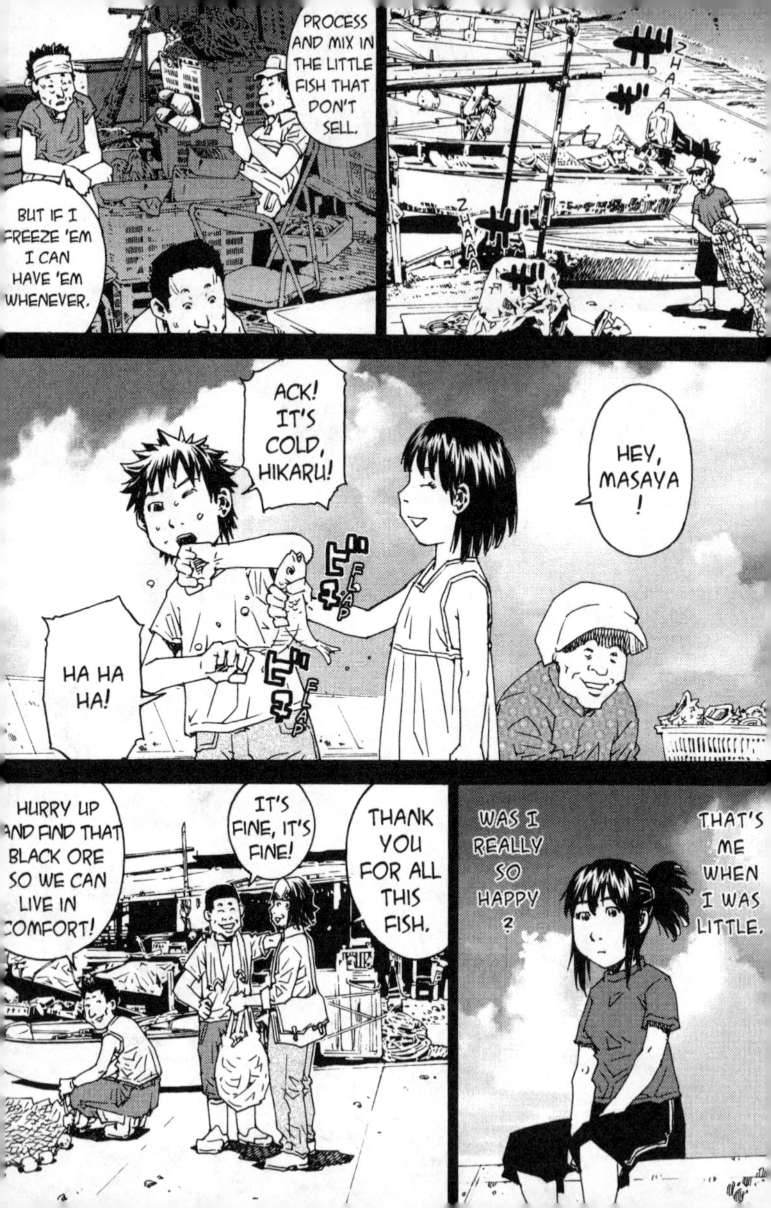
ZHAAA
ZHAAA
PROCESS AND MIX IN THE LITTLE FISH THAT DON'T SELL.
BUT IF I FREEZE 'EM I CAN HAVE 'EM WHENEVER.
HEY, MASAYA!
ACK! IT'S COLD, HIKARU!
FLAP
FLAP
HA HA HA!
THAT'S ME WHEN I WAS LITTLE.
WAS I REALLY SO HAPPY?
THANK YOU FOR ALL THIS FISH.
IT'S FINE, IT'S FINE!
HURRY UP AND FIND THAT BLACK ORE SO WE CAN LIVE IN COMFORT!

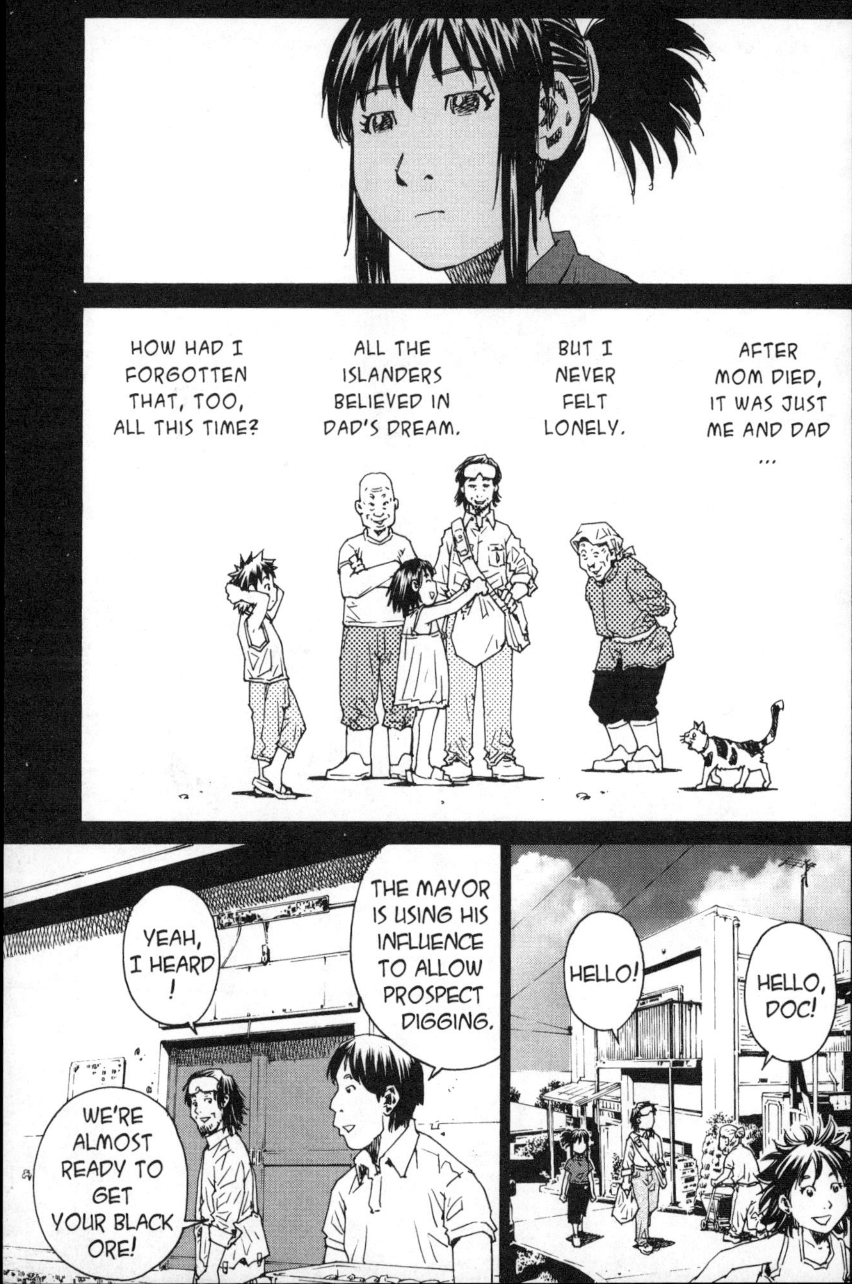
AFTER MOM DIED, IT WAS JUST ME AND DAD ...
BUT I NEVER FELT LONELY.
ALL THE ISLANDERS BELIEVED IN DAD'S DREAM.
HOW HAD I FORGOTTEN THAT, TOO, ALL THIS TIME?
HELLO, DOC!
HELLO!
THE MAYOR IS USING HIS INFLUENCE TO ALLOW PROSPECT DIGGING.
YEAH, I HEARD!
WE'RE ALMOST READY TO GET YOUR BLACK ORE!

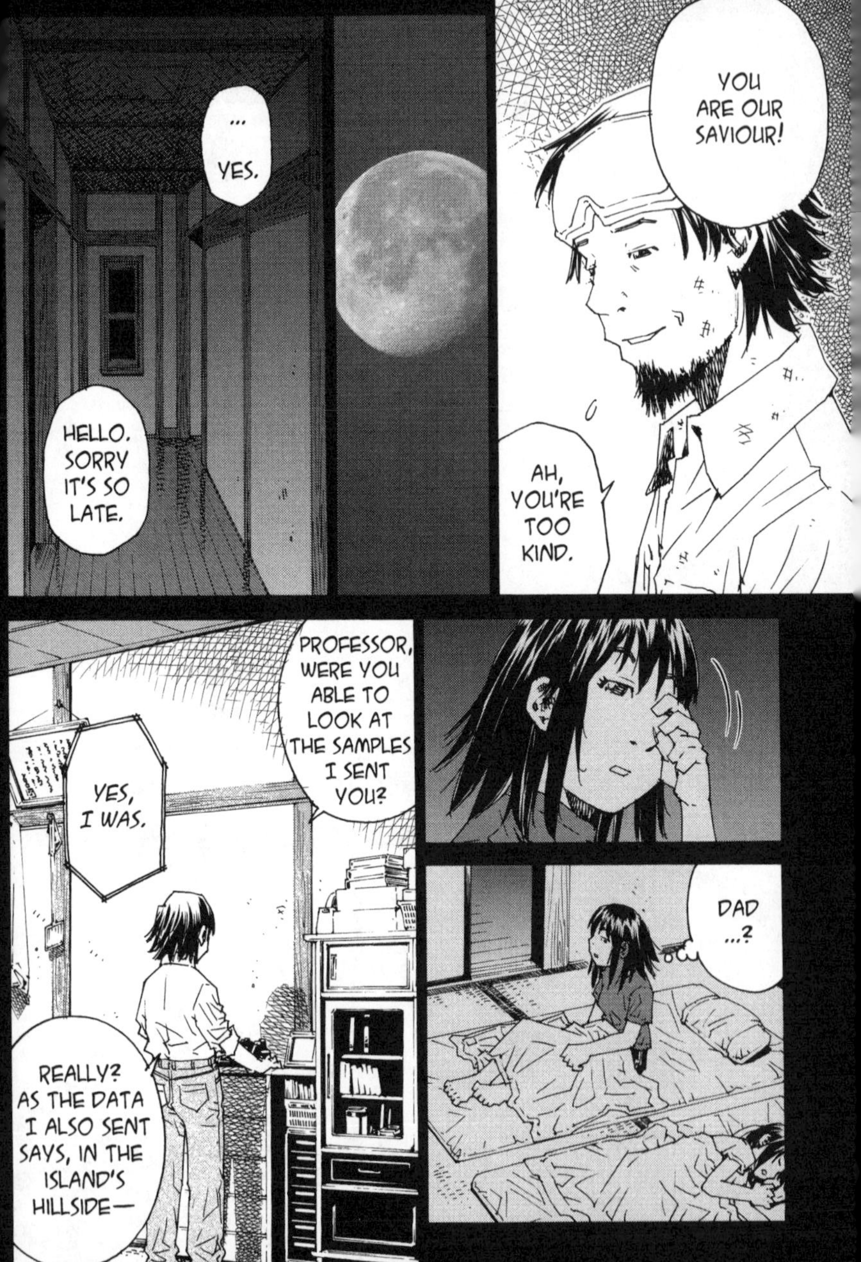
YOU ARE OUR SAVIOUR!
AH, YOU'RE TOO KIND.
... YES.
HELLO. SORRY IT'S SO LATE.
DAD ...?
PROFESSOR, WERE YOU ABLE TO LOOK AT THE SAMPLES I SENT YOU?
YES, I WAS.
REALLY? AS THE DATA I ALSO SENT SAYS, IN THE ISLAND'S HILLSIDE—

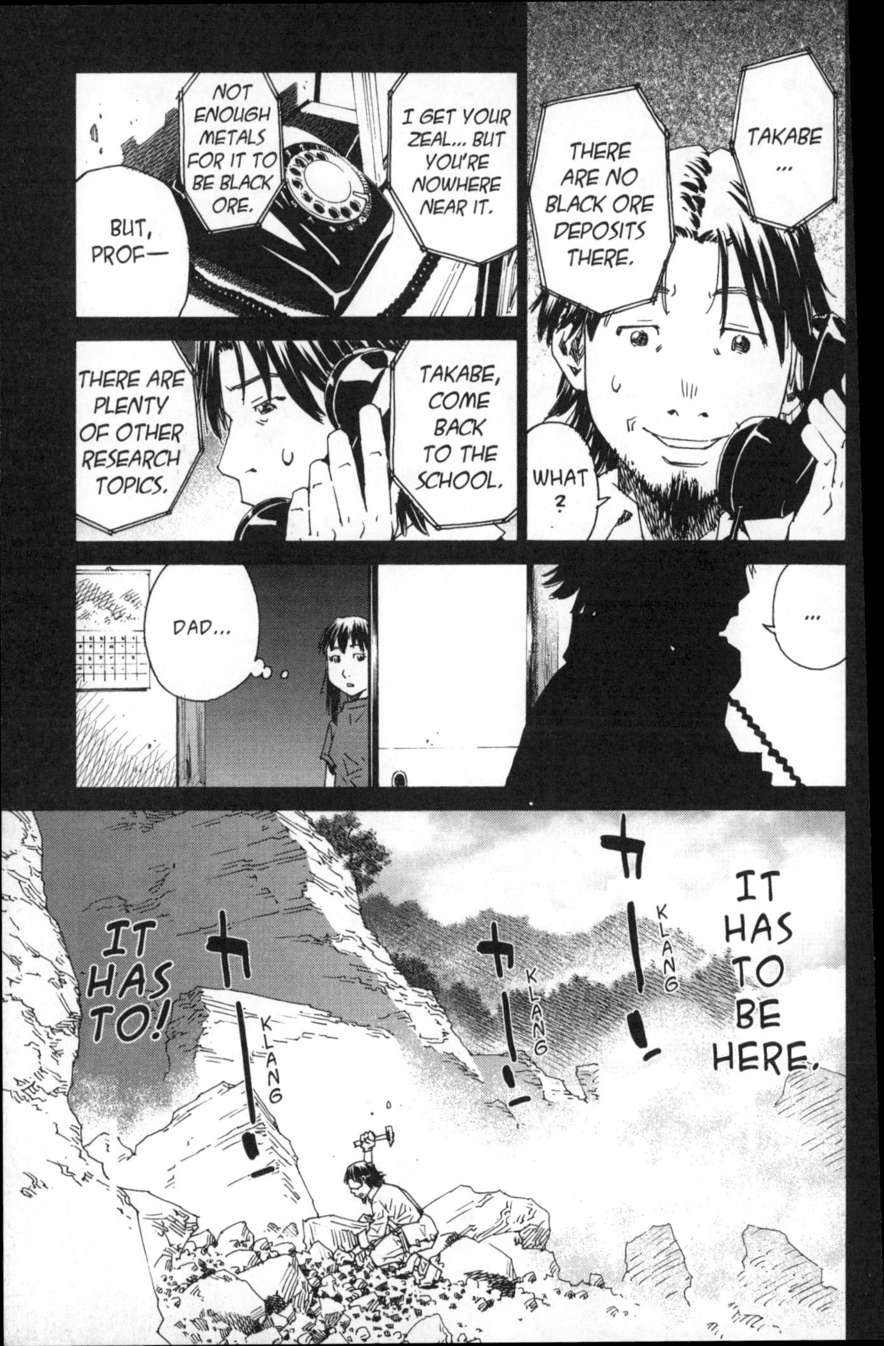
TAKABE ...
THERE ARE NO BLACK ORE DEPOSITS THERE.
I GET YOUR ZEAL... BUT YOU'RE NOWHERE NEAR IT.
NOT ENOUGH METALS FOR IT TO BE BLACK ORE.
BUT, PROF—
WHAT ?
TAKABE, COME BACK TO THE SCHOOL.
THERE ARE PLENTY OF OTHER RESEARCH TOPICS.
...
DAD...
IT HAS TO BE HERE.
KLANG
KLANG
KLANG
IT HAS TO!

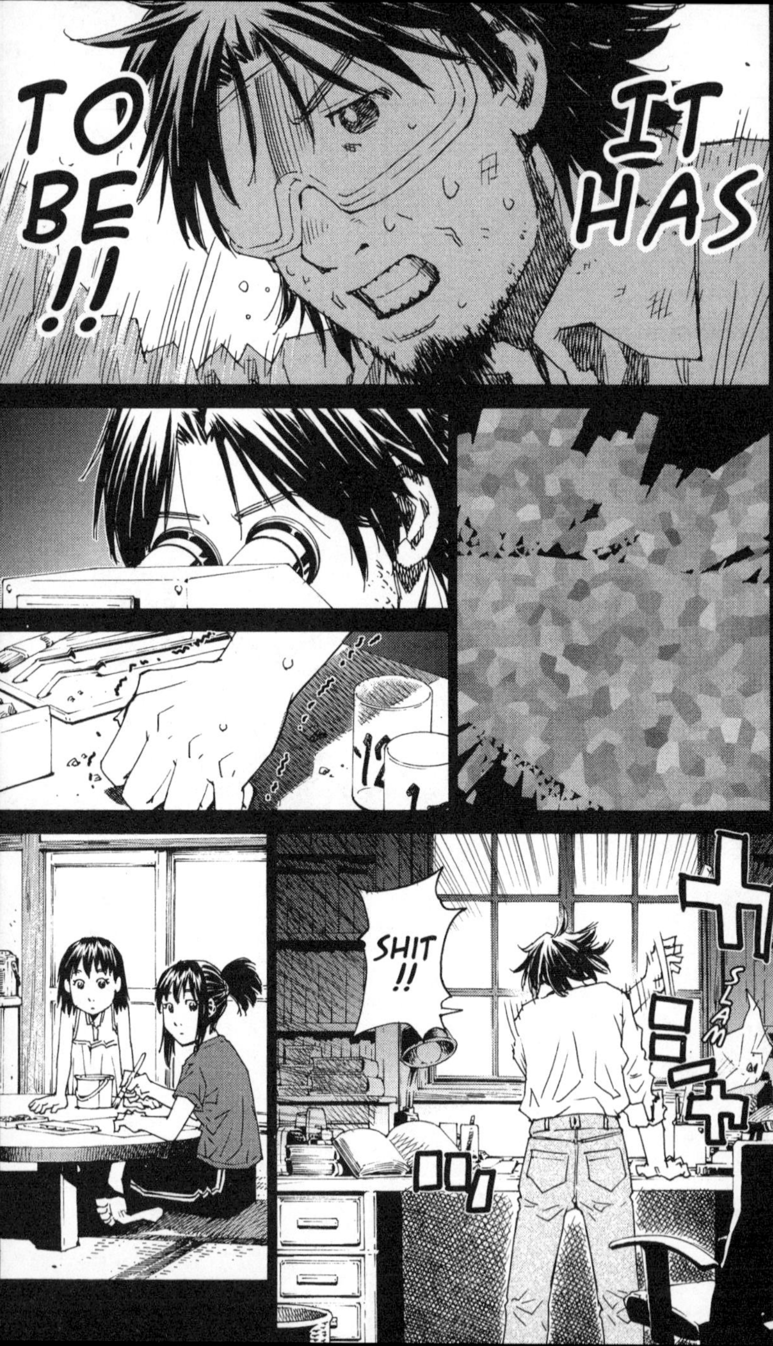
IT HAS
TO BE!!
SLAM
SHIT!!

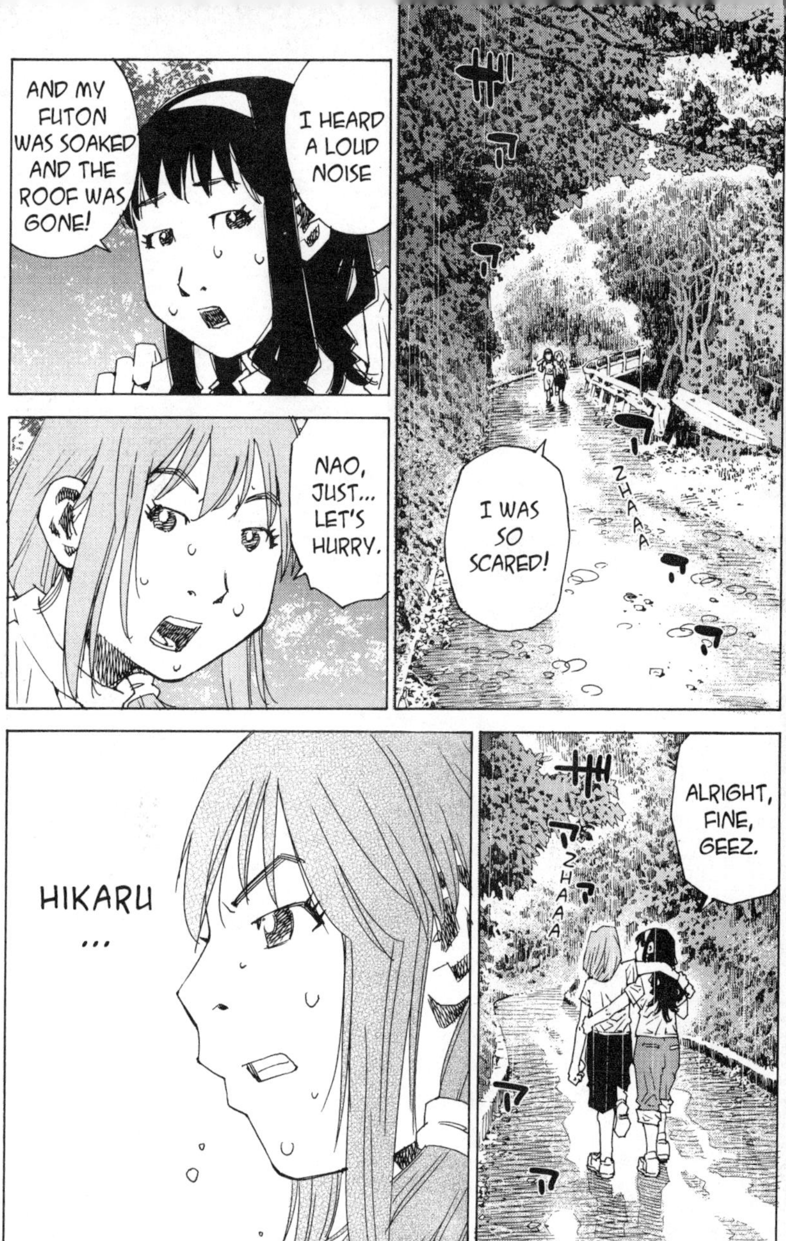
ZHAAA
I WAS SO SCARED!
I HEARD A LOUD NOISE
AND MY FUTON WAS SOAKED AND THE ROOF WAS GONE!
NAO, JUST... LET'S HURRY.
ALRIGHT, FINE, GEEZ.
ZHAAA
HIKARU ...

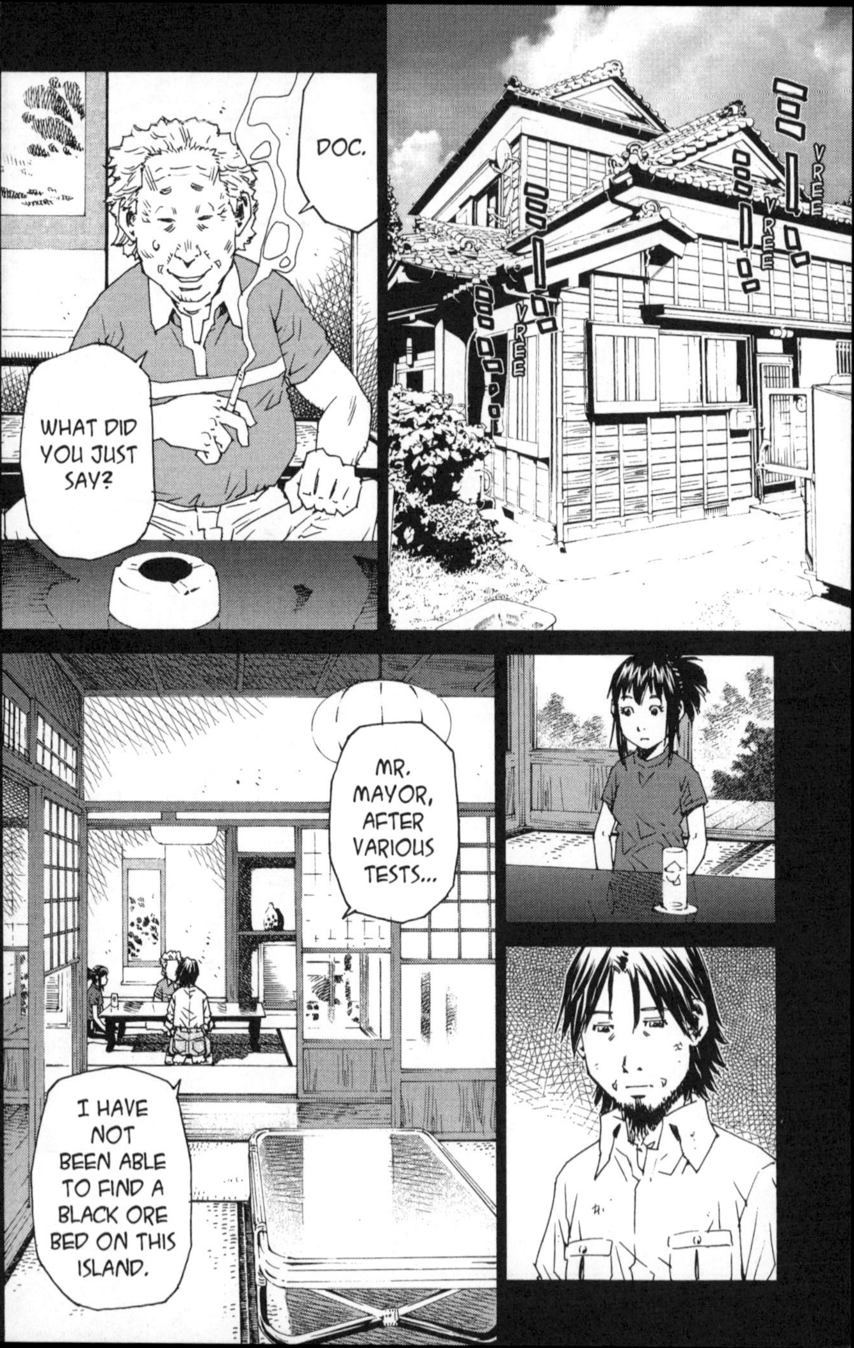
VREE
VREE
VREE
DOC.
WHAT DID YOU JUST SAY?
MR. MAYOR, AFTER VARIOUS TESTS...
I HAVE NOT BEEN ABLE TO FIND A BLACK ORE BED ON THIS ISLAND.

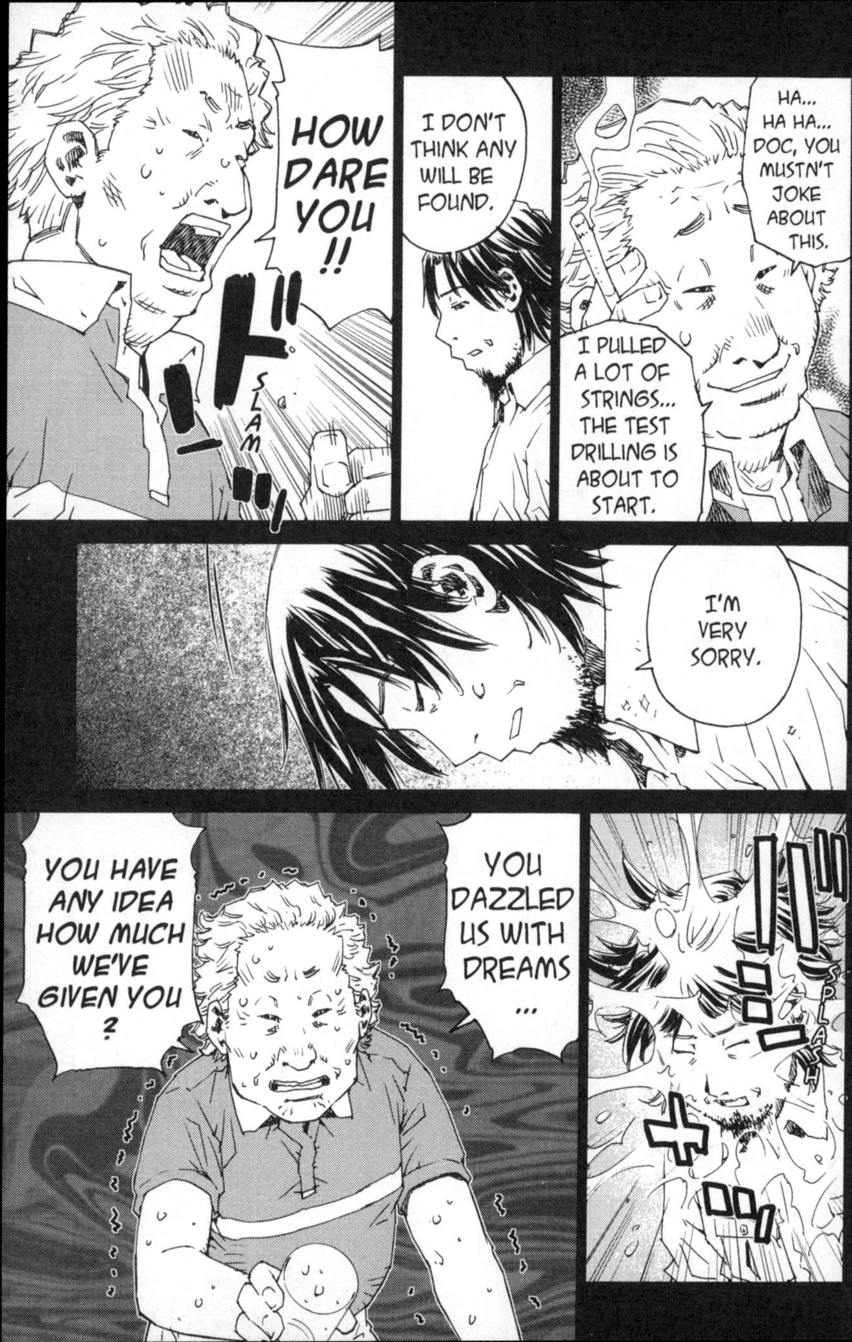
HA... HA HA... DOC, YOU MUSTN'T JOKE ABOUT THIS.
I PULLED A LOT OF STRINGS... THE TEST DRILLING IS ABOUT TO START.
I DON'T THINK ANY WILL BE FOUND.
HOW DARE YOU !!
SLAM
I'M VERY SORRY.
SPLASH
YOU DAZZLED US WITH DREAMS ...
YOU HAVE ANY IDEA HOW MUCH WE'VE GIVEN YOU ?

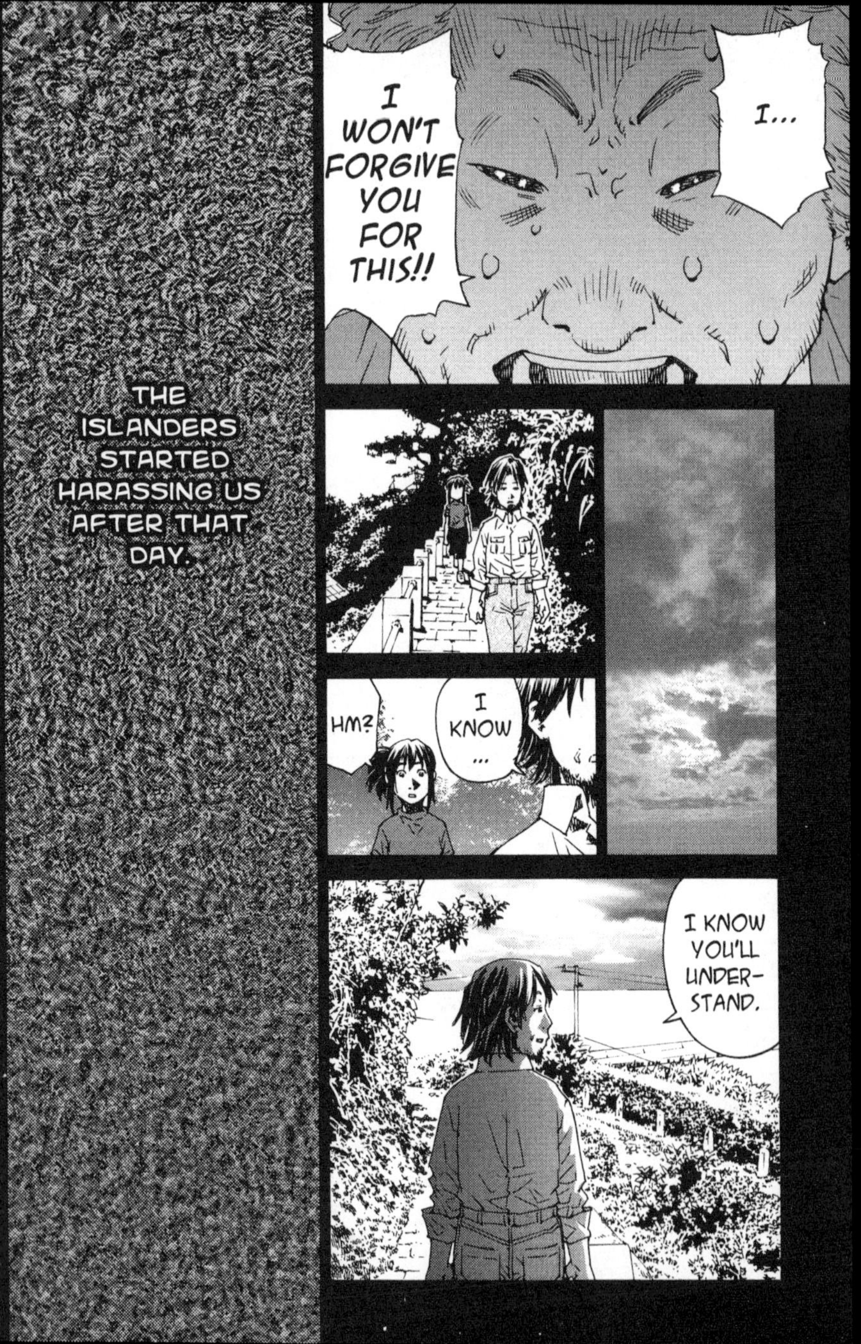
I...
I WON'T FORGIVE YOU FOR THIS!!
I KNOW ...
HM?
I KNOW YOU'LL UNDER-STAND.
THE ISLANDERS STARTED HARASSING US AFTER THAT DAY.

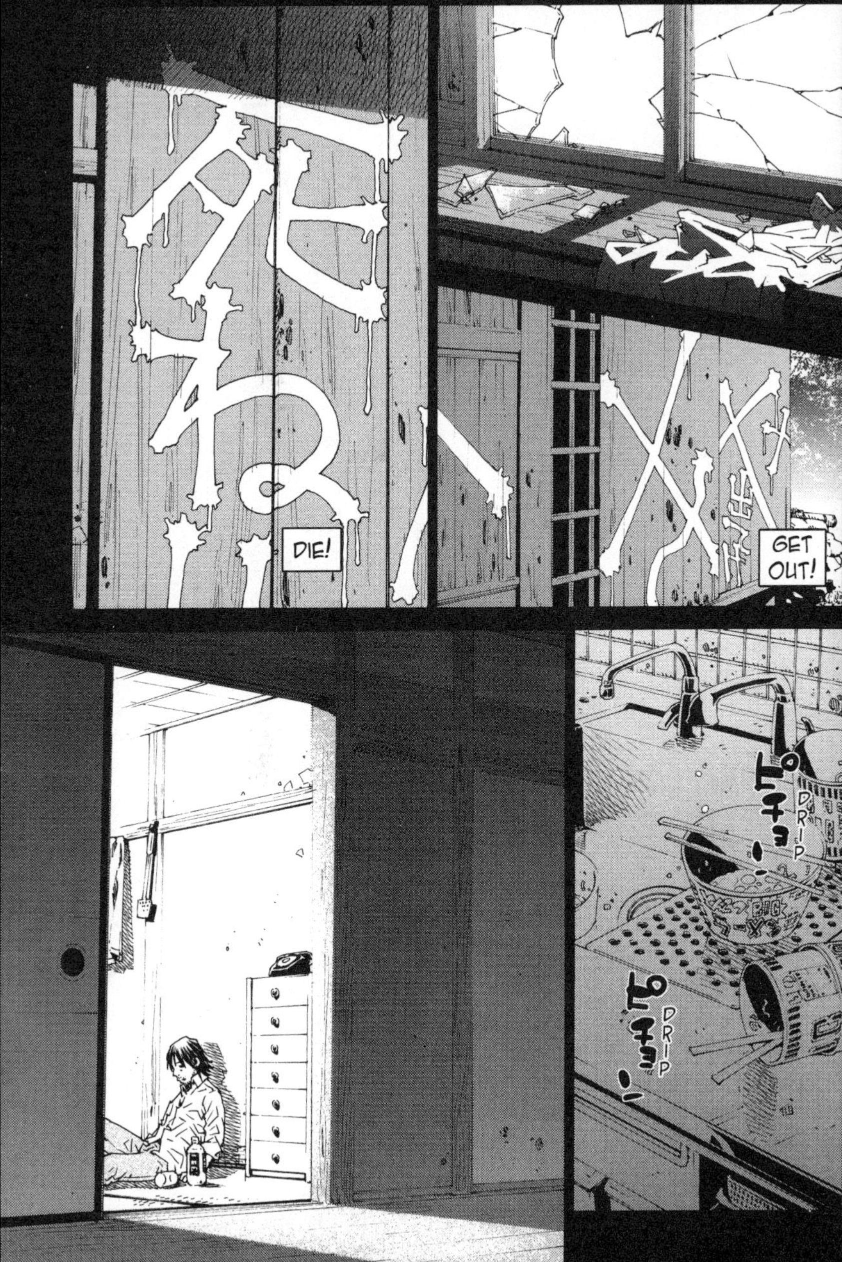
GET OUT!
DIE!
DRIP
DRIP

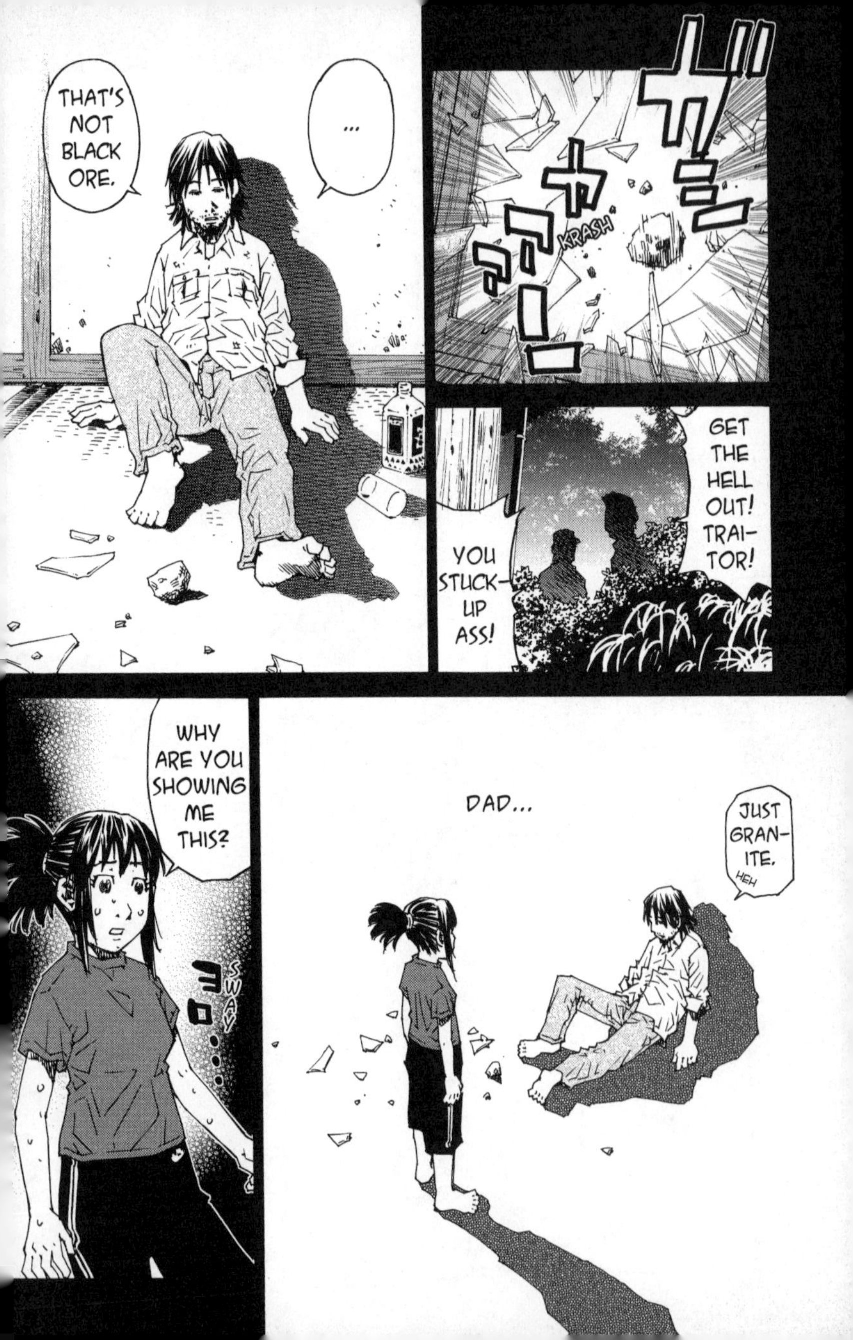
KRASH
GET THE HELL OUT! TRAITOR!
YOU STUCK-UP ASS!
...
THAT'S NOT BLACK ORE.
JUST GRANITE.
HEH
DAD...
WHY ARE YOU SHOWING ME THIS?
SWAY

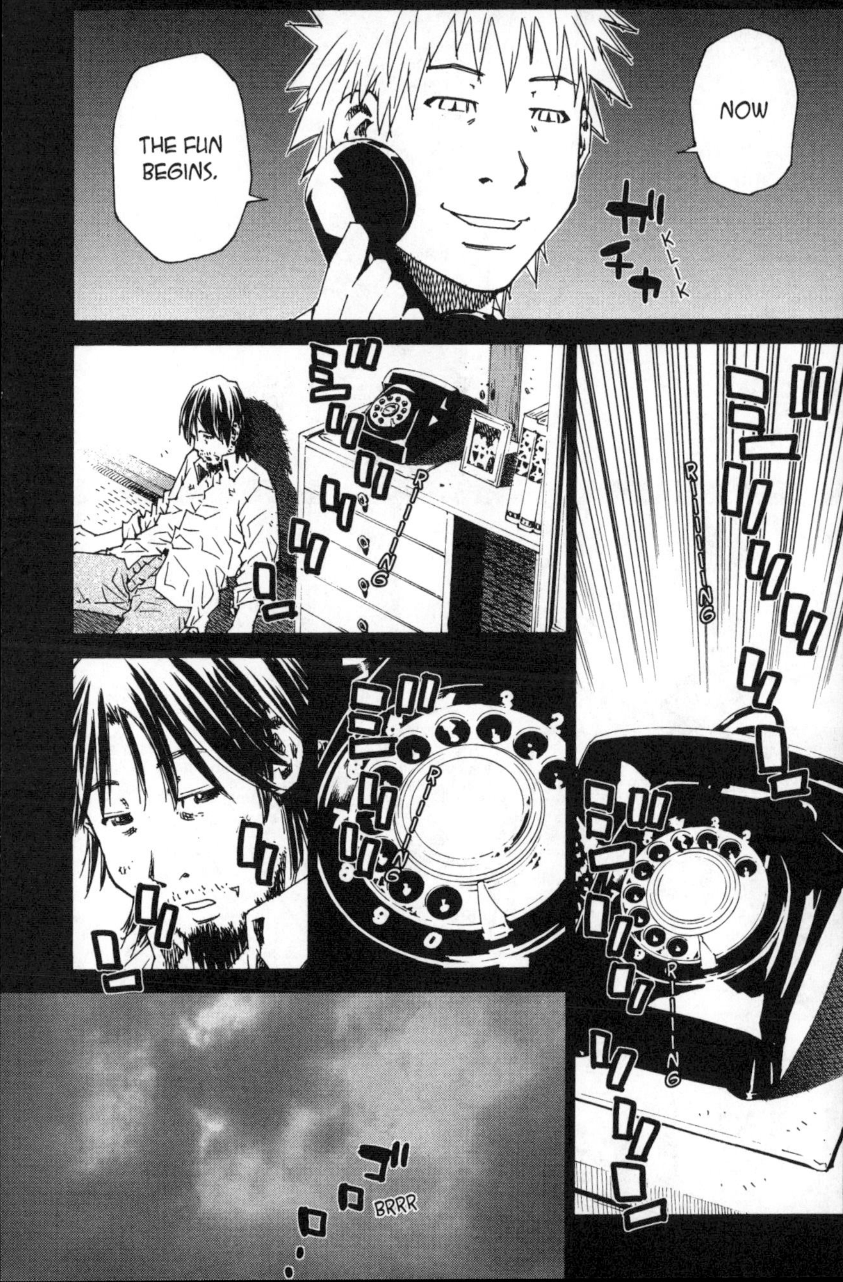
NOW
ガチャ
KLIK
THE FUN BEGINS.
RIIIING
RIIIING
RIIIING
RIIIING
ゴロロ
BRRR

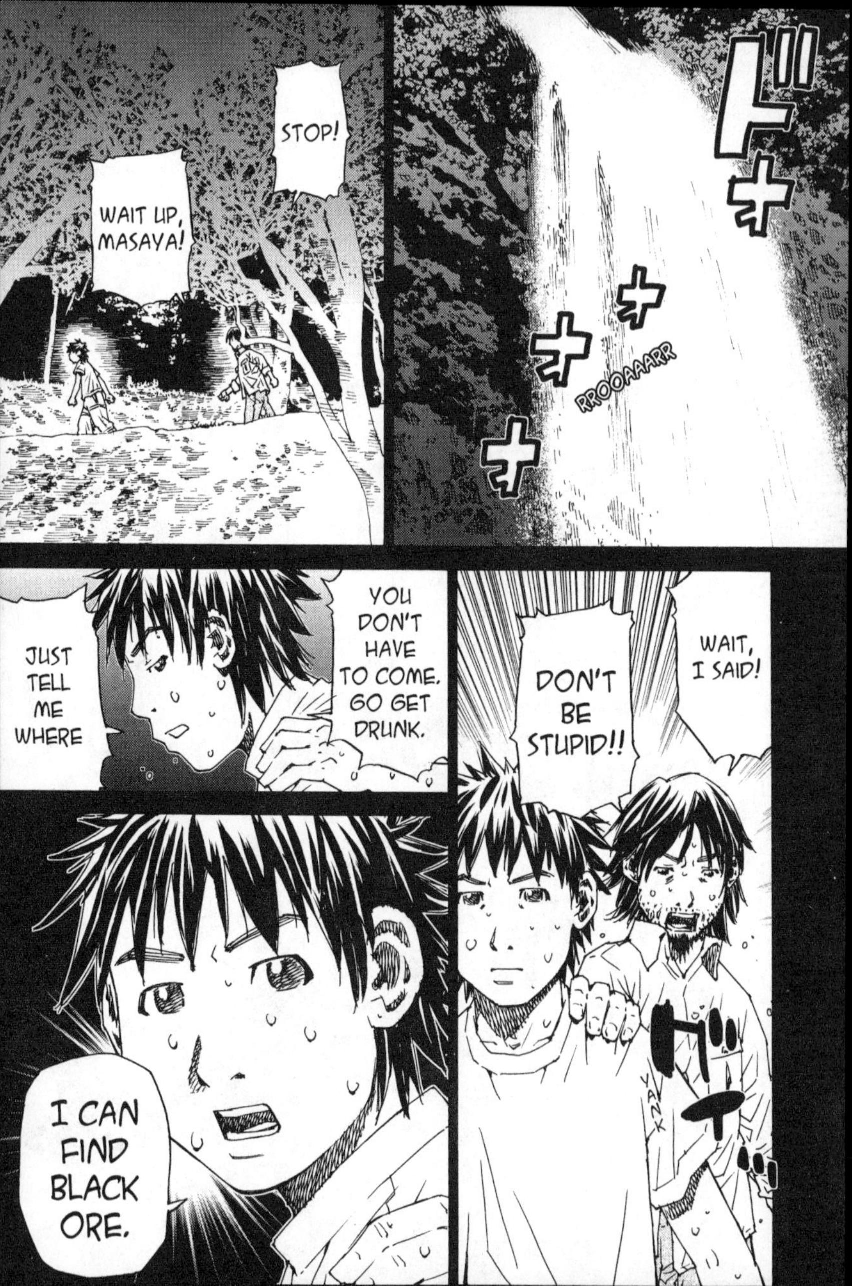
RROOAAARR
STOP!
WAIT UP, MASAYA!
WAIT, I SAID!
DON'T BE STUPID!!
YANK
YOU DON'T HAVE TO COME. GO GET DRUNK.
JUST TELL ME WHERE
I CAN FIND BLACK ORE.

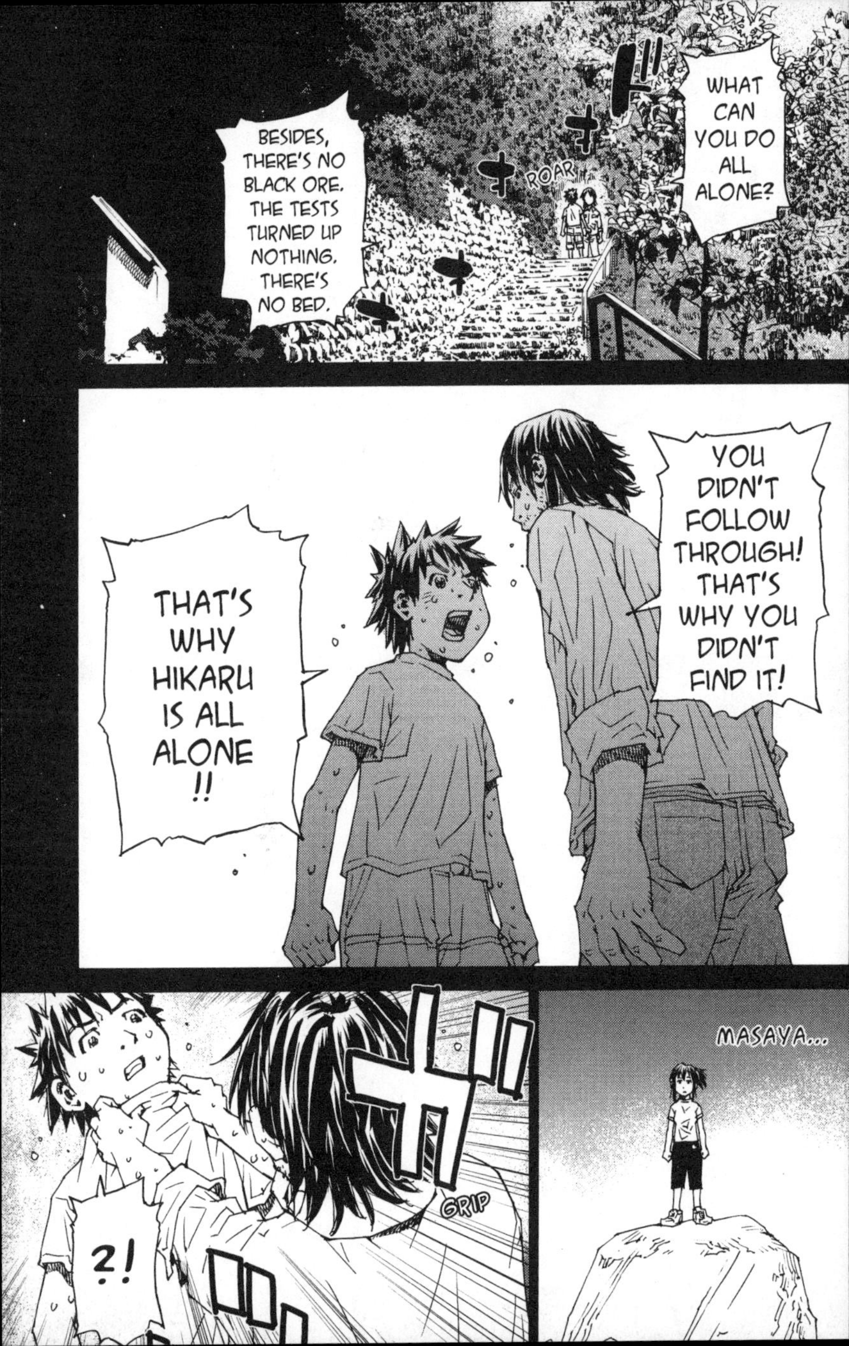
WHAT CAN YOU DO ALL ALONE?
ROAR
BESIDES, THERE'S NO BLACK ORE. THE TESTS TURNED UP NOTHING. THERE'S NO BED.
YOU DIDN'T FOLLOW THROUGH! THAT'S WHY YOU DIDN'T FIND IT!
THAT'S WHY HIKARU IS ALL ALONE !!
MASAYA...
GRIP
?!

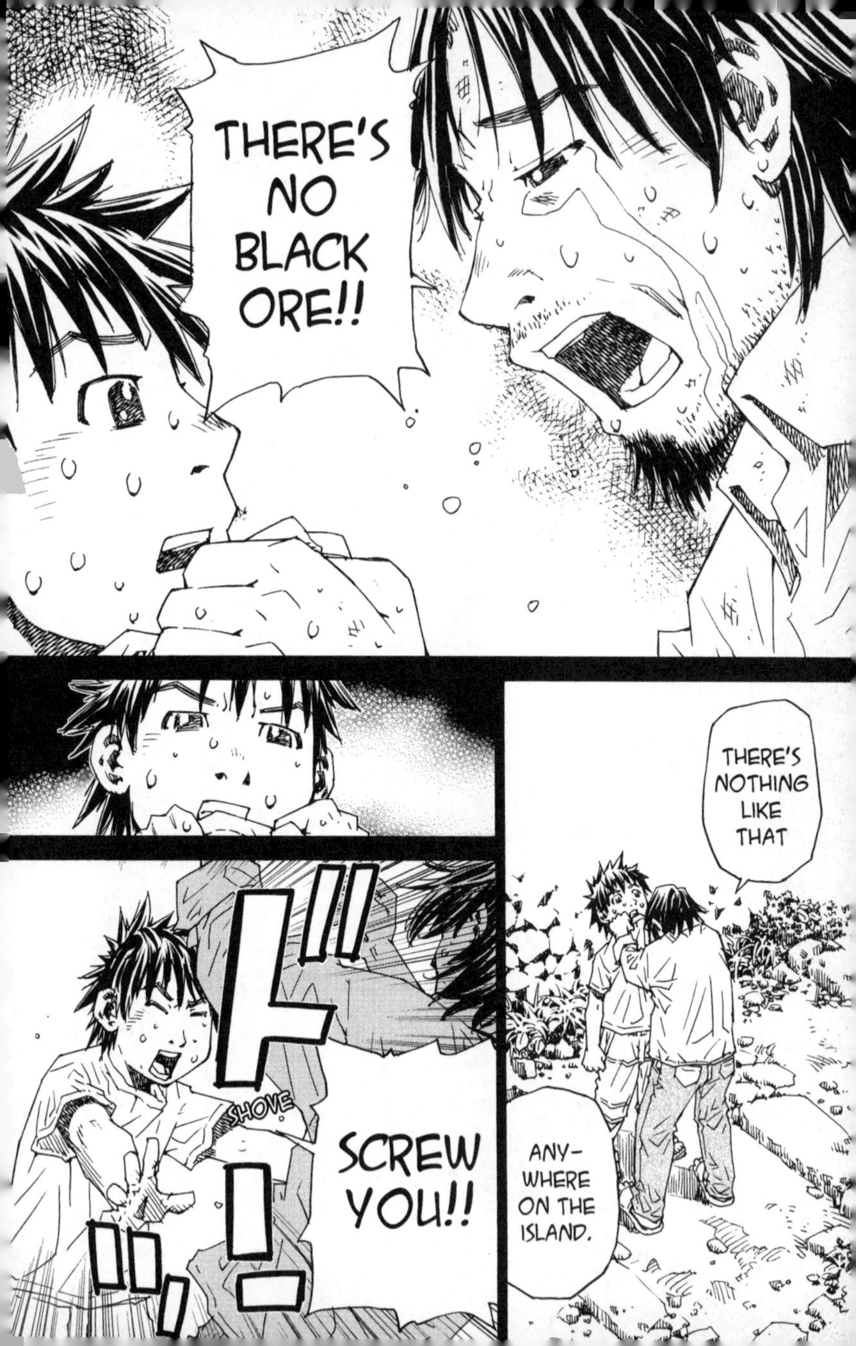
THERE'S NO BLACK ORE!!
THERE'S NOTHING LIKE THAT
ANY-WHERE ON THE ISLAND.
SHOVE
SCREW YOU!!

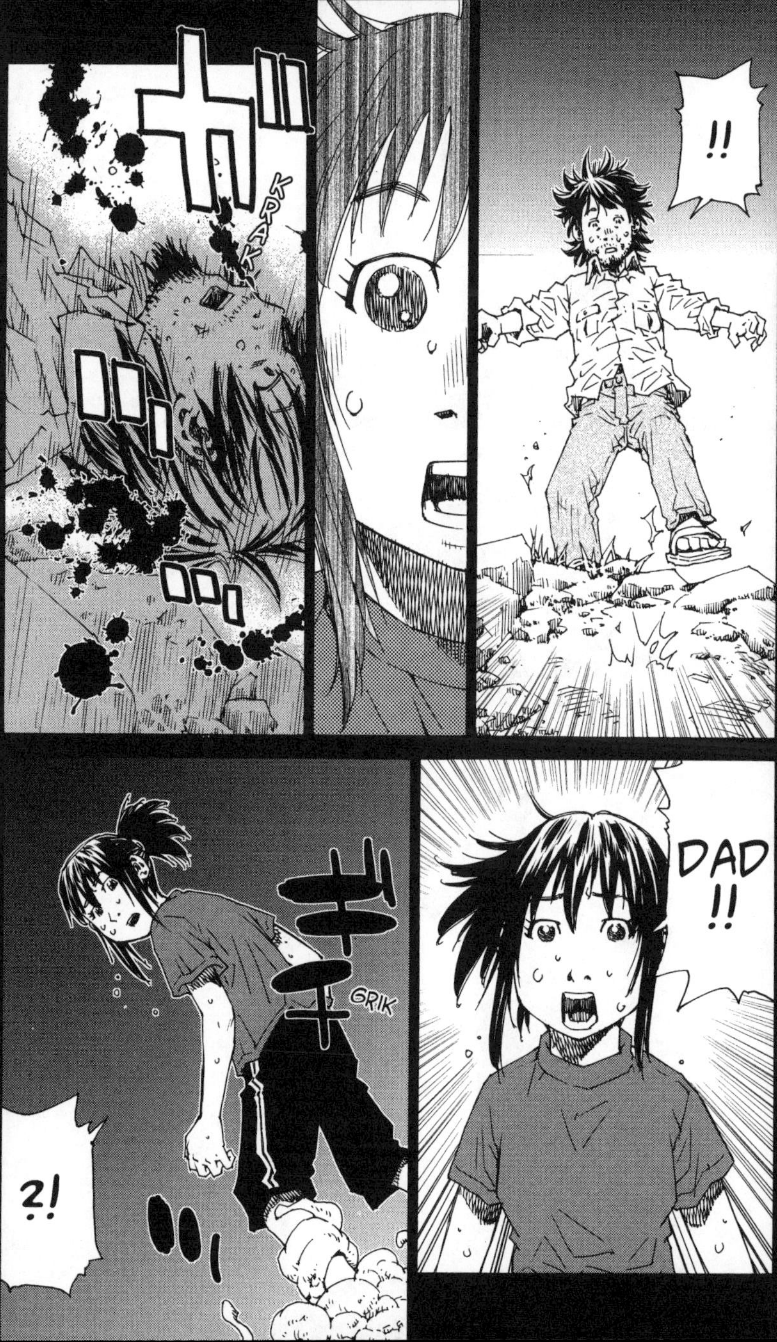
!!
KRAAK
DAD !!
GRIK
?!

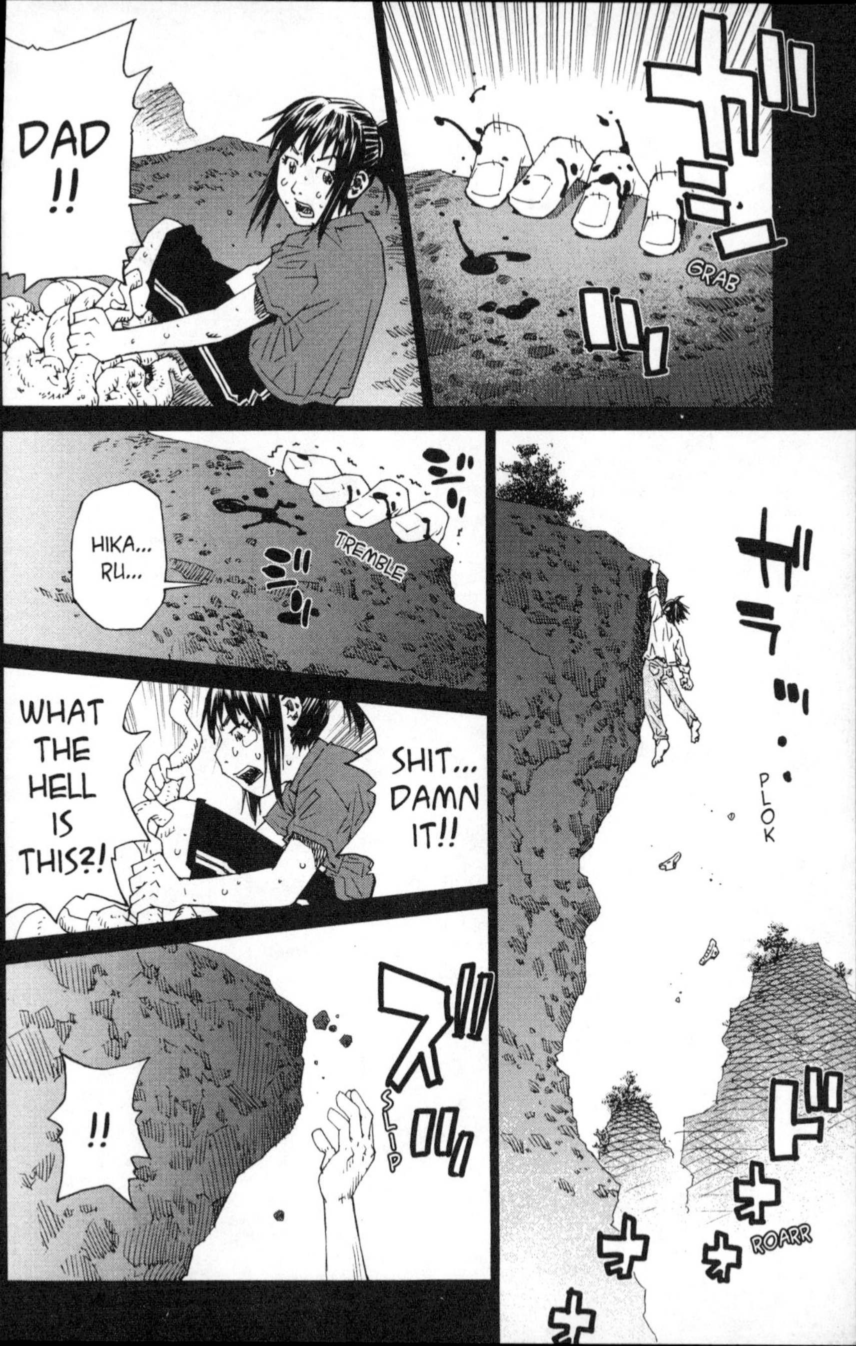
GRAB
DAD!!
PLOK
ROARR
HIKA... RU...
TREMBLE
WHAT THE HELL IS THIS?!
SHIT... DAMN IT!!
SLIP
!!

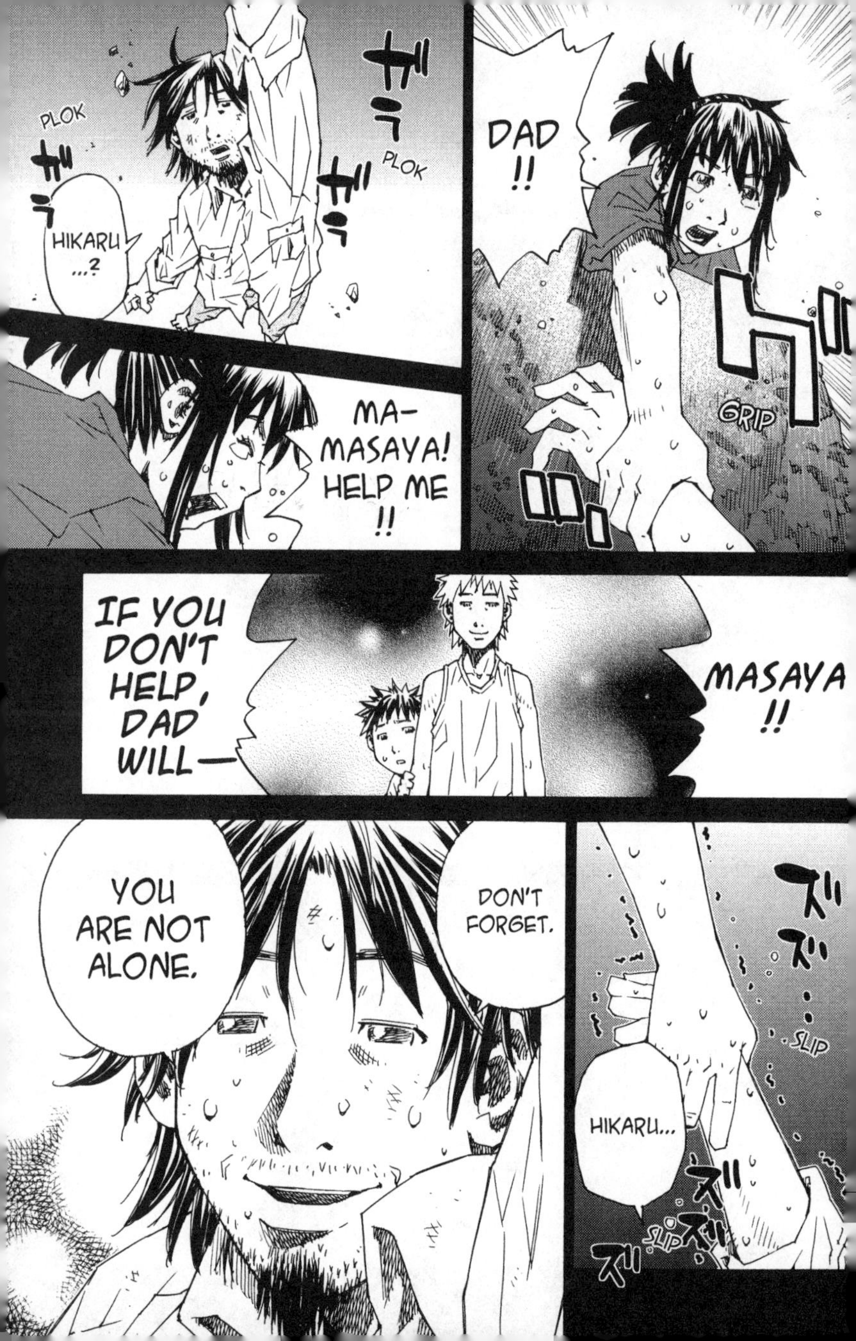
DAD !!
GRIP
PLOK
PLOK
HIKARU ...?
MA-MASAYA! HELP ME !!
MASAYA !!
IF YOU DON'T HELP, DAD WILL—
SLIP
SLIP
HIKARU...
DON'T FORGET.
YOU ARE NOT ALONE.

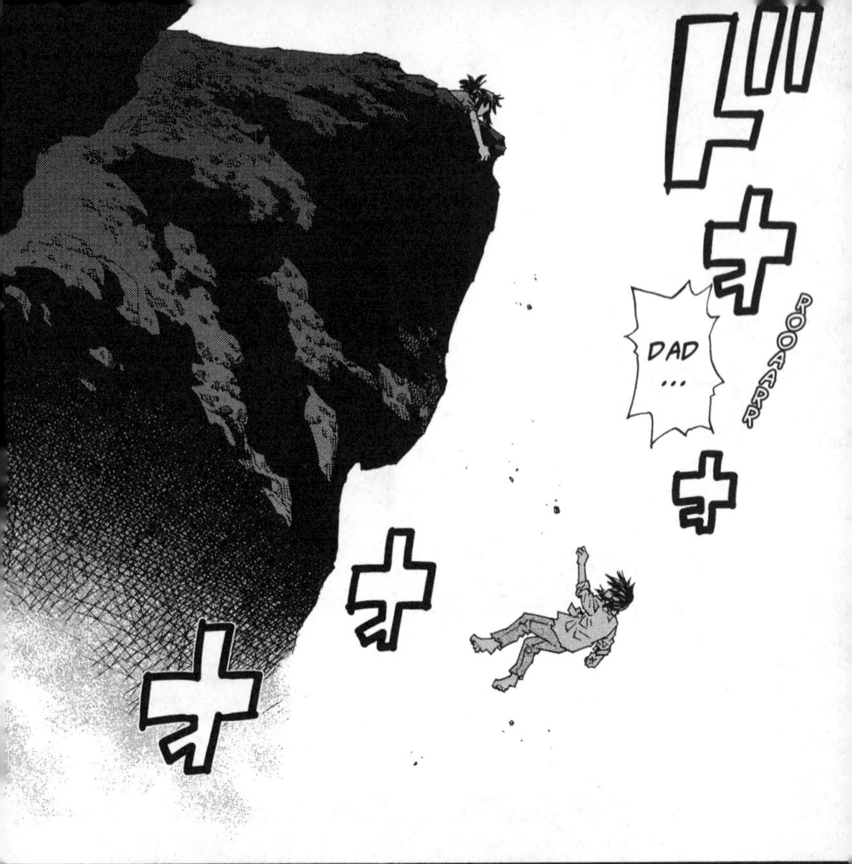
ROOAARRR
DAD ...
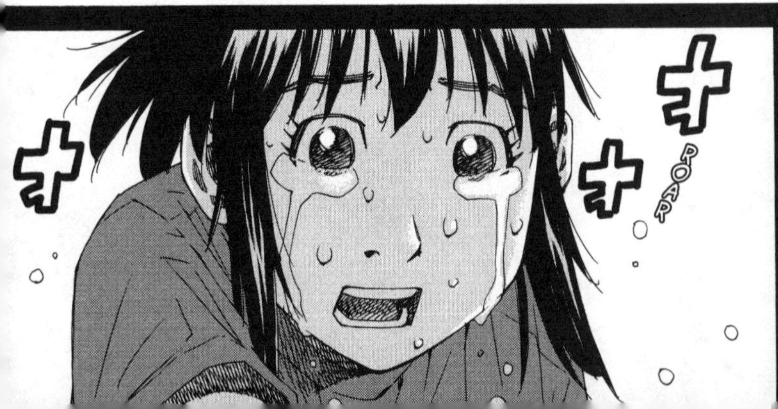
ROAR

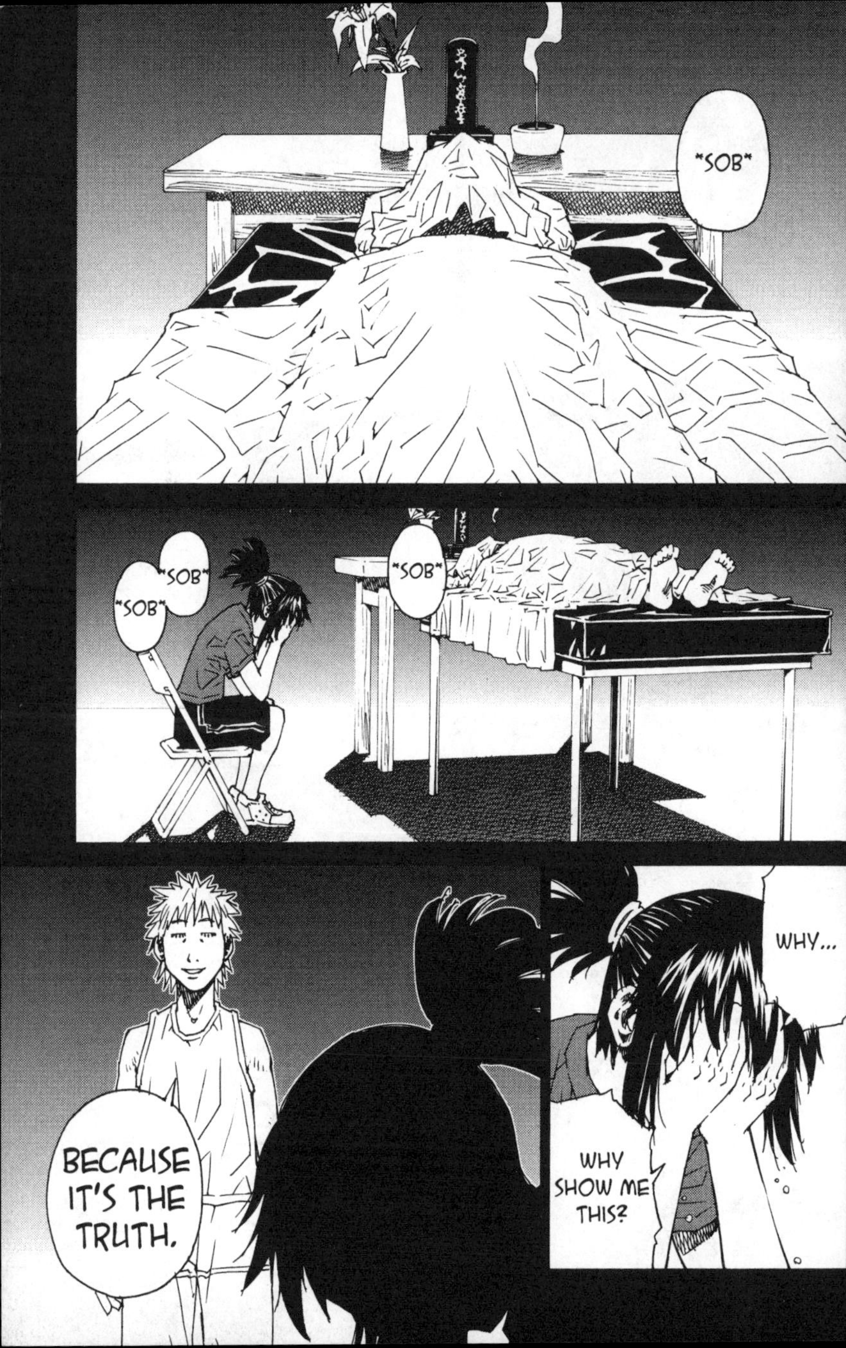
SOB
SOB
SOB
SOB
WHY...
WHY SHOW ME THIS?
BECAUSE IT'S THE TRUTH.

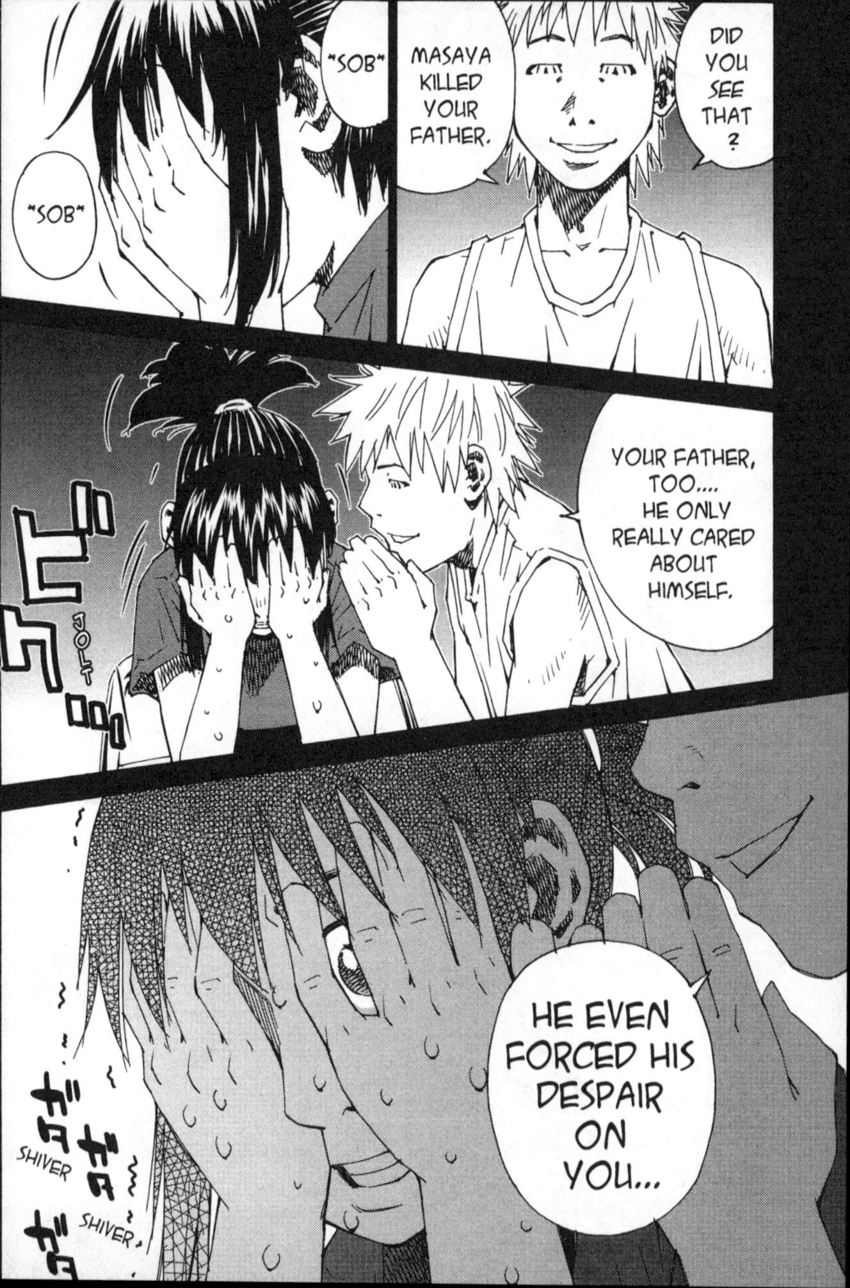
DID YOU SEE THAT?
MASAYA KILLED YOUR FATHER.
SOB
SOB
YOUR FATHER, TOO.... HE ONLY REALLY CARED ABOUT HIMSELF.
JOLT
HE EVEN FORCED HIS DESPAIR ON YOU...
SHIVER
SHIVER

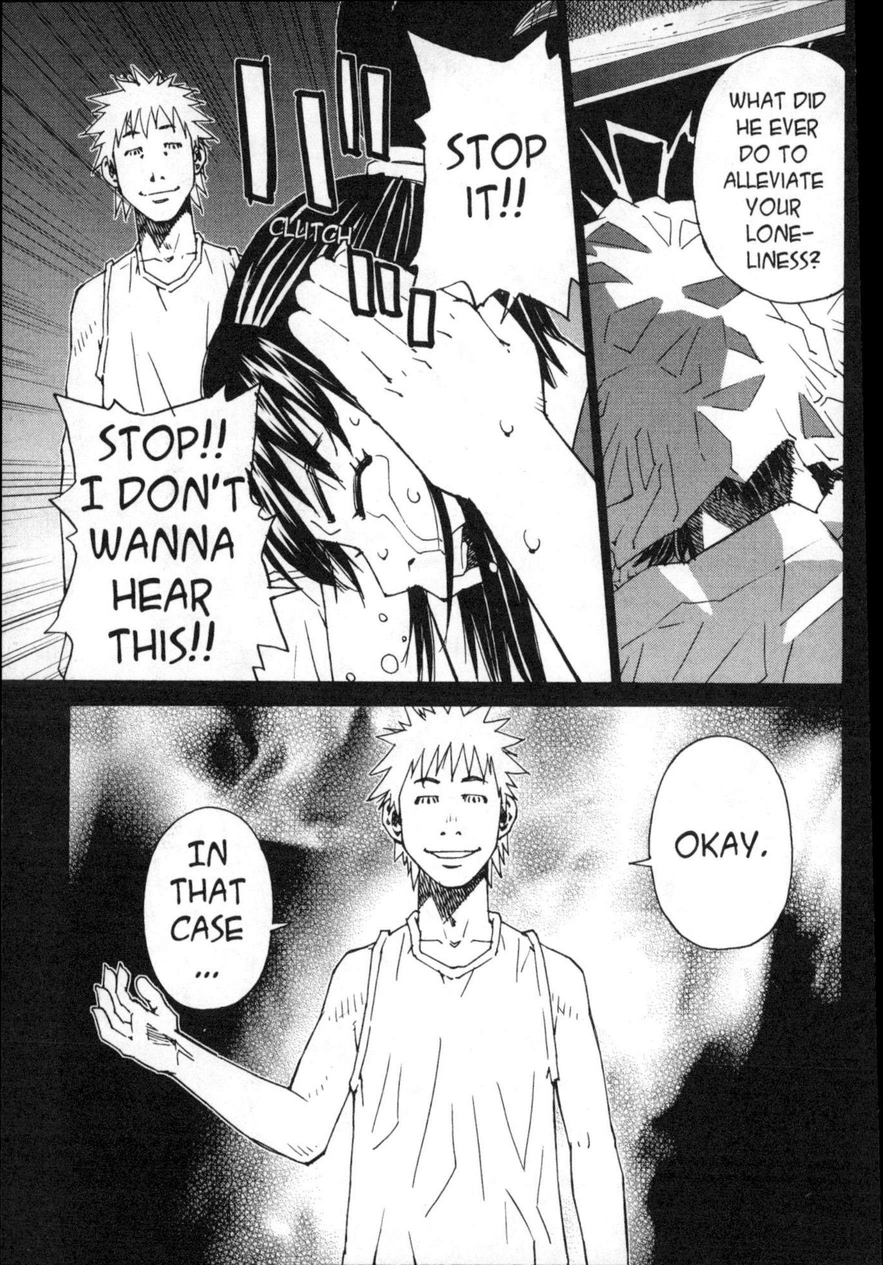
WHAT DID HE EVER DO TO ALLEVIATE YOUR LONE-LINESS?
STOP IT!!
CLUTCH
STOP!! I DON'T WANNA HEAR THIS!!
OKAY.
IN THAT CASE ...

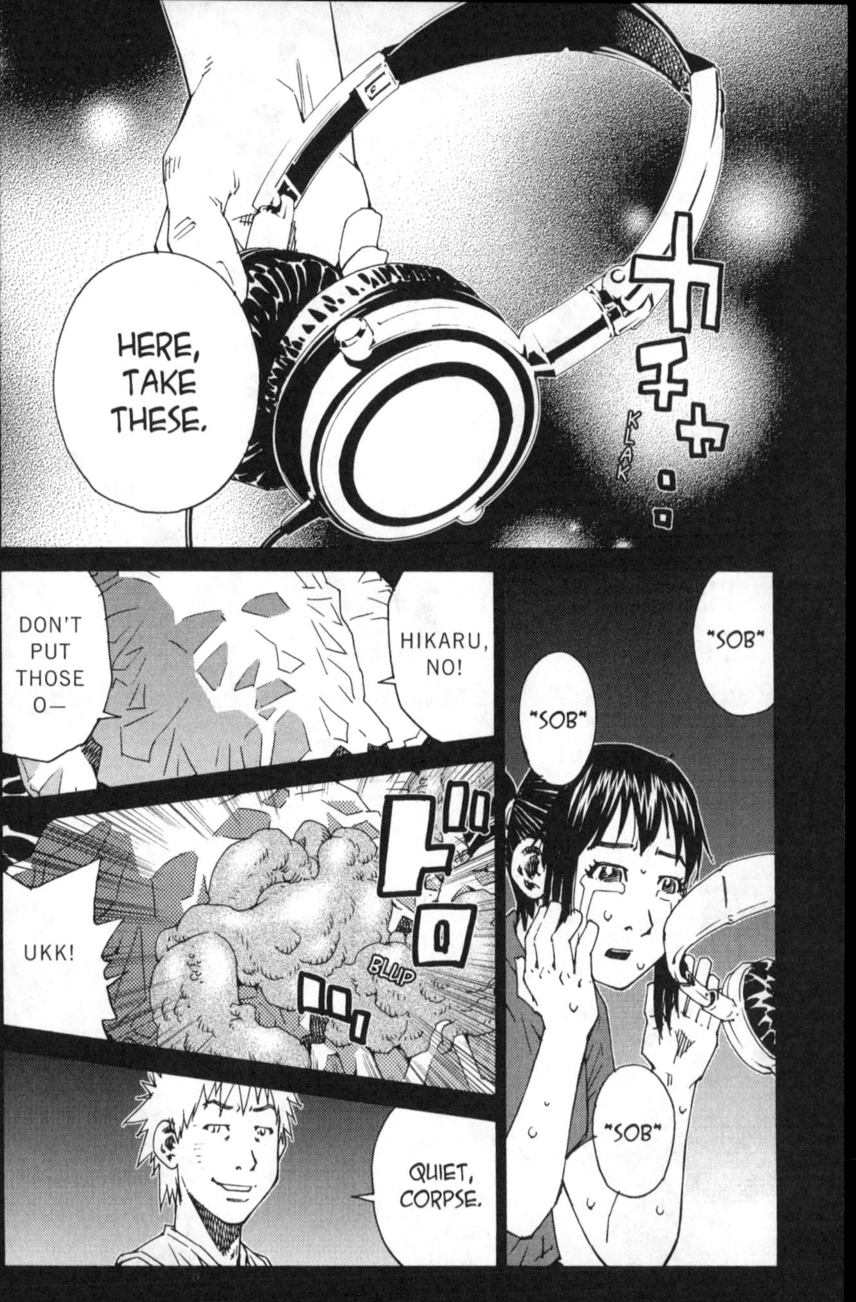
HERE, TAKE THESE.
KLAK
"SOB"
"SOB"
"SOB"
HIKARU, NO!
DON'T PUT THOSE O—
UKK!
BLUP
QUIET, CORPSE.

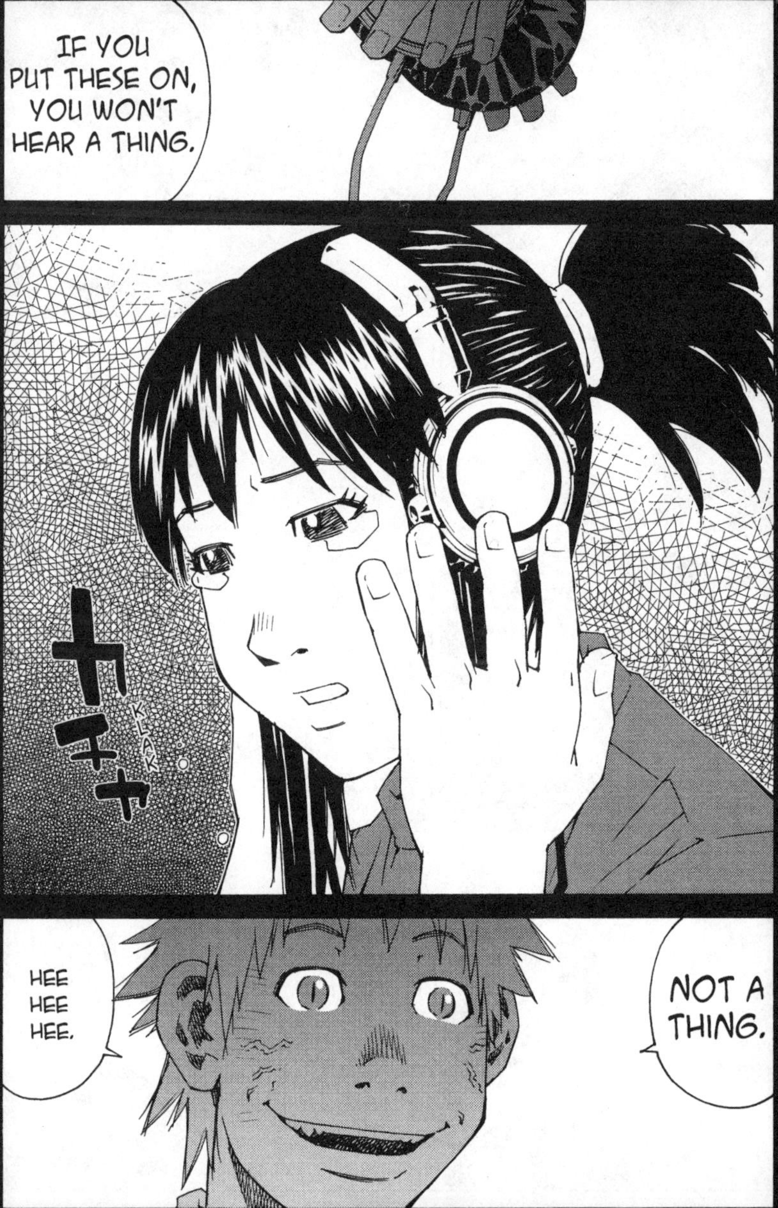
IF YOU PUT THESE ON, YOU WON'T HEAR A THING.
KLAK
NOT A THING.
HEE HEE HEE.

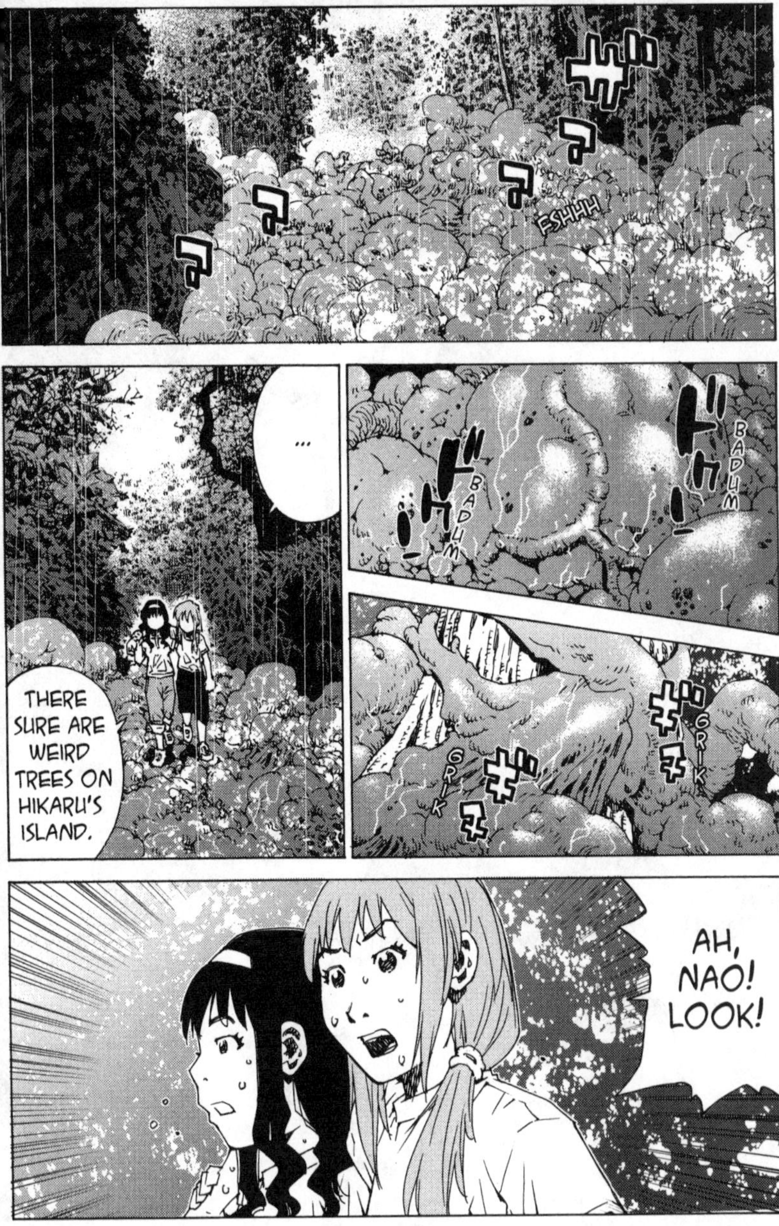
FSHHH
BADUM
BADUM
GRIK
GRIK
...
THERE SURE ARE WEIRD TREES ON HIKARU'S ISLAND.
AH, NAO! LOOK!

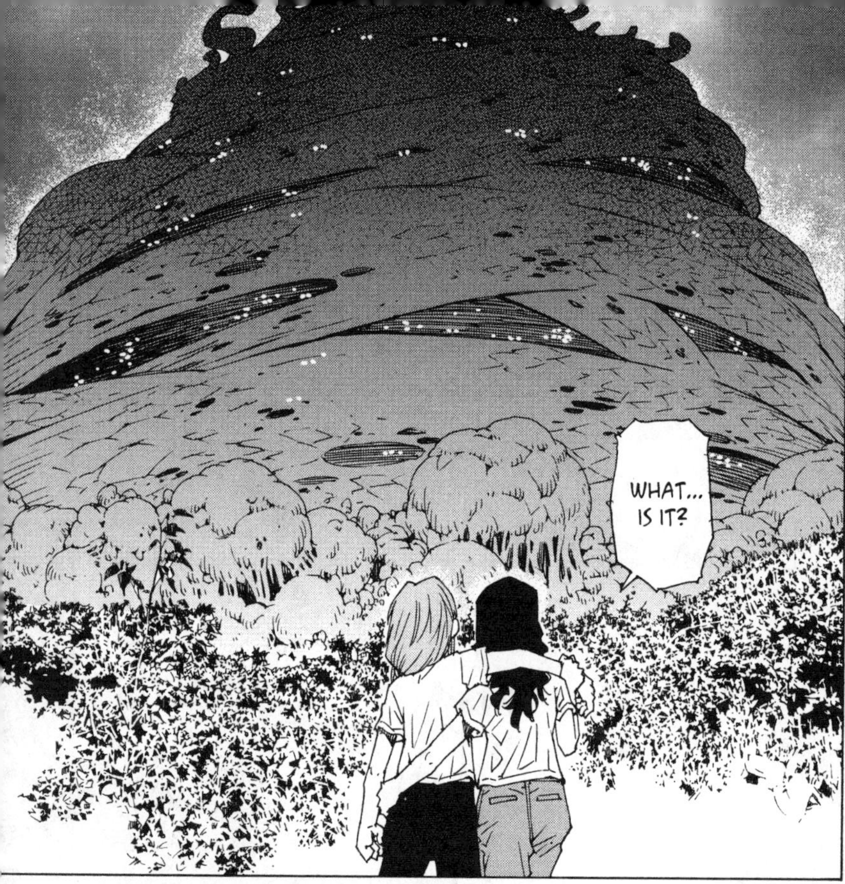
WHAT... IS IT?

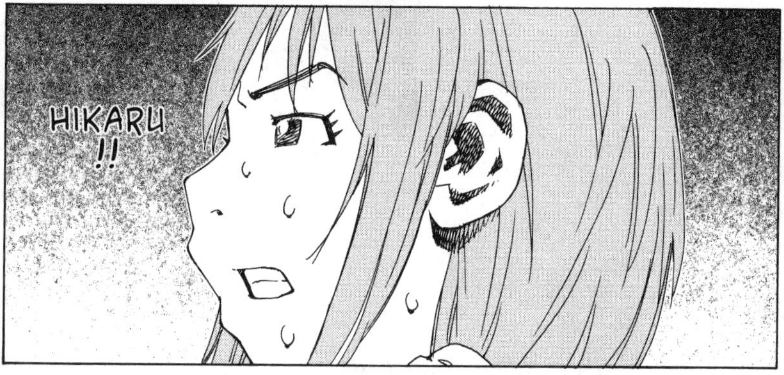
HIKARU !!

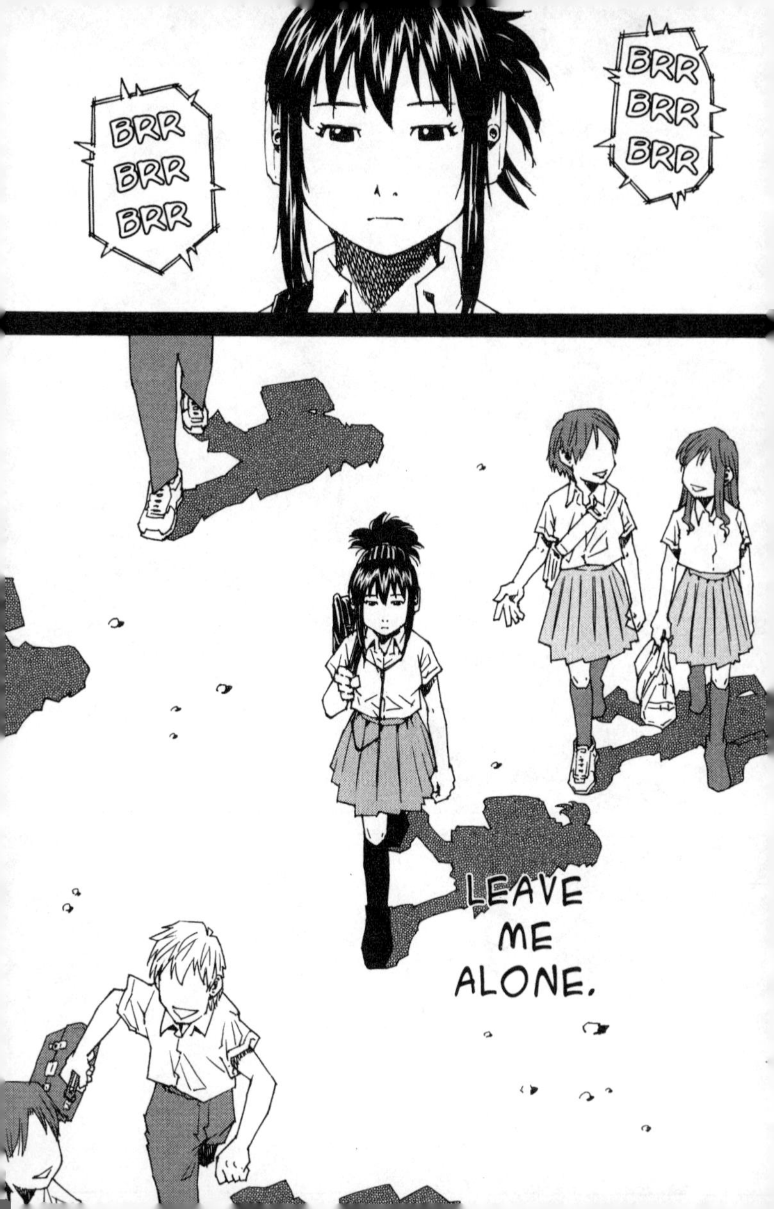
BRR BRR BRR
BRR BRR BRR
LEAVE ME ALONE.

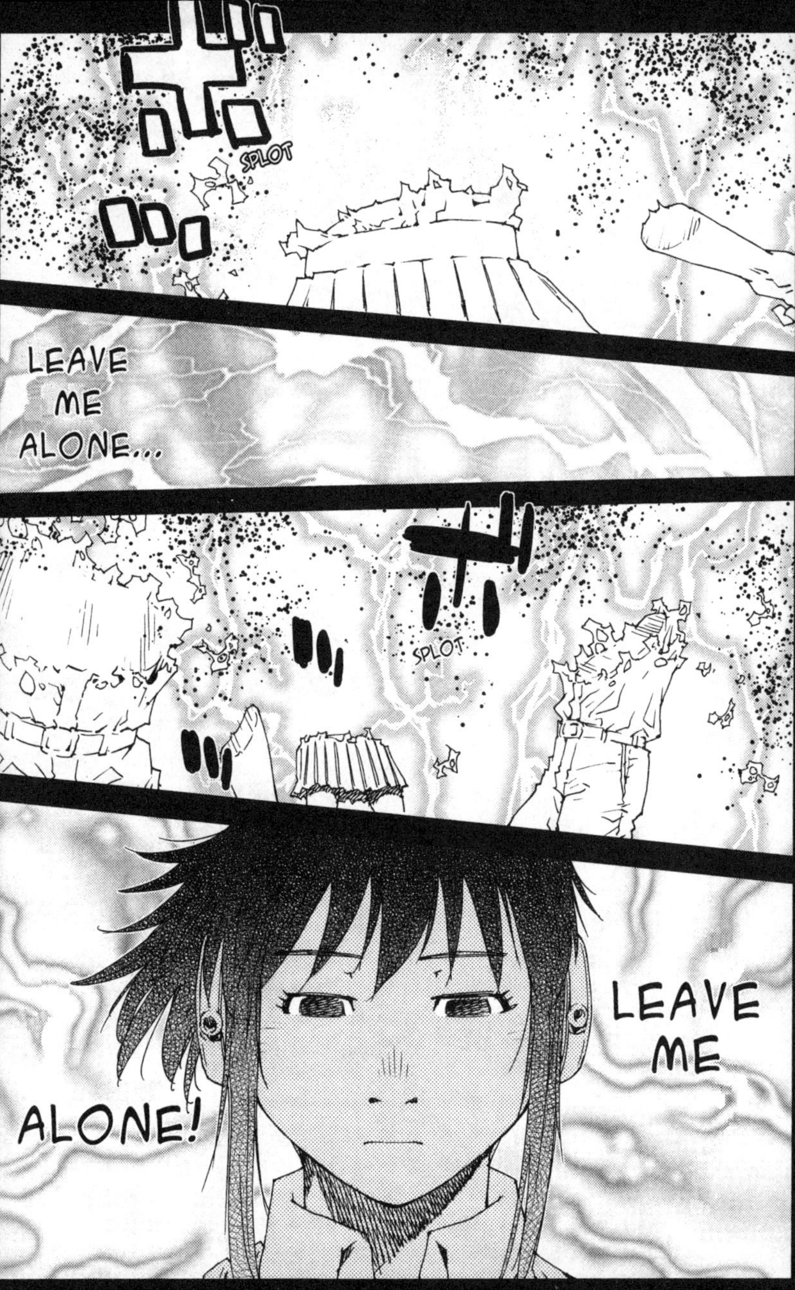
SPLOT
LEAVE ME ALONE...
SPLOT
LEAVE ME
ALONE!

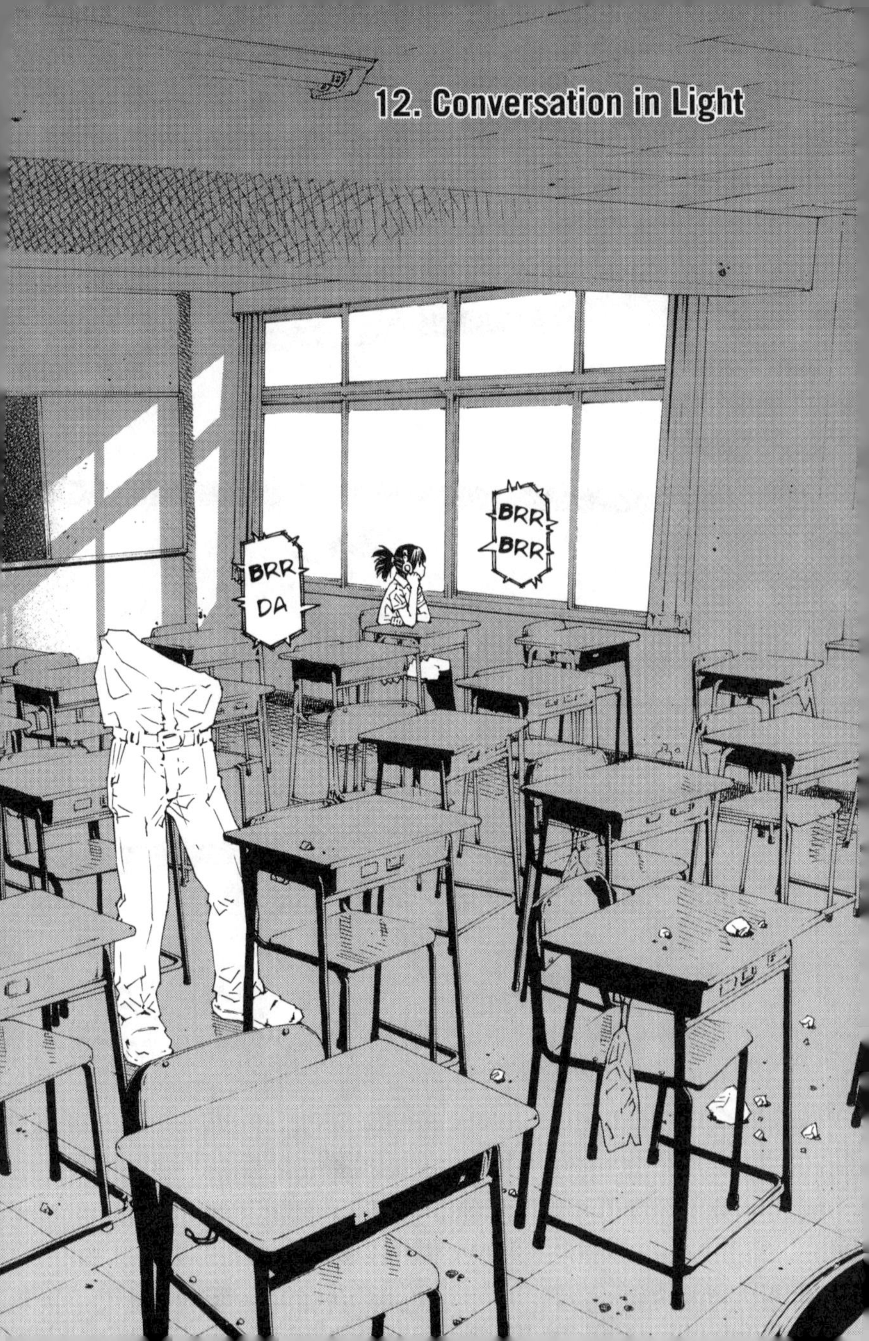
12. Conversation in Light
BRR BRR
BRR DA

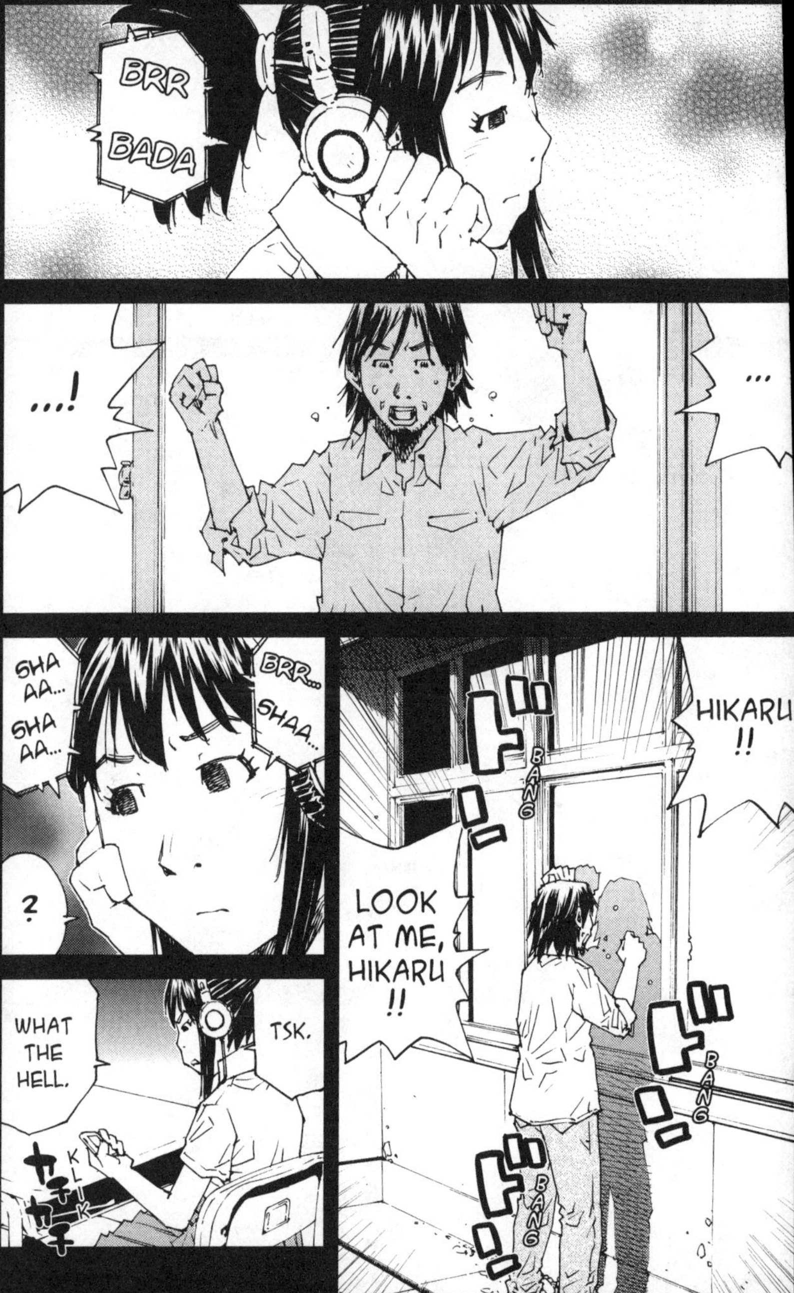
BRR
BADA
...
...!
HIKARU !!
BANG
LOOK AT ME, HIKARU !!
BANG
BANG
BRR... SHAA...
SHA AA... SHA AA...
?
TSK.
WHAT THE HELL.
KLIK

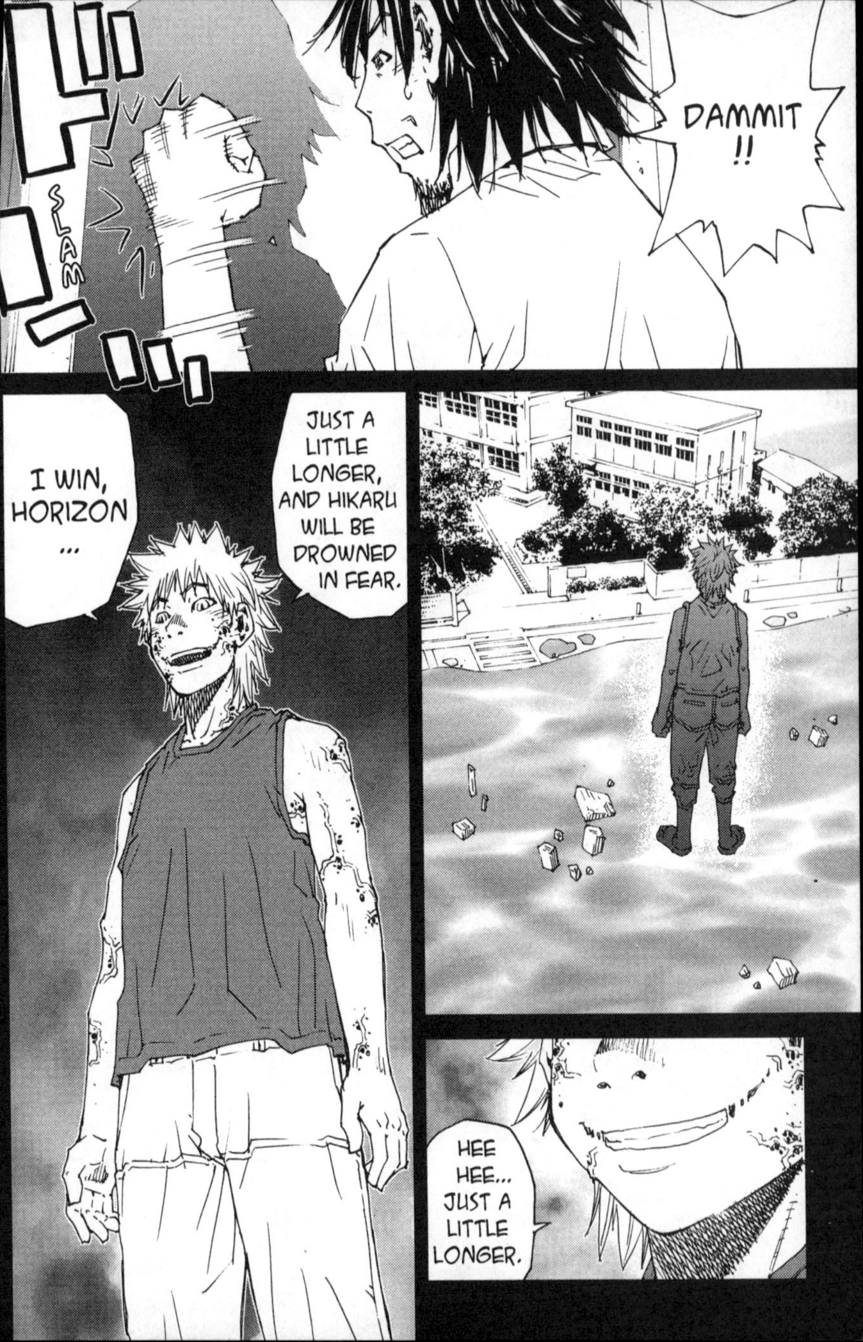
DAMMIT !!
SLAM
HEE HEE... JUST A LITTLE LONGER.
JUST A LITTLE LONGER, AND HIKARU WILL BE DROWNED IN FEAR.
I WIN, HORIZON ...

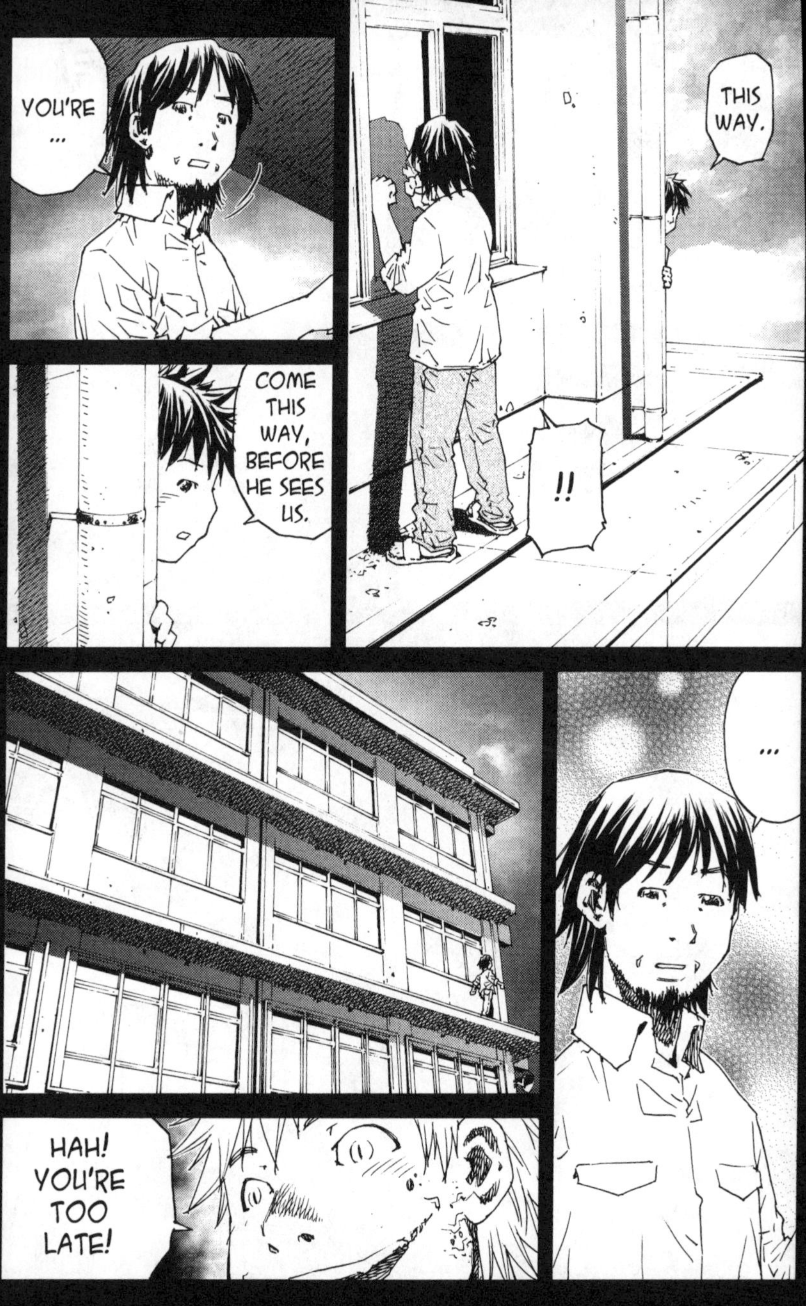
THIS WAY.
!!
YOU'RE ...
COME THIS WAY, BEFORE HE SEES US.
...
HAH! YOU'RE TOO LATE!

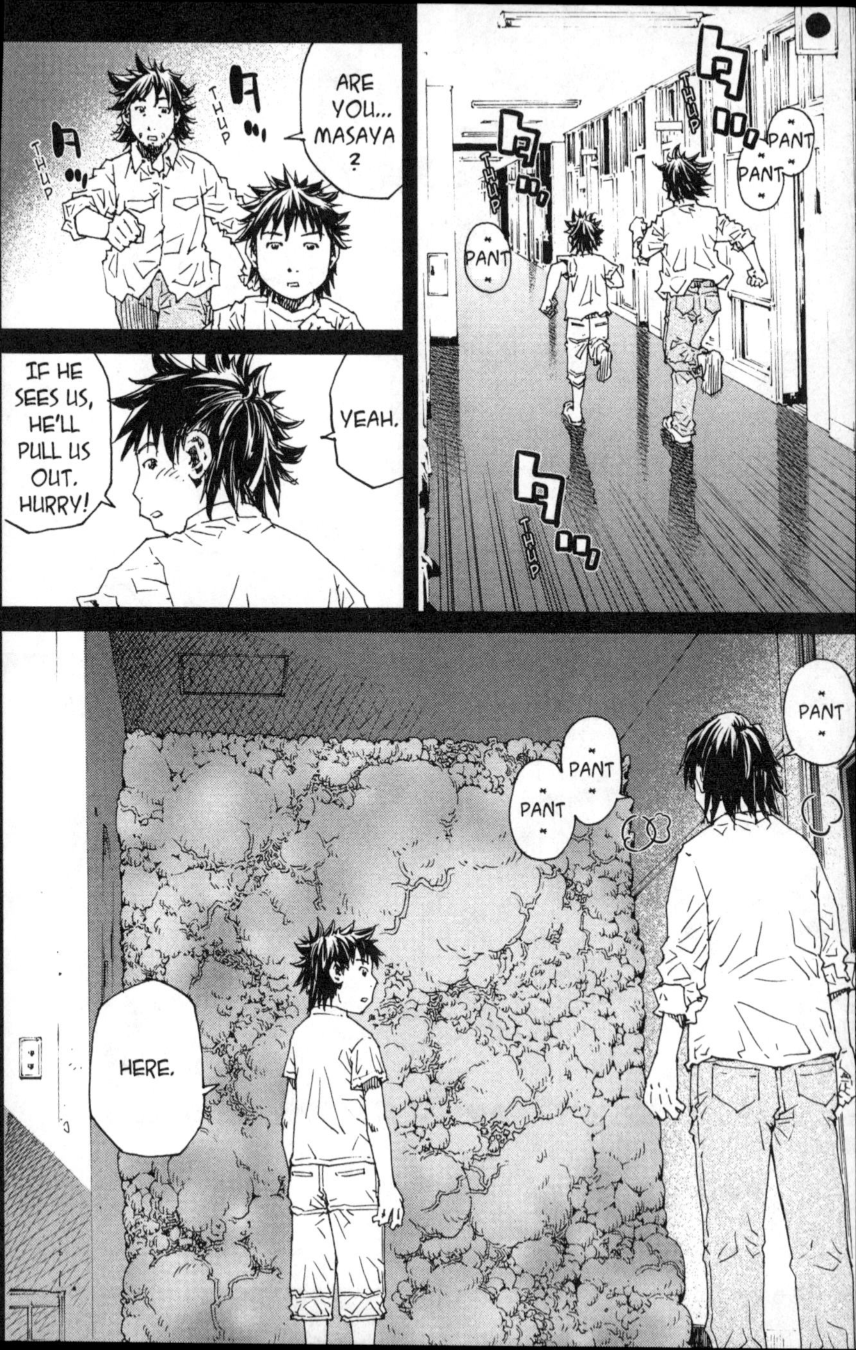
PANT PANT
THUP
THUP
PANT
THUP
ARE YOU... MASAYA?
THUP
THUP
IF HE SEES US, HE'LL PULL US OUT. HURRY!
YEAH.
PANT
PANT
PANT
HERE.

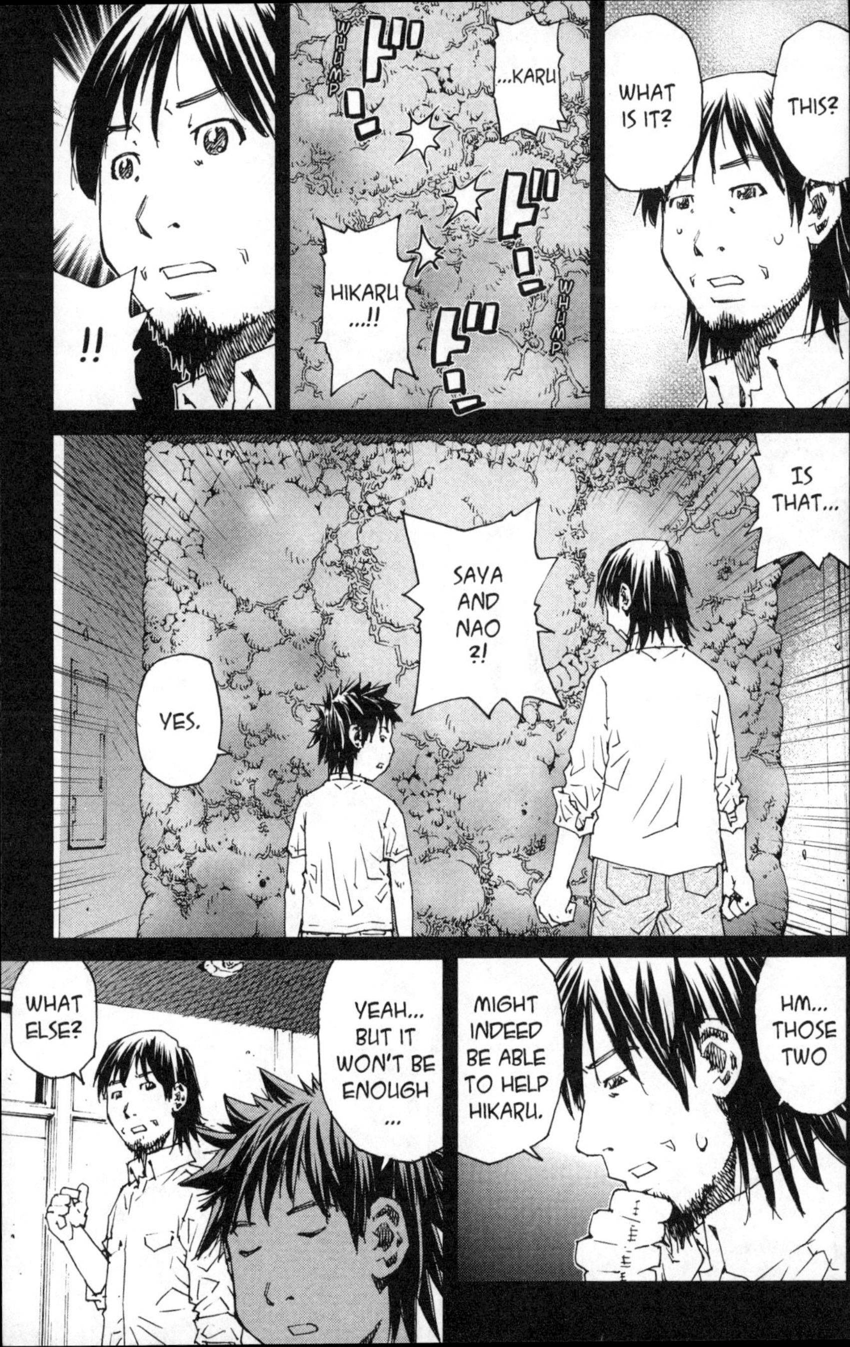
THIS?
WHAT IS IT?
...KARU
WHUMP
HIKARU ...!!
WHUMP
!!
IS THAT...
SAYA AND NAO ?!
YES.
HM... THOSE TWO
MIGHT INDEED BE ABLE TO HELP HIKARU.
YEAH... BUT IT WON'T BE ENOUGH ...
WHAT ELSE?

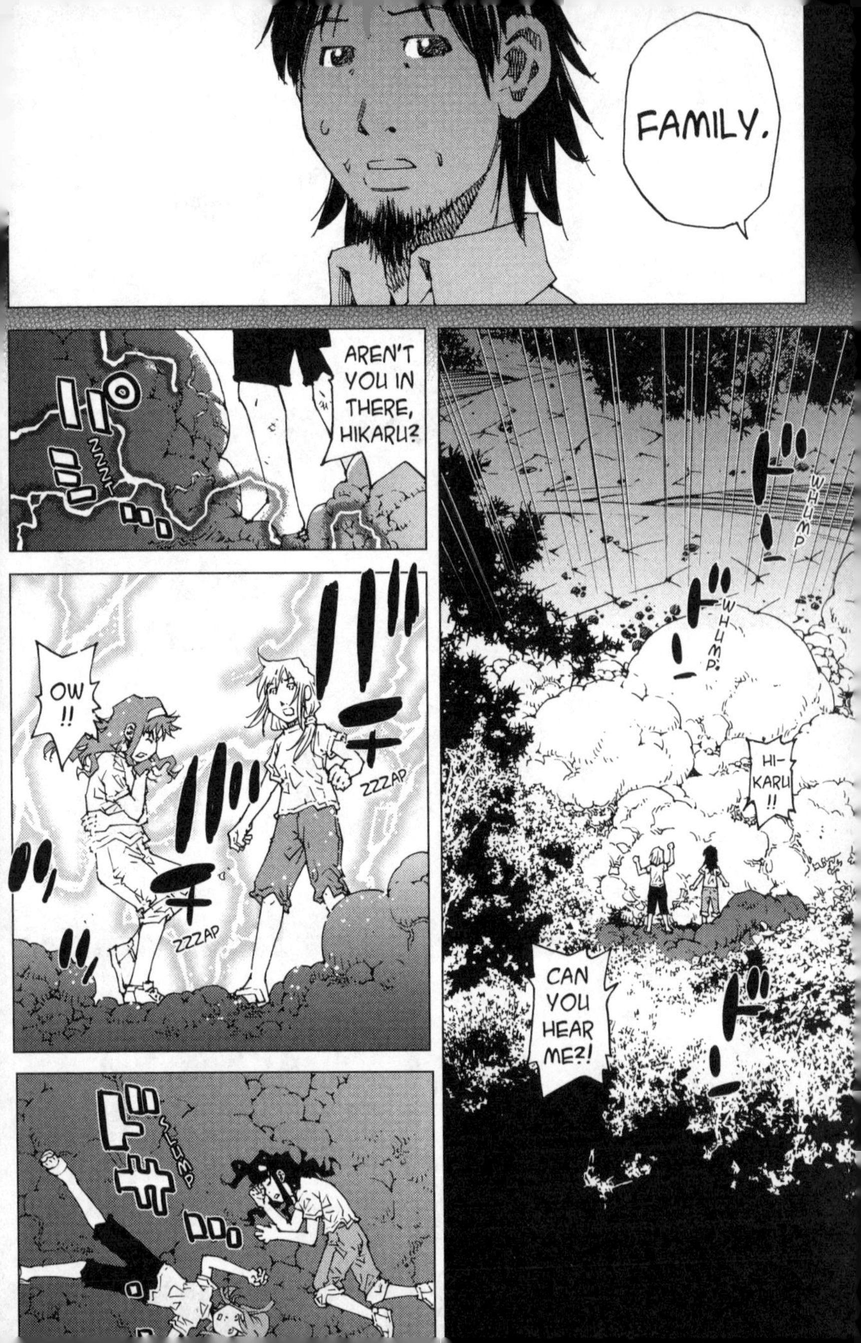
FAMILY.
WHUMP
WHUMP
HI-KARU!!
CAN YOU HEAR ME?!
AREN'T YOU IN THERE, HIKARU?
NNNT
OW!!
ZZZAP
ZZZAP
SLUMP

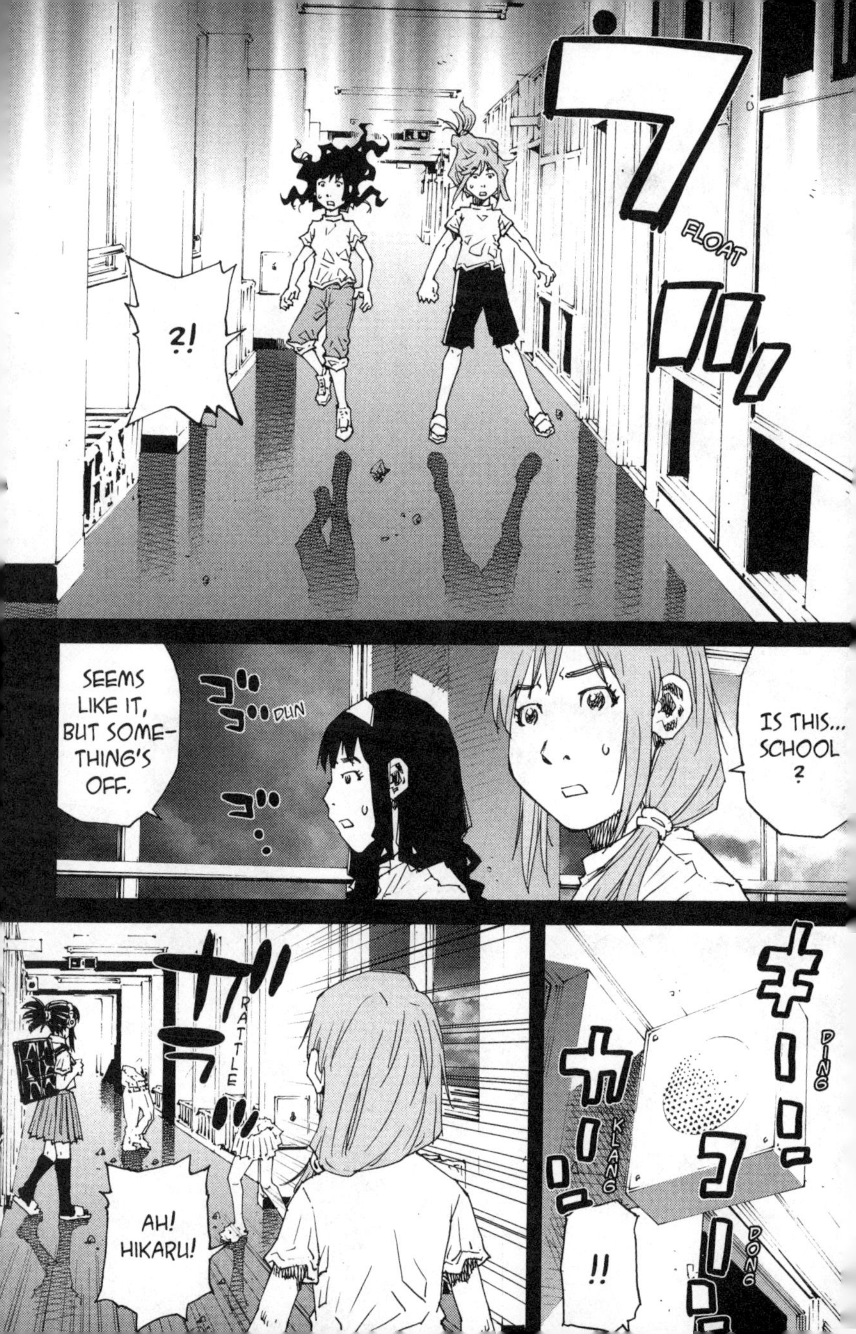
FLOAT
?!
IS THIS... SCHOOL ?
DUN
SEEMS LIKE IT, BUT SOME-THING'S OFF.
DING
KLANG
DONG
!!
RATTLE
AH! HIKARU!

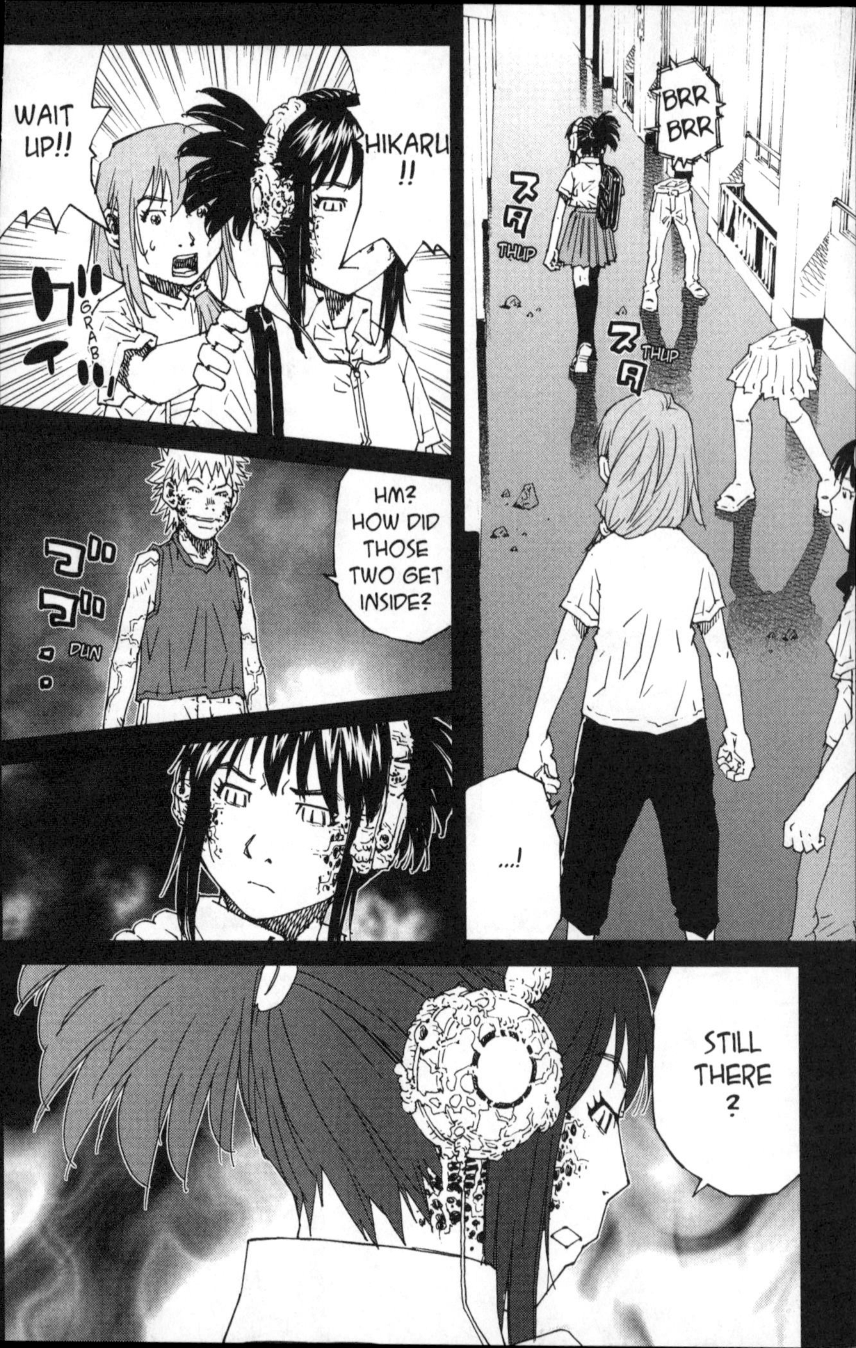
BRR BRR
THUP
THUP
...!
WAIT UP!!
HIKARU !!
GRAB
HM? HOW DID THOSE TWO GET INSIDE?
DUN
STILL THERE ?

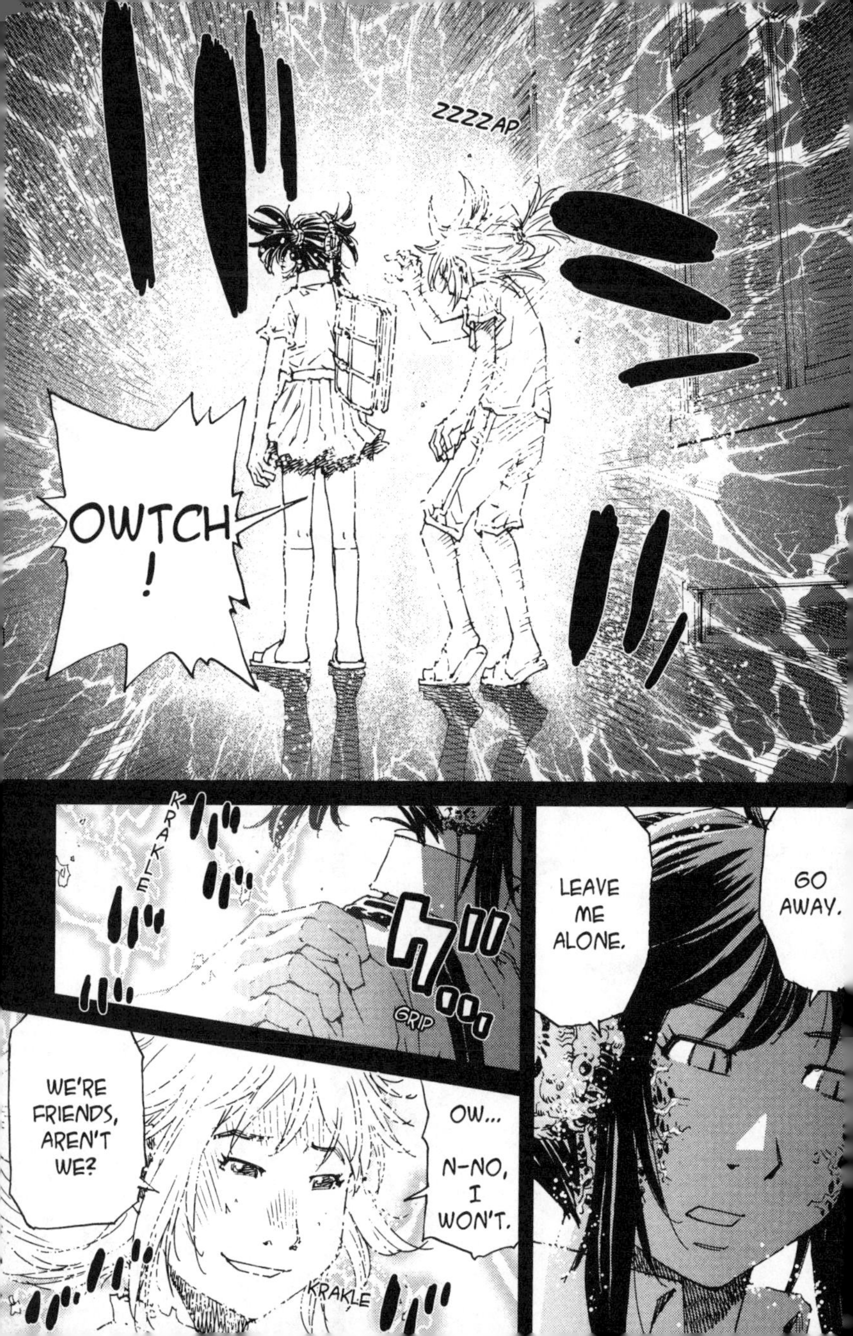
ZZZZAP
OWTCH!
GO AWAY.
LEAVE ME ALONE.
KRAKLE
GRIP
OW...
N-NO, I WON'T.
WE'RE FRIENDS, AREN'T WE?
KRAKLE

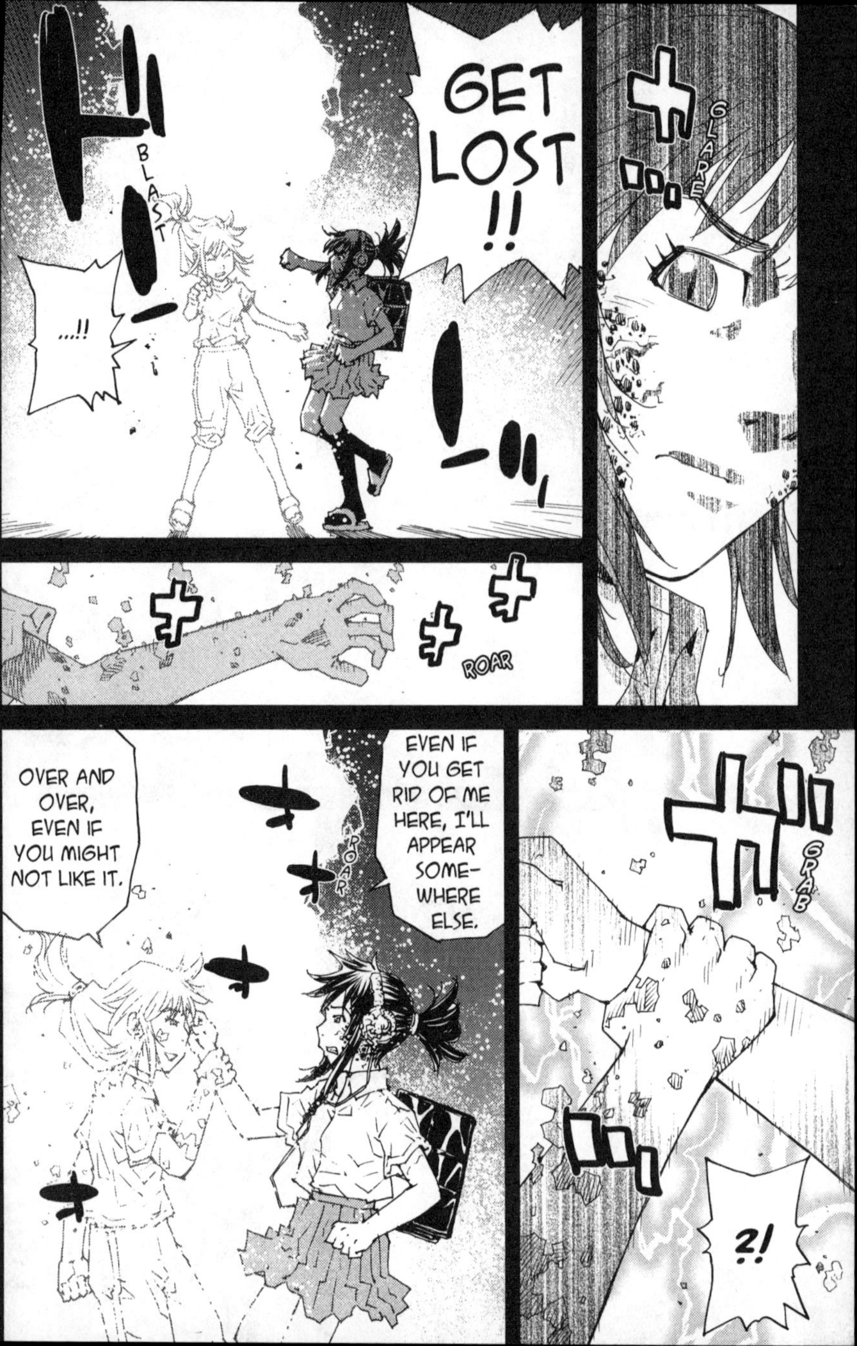
GLARE
GET LOST !!
BLAST
...!!
ROAR
GRAB
?!
EVEN IF YOU GET RID OF ME HERE, I'LL APPEAR SOME-WHERE ELSE.
ROAR
OVER AND OVER, EVEN IF YOU MIGHT NOT LIKE IT.

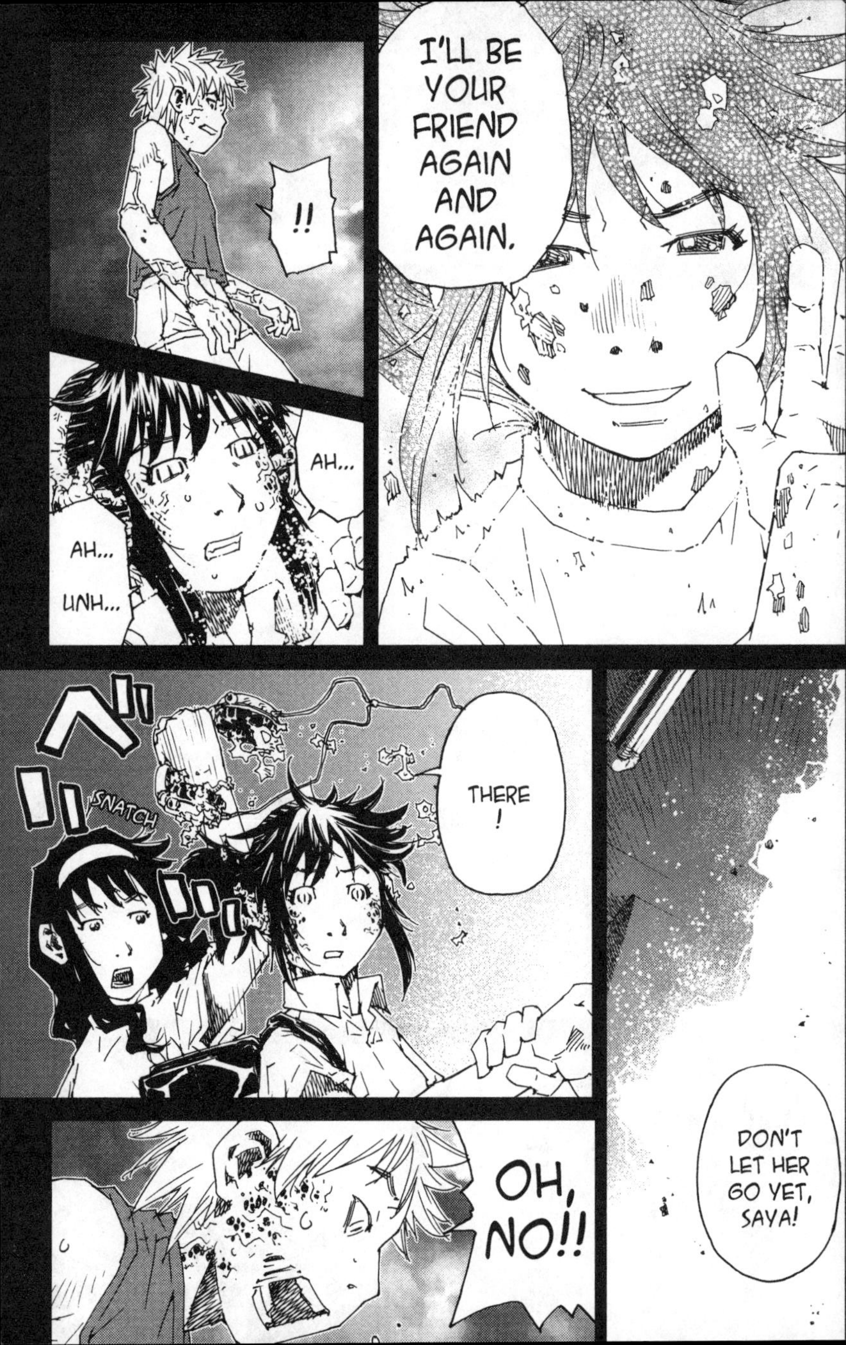
I'LL BE YOUR FRIEND AGAIN AND AGAIN.
!!
AH...
AH...
UNH...
DON'T LET HER GO YET, SAYA!
THERE!
SNATCH
OH, NO!!

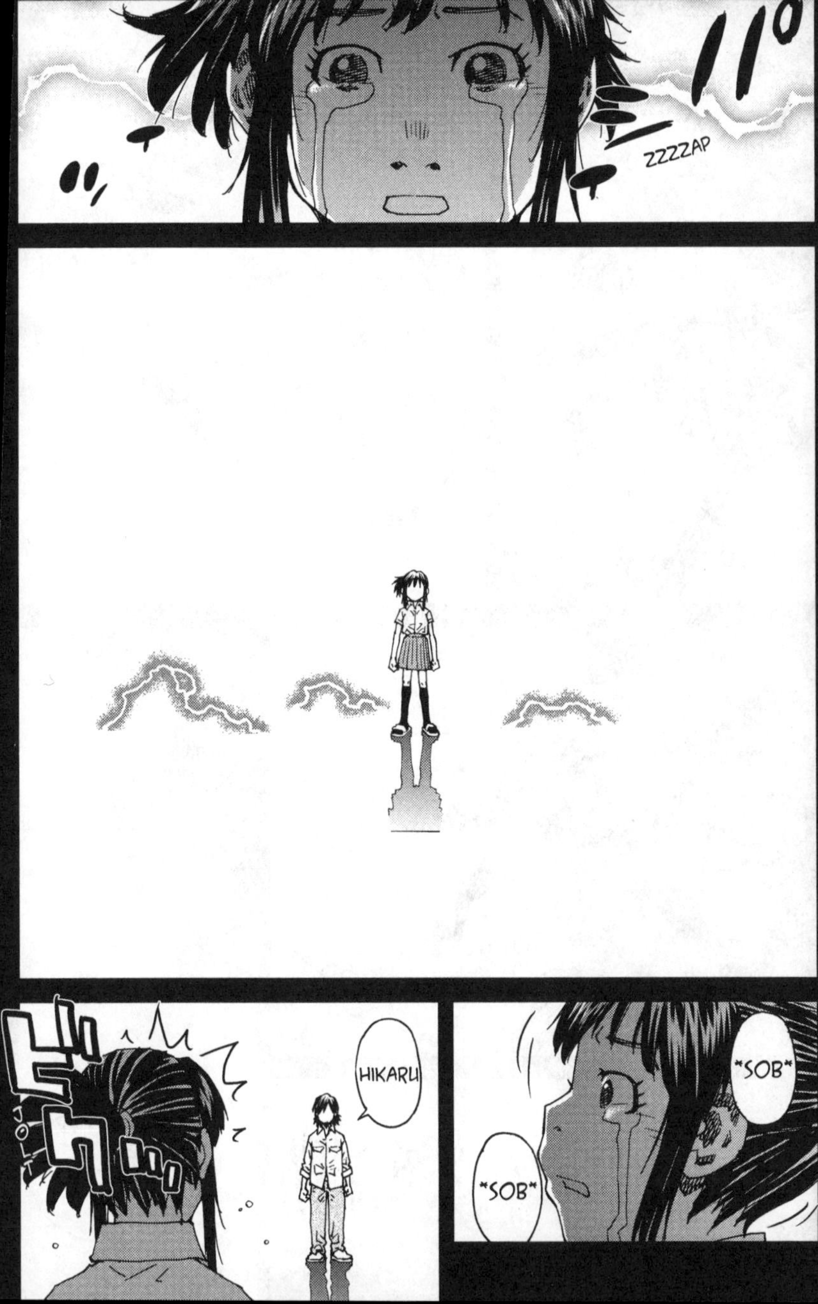
ZZZZAP
SOB
SOB
HIKARU
JOLT

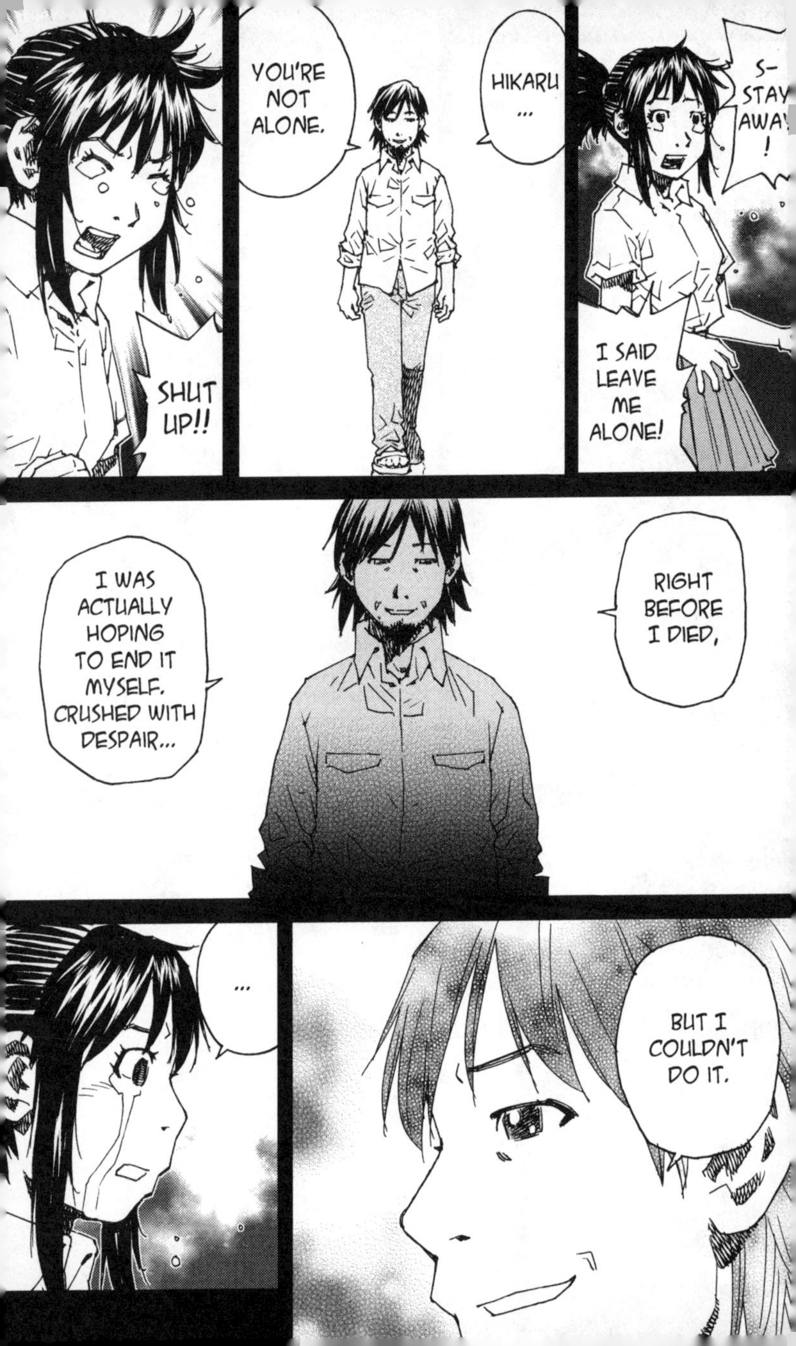
S-STAY AWAY!
I SAID LEAVE ME ALONE!
HIKARU...
YOU'RE NOT ALONE.
SHUT UP!!
RIGHT BEFORE I DIED,
I WAS ACTUALLY HOPING TO END IT MYSELF. CRUSHED WITH DESPAIR...
BUT I COULDN'T DO IT.
...

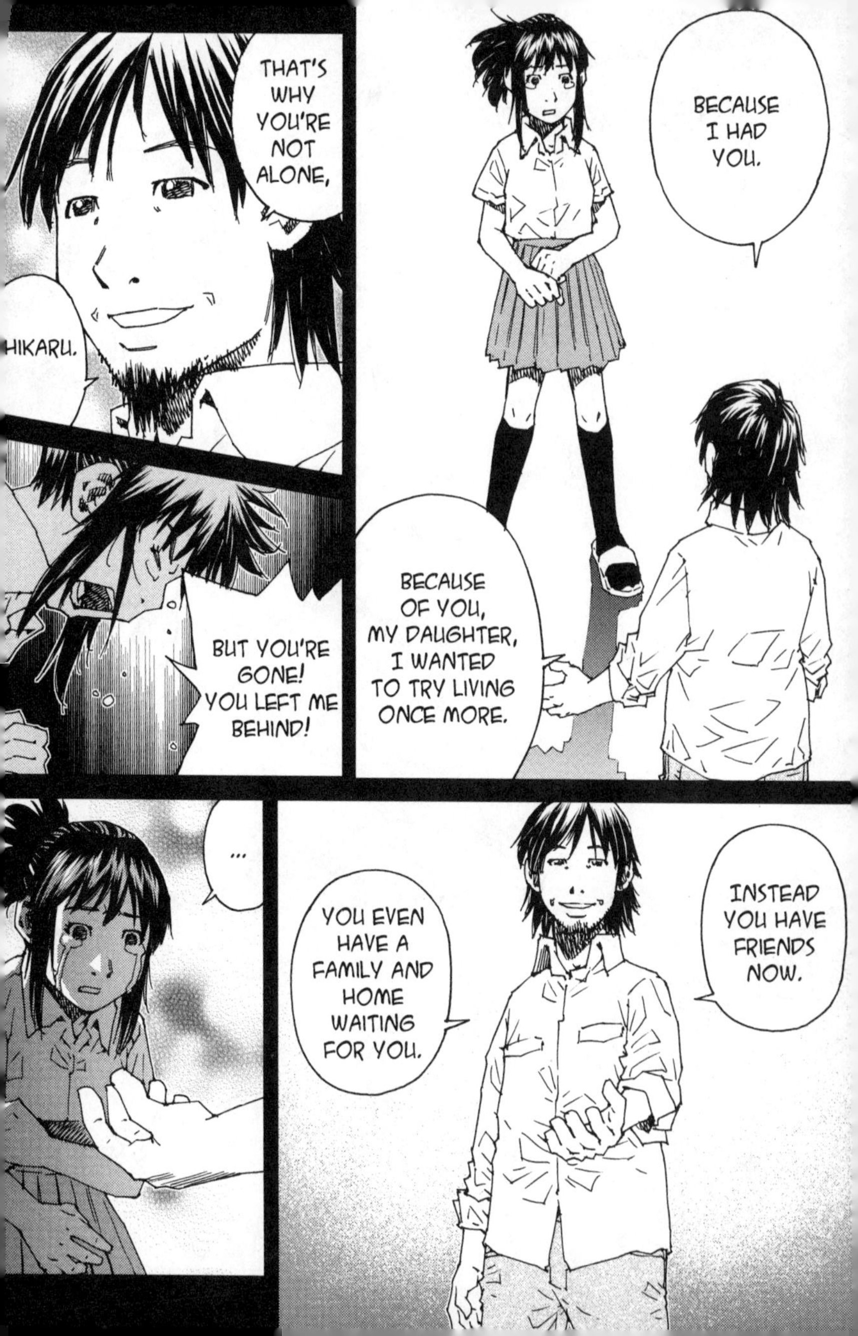
BECAUSE I HAD YOU.
BECAUSE OF YOU, MY DAUGHTER, I WANTED TO TRY LIVING ONCE MORE.
THAT'S WHY YOU'RE NOT ALONE,
HIKARU.
BUT YOU'RE GONE! YOU LEFT ME BEHIND!
INSTEAD YOU HAVE FRIENDS NOW.
YOU EVEN HAVE A FAMILY AND HOME WAITING FOR YOU.
...

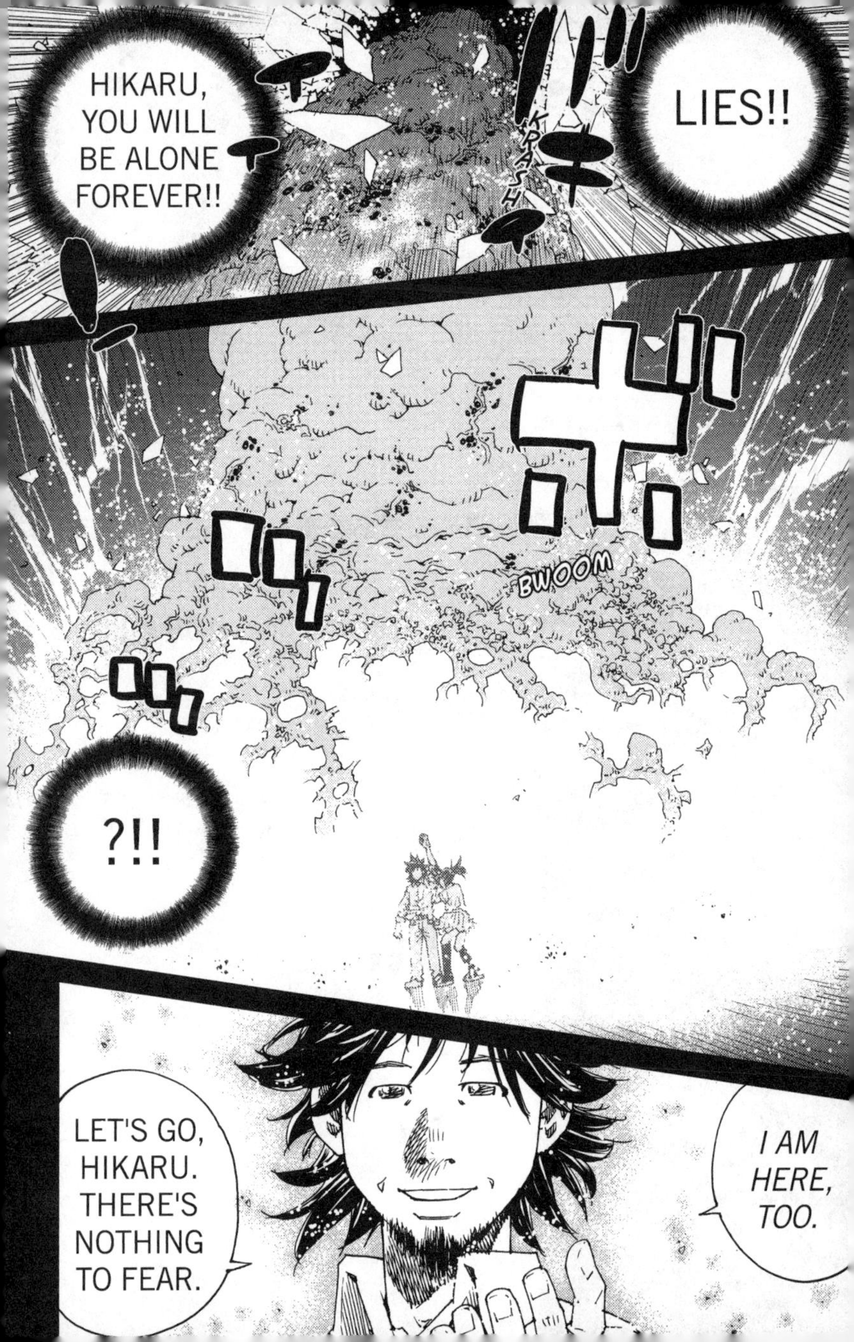
LIES!!
KRASH
HIKARU, YOU WILL BE ALONE FOREVER!!
!
BWOOM
?!!
I AM HERE, TOO.
LET'S GO, HIKARU. THERE'S NOTHING TO FEAR.

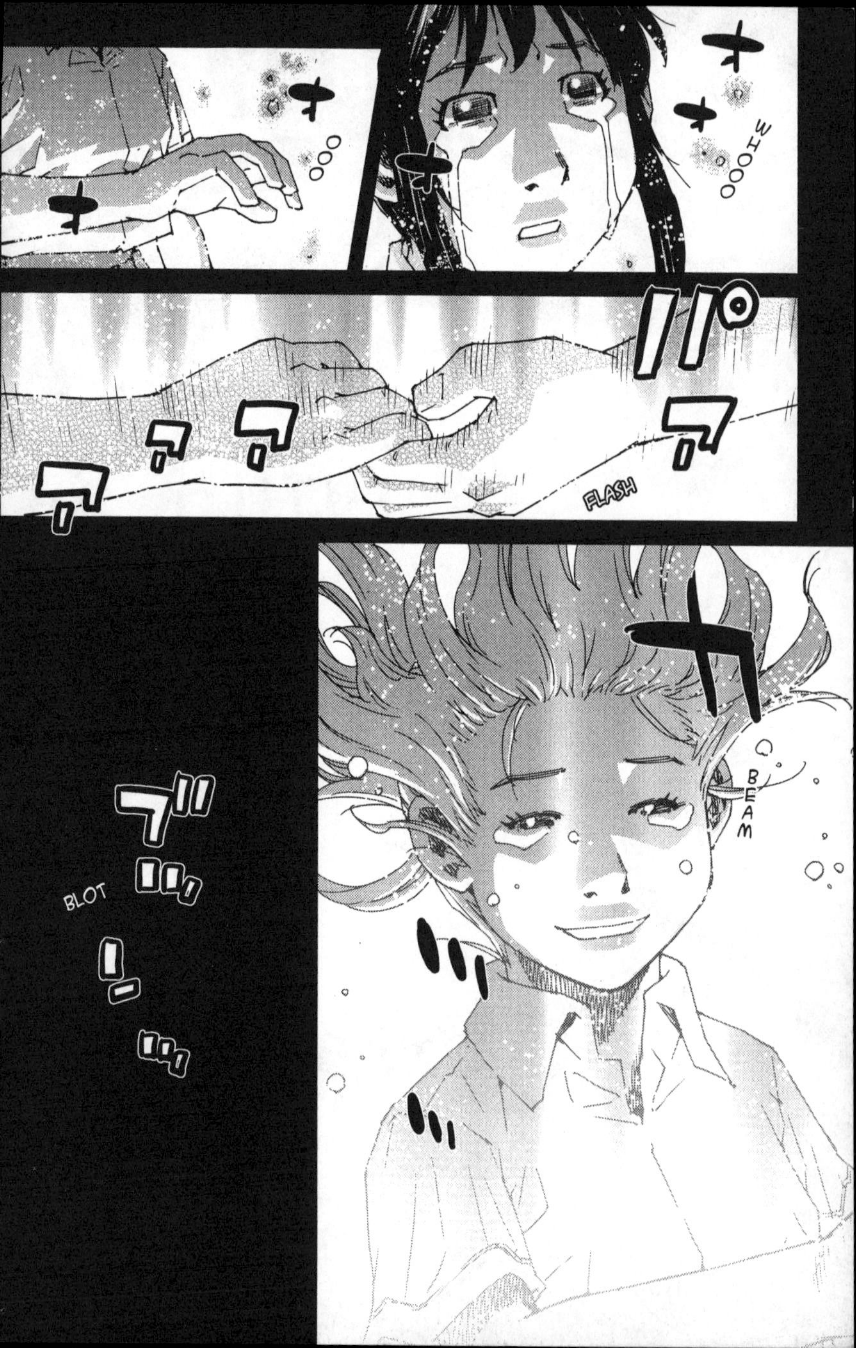
WHOOO
FLASH
BEAM
BLOT

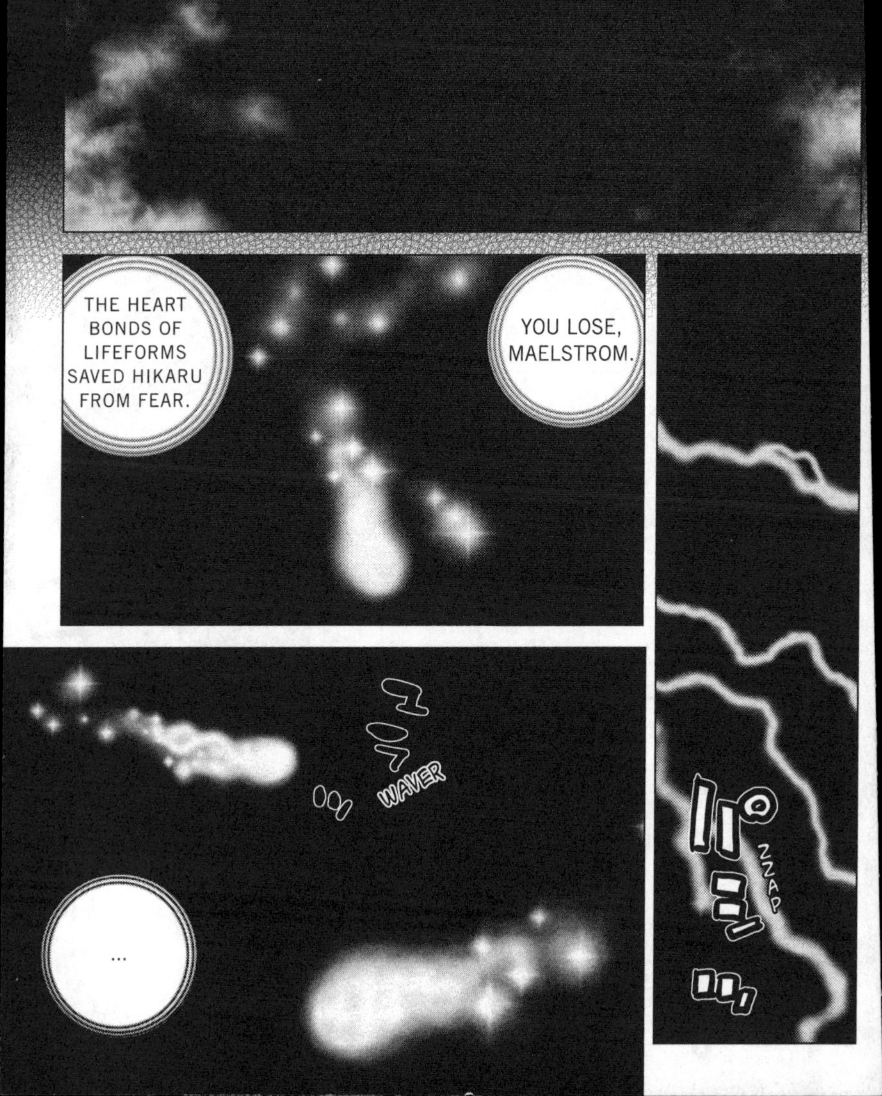
ZZAP
YOU LOSE, MAELSTROM.
THE HEART BONDS OF LIFEFORMS SAVED HIKARU FROM FEAR.
WAVER
...

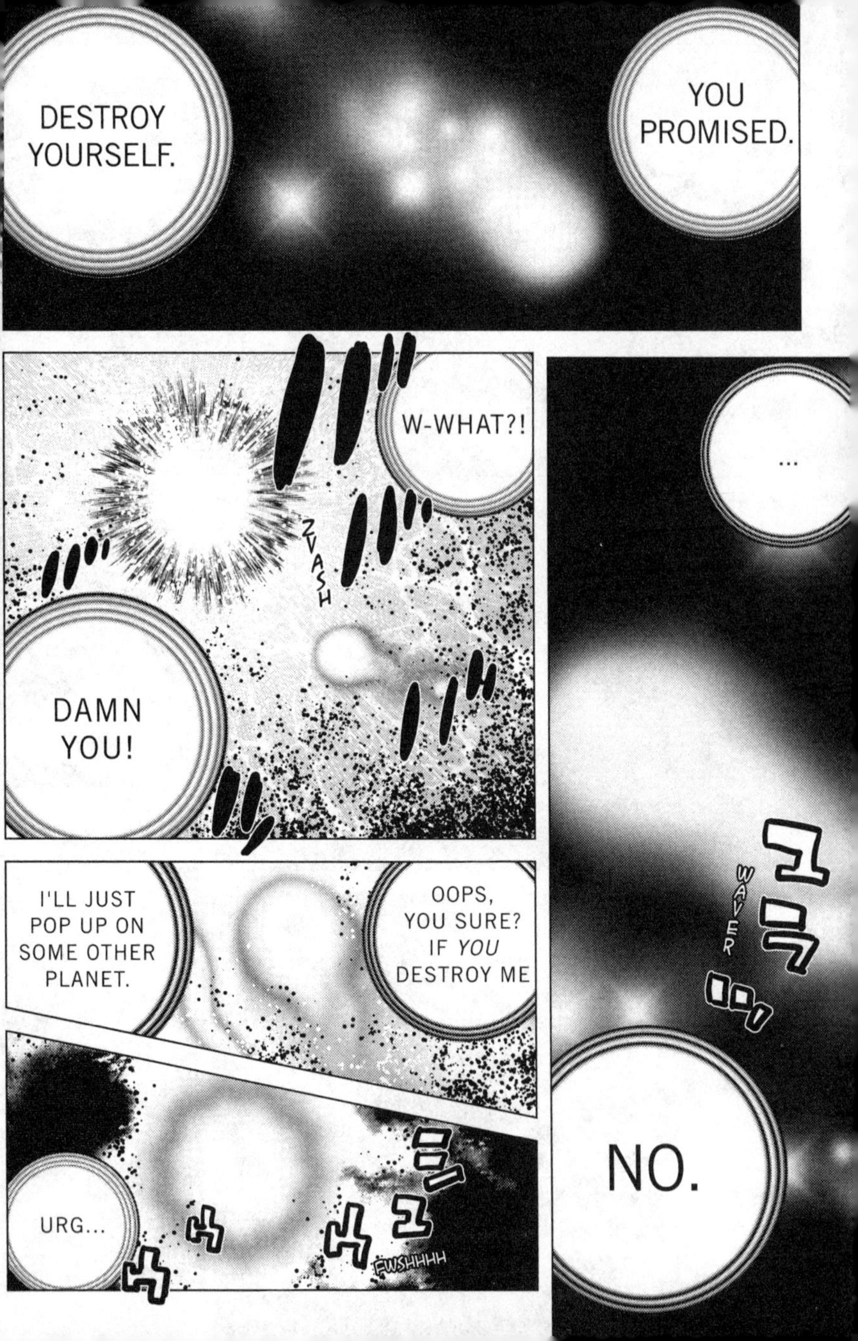
YOU PROMISED.
DESTROY YOURSELF.
...
WAVER
NO.
W-WHAT?!
ZVASH
DAMN YOU!
OOPS, YOU SURE? IF *YOU* DESTROY ME
I'LL JUST POP UP ON SOME OTHER PLANET.
FWSHHHH
URG...

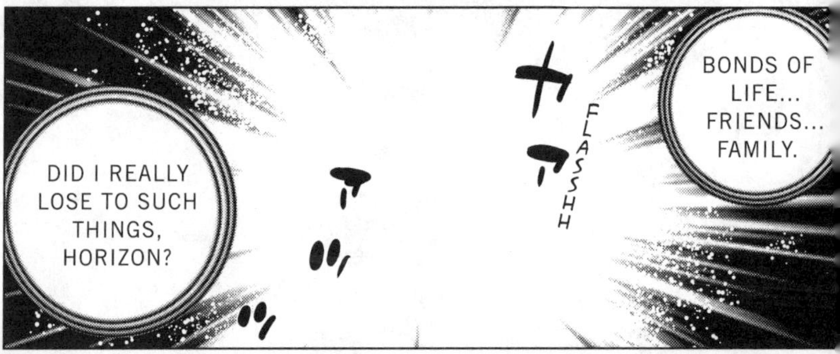
BONDS OF LIFE... FRIENDS... FAMILY.
FLASSHH
DID I REALLY LOSE TO SUCH THINGS, HORIZON?

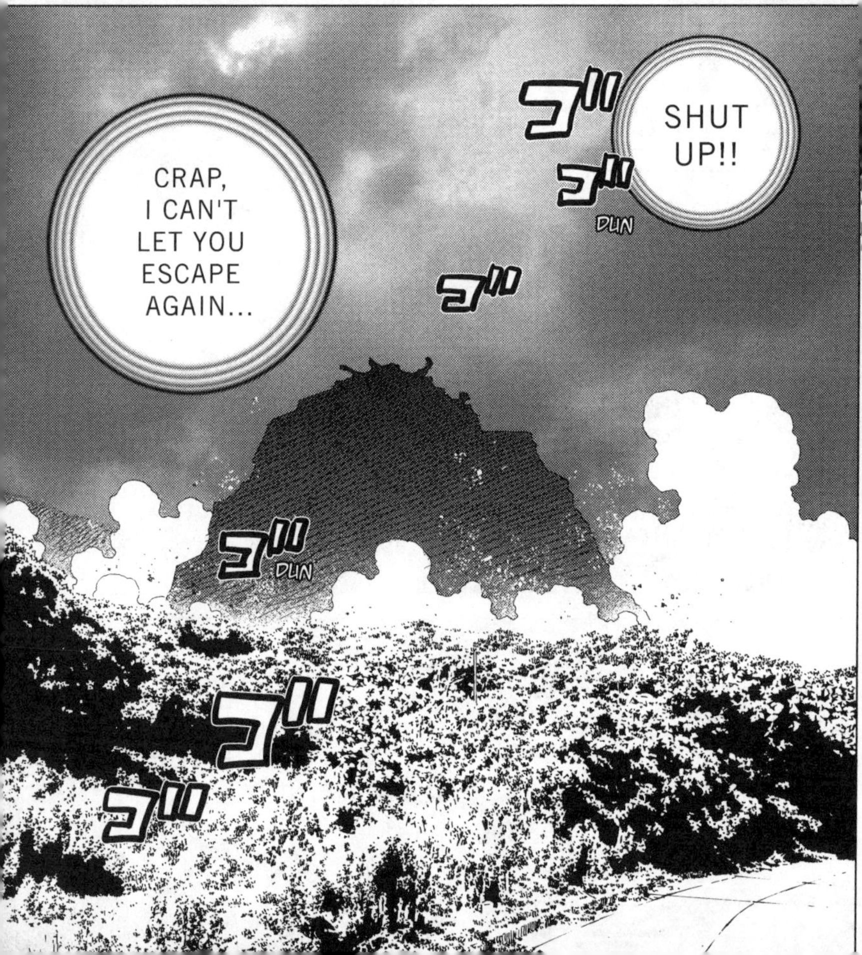
SHUT UP!!
DUN
CRAP, I CAN'T LET YOU ESCAPE AGAIN...
DUN

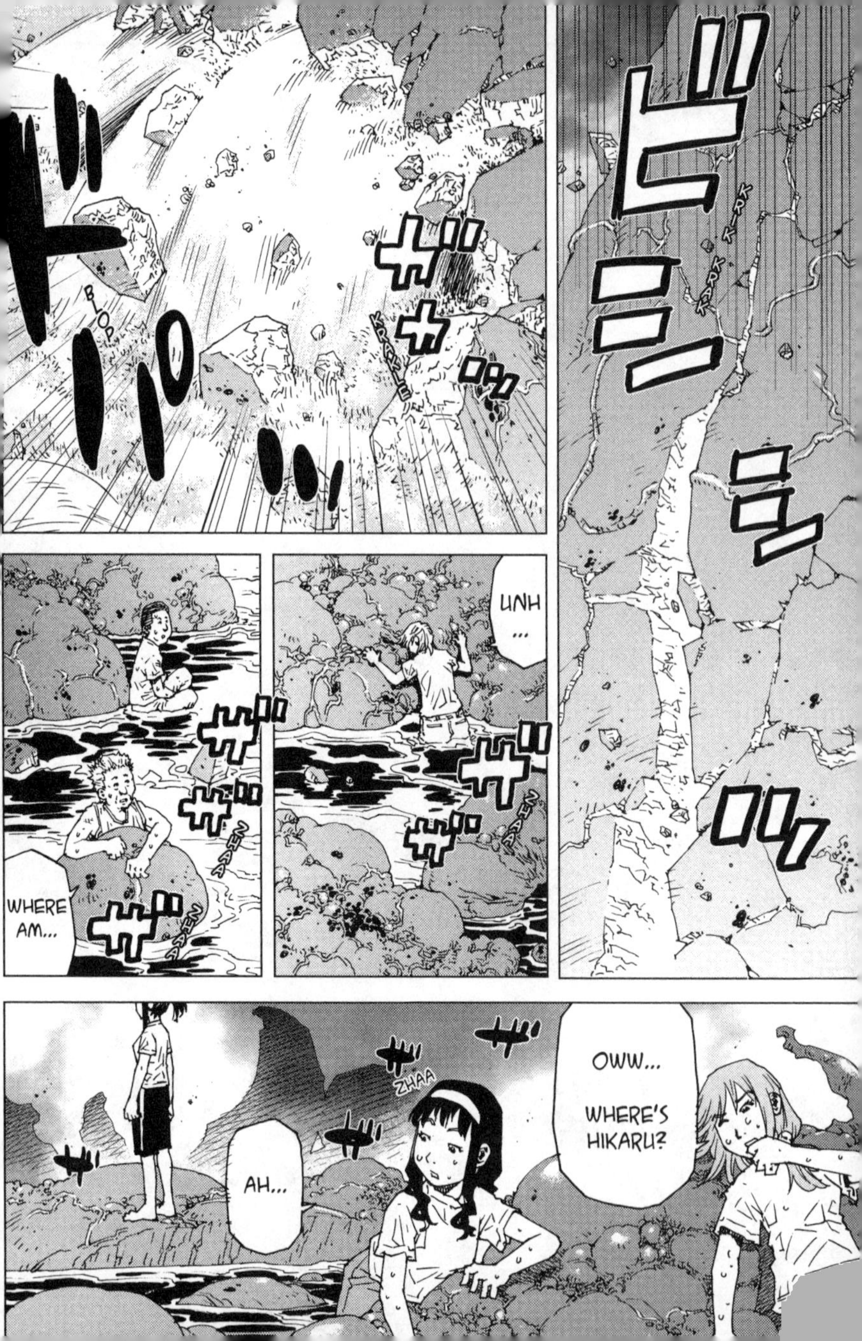
KRIK
KRAK
KRAKLE
BLOP
UNH ...
ZHAA
WHERE AM...
ZHAA
OWW... WHERE'S HIKARU?
ZHAA
AH...

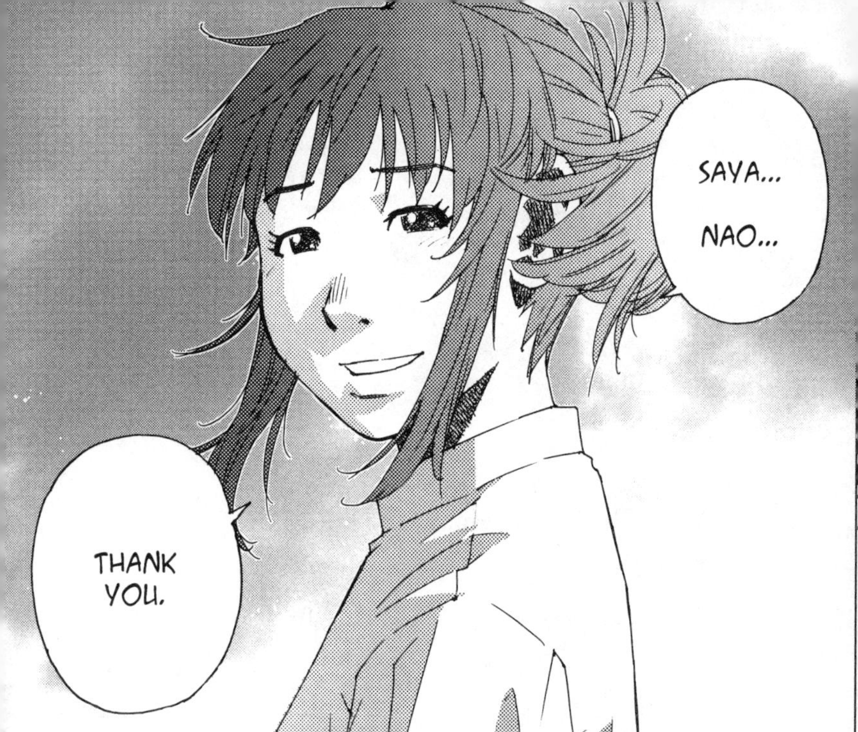
SAYA... NAO...
THANK YOU.
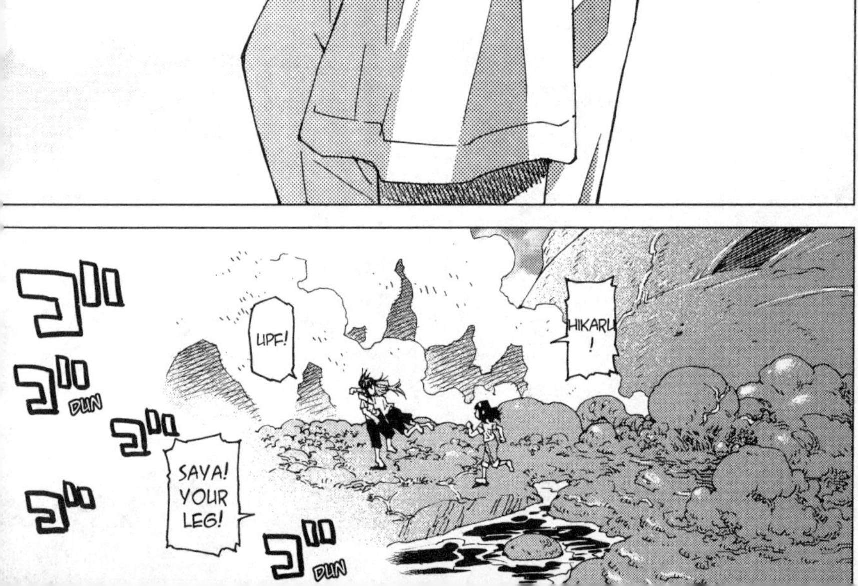
HIKARU!
UPF!
SAYA! YOUR LEG!
DUN
DUN

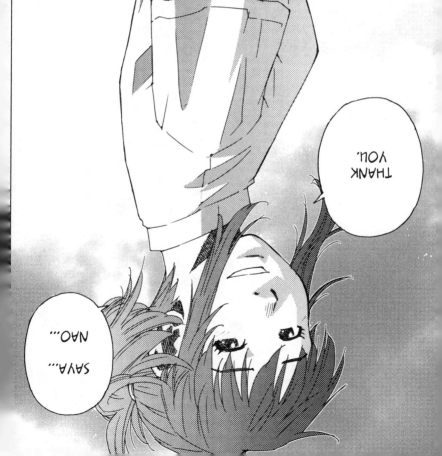

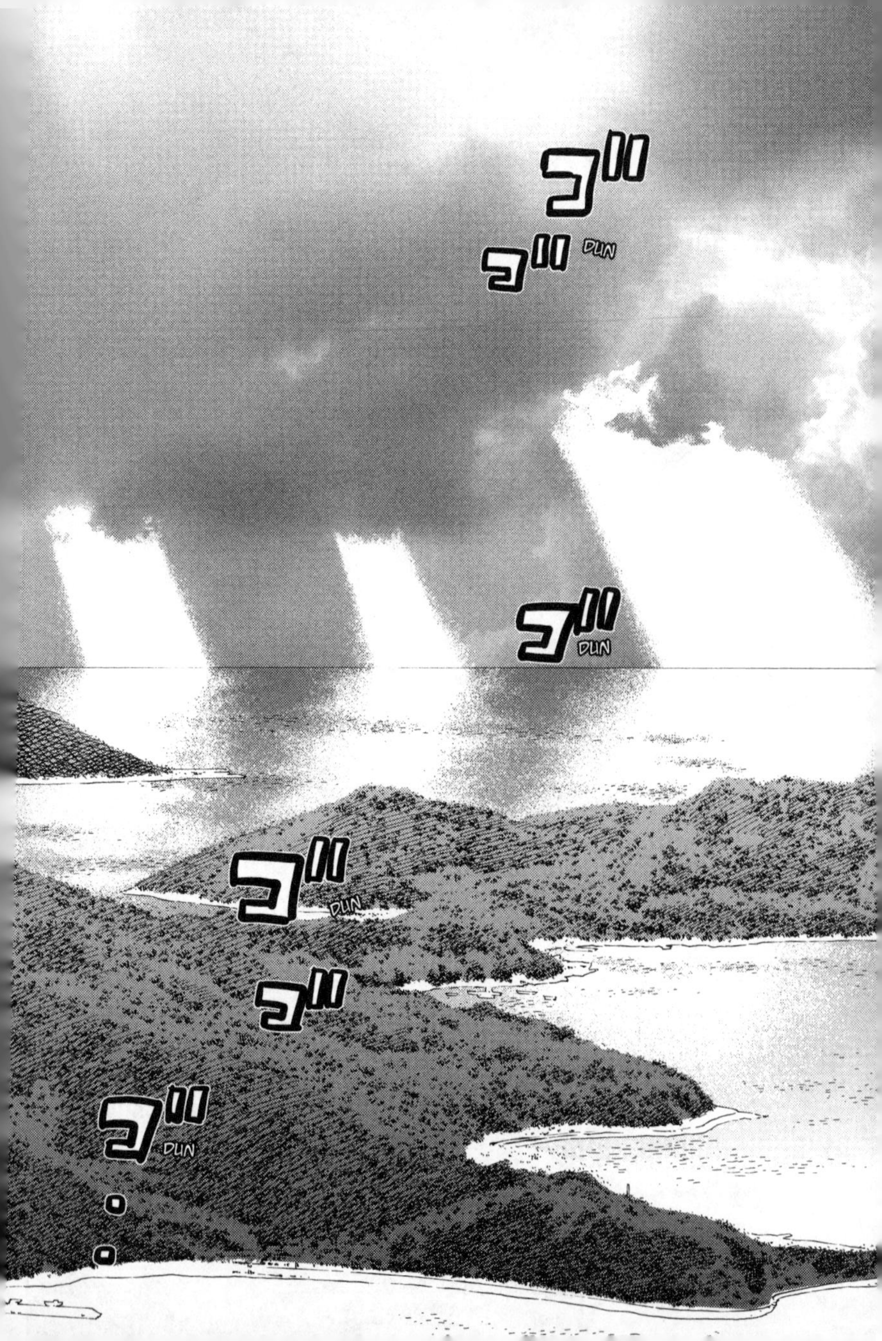
ゴ
ゴ DUN
ゴ DUN
ゴ DUN
ゴ
ゴ DUN

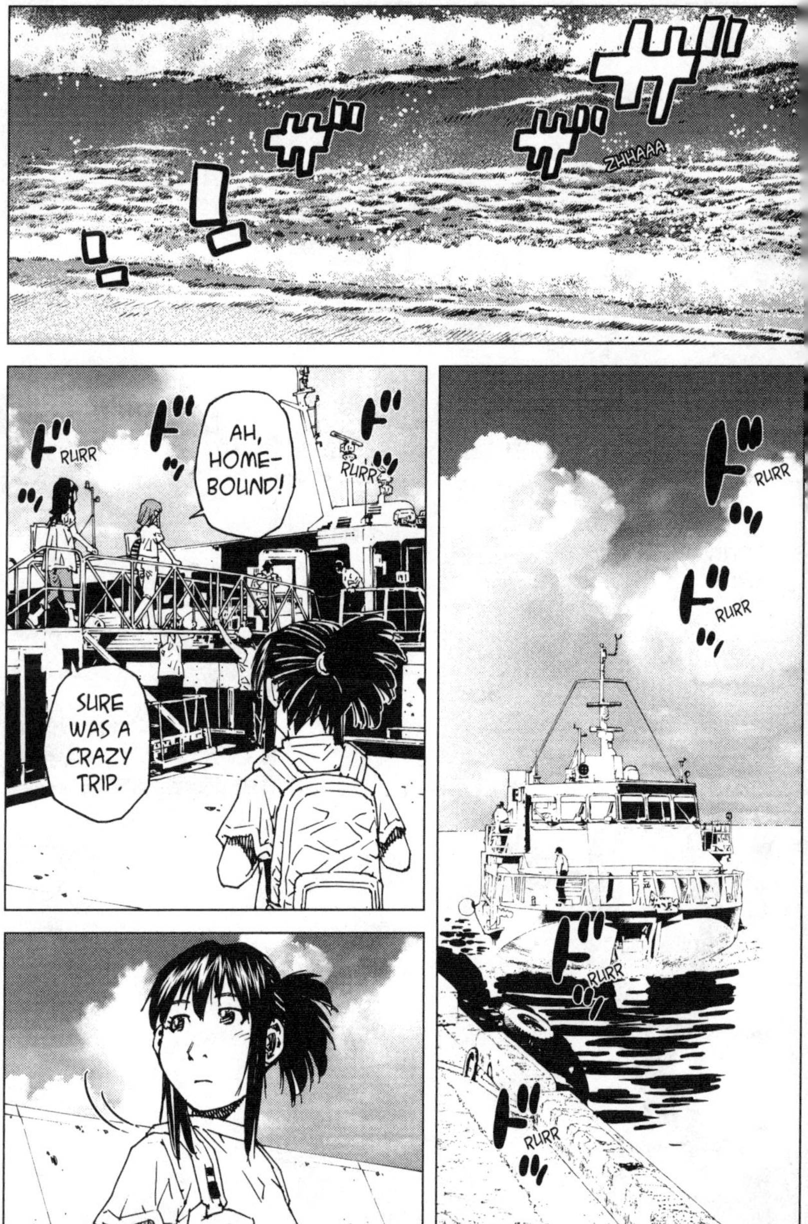
ZHHAAA
RURR
RURR
RURR
RURR
RURR
AH, HOME-BOUND!
RURR
SURE WAS A CRAZY TRIP.
RURR

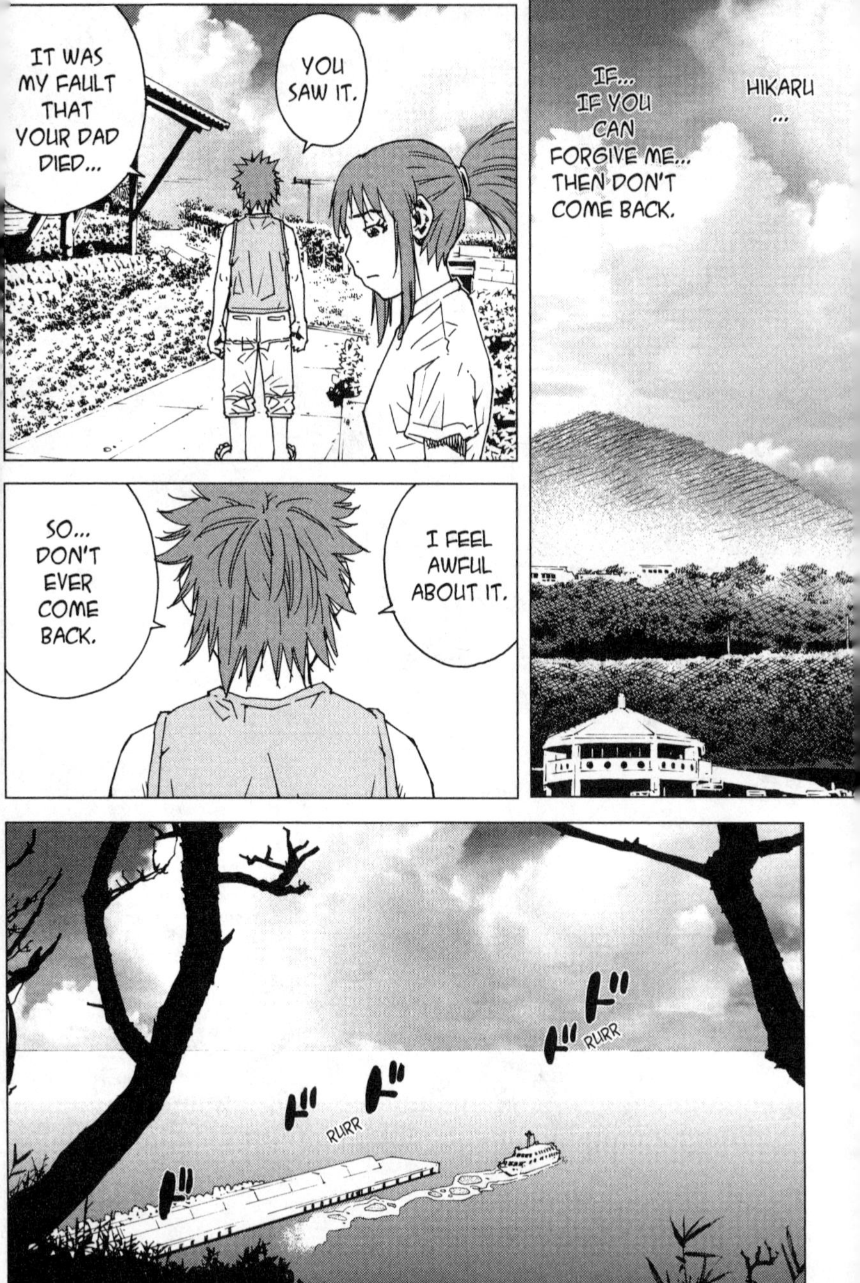
HIKARU
...
IF... IF YOU CAN FORGIVE ME... THEN DON'T COME BACK.
YOU SAW IT.
IT WAS MY FAULT THAT YOUR DAD DIED...
I FEEL AWFUL ABOUT IT.
SO... DON'T EVER COME BACK.
ドド
RURR
ドド
RURR
ド

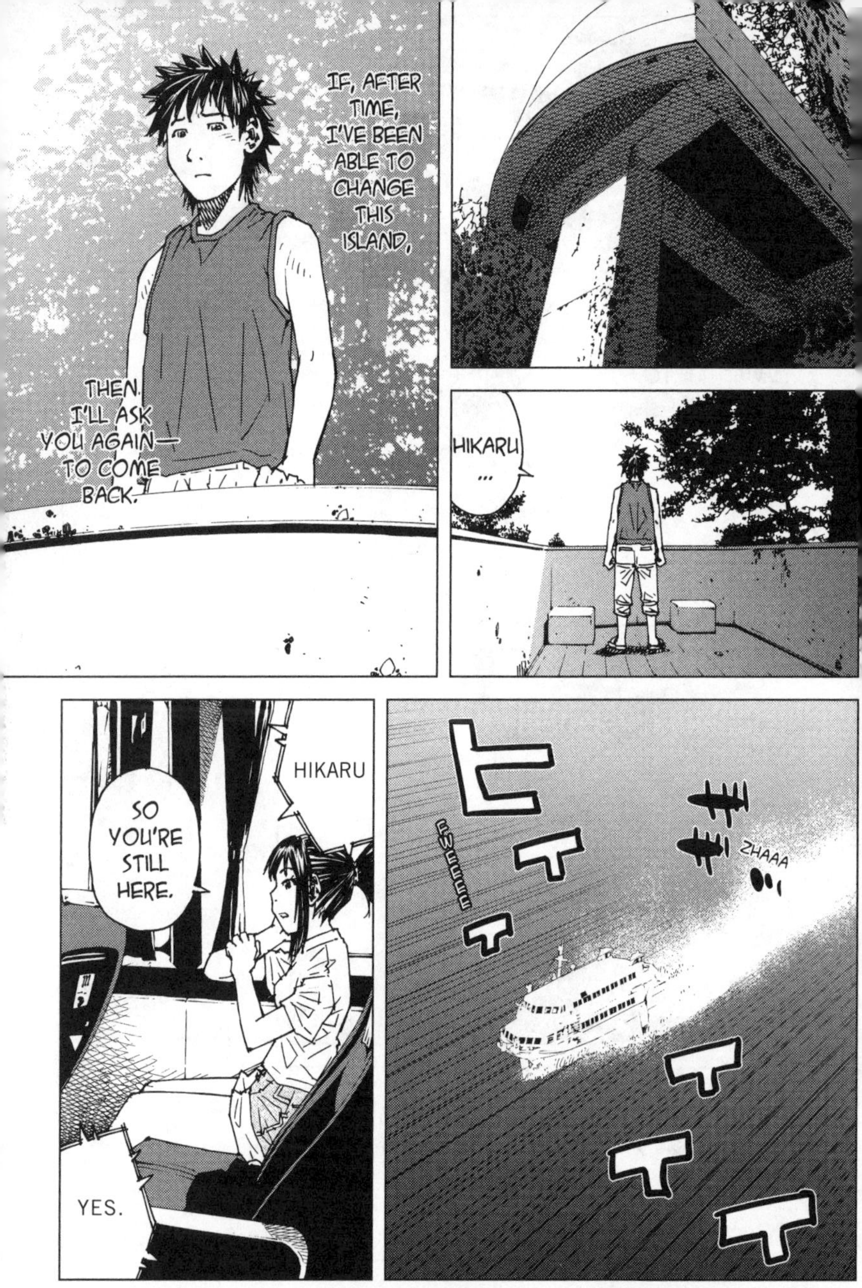
HIKARU
...
IF, AFTER TIME, I'VE BEEN ABLE TO CHANGE THIS ISLAND,
THEN. I'LL ASK YOU AGAIN— TO COME BACK.
FWEEEE
ZHAAA
HIKARU
SO YOU'RE STILL HERE.
YES.

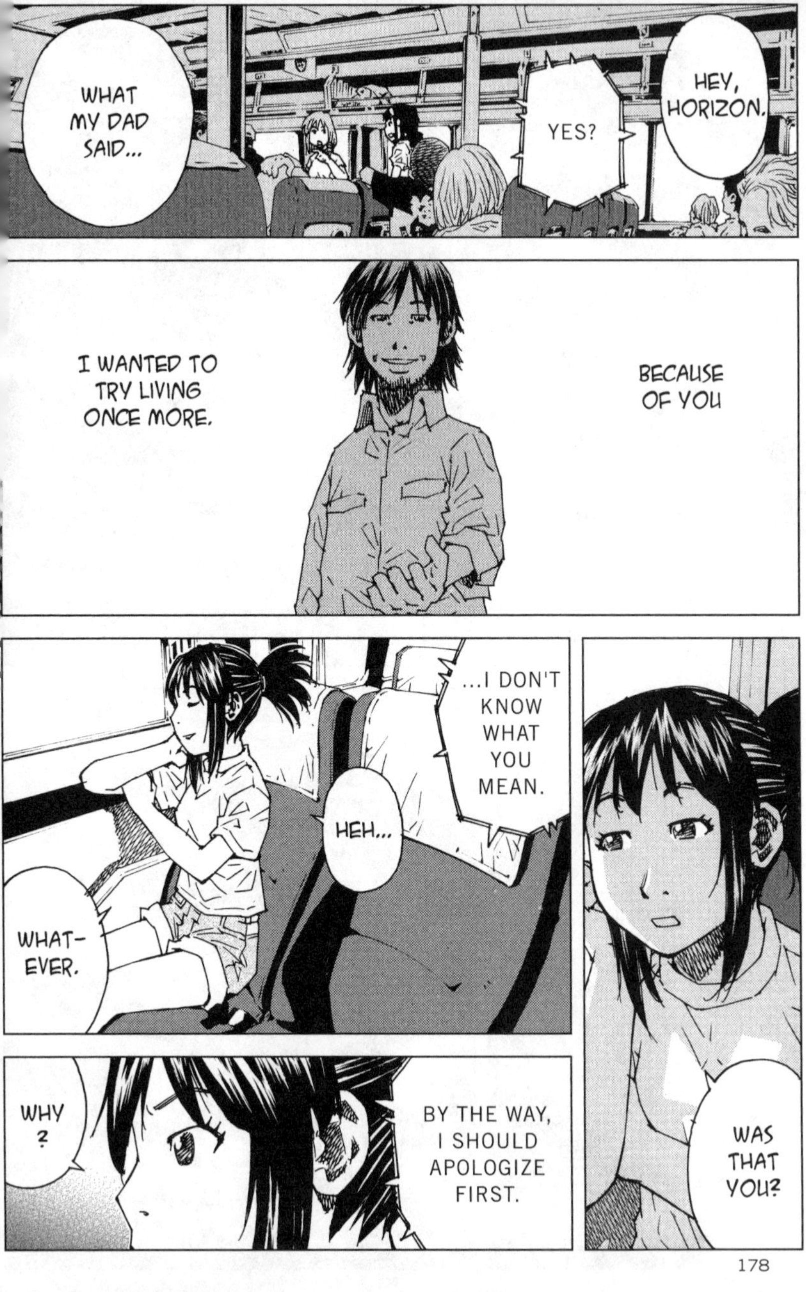
HEY, HORIZON.
YES?
WHAT MY DAD SAID...
BECAUSE OF YOU
I WANTED TO TRY LIVING ONCE MORE.
WAS THAT YOU?
...I DON'T KNOW WHAT YOU MEAN.
HEH...
WHAT-EVER.
BY THE WAY, I SHOULD APOLOGIZE FIRST.
WHY ?

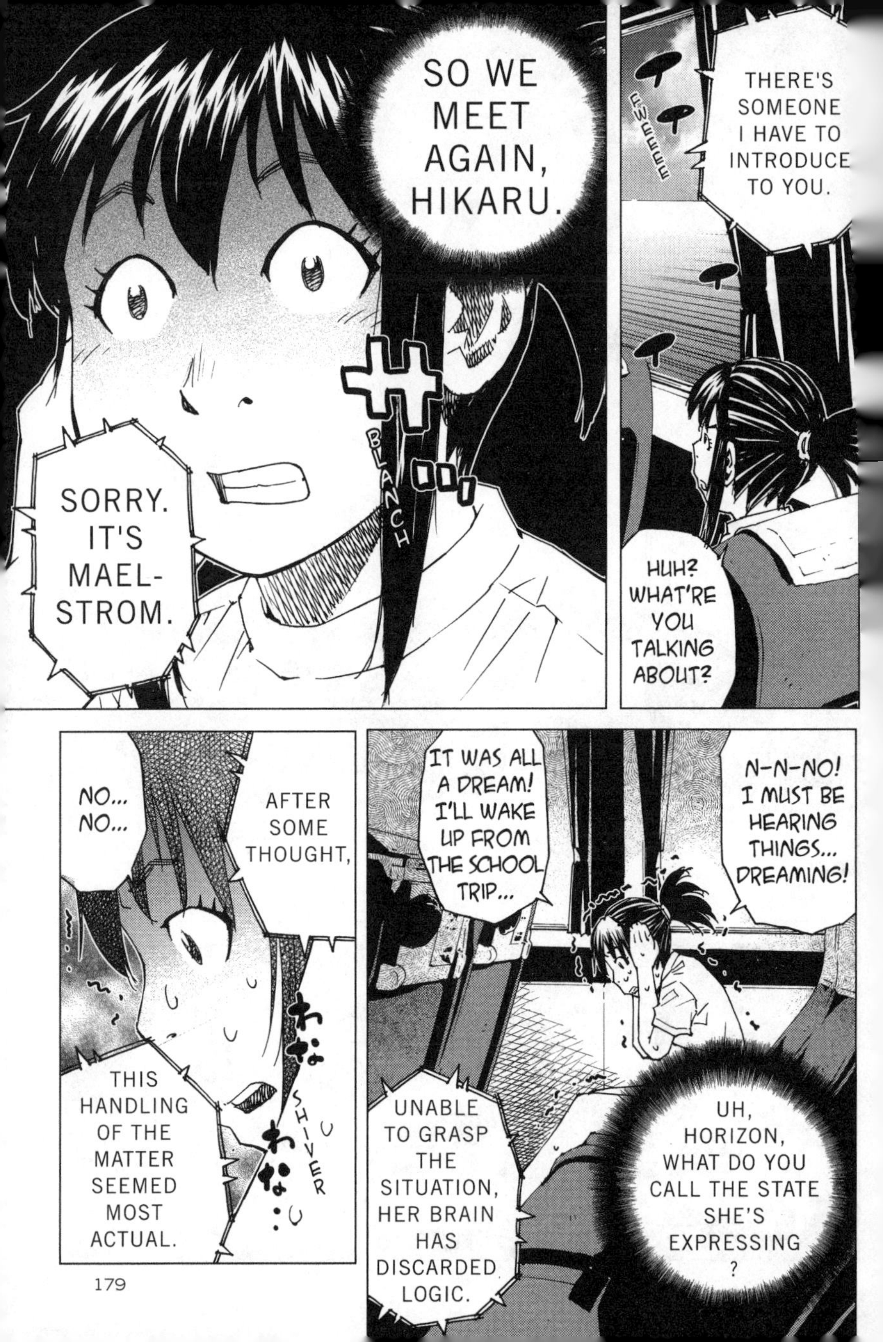
THERE'S SOMEONE I HAVE TO INTRODUCE TO YOU.
FWEEEE
HUH? WHAT'RE YOU TALKING ABOUT?
SO WE MEET AGAIN, HIKARU.
BLANCH
SORRY. IT'S MAEL-STROM.
N-N-NO! I MUST BE HEARING THINGS... DREAMING!
IT WAS ALL A DREAM! I'LL WAKE UP FROM THE SCHOOL TRIP...
UH, HORIZON, WHAT DO YOU CALL THE STATE SHE'S EXPRESSING ?
UNABLE TO GRASP THE SITUATION, HER BRAIN HAS DISCARDED LOGIC.
AFTER SOME THOUGHT,
NO... NO...
SHIVER
THIS HANDLING OF THE MATTER SEEMED MOST ACTUAL.

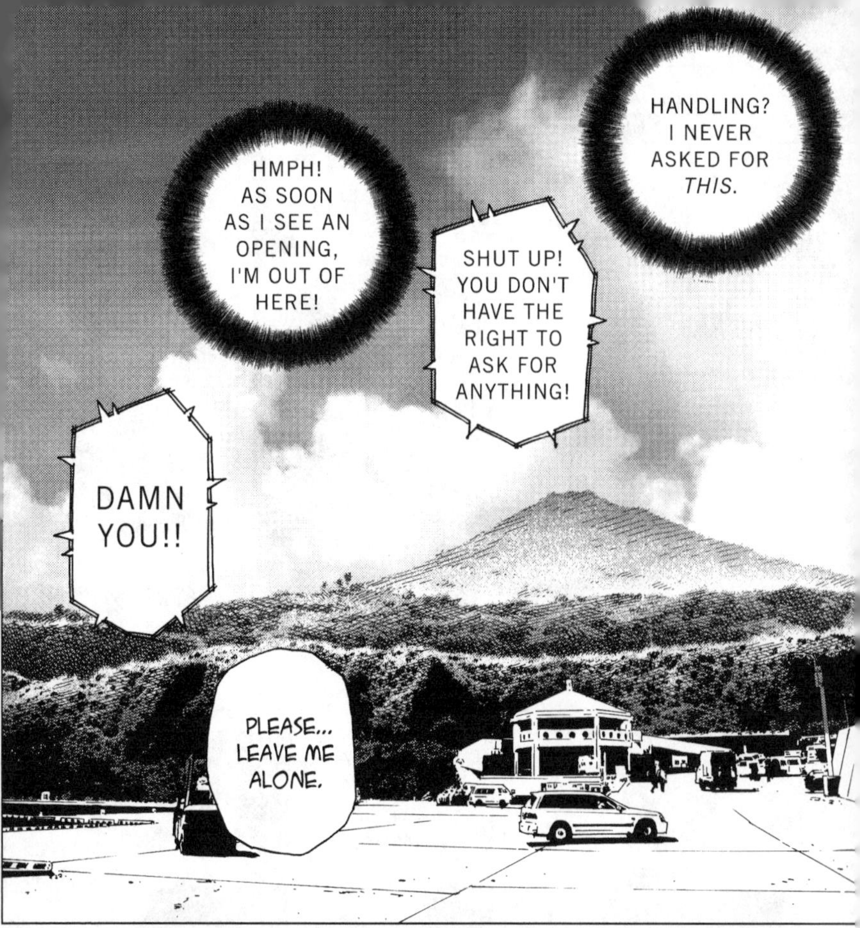
HANDLING? I NEVER ASKED FOR *THIS*.
SHUT UP! YOU DON'T HAVE THE RIGHT TO ASK FOR ANYTHING!
HMPH! AS SOON AS I SEE AN OPENING, I'M OUT OF HERE!
DAMN YOU!!
PLEASE... LEAVE ME ALONE.

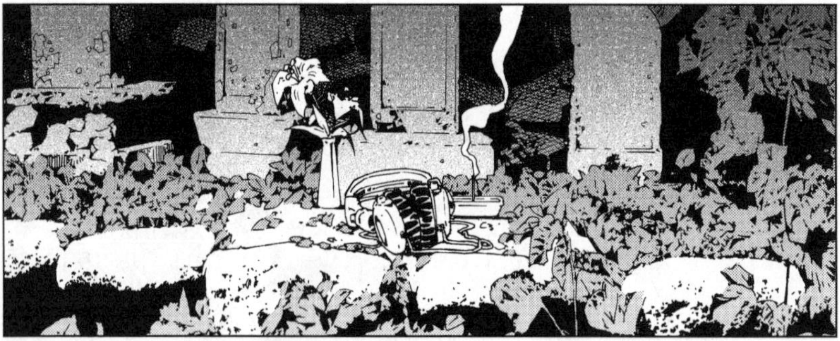

7BILLION NEEDLES

End of Volume 2

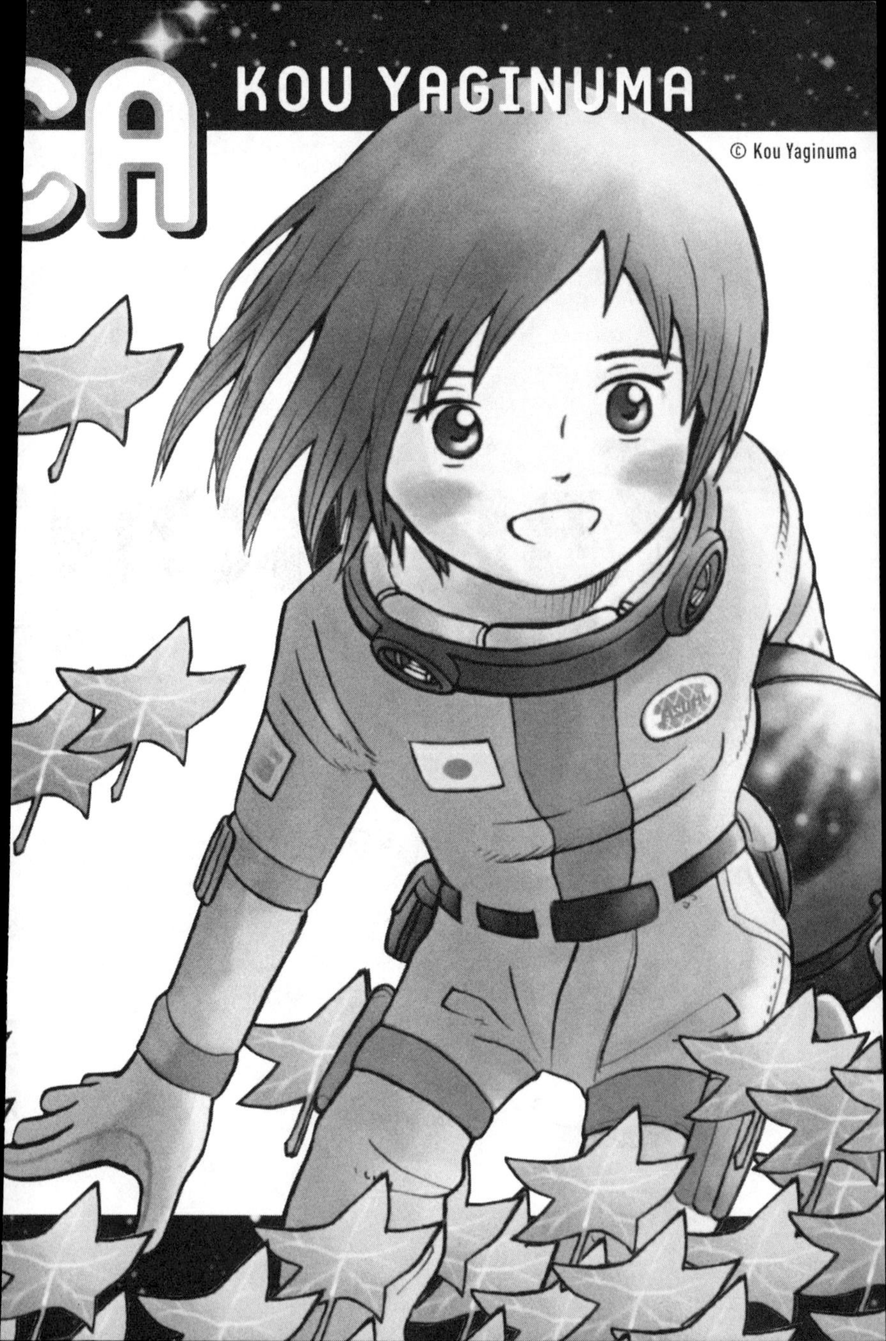
CA
KOU YAGINUMA
© Kou Yaginuma

TWIN SP

Space has never seemed so close and yet so

"It's easy to see why the series was a smash hit in its native land...
Each page contains more genuine emotion than an entire space fleet's
worth of similarly themed stories."
—*Publishers Weekly*

**Volumes 1-4
now available!**

$10.95/$12.99 each

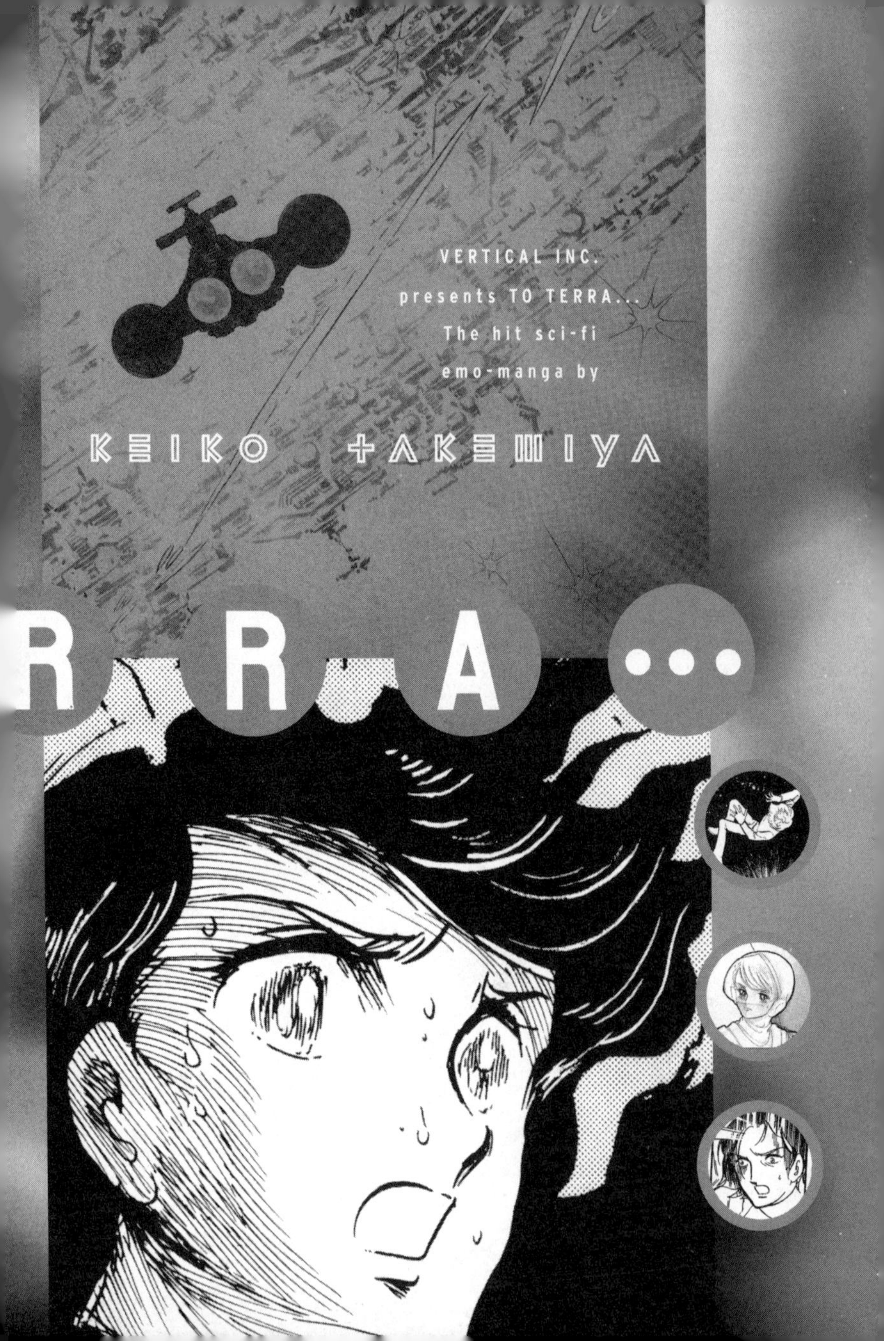
VERTICAL INC.
presents TO TERRA...
The hit sci-fi
emo-manga by
KEIKO TAKEMIYA
RRA...

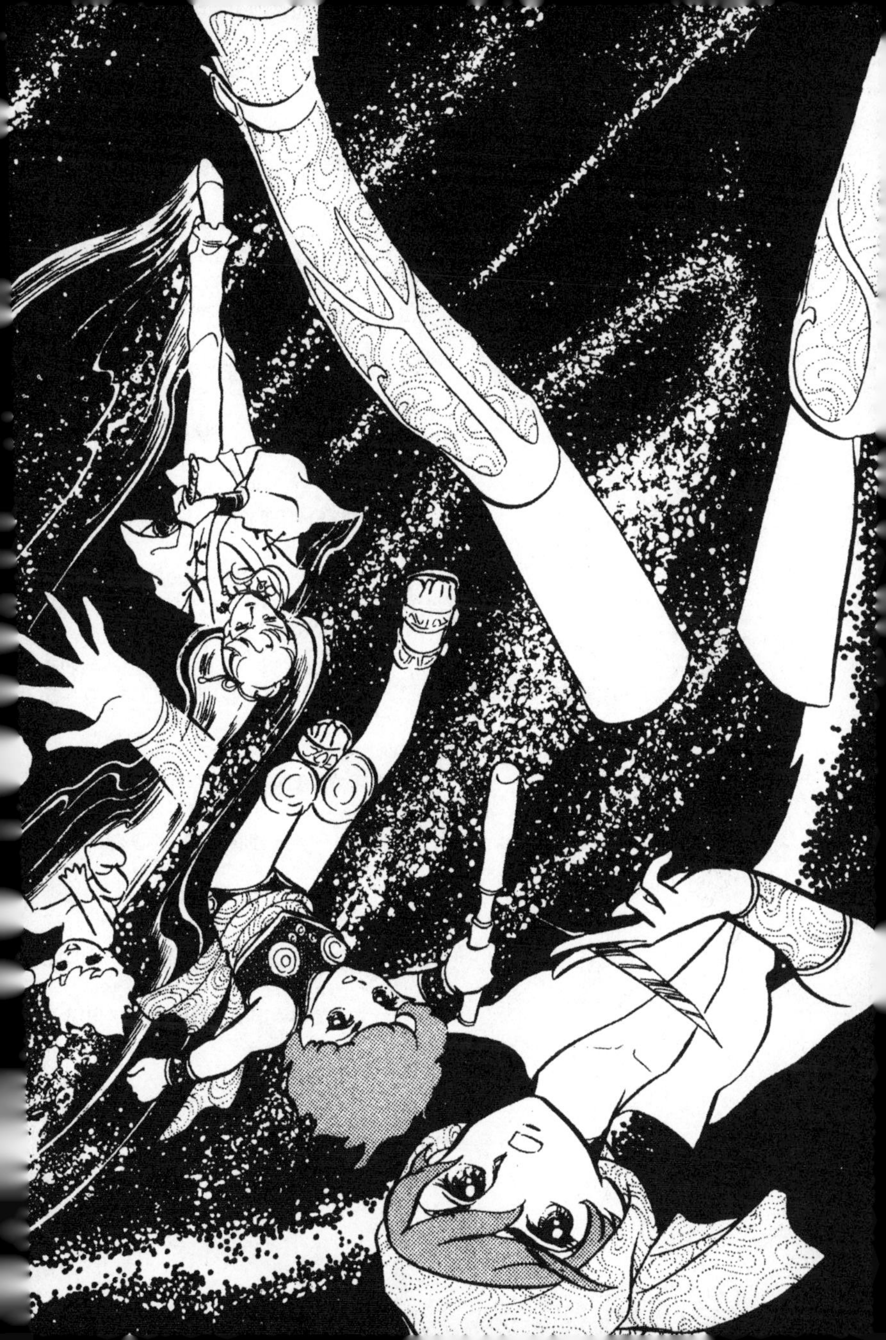

7 Billion Needles, Volume 2

Production - Glen Isip
    Hiroko Mizuno
    Tomoe Tsutsumi

Published by Vertical, Inc., New York

Originally published in Japanese as *70 Oku no Hari*
by MEDIA FACTORY, Inc., Tokyo 2009

70 Oku no Hari first serialized in Gekkan Comic Flapper,
MEDIA FACTORY, Inc., 2008-2010

This is a work of fiction.

ISBN: 978-1-934287-95-8

Manufactured in the USA

First Edition

Vertical, Inc.
1185 Avenue of the Americas, 32nd Floor
New York, NY 10036
www.vertical-inc.com